GARDEN *of the* CURSED

ALSO BY KATY ROSE POOL

The Age of Darkness series

There Will Come a Darkness
As the Shadow Rises
Into the Dying Light

GARDEN *of the* CURSED

KATY ROSE POOL

HENRY HOLT AND COMPANY
NEW YORK

Henry Holt and Company, *Publishers since 1866*
Henry Holt® is a registered trademark of Macmillan Publishing Group, LLC
120 Broadway, New York, NY 10271 • fiercereads.com

Our books may be purchased in bulk for promotional, educational, or business use. Please contact your local bookseller or the Macmillan Corporate and Premium Sales Department at (800) 221–7945 ext. 5442 or by email at MacmillanSpecialMarkets@macmillan.com.

Library of Congress Cataloging-in-Publication Data is available.

First edition, 2023
Cover illustration by Michael Rogers
Book design by Samira Iravani
Printed in the United States of America

ISBN 978-1-250-84666-2 (hardcover)
1 3 5 7 9 10 8 6 4 2

For Brian

Your trust in me as a writer is the real magic

ONE

They say summer storms in Caraza bring more than rain. When lightning crackles across the sky and the air gets thick enough to chew, it means trouble isn't far behind.

Marlow wasn't one for superstition, but when the sky broke open the moment she stepped onto the dock at Breaker's Neck, even she had to admit the timing was portentous.

On the muddy isthmus below the dock, husks of rust and steel sat beached like whale carcasses, some of them nearly intact and some already gutted. Laborers stripped the hulls like scavengers picking the bones of some great behemoth, the crash of falling debris indistinguishable from the thunder shaking the sky.

Generally, Marlow avoided Breaker's Neck as much as possible, and not just because of the noise and the thick stench of scorched metal and brine that emanated from the ship-breaker's yard. Most parts of the Marshes were loud and smelly, but Breaker's Neck presented an additional threat—it was Copperhead territory. A dangerous place for anyone in the Marshes to find themselves, but especially risky for Marlow.

But it wasn't like she had much of a choice. This case had dragged on for almost two weeks, and time was up. Tonight was the grand premiere of *The Ballad of the Moon Thief*, and if its prima ballerina had any hope of performing, Marlow was going to have to brave the danger.

Tugging the hood of her jacket over her head, she sloshed across the crooked plankway that sagged along the isthmus, heading for the rusted remains of an empire dreadnought. The ship was keeled over and half sunk in the mud, but unlike the other ships around it, there was no one stripping this one apart.

Marlow carefully climbed down the steel ladder that rose from the dreadnought's cavernous belly, hopping down the last few rungs and landing on what had once been the bulkhead of one of the compartments. A hermetic hatch led to the main deck. Pushing a wet strand of hair out of her face, Marlow marched over to it.

"Nightshade." As she uttered the password, the handle spun and the hatch swung inward.

With her stomach squirming like a bucket of crayfish, Marlow stepped into the Blind Tiger.

Bioluminescent lamps glinted off the corrugated walls of the dreadnought, turning the whole bar a malevolent dark purple. Voices clambered over one another, punctuated by the high notes of clinking glasses. This early in the evening the crowd was thin, with no real entertainment save a lone zither player plucking in the corner.

Marlow made a slow circuit of the speakeasy, cataloging each face: The soothsayer reading some bright-eyed young woman's fortune, the bracelets on her arms jangling as she shook a bowl of runestones. A man drinking alone, gaze darting around the room as though worried someone might catch him there—an off-duty cop, or a cheating husband, Marlow guessed. A group of gamblers clustered around one of the tables, arguing over dice.

But none matched the description of one Montgomery Flint. Marlow's curse dealer contact had provided a fairly detailed account—long dark hair, a mole under his lip, and a jade earring stud in one ear.

There was still no sign of Flint by the time Marlow reached the long, curved bar that took up the stern of the hollowed-out deck.

Sliding onto one of the silver stools, she waved the bartender over and ordered a Maiden's Prayer. She leaned back in her seat as if she were merely taking in the atmosphere rather than keeping an eye out for Flint.

Her gaze lingered on a tall woman who sat a few stools down, simply but elegantly dressed in a sharp black suit. Short-cropped dark hair fell in a gentle wave over her eye and a row of silver earrings glinted against the shell of her ear. One slender hand was curled around a thick-rimmed tumbler, and when she noticed Marlow staring at her, she raised the glass in a tiny salute before taking a sip.

Marlow's pulse picked up, and it took her a second to realize why. She'd seen this woman before—not long ago, in fact. She'd boarded the same water-taxi that had ferried Marlow to Breaker's Neck.

Marlow turned back to her drink, heart hammering as she raised it to her lips. The cocktail burned on its way down.

It didn't necessarily mean anything. Lots of people took water-taxis. And lots of people came to speakeasies, even ones owned by Copperheads. But that thought did little to soothe the unease prickling up Marlow's spine.

Because for the past few weeks, Marlow had been growing more and more convinced that she was being followed. Coincidence after coincidence—seeing the same old man pass by the spellshop where she worked some days, and again browsing a crayfish stall at the Swamp Market. A messenger boy that Marlow had seen not twice but three times in a single day earlier that week.

It was a pattern. And in Marlow's line of work, patterns didn't go unexamined.

You're here for a case, Briggs, she reminded herself. *Don't get distracted.*

A flash of movement at the very end of the bar seized her attention. Marlow watched as a man with long dark hair swept into a shadowy corridor that branched off from the main deck. Caught in the glow of the violet light, a jade stud winked in his earlobe.

There you are. Marlow threw back the rest of her drink and pushed away from the bar to follow, the elegant woman forgotten for the moment.

The corridor that Flint had disappeared into was empty, and dimly lit with sickly green bioluminescent lamps. Three lavatory doors lined the right side, with lights above the doorknob indicating whether they were occupied. Only the nearest one was illuminated.

Marlow rolled her shoulders against the wall across from the door and waited. She toyed with her lighter, flicking it open and shut as she hummed softly along to the faint twang of the zither, trying to remember the name of the song. As the notes reached a crescendo, the lavatory door swung open.

"Hi there," Marlow said as her mark stepped into the hallway. He glanced at her, surprised but not scared. Not yet.

"Can I help you, sweetheart?" he drawled.

Sweetheart? It was like he wanted to get hexed.

"You sure can!" she chirped, shouldering off the wall. "You can start by telling me why you cursed the prima ballerina of the Monarch Ballet."

He stilled. "I don't know what you're talking about."

"Here's how this is going to go," Marlow said, pushing her hands into her jacket pockets. "I'm going to ask you once, very nicely, to hand over the curse card. And if I have to ask a second time, well—I won't be as nice."

Flint stared at her, weighing his options. Then, without warning, he shoved Marlow back and bolted down the corridor. Marlow stumbled, her legs slipping out from under her as she careened against the wall. But she already had the hex card pinched between her thumb and her knuckle.

"*Congelia*," she muttered. Glowing red glyphs swirled out from the card and shot toward her target like an eel slicing through dark water. The spell struck him between the shoulder blades and he crumpled like wet paper.

Marlow climbed to her feet and stalked toward him.

"I lied," she said, nudging his arm with her boot as he groaned in pain. "I'm not going to ask a second time."

She rolled him over and briskly patted down his jacket while he let out a few thready breaths and whines of pain. Marlow resisted rolling her eyes. It was just a simple Immobilizing hex. No need to be such a child about it.

Something crinkled in one of his inner pockets. Throwing a glance over her shoulder to make sure they were still alone in the corridor, Marlow withdrew a pamphlet.

No, not a pamphlet. A playbill, emblazoned with the same black-and-gold promotional image that Marlow had seen plastered across the city for the past few weeks. The golden Sun King's court and the face of the prima ballerina, Corinne Gaspar, staring up at it, her dark skin luminous against the silver moon. *The Ballad of the Moon Thief*, the playbill read in bold, dark letters.

Marlow thumbed through the playbill. Tucked inside was a ticket to the ballet and a black curse card, marked with stripes of interlocking gold diamonds. She turned the card over, revealing an intricately etched illustration of a girl dancing with music notes floating above her. The illustration moved, showing the girl falling back, one arm thrown dramatically over her face. Gold and white glyphs ran along the edges of the card. Marlow could tell that the spell had been cast because the glyphs were no longer glowing, their magic used up.

"What's this?" Marlow said, waving the curse card in Flint's panicked face as she pocketed the ticket. "A curse that afflicts its subject with debilitating vertigo every time they hear a certain piece of music. Such a strange coincidence, because I happen to know that Corinne Gaspar is suffering from this exact problem. How do you suppose that happened?"

Flint gurgled in reply, his face locked in a rictus of surprise. Seizing a handful of his gold silk shirt, Marlow hauled him upright so he wouldn't choke on his own spit.

"You want to tell me why a midlevel ship-breaker foreman spent over two hundred pearls to curse the prima ballerina in the Monarch Ballet?"

She'd considered a host of theories about who was behind Corinne's curse and what had motivated them. Corinne had suspected a jealous ex-boyfriend out to sabotage her—an easy, if obvious, answer. But the ex-boyfriend had turned out to be a dead end, and Marlow had turned her attention to the Monarch Ballet's biggest competitor, the Belvedere Theater. After all, what better way to ensure the Monarch took a loss than to sabotage their biggest draw? But she hadn't been able to link them to Flint. The only things she knew about him were his name and that he'd bought this curse off a dealer who, as luck would have it, owed Marlow a favor.

"You want to know?" Flint slurred. "I'll tell you."

He spat in Marlow's face. A glob of saliva landed wetly on her cheek, and for a moment Marlow was stunned into silence. Slowly, deliberately, she wiped her face and said, in a taut voice brimming with violence, "You're *really* going to regret that."

But before she could make good on her threat, a chillingly familiar voice sounded from the end of the hallway.

"Do my eyes deceive me? Or is that Marlow Briggs I see skulking around this very fine establishment?"

Marlow rose on shaking legs and swung around to face Thaddeus Bane—second-in-command of the Copperheads, and the second-to-last person she ever wanted to see anywhere, but especially here. He took up nearly the breadth of the hallway, his barrel-like chest stuffed into an ostentatious purple waistcoat bedizened with shining gold-linked chains.

Two Copperhead lackeys stood on either side of him, wearing slightly more subdued threads, but the same bronze snake tattooed around their throats.

"You know, when our doorman said he'd seen you come in, I thought he must be mistaken," Bane went on in a lazy burr. "Surely the brilliant *Marlow Briggs* wouldn't be stupid enough to set foot in a Copperhead joint again."

He bellowed her name like an announcer at a pit fight, his eyes gleaming manically in the green light. A cold trickle of fear slid down Marlow's spine. Thaddeus Bane had every reason to want revenge on Marlow after she had humiliated him and his boss, Leonidas Howell, nine months ago—and it seemed his chance had finally arrived. He was incandescent with delight.

"Guess you're not as smart as you think you are," he sneered.

"Still smarter than you, Thad," Marlow replied sweetly.

Bane chuckled, shaking his head as he strolled toward her with the air of an indolent predator who knew its prey was cornered. "And you came alone. Where's your friend Swift? Been a while since we've seen him, and we miss him something awful."

Bane's two cronies pushed deeper into the hall, flanking Marlow. She stood her ground, sizing them up. The one with a red beard she vaguely recognized, and the other, a wiry youth with a squid beak nose, looked like he couldn't be much older than she was. A new recruit. Maybe even Swift's replacement.

Marlow smiled as she slipped a hand into the pocket of her rain jacket. "Actually, he had a message for you."

"Oh?"

"He says he's really flattered, but this obsession your boss has with him is starting to get embarrassing."

Bane flashed a crocodile grin, advancing. "Speaking of, I wish the boss was here now. But don't worry—I'll be sure to describe your screams in detail to him later."

For a moment Marlow's fear dulled the edges of her mind. She swallowed it down and forced herself to meet Bane's cruel gray eyes with another smile.

"With all the time I've spent occupying that vacant head of yours, you should really think about charging rent," she said, thumbing through the slim stack of spellcards in her pocket and hoping she could somehow divine by touch which one she needed.

"You really think you're better than the rest of us," Bane snarled. "Because you used to rub shoulders with the noblesse nouveau. But then your bitch of a mother dumped you back in the Marshes, didn't she?"

Marlow clenched her jaw, fury pouring through her veins like hot acid.

"Guess she figured out what the rest of us already knew—you can't wash the swamp off the swamp rat."

His cronies guffawed. Marlow's fingers closed around what she deeply hoped was a temporary Blinding hex.

As she opened her mouth to cast it, the red-bearded crony flicked open a switchblade and held it to her throat.

"Hands where we can see them," he said in a low voice.

Marlow sucked in a breath that felt closer to a sob and jerked her hands up, showing them her palms. Squid Beak pushed right into her space, roughly grabbing her wrists and pinning them behind her back.

She was alone. Swift and Hyrum had no idea where she was. And she couldn't talk, think, or hex her way out of this.

The blade pressed into her skin, and Marlow bit down on a pathetic whimper as Bane leaned into her, his breath on her cheek as warm and wet as a summer storm.

"Tell you what," he said conspiratorially. "I'll let you choose what we take from you, how's that? A few ounces of blood, perhaps? Or I could take your nose, so you'll stop poking it where it doesn't belong. Or maybe you'd rather I take some of your memories—all your memories of dear old mommy, perhaps?"

Marlow growled low in her throat.

"What'll it be, Briggs?" Bane asked. "Make it quick, before I lose patience and take all three. Our spellwrights could always use the ingredients."

There was no doubt in her mind that Bane would love nothing more than to carve her up for spare parts to make more illegal curses. Tears stung her eyes. She squeezed them shut. Whatever horror Bane was planning to inflict on her, she wouldn't give him the satisfaction of seeing her cry.

"Put the knife down," a voice said, crystal clear and commanding.

Marlow opened her eyes to the sight of a woman leaning casually against the wall at the end of the hallway. Marlow's heart jolted as she recognized the elegant woman from the bar. The one who'd been on Marlow's water-taxi.

Definitely not a coincidence, then.

"Sweetcakes, maybe you don't understand how things work around here," Bane said, rounding on her. "Or maybe you just don't know who you're talking to."

A thin smile curled the corner of the woman's lips. "I know exactly who you are, Thaddeus Bane. The real question is whether you know who I am."

Bane stared at her for a moment and then erupted into braying laughter. Following their leader's cue, the others guffawed along.

The woman pushed one sleeve of her jacket up, subtly flashing a black tattoo. It was too fast for Marlow to make out the shape, but it seemed to have the desired effect—Bane stopped laughing abruptly, his jaw slack, eyes bulging.

"Oh, so you *do* know who I am," the woman said, tilting her head. "Now tell your friends here to let the girl go."

"Who are you to order us around?" Red Beard demanded. "This is *our* territory."

"That's a bit above your pay grade, I think," the woman said, flicking her gaze back to Bane.

"Let her go." Bane straightened his shoulders, doing his best not to look rattled in front of his men. But the damage had already been done. "She's not worth our time anyway."

The two men backed away from Marlow haltingly, obviously wrong-footed by their boss's sudden change of heart, although they didn't dare question it. As soon as their hands left her skin, Marlow jerked away, steadying herself against the wall, gaze flickering from Bane to the woman and back.

"Come along now." The woman cast one final appraising look at Bane and spun on her heel, striding effortlessly across the speakeasy floor, clearly expecting Marlow to follow.

Marlow hesitated at the edge of the room, weighing her options. In the end, her unrelenting hunger for answers won out, the way it always did.

Tossing a regretful glance at the still-immobilized Flint, she trailed the woman across the bar, back through the hatch, and up the ladder into a damp, muggy twilight. The storm had subsided, but the air was still sharp with the taste of lightning.

"Hold on," Marlow commanded, halting at the edge of the plank-way. "Stop right there and tell me who you are and why you've been following me."

She brandished her Blinding hex in one hand.

The woman spun in a wide circle to face her, her short dark hair falling over her eye. "A thank-you wouldn't be out of order. What do you think Thaddeus Bane would have done to you if I hadn't stepped in?"

"I didn't need your help," Marlow lied. "I've handled him before."

"I know," the woman replied. "Which raises the question of how exactly a seventeen-year-old girl managed to piss off the most ruthless street gang in Caraza."

Marlow flashed a blithe smile. "I just seem to have that effect on people."

The woman's lips twitched and she held up her hands. "You can put away the spell. I'm not going to hurt you."

The sleeve of her jacket had slipped down, revealing the tattoo that Marlow had only glimpsed in the bar. A flower of midnight black bloomed over her forearm, its petals as sharp and dangerous as fangs. Marlow had the sense that the woman wasn't letting her see it by accident.

"That's not a gang emblem I've seen before," Marlow said warily.

"That's because it's not a gang emblem."

Marlow met the woman's gaze again. She looked back at Marlow, an anticipatory gleam in her amber eyes.

Marlow's skin prickled, hair standing on end. It was a feeling she knew well. The feeling she got when something didn't quite fit, when she noticed something that most others didn't. When that strange, unknowable part of her—the thing she called *instinct*—slotted a clue into place, connecting two seemingly innocuous truths together.

But it wasn't Corinne's case or even the Copperheads that Marlow's mind went to.

Instead, it was her mother, and a memory of the night she'd disappeared.

It wasn't a memory Marlow revisited often anymore, but when she did, it was like she was transported instantly back to their lavish quarters in Vale Tower. Like she could still smell the burning candle and the hint of vetiver and bergamot perfume beneath it, could still see her mother sitting at her writing desk, holding a spellcard to the flame.

"What are you doing?" Marlow had asked, standing in the doorway.

Her mother had startled, knocking her elbow into a bottle of perfume, which spilled across a pile of papers on the desk. "Minnow! I didn't hear you come in."

The spellcard caught fire, the flames chewing quickly through it, leaving ash in their wake. But not before Marlow spotted a symbol on the back—a black flower, with claw-sharp petals.

Marlow slammed the door on the memory before it went any further. She raised her eyes back to the woman, and saw in the slight glint of satisfaction that she knew Marlow recognized the symbol.

A crash of thunder split the air. Marlow startled despite herself, throwing her gaze to the sky on instinct. The storm clouds had dissipated, the evening clear, and Marlow realized belatedly that the sound had come from the ship-breaker's yard. Of course.

When she looked back to the woman with the tattoo, she was gone.

TWO

It had been over a year since the last time Marlow had entered Evergarden. Through the cable car window, she could see the gleaming skyline rising from the center of the city. The last rays of the sun splashed vermilion across the spokes of the five canals radiating out from Evergarden's center, so different from the twisted, muck-filled waterways of the Marshes.

As the cable car zipped over the outermost edge of the Marshes, Marlow couldn't shake the chill crawling up her spine after the encounter with Bane and the woman with the black flower tattoo. Part of her wished she could just go home, curl up on the couch with Toad, and play a game of Casters with Swift, but the job wasn't finished.

With her feet propped up against the side of the cable car, Marlow paged through the playbill she'd lifted off Flint, worrying at her lingering questions like a scab she couldn't stop picking at. Yes, she could break the curse, but she'd never figured out who Flint was or why he'd cast a curse on Corinne in the first place.

If there was one thing Marlow couldn't stand, it was unanswered questions.

The cable car swung to a stop at Pearl Street Station, and Marlow shoved the program back into her jacket and disembarked onto the platform.

The air on this side of the city was far sweeter than the sulfurous stench that clung to every crevice of the Marshes, in part because it was upwind, but mostly because every conceivable surface was blanketed with bougainvillea and jasmine vines. The scent instantly propelled Marlow back in time, to over a year ago when she'd called this part of the city home.

But that was a different time. And she was a different Marlow now.

Evergarden hummed with magic. The broad promenades were charmed to remain gleaming and pristine no matter how many feet treaded over them. Planters filled with mosquito-repelling blossoms floated above the canals. Marlow made her way down Pearl Street, the main shopping district of the Outer Garden. Soothing scents wafted from perfumeries and salons selling magic elixirs that promised flawless skin and everlasting youth. Ateliers showcased the latest fashions, from cloth made of enchanted flames to dresses that changed color according to the wearer's mood. A charming patisserie offered free samples of mood-lifting candies and colorful meringue confections with a variety of effects according to flavor. Spell emporiums far grander than any dingy spellshop in the Marshes sold nearly endless selections of spellcards and enchanted objects.

There was more magic in a single block of the Outer Garden District than in all of the Marshes combined—though of course, none of these flashy enchantments and charms would even exist without ingredients culled from the people who lived in the Marshes.

As Marlow crossed Azalea Bridge to Starling Street, the lanterns were just beginning to glow, painting the paved bricks scarlet and gold. The Monarch's crown-shaped facade reigned over the square at the end of the street. *The Ballad of the Moon Thief Grand Premiere!* declared the crimson-and-gold marquee.

Marlow paused beside one of the terra-cotta planters that lined the square and picked a handful of coral amaryllis blossoms before climbing the steps to the gleaming gold doors of the Monarch Theater.

A doorman dressed in a sharp crimson dinner jacket trimmed with intricate gold embroidery eyed Marlow as she approached, his face pinched in disapproval.

"Doors don't open for another thirty minutes," he intoned.

Fixing him with her most winning smile, Marlow clutched the flowers against her chest and simpered, "I just want to wish my friend good luck on the show tonight. She's been so nervous all week, and I know she'd love to have the extra encouragement before she goes out there."

She couldn't just tell the doorman the real reason she was here—for one, Corinne had begged her to keep the curse quiet, and Marlow knew how to be discreet. And for another, it seemed like a stretch that this doorman would believe her anyway.

"Your friend. I'm sure," the doorman replied with a rather scathing look at Marlow's attire—an oversized olive-green rain jacket thrown over a thin black top and ratty shorts. Practical for running around in the summer humidity, but not exactly presentable for a night at the theater. "Doors still open in thirty minutes."

Marlow held out the ticket she'd lifted off Flint. "I have a ticket."

"Ticket or no ticket, doors are open in—" His gaze dropped to the ticket and he stopped talking abruptly. "My apologies," he stuttered. "I didn't realize you were a friend of Miss Sable's!"

Marlow blinked at him. After a too-long pause, she said, "Miss Sable. Right. That's the friend I was talking about. How did you . . . know that?"

"The ticket?" he said, waving it in front of Marlow. "It's one of her comped seats. Both leads get their own private box for opening night."

"Leads?" Marlow echoed.

"She didn't tell you?" the doorman asked. "Miss Sable is playing the role of the Moon Thief tonight. Of course it must be devastating for Miss Gaspar to miss opening night—but I know Miss Sable will make a stunning Moon Thief. She must be so excited to finally debut as the prima ballerina after all those years of falling short. She really didn't say anything?"

"I'm sure she wanted it to be a surprise," Marlow replied faintly, her mind whirring to slot this new information in place.

The doorman's eyes narrowed. "How did you say you knew Miss Sable again?"

"We grew up together," Marlow lied smoothly. "Are you going to let me go congratulate her, or do I have to stand outside explaining myself to you while Viv has a breakdown about her debut?"

He let her inside before Marlow could contemplate using her Blinding hex on him. She blew through the front doors, charging across the gilded floor of the atrium, past the grand, sweeping staircase.

Marlow had learned a long time ago that people rarely tried to stop you if you looked like you knew where you were going and strode with purpose, so she was halfway down the corridor that led backstage before she was stopped by a girl dressed in all black, her dark hair pulled back into a neat ponytail.

"You can't go in here," she said.

"I'll just be a second," Marlow said, maneuvering toward the open door of the greenroom, where she could see dancers and technicians preparing for the night's show, applying glittering makeup and getting dressed in elaborate costumes.

"I can't let you—"

"Marlow, is that you?" Corinne's musical voice called over the din. Marlow spotted her floating toward them, her face bare and her simple cloth robe flowing behind her like a cape. She looked much like Marlow felt—utterly exhausted—but she danced across the room like the prima ballerina she was. "Teak, let her in."

The black-clad girl stepped away from the threshold immediately, and Marlow made a beeline for Corinne, ducking around two stagehands carrying a large golden throne.

Corinne reached for Marlow's hand as she approached. "I'm so glad you're here. They just told me a few hours ago that I can't—" She took a breath, holding back tears. "That I won't be performing tonight. With the"—she lowered her voice—"the *curse*, they said it's too big a risk. Please tell me you have some kind of lead."

"Oh, I have better than that," Marlow promised. "Come with me."

She looped her arm through Corinne's, dragging her toward the row of lit-up mirrors where a few of the dancers were getting their makeup applied and their hair styled.

"Marlow, what are you—?"

Marlow ignored her, marching over to the dancer preening at the last mirror, her raven hair piled on her head, silver glitter shimmering on her pale skin. She looked just like her picture in the program.

"Vivian Sable?" Marlow asked, coming to a stop at her elbow.

"Y-yes?" Vivian replied, blinking at Marlow's reflection in the mirror.

"I just wanted to congratulate you," Marlow said, "on getting the starring role of the Moon Thief. In fact, I was hoping you could sign something for me."

She pulled out Flint's curse card, slapping it down on the vanity in front of Vivian.

"I don't . . . I don't understand," she said, going white.

"Sure you do," Marlow replied. "You got your boyfriend or whoever to buy a curse on the black market to make sure Corinne couldn't perform in the show. Leaving you, her understudy, to take over the role."

Marlow could see Corinne's face in the mirror, her mouth going slack with shock, her dark eyes clouding with hurt.

"That . . . that isn't true," Vivian said meekly, her bright green eyes filling with tears. "Corinne, I would *never*—"

"Save the theatrics for the stage," Marlow advised. "Or not, I guess, since you won't be performing tonight once I break the curse and you explain to the producers what you did."

"I *swear*—" Vivian started.

"Oh, and if you don't?" Marlow added. "I'm going to curse your feet to rot off."

She didn't actually have such a curse, but it made for a better threat than the Blinding hex.

Vivian burst into noisy tears. "I'm sorry," she sobbed into her hands. "Corinne, I'm so sorry, I *never* wanted to hurt you. I just—I've danced with this company for *years*, and every time I think I've finally made lead, I lose out to the shiny new star. I couldn't take it anymore!"

"And you knew you couldn't earn it on your own," Marlow said. "Because Corinne is five times the dancer you'll ever be."

Corinne just stared at Vivian, stunned. "I never thought you'd be capable of something like this. You were my *friend*."

Marlow recognized the devastation in her voice. She was learning the lesson Marlow already knew too well—that the people you cared about would only let you down in the end.

Vivian blinked at her through watery green eyes, but Marlow knew she wasn't sorry for what she'd done, just that she'd been caught.

Marlow waved the ponytailed stage manager over. "You. Take Miss Sable here to see the producers. She has something very urgent she needs to tell them."

With a quick, confirming glance at Corinne, the stage manager led a sniffling Vivian away. The scene she was making had begun to draw the attention of the other dancers and show technicians, but Marlow's focus was on Corinne as she moved slowly toward the curse card sitting on the vanity, touching it with a shaking hand.

Marlow dug into another jacket pocket and held out her lighter. "You want to do the honors?"

Corinne swallowed, taking the lighter. "I burn it? And the curse will break, just like that?"

"Just like that."

With a fortifying breath, Corinne flicked open the lighter. It took a few tries to ignite it, but finally Corinne held the curse card over the flame. Instead of catching fire, the curse card glowed a dark purple—and so did Corinne, a shadowy aura threaded with black veins that drew toward the curse card like water being sucked through a straw. The curse card absorbed the magic and then the glow died out, the card flickering purple before turning a dull graphite.

Corinne stood holding the spent curse card and the lighter, stunned.

"Well?" Marlow said.

Corinne handed her the card and the lighter, spun in a neat circle, and flew over to a dark-haired boy with a violin slung over one shoulder.

"Xander! Play 'A Thief in the Sun King's Court.'"

He did at once, the first chords of the song curling through the room like smoke. Corinne snapped into position, her body moving in precise, controlled lines as she danced the number that, until one minute ago, she hadn't been able to hear without fainting. Even dressed in a simple robe instead of the intricate costume of the Moon Thief, she was captivating.

Applause erupted through the room as the other dancers and musicians watched Corinne leap and dance, their relief and joy at having their prima ballerina back palpable. She was going to be incredible tonight. No one would be able to keep their eyes off her.

Marlow smiled as she slipped the burned-out curse card into her pocket. Its power was entirely used up, and it would never hurt anyone again. But for Marlow it was a reminder—that as long as there were curses, she would go on breaking them.

"I don't know what you did, exactly, but thank you."

Marlow turned and found the stage manager with the sleek ponytail—Teak—standing beside her, watching Corinne move to the crescendoing violin.

"I just did my job," Marlow replied easily.

"Well, you saved the ballet," Teak replied. "All the critics come on opening night, and if we'd had to premiere with Vivian playing the Moon Thief, we'd be waking up to some pretty unpleasant words in the morning papers. Not to mention, I heard a rumor from one of the ushers that the Five Families scions are attending tonight's show. I can't even imagine the embarrassment if—"

"What?" Marlow asked abruptly, her ears ringing. "The Five Families scions are coming here? Tonight?"

Teak gave her an odd look. "Yes, but no offense, I doubt you'll be able to stage an accidental-on-purpose run-in with Adrius Falcrest, if that's what you're thinking."

A high, hysterical laugh squeaked out of Marlow. "I can promise you that is *not* what I was thinking."

Teak narrowed her eyes. "All right. I'm just saying this from experience. Not that *I've* tried to—"

"Right, yes, got it," Marlow replied. "Listen, tell Corinne I'll be in her dressing room when she's ready to settle. I should probably get out of here before the crowds show up."

"You're not going to stay and watch?"

Marlow smiled, tight-lipped. "Maybe another time. I'm sure Corinne will be great. But I've had a pretty long day and I just need to get out of here."

As fast as she possibly could.

The doorman had evidently begun letting people inside. When Marlow reentered the lobby, her jacket pockets a few pearl strings heavier, it was teeming with people. Everyone wore their finest—suits and gowns in rich jewel tones with exaggerated silhouettes and magical flourishes—all for the dubious honor of being noticed amongst the crowd and hopefully mentioned in tomorrow's fashion columns.

Marlow accrued her own fair share of notice for entirely different reasons, though she supposed she'd be a shoo-in for the Fashion Follies section with her still-damp jacket, muddy boots, and the tangle of dirty-blond hair hanging at her shoulders.

Even more reason to make a clean getaway.

That plan came to a crashing halt the moment she descended into the atrium and stopped cold—along with the rest of the crowd. It seemed every gaze in the lobby was pinned to Gemma Starling and Amara Falcrest as they sailed through the doors. Murmurs bubbled through the room like fizz in a bottle of sparkling wine.

Amara and Gemma paid their onlookers no mind, accustomed to such attention. Gemma shimmered beneath the light of the chandelier in a daring fuchsia dress with a voluminous train that resembled the plumage of an exotic bird. Golden circlets floated up her arms, adorned with jewel beads orbiting like little planets. Her rose-colored curls were gathered in an elaborate updo, and her face was painted with a stripe of gold across her eyes that deepened to a rich bronze along the ridge of her brow.

Amara wore a dramatic, sculptural gown in deep amethyst, her pin-straight midnight-black hair coiled like a crown around her head and studded with pearls. Smaller pearls flecked the corners of her eyes and along her high cheekbones. Marlow's gaze lingered on the delicately filigreed silver carcanet encircling her throat—an accessory usually only worn by women engaged to be married.

Marlow stood frozen on the steps as they neared, snatches of their conversation floating toward her.

"—if Adrius wanted us to wait up for him, then he shouldn't have wasted all that time flirting with what's-her-name at the teahouse. I swear, by now he must have bedded every suitable prospect in Evergarden."

"And plenty of the unsuitable ones," Amara added cuttingly.

Gemma trilled with laughter, and Marlow let out a relieved breath as they breezed past without a glance.

But because it seemed her luck today was determined to be dismal, a second later she heard Amara's voice again.

"Gemma, hold on—is that *Marlow Briggs*?"

Bullfrog butts. She'd been made. Ducking her head low, Marlow slunk toward the exit.

Gemma laughed loudly. "Right, because I'm sure Marlow Briggs frequents the— Gods, that *is* her. Marlow!"

Marlow cast a desperate glance at the open doors, wondering if she could simply make a break for it before Amara and Gemma reached her.

Instead, she pulled in a bracing breath and spun to face them.

"Hi, Gemma," she greeted as amicably as she could manage. "Amara."

Gemma let out a low whistle. "Wow, Marlow Briggs. It's been *ages*."

A year and five weeks, but who could remember the exact day Marlow's mother had vanished, taking Marlow's entire life with her?

"We thought you must've disappeared like your mom," Gemma went on, with no indication that she'd considered whether this might be a sore subject. "What are you doing at the Monarch? Do you *work* here?"

She sounded dubious, though Marlow was unsure if it was the concept of work itself she objected to or the thought of Marlow being employed by a place as glamorous as the Monarch. Marlow couldn't exactly fault her for the latter—she had no doubt that the rest of the crowd, still buzzing over Amara and Gemma's arrival, were wondering what exactly Caraza's most sought-after socialites were doing talking to her.

"I just came by to help a friend," Marlow answered. There was an awkward pause, and it seemed like as good an opening as she'd get to make her retreat. "Anyway, so fun seeing you, but I have to—"

"Marlow?" A rich, deep voice joined the fray as Darian Vale approached. "Gods, it's been—"

"Ages," Marlow finished for him. "Or so I've been told."

Darian pulled up next to Amara, winding an arm around her waist. Marlow's gaze tracked Amara's delicate hand as it smoothed over Darian's cobalt waistcoat to fix his herringbone cravat. She glanced again at Amara's silver carcanet, making the connection. They were engaged.

Marlow felt suddenly, immeasurably distant from the girl she'd been a year ago, when she'd been completely ensconced in the social world of these people, kept abreast of every tryst and dramatic separation. It was just the air she'd breathed back then, an inescapable part of life amongst the noblesse nouveau.

At Darian's heels was his brother, Silvan, unmistakable with his long, ice-blond hair, the haughty look on his angular face, and the pet snake curled indolently around his arm, a shock of bright blue against Silvan's pearlescent silver sleeve. Indifference sharpened to sneering contempt as his gaze glided over Marlow and landed on the crowd, a clear dismissal.

Marlow's pulse drummed in her head, not because she cared that Silvan detested her—which he did, although she was hardly unique in that regard—but because if he was here, then that meant, without a doubt, that his best friend was, too.

"Well, how have you been?" Darian asked politely. Unlike his brother, his good manners were always on display. Marlow assumed it was because there was very little substance beneath his strong jaw and honey-blond hair.

Gemma, on the other hand, was not so constrained by civility. "Seriously, where *did* you disappear to?"

Marlow knew her curiosity didn't derive from any sense of friendship.

Her interest in Marlow was the same interest a child might have for a shiny new toy. There had never been any chance of friendship, even when Marlow had been part of Evergarden society. Girls like Amara and Gemma didn't have friends, they had sycophants and victims. Even back then, Marlow was too thick-skinned to make a satisfying victim, and too wary to be a biddable sycophant. She had therefore been largely invisible to them, which had suited her just fine.

She wasn't the daughter of some lesser lord, but the daughter of the former Vale chevalier—not quite a commoner, but definitely not noblesse nouveau, though she'd been allowed to be educated alongside them. A rare allowance for someone of her status, and one she was grateful for, even now.

It was precisely that education that had taught her enough about spellcraft to become such a successful cursebreaker.

But none of these scions, the upper echelon of the upper echelon, had been Marlow's *friends*. None, of course, except—

Marlow stumbled over her answer to Gemma's question as she caught sight of a familiar head of carefully tousled chestnut curls. The crowd parted as neatly as curtains before a stage, and Adrius Falcrest emerged, his flame-gold dress coat sweeping out behind him, a matching cravat peeking out from his ruby waistcoat. Gilded by the light of the chandelier, he strode across the lobby with the leonine grace of someone perfectly aware that he commanded every set of eyes in the room—and perfectly content to.

Marlow could tell that he hadn't yet realized who it was his friends had accosted in the middle of the Monarch's lobby. Vindication fizzed in her chest as she watched him recognize her. The affable charm faded from his face, his smooth gait faltered for a split second before he recovered himself, an insouciant grin sliding comfortably into place.

Even the other scions, Marlow knew, were not unaffected by the inexorable glow of Adrius's presence. She felt them shift around her, accommodating Adrius and drawing toward him, like flowers seeking the sun.

"Well, this is certainly shaping up to be an interesting night," Adrius said, his whiskey-gold eyes lighting on Marlow, one elegant dark eyebrow cocked. "If you wanted to see me this badly, you didn't need to follow me all the way to the ballet, Minnow."

Marlow seethed, mortification kindling her anger. No one had called her that in over a year. The only two people who ever had were her mother and Adrius, who'd read it off a note her mother had slipped her on her very first day of classes in Evergarden. He'd refused to call her anything else since. It hadn't bothered her back then—or rather, it had bothered her in an entirely different way. Before Marlow recognized it for the cruel jab it was.

"Just an unlucky coincidence," Marlow replied, clipped. She considered, briefly, the appeal of wasting her last hex on Adrius, just for the fun of it. "I was on my way out, actually."

"So soon?" Adrius asked, brows pinching together with mock concern. "If it's a matter of affording a seat, I'm sure we can find room in the box, you need only ask. We are old friends, after all—aren't we?"

Gemma stifled a high-pitched giggle, and Amara elbowed her sharply. Silvan's gaze climbed skyward, as though he was praying for the Ibis God to swoop down from above and put an end to this awkward reunion. Marlow found herself in the unfamiliar position of wholeheartedly agreeing with him—although at this point, she'd also welcome the Crocodile Goddess rising from the depths of the swamp. Or better yet, snapping Adrius up in her jaws.

"Speaking of our private box, shouldn't we head up?" Silvan groused, shooting Adrius a pursed look. "I feel it's high time we take our leave of the . . . crowds." He punctuated this with an unsubtle glance at Marlow.

Adrius, however, made no sign he'd heard him, fixing Marlow with a taunting smirk as he awaited her riposte.

She was delighted to disappoint him. "Thanks for the offer, but I'll have to pass." She couldn't resist tacking on a sarcastic smile. "Enjoy the show."

She turned her back, but her escape was immediately thwarted by Teak, the stage manager she'd met in the green room.

"Miss Briggs!" Teak exclaimed. "I'm glad I caught you before you left."

"Corinne already paid me," Marlow said, stepping around her to reach the doors.

"Of course," Teak said, hurrying to follow. "The producers just wanted to extend their thanks—for your help as well as your discretion. Please accept this as a token of their gratitude."

She thrust a pair of tickets at Marlow, and Marlow, aware that Adrius and the others were still staring, took them without argument.

"They're valid for any night you wish to attend. The doorman will let you in on sight," Teak explained. "If you're ever in need of something the Monarch can provide, we'd be happy to assist you."

"I'll keep that in mind." Marlow could not imagine a scenario where she might require the aid of a ballet company, but she'd learned that it never hurt to have someone indebted to you. In Caraza, favors were often a more powerful currency than pearls. Especially for a cursebreaker.

As Teak marched away, ponytail swinging, Marlow was at last free to make her escape. She could feel Adrius's eyes on her back as she fled out the doors. Anger and mortification burned in her gut, but she was content at least with the knowledge that in less than an hour she'd be back in the Marshes where she belonged, and she'd never have to see Adrius Falcrest again.

THREE

Marlow sat on the counter of the Bowery Spellshop, chocolate-stuffed biscuit in hand, enchanting a cup of tea with a pilfered heating spellcard. Beside her, Swift fussed with his newest acquisition from the pawnshop next door, some kind of Aristan machine that, as far as Marlow could tell, had been invented to make a lot of unpleasant crackling noises.

The shop was empty now, but the morning had been an unusually busy one. Marlow didn't mind dealing with customers, but she preferred times like this when the shop was quiet and she could spend her time bothering Swift and sorting through new spells and cataloging ingredients.

Shoved unceremoniously between a soothsayer's office and a pawnshop, the Bowery was one of the oldest spell dealers in the Marshes. Its cramped quarters were stuffed full of spellcards of all kinds—simple Cleaning spells, Levitating charms, spells to ease bad dreams or bestow good luck, hexes to make someone's tongue swell up when they lied, enchantments to make one braver, or more desirable.

"That's a waste of magic," Swift grumbled, wiping a bead of sweat from his forehead and eyeing Marlow as she balanced her biscuit across the top of the now-steaming teacup. "It's already sweltering in here. Why do you need hot tea?"

"So it'll melt the inside of the biscuit and make it all gooey and delicious," she explained.

He squinted at his machine, his handsome features crinkled in dismay. "There is something very wrong with you."

"You have your luxuries, and I have mine," she replied serenely, gesturing at the machine, which was now emitting a low whine as Swift smacked the top of it. Through a bite of perfectly gooey chocolate she suggested, "Try hitting it harder."

Swift glared. "If you're not going to be helpful—"

"Why did you even buy that thing?"

"It's called a *radio*, and I bought it because I'd like to know what's going on in the world outside the Marshes."

The radio crackled to life, and a brassy song filled the shop before fading out as a voice rang out.

"*The Ballad of the Moon Thief* had its worldwide premiere last night, and it was a hit! Tickets are on sale now, so hurry and get yours before they sell out!"

There was something decidedly unsettling about listening to a stranger's disembodied voice try to sell theater tickets, but Swift looked absolutely thrilled.

"Oh right, how'd that case turn out?" he asked, drowning out the voice as it continued to chatter on. "You must've broken the curse if the show opened."

"Or that radio of yours is lying to you."

"I highly doubt you'd be sitting here, pestering me, if you hadn't," Swift replied. "So what happened? Who did it?"

She sipped her tea, avoiding his gaze. "Her understudy."

"Seriously?" Swift asked. "That's it? No more details? Come on, this case was a huge deal! Give me a little intrigue, a little Marlow pizzazz!"

Usually, Marlow was happy to regale him with sordid tales of scorned lovers and bitter rivals—and the Moon Thief case had certainly had its fair share of excitement. But it was precisely the exciting parts that she hoped to keep to herself.

Swift jostled her shoulder. "You never even told me how Orsella's lead panned out."

It was more *where* the lead had taken her that Marlow didn't want to divulge. "What's there to tell? I found the guy, I broke the curse, I saved the girl, same old story. Why don't we talk about what *you've* been up to? Met any more charming raconteurs lately?"

"Marlow." Swift's voice turned suspicious. "What are you not telling me?"

He was way too smart for his own good.

"It's very annoying when you do that," she complained.

"Good, now you know how the rest of us feel," Swift replied. "I can't change my *breakfast order* without you dredging up my deepest, darkest secrets. So what is it?"

"Before I tell you," Marlow hedged, "I would like to point out that I am sitting here, perfectly intact, and I *barely* even—"

"Marlow, I swear to the Crocodile Goddess—"

"I was at the Blind Tiger," Marlow said in a rush. "Orsella said I'd find the guy who bought Corinne's curse there."

Swift was silent for a long moment, which was honestly a lot worse than if he'd started yelling right off the bat. Finally, he asked, "So did you?"

"Yes," Marlow replied. "I hexed him, got the curse, and left."

"And?" Swift prompted. When she didn't offer more, he continued, "Let me guess: You ran into some Copperheads there. Because it's a *Copperhead bar*. How could you be so reckless?"

"I wasn't being *reckless*, Swift, I was doing my job," Marlow replied hotly. "Sometimes there are risks involved. I'm a cursebreaker, not a—"

"Not a what? A spellshop clerk?"

"Well, technically, I'm that, too," Marlow allowed. "Look, I didn't mean it like that. I'm *glad* Hyrum hired you. I'm glad you're safe now. If anyone deserves that, it's you."

"Just because we warded my flat to make it impossible to find doesn't mean I'm *safe*," Swift spat. He adjusted his left sleeve where it was pinned just under his elbow to cover the missing part of his arm. "Bane could still show up here to *pay you a visit*."

"Even Bane isn't stupid enough to make trouble in Reaper territory," Marlow said dismissively. The Reapers and the Copperheads were the two biggest gangs in the Marshes and had developed a bitter, bloody rivalry. No matter how much the Copperheads had it out for Marlow and Swift, they wouldn't touch them in Reaper territory.

Swift shook his head. "I owe you a lot, Marlow, and you know I couldn't love you more if you were blood, but sometimes it's like you don't see anything except the mystery you're trying to solve."

A chord of hurt throbbed in her chest. Which meant, of course, that Swift had hit home. It wasn't anything she didn't already know about herself, but coming from Swift it held more weight. And not just because he was right, but because she could see the raw fear in his dark eyes, and she was ashamed to have put it there.

It took her right back to those first few weeks after her mother's disappearance, when she'd finally found Swift again. But he'd been nothing like the exuberant, goofy boy she'd known as a kid, the boy she'd bossed around and played Swamp Monster with. The Swift she had returned to had been a hollow, hunted creature, less whole than he was now. The Copperheads' curse may have claimed his arm, but that was a small price to pay for his freedom.

His was the first curse Marlow had helped break, and it was the reason she'd gotten into the business of cursebreaking to begin with. The look on

Swift's face the moment the curse had lifted and the Copperheads' hold on him was finally severed had stayed with her ever since. A reminder of the kind of good she could do by changing even just one life.

And it was precisely that memory that made Swift's disappointment so hard to bear. She felt like crying.

"Promise me you won't go back to Breaker's Neck," Swift said seriously.

She wouldn't lie to him. "I have to go where the case takes me, Swift. It's not like I was there looking for trouble."

His expression was bitter, resigned. "No, Marlow, you're never looking for trouble, yet it always seems to find you anyway, doesn't it?"

The radio droned on in the silence, now playing what sounded like a weather report.

The door of the shop swung open, and they both jumped, veering to face Hyrum as he stomped inside, shaking rain from his mane of dark hair.

"Am I paying the two of you to stand around and gossip?" he asked, glancing from Swift to Marlow and back. "Go organize the wards shelf or something."

With a last glare, Swift stalked off to the far corner of the shop.

Marlow hopped down from the counter, circling Hyrum like a pelican spotting its dinner.

"Yes?" Hyrum grunted, shoving aside the curtain to the back storage room.

"You know a lot about the Marshes," she began.

"I've lived here my entire life, so I'd say I know a bit," Hyrum retorted. He spoke to the wall of spell ingredients—canisters full of baby teeth, blood, shimmering gold luck, ghostly memories suspended in smoke. Jars that appeared empty but really contained someone's voice, or their last breath. All bought from people desperate enough to sell pieces of themselves for a few pearls.

There wasn't much profit in selling enchantments to folks in the Marshes, who often could barely afford to feed their families, much less buy protection wards and mood-lifting charms. So like most spellshops in the Marshes, the Bowery also bought ingredients and sold them to the Five Families for a small cut. And if Hyrum, on occasion, siphoned off ingredients to sell on the black market, well, that was just good business.

Marlow nudged aside an overturned box with her foot. "Have you ever heard of a gang that uses a black flower symbol as their emblem?"

Hyrum dropped the box in his hands and wheeled around to face her. "Is this for a case?"

His tone was deliberately cool, but it could not hide his initial reaction to the question.

"Sort of," Marlow hedged.

"Because if it *is* about a case, it would be my professional advice to drop it."

"So you *do* know something about it." Taking a gamble, she pressed, "Did Mom mention it to you?"

Something flickered across his weathered face, lightning-quick, but it was gone before Marlow could decipher it. "No, Cassandra never said anything to me, and if you're as smart as I think you are, you won't bring up anything to do with the Black Orchid to me, or anyone else in—"

"The Black Orchid?"

Hyrum cringed, plunging his face into one broad palm. "*Forget* you heard that. And shut up about this, I mean it. Let it go, Marlow."

He never called her by her first name. It was always "get back to work, Briggs" or "stop bothering me, kid." Hearing it now, she knew it meant he was deadly serious. Hyrum was many things—taciturn, aggravatingly stuck in his ways, at times an infuriating bastard—but he wasn't irrational. If he wanted Marlow to stay away from this, there was a good reason.

But letting things go wasn't really in Marlow's nature. And this was about her mother, the great unsolved mystery of her life. The question that lived under her skin, that prodded at her when her thoughts were otherwise quiet. It sat like a lake in her mind. On the surface were the obvious questions that lapped against the shore.

Where was she?

Why had she left? Had it been by choice, or by force?

Was she even still alive?

But these questions were more than questions—they were clues to the mystery that pulled Marlow into the depths below. The mystery of who her mother really was.

Hyrum must have recognized the look on her face and what it meant, because he sighed. "Your mother kept secrets to protect you."

"Secrets can't protect me," Marlow replied. "Only the truth can."

Marlow owed Hyrum a lot. He'd known her since she was a kid, having been one of Cassandra's closest friends in the Marshes. He'd been the one to pick up the pieces and give Marlow a home after she'd lost everything.

But if he wasn't going to budge on this, she would just have to find the answers she wanted without his help, or his knowledge. He couldn't complain. He *knew* who Marlow was, and he knew there was no letting go of this. Not for her.

With both Swift and Hyrum ticked off, Marlow spent a miserable afternoon cataloging ingredients in the Bowery's sweltering back room. She'd never been so relieved when Hyrum told her she didn't have to help close up.

Another brief but torrential afternoon storm had left the street soggy with mud, but her stomach rumbled with hunger, so Marlow dragged herself down to the dock and the boats moored there, selling fish fry and turtle soup.

Caraza was built on the low-lying wetlands between Tourmaline Bay and the Pearl River. The city architects had dredged the bay side of the city, carving out an efficient, organized network of canals. That part of the city became Evergarden and the Outer Garden District.

The project had more or less drowned the land to the west, already prone to flooding from the river. The people of the Marshes, as this part of the city had come to be called, had no real choice but to adapt to their new environment. They built their homes on stilts, laid down makeshift roads and bridges of wood and scavenged materials, turned fishing boats into homes and storefronts.

"You got time for a game, Marlow?"

Marlow glanced over at Fiero and Basil sitting in their usual spot on the end of the dock, a Pento board between them.

"Just getting dinner," Marlow replied, nodding over to the boats. "You want anything?"

Fiero twirled a Pento tile between his fingers and watched Basil sign rapidly. He'd sold his voice to a spellshop almost two decades ago to pay off a debt. "Baz says you're just embarrassed by how badly he beat you last time."

"It was a lousy draw!" she shouted over her shoulder, heading toward the boats.

She bought three fish frys with pickled onions and spicy sauce, piping hot and wrapped up in newspaper. She dropped two of them off with Fiero and Basil before carrying her own up to her tiny flat above the Bowery.

It smelled so delicious and she was so hungry that she ended up unwrapping it to eat as she climbed the creaking stairwell to the third landing, chewing as she mulled over where to start looking for answers about the Black Orchid.

She was still lost in thought when she unlocked her front door, balancing her dinner in one palm.

Perhaps that was why it took her several long seconds to notice that someone was sitting in her chair, feet propped up on the desk, one hand stretched above his head, the other scratching Toad affectionately between the ears.

The fish fry tumbled out of Marlow's hand, plopping onto the floor. She caught the gray flash of Toad's furry tail as she bounded over to investigate, but Marlow's attention was fixed on the boy at her desk.

Adrius said, "So, this is where you've been hiding all this time."

FOUR

Marlow wondered, as her pulse thundered in her head, which god in the Pantheon of the Ever-Drowning Mangrove she'd pissed off this time. Because clearly, someone was out to ruin her life.

"What, no hello?" Adrius asked, swinging his legs off the desk. Today's rich carmine jacket and open-collared cream shirt were much more casual than the outfit he'd worn at the theater the night before, but he still looked perfectly polished. "Do they not have hospitality in the Marshes?"

It took Marlow several calming breaths to find her voice. "How did you get in here?"

He drummed his fingers on the desk. "Pretty simple Lock-picking spell. You should really update your wards."

Marlow wanted to laugh. "If I'd known I was in danger of surprise visits from you, I would have."

Not that it would have mattered. As a scion of one of the Five Families, Adrius had access to spells she couldn't even *dream* of. No ward would be strong enough to keep him out.

The corner of Adrius's mouth quirked up. "You never complained about my surprise visits before."

Back in Evergarden, it had not been unusual for Marlow to find Adrius much like this, lounging in the apartment she shared with her mother. He usually appeared whenever there was some function at Vale Tower—inevitably Adrius would slip away and show up in Marlow's living room complaining that the party was so dull, or that Silvan was being particularly irritating that day. He'd then inform Marlow it was her responsibility to entertain him. Sometimes, Marlow indulged him, teaching Adrius to play Casters or roping him into silly pranks. Other times, she would insist she had schoolwork or chores, and inevitably Adrius would end up coaxing her away from her obligations anyway.

From the beginning, their friendship had existed on Adrius's terms.

She drew her spine straight. "Are you planning on telling me what in the mucking brack you're doing in my house?"

"Do you call this a house?" he wondered, his gaze sweeping from the boxy kitchen huddled in the corner, over the slouching table propped up by old boxes from the Bowery, to the tattered sheet that hung across the far wall. "I didn't know they made flats this small. It's . . . cozy."

It was cluttered and cramped and felt somehow even smaller with Adrius inside it. As if his presence spilled out into every nook and cranny like incendiary light.

She needed him gone.

"You haven't answered my question." She eyed Toad, who was cheerfully licking at the dropped fish fry.

"What am I doing here?" He circled around the desk to perch on the edge, arranging the lean, elegant lines of his body to greatest advantage. Marlow wondered if he even realized he was doing it, or if posing and posturing just came second nature to him. "I thought I might hire a good cursebreaker. Know any?"

He was looking at her in that arch way of his, honey-gold eyes framed by thick, dark lashes, full lips pressing down a smile, like maybe all this was a joke and he hadn't yet decided if he was going to let her in on it.

"Why would a Falcrest scion need a cursebreaker?"

"I imagine for the same reason anyone needs a cursebreaker."

It *had* to be a joke. "Let me see if I have this right. Someone cast a curse on the son of the man responsible for producing half the spells in this city, and you want *my* help to break it?"

"No, I want your help to plan the Falcrest Midnight Masquerade," Adrius replied.

Marlow knew well enough to expect the flippant reply, but beneath the careless, charismatic Falcrest veneer, she detected something troubled. It showed itself in the way his long fingers gripped the edge of her desk just a little too tight. Whatever had happened to him, he was worried enough not only to have crossed the city to the Marshes—somewhere he'd probably never before set foot in his entire charmed life—but had come to *Marlow*. To ask for her *help*.

It must have rankled him to have to admit that he needed anything from someone as insignificant as her.

"Last night, at the ballet, I overheard you talking to that woman," he explained. "She told me the whole story of how you single-handedly rescued the star of the Monarch Ballet and saved the entire theater from utter financial ruin."

Of course. Teak, the stage manager who was apparently easily dazzled by the glamour of the noblesse nouveau. So much for discretion.

"It was quite a tale," Adrius went on. "So I figured, if you're really that good at breaking curses, you'll be able to help me with my . . . problem."

Marlow folded her arms over her chest. "What would give you the idea that I'm at all interested in helping you?"

"You wound me, Minnow," Adrius said, clutching his chest dramatically. "It's been over a year since we've seen each other, and this is the treatment I get? Come, you can tell me the truth. I know you've missed me."

She held up her hands in surrender. "You got me. I stare out my bedroom window every morning, pining and praying that today will be the day Adrius Falcrest appears in my living room."

His golden eyes darkened for a moment so brief she wondered if she'd imagined it. "See, that wasn't so hard."

Having grown bored of the fish fry, Toad slinked over to Adrius, winding around his ankles and meowing plaintively. She stared up at Marlow, her pupils going huge and glowing like a pair of iridescent moonstones.

"Gods," Marlow said, looking from Toad's glowing pupils back to Adrius. "You're serious, aren't you?"

Adrius leaned away from Toad. "Did your cat just . . . ?"

"Toad can detect curses," Marlow said. "Don't ask me how or why. I found her like that. But she's never wrong, which means you really *are* cursed."

"Why else would I be here?"

"To ruin my evening?" Marlow suggested.

Adrius looked at her, smug. "You're considering helping me, aren't you?"

She didn't deny it. Her curiosity was more than piqued, and it was almost enough to overwhelm the part of her that warned to stay away from Adrius Falcrest at all costs.

There was another reason to accept the offer, one that beat like a drum in her chest. Agreeing to help Adrius meant returning to Evergarden—the place that held the ghosts of her past and, quite possibly, the key to finally putting them to rest. If there was an answer to what had happened to her mother, it was in Evergarden.

"There's hundreds of cursebreakers in this city," she said, stalling. "I'm sure with all those piles of pearls you'd have no trouble finding one."

"I don't know any of those cursebreakers," Adrius replied easily. "I know you."

No, you don't, Marlow wanted to say. He knew the girl she'd been a year ago, and he imagined that somehow despite all the upheaval Marlow had endured in that time, she hadn't changed. That she was still that guileless little girl, easy to charm and even easier to manipulate.

"Come on," he pressed. "For old times' sake?"

Marlow clenched down on a seething smile. She'd avoided approaching him the entire time he'd been in her flat, afraid somehow that coming closer would mean getting pulled into his orbit like a wayward moon. But now her anger overrode any sense of self-preservation and she found herself crossing the distance without thought.

"Time to go," she bit out, dragging him to the door by a fistful of his jacket as if he were anyone else.

"Hold on," he protested. "I only meant that—you must at least be curious what the curse *is*. You don't want to—?"

Of *course* she was curious. There was a huge part of her that burned to know, if only because she found the mere idea of an unsolved mystery unbearable. And she wasn't so deep in denial that she couldn't admit the thought of knowing one of Adrius Falcrest's secrets still held undeniable allure.

"Get out of my house," she hissed.

He must have recognized how grave his error had been and how dangerously pissed off Marlow was, because he relented with surprising ease. Marlow barely even had to steer him out. On the landing, he turned back to her as she gripped the door, more than ready to slam it shut.

But the look on his face stopped her.

It was an expression she wasn't used to seeing, even back when—when she hadn't known his true character. Brow drawn tight, mouth soft, eyes troubled. He looked young. He looked vulnerable. He looked . . . lost.

Marlow hesitated. Because they'd been friends once, and maybe she still remembered how it had felt to bask in the golden glow of Adrius's attention, to imagine she could see past the blinding light of his charm to the boy beneath the facade.

But it didn't matter. It wasn't real. *He* wasn't real, not then, and not now, and maybe if Marlow told herself that enough times, she'd finally start believing it.

But she still didn't close the door. Even when Adrius looked away, turned in a slow half circle, and started to descend the creaking wooden stairs.

She was still so godsdamn soft. With a steadying breath, she stomped back to her desk, past an alarmed Toad, and threw open the top drawer to pluck out one of the cards before rushing down the stairs after him.

"Adrius."

She caught him just below the second landing. He whipped around, eyes bright. He stood a step below her, and it felt strange to look at him from that angle, like a portrait that was just ever so slightly *off.*

She thrust the card at him. "Here. The address of another curse-breaker I trust. I've worked with her; she knows her stuff, I promise. And she values discretion."

"Oh." His eyes dropped to her hand as he took the card carefully, pinching it between his fingers without so much as grazing Marlow's thumb. Then he met her gaze again, lips curling into a smile. "I don't suppose I'll run into you at the ballet again, will I?"

She snorted. "That's not really my kind of place."

"It was, once."

"No, it really wasn't." She cleared her throat. "Good luck, Adrius."

She spun on her heel, scrambling back up the stairs before she let herself say anything more.

A familiar rap against Marlow's door woke her the next morning. Groaning, she wiped a hand over her sleep-crusted face and rolled out of bed, shuffling past Toad, who was pawing dolefully at her empty food bowl.

"Swift, you better be in immediate physical peril right now," she said, unlatching the door.

"It's almost midday," Swift said with a judgmental look. "Were you really still asleep?"

"It's my day off, and I had a long night," she replied, moving to let him inside.

He predictably made a beeline for Toad and leaned down so she could rub her head happily against his face.

Marlow hadn't been able to settle her thoughts after Adrius left the night before, and even after frantically cleaning up her dropped dinner and then the entire rest of her flat, she hadn't been able to burn out the frenetic energy buzzing under her skin. The more she replayed their conversation, the angrier she became, until she stopped being able to tell who it was she was angry at.

"Did you want to yell at me some more?" she asked Swift as she set about getting breakfast for Toad and boiling water for tea on the woodstove.

He scratched at the back of his neck. "I actually came to apologize."

"You didn't say anything that wasn't true."

"It wasn't fair. The only reason the Copperheads even know about you is because of me." Marlow did not like seeing the shadow of shame in his dark eyes. "I think I just . . . I don't know. I just feel so guilty, that you could get hurt because of me. And I feel so stupid because I'm *terrified*, and you . . . you never seem to be afraid of anything."

"That's *far* from true," she said with a snort. "I'm scared of plenty of things."

"Well, you never show it."

It was half compliment and half reproach. A reminder that even though she trusted Swift, relied on Swift, there were still things she held back.

The teapot whistled and Swift darted into the kitchen to pour the tea.

"By the way," he said over his shoulder, "there's a package sitting outside. I would've brought it in but it's kind of unwieldy to carry with one hand."

Grateful for the change in subject, Marlow poked her head out the front door. A large, rectangular box sat on the landing, wrapped in white paper and silver ribbon. Uneasy, Marlow carried it back to her desk.

There was no card or address of any kind. Either someone had dropped it off themselves, or they had sent it by magic. With a sinking feeling, Marlow untied the ribbon and lifted off the top of the box.

"Is that a *dress*?" Swift asked, sounding aghast and delighted.

A very expensive one, by the look of it, with a long, flowing skirt the color of Tourmaline Bay and a ruffled bodice embroidered with glittering turquoise gems that resembled sunlight glinting off water. Nestled beside it in the crinkly tissue paper sat a crisp, white envelope.

Marlow lifted her teacup to her lips.

"Who the brack sent you a *dress*?" Swift demanded. "Do you have a rich secret admirer I don't know about? This isn't for a case, is it?"

She glared. "There's no admirer and there's no case. Stop laughing."

He did stop laughing, but only so he could dodge around her to swipe the envelope out of the box. "Is this a love letter? Today is my *favorite* day." The envelope burst open in his hands with a shower of bright sparks and gently lilting music. Swift held out the page within, clearing his throat. "'To our esteemed guest. You are hereby invited to the Summer Solstice Classic Regatta.' *Gods*, Marlow, what *is* this? 'Refreshments to follow at the . . .' blah blah blah. Oh, there's a handwritten bit here at the end—'If you decide to reconsider the offer, find me here tomorrow.' It's not signed."

Of course it wasn't signed. Because who else in this entire muck-filled city would invite Marlow to a *regatta* besides Adrius Falcrest. And send a *dress* with the invite, gods below.

Marlow snatched the invitation out of Swift's hand, crumpled it up, and threw it into the small garbage bin next to her desk.

"You know who sent it," Swift accused, still breathless with laughter.

"Yep."

"And?"

She rolled her eyes. "Adrius Falcrest. What time do you get off work tonight?"

When she looked back at Swift, there was a strange expression on his face, as if she'd just said, "No, thanks, I don't want another chocolate biscuit."

"Adrius Falcrest invited you to a regatta and we're just . . . not going to talk about that?"

"It's not what you think," she said. "He wants to hire me to break a curse."

Swift balked. "And you're not going to take the case? Really? I thought helping people was kind of your whole thing. Even people you hate."

"I don't hate him," Marlow snapped. "I don't feel anything about him. And *please,* he's a Falcrest scion, he'll be fine."

"Yeah, he's a *Falcrest scion*. Which means he has a lot of money. Money he could pay you with." He waggled his eyebrows. "Money that you could use to buy a nice gift for your best pal, Swift."

"I don't want his money," Marlow replied. "I'd rather wade naked through Limewater Lagoon than work for Adrius Falcrest."

Swift stared at her for a long moment, and then blew out a breath, shaking his head. "In that case, can I have the dress? I can pawn it next door. They have this new type of camera that—"

"Yeah, fine, take it," Marlow said with a wave.

She shoved the dress into a bag to make it easier for Swift to carry, and sent him on his way. As soon as the door swung shut behind him, Marlow collapsed back into her chair. Toad climbed up into her lap, her sharp claws digging into the meat of Marlow's thigh.

What did Adrius think he was pulling, sending her an invitation to a regatta? Had she not been clear that she wasn't interested in taking the case?

For old times' sake. Marlow felt like breaking something just thinking of it, the way he'd so callously thrown their past friendship, or whatever it had been, in her face.

The fact of the matter was, they *had* been friends. Or Marlow had been foolish and lonely enough to think that they were. And Adrius had been—Adrius. Charming and captivating and *kind* when no one else even bothered to notice her.

Until he wasn't. Until she'd looked at him one day, and he had looked right past her like she didn't exist. And the *worst* part was, it had taken her weeks to accept what had happened. Weeks of trying to capture his attention again, like trying to catch a firefly in a glass jar. Weeks of waking up each morning hoping that would be the day he showed up at her door, teasing her and calling her *Minnow*, and everything would go back to the way it had been. Weeks of wondering if she'd done something wrong, or if he'd just gotten bored with her, or if it had all been a game from the start.

Even now, it drove her crazy, an itch she couldn't scratch no matter how many times she told herself that it didn't matter, and more important, she didn't care.

Get over it, Briggs. Move on.

That evening, Marlow sat at her desk, picking over a bowl of rice and egg stew as she finished up her notes on the Moon Thief case.

Toad had overturned the waste bin and was amusing herself by batting its contents around the room in a desultory hunt. She had one piece of rubbish cornered at Marlow's feet, and she pounced, tackling her prey and gnawing on it noisily.

You shouldn't let your cat eat trash, an annoyingly Swift-like voice chastised.

With a sigh, Marlow scooped Toad up, rescuing the crumpled piece of paper. With a lurch, Marlow realized it was the invitation to the regatta. She righted the waste bin and shoved it back inside.

Marlow went back to her desk, but found she could no longer focus on her notes. Her attention snagged on the invitation, like she was a fish and it was the bait waiting to reel her in.

It's just a stupid piece of paper, she chided herself. But she felt like it was mocking her.

In a fit of irritation, she fished it out of the waste bin again and reached for her lighter. Smoothing out the invitation, she flicked open the flame and held it to the bottom corner. Unbidden, her eyes scanned the delicate cursive script.

To our esteemed guest, it read. *You are hereby invited to the Summer Solstice Classic Regatta. Refreshments to follow at the reception luncheon aboard the* Contessa.

"Shit," Marlow said to her empty flat. She put the lighter down. "*Shit.*"

In three loping strides, Marlow crossed the flat to the tattered sheet that blanketed the wall beside her bed. With a sharp tug, the sheet cascaded down, revealing Marlow's notes from a much older, much more vexing case: The Case of the Missing Mother.

Clues covered the wall, along with Marlow's own threads of conjecture and, of course, questions. Everywhere, questions.

The wall had been untouched for over six months, which was around the time Marlow had exhausted every possible lead, as well as herself, and Swift and Hyrum had taken it upon themselves to stage an intervention. She'd covered up the wall, packed her questions carefully away, and let the case go cold, knowing deep down that if she was ever going to find the answers she wanted, she wouldn't do it from the Marshes.

Now, Marlow let her eyes scan the clutter of loose paper and half-remembered sketches, her ears ringing. Her gaze, at last, fell on a card pinned in the lower left corner of the wall, beneath a list of things Marlow suspected had been missing from their quarters in Vale Tower the day her mother had disappeared.

In her own cramped scrawl, the card read, *Night before: Saw her writing a message to someone, saying, "Bring it to the Contessa tomorrow night." She seemed panicked when she realized I'd seen it. Who is the Contessa and what does she know?*

With shaking hands, Marlow pinned the invitation up next to the card and wrapped her arms around herself.

The *Contessa* wasn't a person. It was a ship.

And tomorrow afternoon, Marlow was going to be on it.

FIVE

The first thing Marlow thought when she arrived at the regatta was that she would much rather walk into the Blind Tiger and face a hundred Copperheads than be here right now.

The *Contessa*'s viewing deck was crowded with noblesse nouveau dressed in crisp white linens and light, gauzy dresses that resembled the various confections whirling about the deck on enchanted trays. Outside the floor-to-ceiling windows, Tourmaline Bay glistened in the late afternoon sunlight. Dozens of sailboats floated in the near distance, taking their marks at the starting line of the race.

But these were not just any boats—they had been magically conjured out of an assortment of impossible materials. Marlow spotted one made entirely of colored glass, reflecting the sun in a vibrant prism. Another was carved out of iridescent nacre, flying shot silk sails. And on and on—gleaming boats of solid gold, boats assembled out of thousands of bright blossoms, even a boat fabricated out of the same wispy clouds that fleeced the azure sky.

It was a stunning display of magic for most anyone in the world. For the people watching the races from aboard the *Contessa*, it was just another event in their social calendar.

No one paid Marlow much mind as she bobbed through the crowd. There were the usual faces of the noblesse nouveau, most of whom Marlow at least vaguely recognized, as well as a fair amount of high-ranking city officials, and a few younger, sharp-eyed people Marlow guessed might be reporters.

Adrius was easy to spot amidst the crowd, holding court in the middle of the deck with a dozen or so admirers hanging on his every word. He wore a bright-coral linen suit with a slightly open collar that made him look effortlessly put together. Marlow pushed toward him, catching the tail end of what was no doubt a riveting story, judging by how intently the other noblesse nouveau were listening.

". . . and that's the last time I ever let Silvan talk me into skinny-dipping in the Crescent Canal again," Adrius said.

The girl next to him—whose name Marlow couldn't recall—let out a high trill of laughter and laid a hand on his arm. "Oh, Adrius, you are *too* much."

At that moment, Adrius's gaze lifted and met Marlow's. Without a single word to his cadre of sycophants, he broke from the circle and swept over to her. The girl who'd laughed at his story looked put out by the dismissal, and then positively incensed when she saw what—or rather who—Adrius had just deserted her for.

The onlookers began to whisper in confusion, but Marlow's gaze went back to Adrius and the unreadable expression on his face.

She quirked a smile. "What, no hello?"

He swept an assessing gaze over her. "What happened to the dress I sent you?"

She grabbed a flute of sparkling wine off a floating tray. "I pawned it." She took a sip, the bubbly drink zipping straight to her head. "Actually, my friend Swift pawned it. He says thanks for the new camera. Why'd you send me a dress anyway? You thought I didn't own anything nice enough to wear to a regatta?"

She'd had to dig a dress out of the back of her wardrobe. It was a dusky lilac with a simple wrap bodice and a knee-length skirt that flowed out from her waist in gentle waves. She was hardly the most fashionably dressed girl aboard the boat, but she didn't think she stood out *too* badly.

Adrius raised his eyebrows and said mildly, "When I saw you at the ballet, it did raise some questions."

"I was working."

"And you're not now?"

"That's yet to be determined." She glanced around. More than a few eyes were trained on them, including those of the same circle of onlookers Adrius had abandoned, as well as a red-haired woman Marlow pegged as a reporter, and a tall, dark-haired man she didn't recognize. His piercing blue gaze made her spine prickle. "Is there somewhere private we can talk?"

Adrius smirked, and she already knew she was going to hate what came out of his mouth next. "Most of the girls here want to get me alone, you know. Probably half the boys, too."

"And yet, it was *my* living room you showed up in two days ago, begging for help."

His grin widened.

"Spare me whatever it is you're about to say," she said, before he could open his mouth.

To her amazement, he did as she asked, his lips pressing together. She narrowed her eyes. For as long as she'd known him, Adrius had been a fount of sarcastic comments. She couldn't remember a time when he'd actually kept his mouth shut, no matter the consequences.

The bracing blare of the starting horn cut through the air. The crowd around them shifted as people moved toward the windows to watch the boats.

Adrius reached for Marlow's wrist. "Come on," he said, jerking his head toward the double doors. "While everyone's distracted."

He wove expertly through the crowd, Marlow in tow. She didn't like the proprietary way he gripped her wrist, but she didn't say anything or try to pull away until they were safely outside, at which point he let her go. He led her up a set of stairs and Marlow took note of the branching corridors, already planning her own search through them once she was done with Adrius.

At the top of the stairs, Adrius took a right down another gilded corridor and pushed open a sliding door that revealed a small, sun-drenched lounge, just a few couches surrounding a low table. The windows on the far side of the room stretched floor to ceiling, looking out onto the sparkling bay.

"This is where Silvan usually sneaks off to during these things," Adrius explained. He gestured Marlow inside.

"You first," she said, watching him carefully.

He shrugged and sauntered in, flopping down on one of the couches with affected indifference.

Marlow stepped inside after him, sliding the door shut behind her and circling the table to lean up against the armrest of the couch facing him.

"So ask me," Adrius said.

She crossed her arms over her chest. "Ask you what?"

"Don't play coy," he said. "You must be dying to know. I bet you haven't stopped wondering about it since the other night—what kind of curse could I *possibly*—"

"Get up."

For a moment Adrius just stared at her. A muscle twitched in his jaw, and he exhaled audibly through his nose. He seized for a moment, all the languid nonchalance sapping out of him as he lurched stiffly to his feet.

"Shit," Marlow said under her breath, sinking down onto the couch. Suspicion confirmed. She remembered how easily Adrius had left her flat the other night when she'd ordered it, and how he'd fallen silent just a few minutes ago on the observation deck. "A Compulsion curse."

"So you've seen this before," he said blandly.

"No, I haven't," Marlow replied. "*No one* has. At least not in a few centuries."

"What?"

Marlow sighed. "The only known recipe for a Compulsion curse—a real Compulsion curse that forces the cursed person to follow any direct order—was invented by Ilario the Terrible five hundred years ago. He used it to do a whole bunch of terrible shit, because he was an evil sorcerer and that was kind of their whole thing. And his spellbook, *Ilario's Grimoire*, was destroyed along with every other spellbook deemed too dangerous by the Five Families when they—*you*—established the spellcraft academies two centuries ago. Or at least, it was supposed to have been destroyed."

Adrius stared at her. "How do you *know* all that?"

"Well, for one, it's my job to know all that," Marlow said, "and also, unlike *you*, I actually paid attention in our History of Spellcraft lectures."

"Is that what that tedious man was droning on about? I suppose I had more interesting things to occupy myself with," he said with a pointed smirk.

"Too busy gazing adoringly at your own reflection in the window?"

"That, and mentally composing odes to the studious blond who sat next to me."

"Silvan must have been so flattered," Marlow replied coolly.

Adrius's lips twitched, and immediately Marlow chastised herself for letting him draw her into his game of provocation.

She blew out a heavy breath. "Of course you'd manage to get yourself not only cursed, but cursed with a spell that shouldn't even *exist* anymore due to how notoriously horrific it is."

"So you can see why I didn't want to take this case to just anyone," Adrius said, that same bland nonchalance blunting his words.

She did see. The potential to take advantage of not just Adrius, but the entire Falcrest family, was boundless. Anyone with knowledge of Adrius's curse could have him completely under their control.

Marlow paced the length of the lounge restlessly. "I'm serious. This is *bad*, Adrius. A Compulsion curse is—someone could order you to hurt your family. Your friends. Yourself. They could—"

"I know." His eyes flashed with something sharp, dangerous. "No one can know about this. *No one.*"

"You haven't told anyone."

"I—can't."

It took Marlow a moment to understand what he was saying. "You mean you've been ordered not to."

"I guess," Adrius replied. "I don't know. I don't *remember* being ordered not to tell anyone, but whenever I try I just . . . can't get the words out."

"And no one's figured it out?" Marlow asked. "It took me all of five minutes."

Adrius laughed. "Well, that's where you and most of the people on this boat differ, Minnow. Because no one else here would be caught dead issuing orders to a Falcrest scion."

"What about your father?"

He smiled thinly. "That would require him to pay attention to me for longer than five minutes."

Marlow had never really understood Adrius's relationship with his father. Aurelius Falcrest was known to be an unpleasant man, acerbic to even his closest allies and contemptuous of anyone who didn't live up to his expectations—a category that seemed to include just about everyone, but especially his son. Marlow had always gotten the sense that Adrius had long ago abandoned any attempt to make him proud, and instead turned disappointing him into an art form.

"You're the only one who knows," Adrius said.

Marlow abruptly stopped her restless pacing, her gaze landing on his troubled face. This was more than just him asking her for help, she saw that now. There was no one else he could turn to. He was trusting her with his life.

He *needed* her, and she could see how much he hated that he did.

"Except I'm not," she pointed out quietly. "There's one other person who knows—whoever did this to you."

Adrius's jaw tightened.

"You have absolutely no idea who it was? Not even a guess? Someone you pissed off recently, maybe? That must be a long list."

"What do you mean? Everyone adores me."

"Of course. How could anyone mistake your charm for obnoxious arrogance?" She cleared her throat. "When exactly did this curse start?"

"About three weeks ago," Adrius answered. "Does this mean you're taking my case?"

"We haven't discussed payment," she said. "A thousand pearls. Half up front, half when the curse is broken. Plus expenses."

It was twice her usual fee, but Adrius didn't need to know that.

He arched an eyebrow. "And if you can't break the curse?"

"Well, it's never happened before," she said. "But I guess anything's possible."

He gazed up at her through his dark lashes, mouth tilting into a smirk. "Now who's arrogant?"

Before Marlow could point out that it wasn't arrogance if it was *true*, the door slid abruptly open and three teenagers burst inside.

"Adrius, how *dare* you ditch us with all those boring stiffs downstairs. I hope you're not—" Gemma stopped in her tracks as her gaze fell on Marlow. "*Oh.*"

Marlow had tumbled back onto the couch in surprise when the door opened, resulting in a tableau she was sure looked far more compromising than it actually was, with Adrius draped along the couch just inches away. Gemma's gaze was flicking back and forth between them, looking a lot like Toad when she caught sight of a bird. If she had a tail, it would be twitching.

Behind her, Silvan looked on with his usual boredom, while his brother wore a polite smile.

"I *knew* it," Gemma crowed. Her hair, Marlow noted, was a different color than it had been at the Monarch—a tart shade of nectarine, which somehow perfectly complemented her frothy, daydream-pink dress. "How long has this been going on?"

Adrius looked like he'd just bitten into an unripened starfruit. "Nothing's *going on*."

"Please, why else would you sneak off before the race even started? We all know how you operate. Just admit it."

Marlow felt like she was watching a disaster in slow motion as Adrius opened his mouth, helpless to defy the order that Gemma had just unwittingly issued.

"We're up here because I asked Marlow—"

It was panic, Marlow told herself later, that made her open her mouth and say what would most likely prove to be the stupidest thing she'd ever said in her life.

"—to be his date!" She flicked a coquettish glance at him and looped an arm through his. "I know you didn't want to tell anyone, but it looks like we don't have a choice."

"Don't tell me *this* is why you were late to the ballet the other night," Silvan scoffed. "Typical. I should've known when we ran into her two minutes before you showed up."

Marlow faked a laugh. "I guess we weren't as discreet as we thought."

"Adrius, are you *blushing*?" Gemma asked.

Darian wrapped an arm around her, trying to usher her and his brother back toward the door. "We'll just leave you two alone, then."

"No, no, it's fine," Marlow said, sensing an opportunity. "I've been monopolizing all of Adrius's time today, haven't I? I was really only supposed to stop by and see the race, but, you know, one thing led to another . . . anyway, I should really get going."

She started to rise, only for Adrius to tighten his hold on her arm.

"Oh, but you don't want to leave me here, do you?" Adrius said, seething with barely concealed anger that hopefully the others would mistake for untamed ardor. "*Darling.*"

"Stay with your friends. I'll see you tomorrow," Marlow promised. "My place, right? Thirteenth bell? Don't be late."

Before she could reconsider, Marlow leaned in and pressed her lips to Adrius's cheek. Her own face heated as she pulled away, stood up, and marched over to the door.

Silvan gave her an almost challenging look as she approached, his pointed chin tipped toward the ceiling. He didn't shift an inch, forcing Marlow to skirt around him to exit the room. She could feel all four pairs of eyes on her back as she turned on her heel and hurried down the corridor.

As Marlow wound through the corridors of the *Contessa*, she tried not to think about what had just transpired and the split-second decision she'd made to keep Adrius's secret. She had a mission to fulfill, and she would not let herself be distracted.

This ship was likely the last place her mother had been before her disappearance. And if that was really the case, then there had to be *some* sort of clue here as to what had happened that night.

The obvious thing to check first would be the ship's logs. Marlow knew from a previous case involving a cursed lobster boat that the log was typically kept in the bridge, so she headed in that direction.

It felt eerie to walk these same halls that her mother had likely traversed on that fateful night. Marlow had gone over the details of that evening in her mind countless times, but now she returned to pick over the memory.

Bergamot and vetiver. Her mother at the writing desk, burning a spellcard. A bottle of perfume, knocked over onto a pile of papers.

"Minnow! I didn't hear you come in." She met Marlow's gaze in the mirror that hung above the writing desk.

"What is that?" Marlow had asked, eyes trained on the spellcard, now nearly just ashes.

"I'm just doing some tidying up," Cassandra had replied. This itself was suspicious, as Cassandra was hardly the tidying-up type. Marlow did most of the cleaning in their apartment. "How were your lessons?"

Marlow flopped across the plush sofa in the center of the sitting room with a groan.

"That bad?" Cassandra asked with a raised eyebrow.

Marlow scrubbed a hand over her face. "Lessons were fine. It's who's *in* them that's the problem."

Cassandra moved from the writing desk to perch on the edge of the sofa by Marlow's head, her fingers running gently through Marlow's hair. "Is this about the Falcrest boy again?"

"No," Marlow muttered, grabbing a pillow and squeezing it to her chest. "I don't want to talk about it."

"He didn't do anything to you, did he?" Cassandra asked, her voice unexpectedly sharp. "Did he say something to you?"

"No," Marlow huffed. "That's the problem."

"Well," Cassandra said, combing through a knot in Marlow's hair with her fingers, "that may be for the best. Nothing good can come of falling for a boy like that, believe me."

Marlow craned her neck to look at her mother. "I didn't *fall* for him. We're friends. Or I thought we were, anyway."

Cassandra hummed noncommittally. "Just be careful, Minnow."

Marlow fully took in her mother's appearance, and noted that she was not wearing the more relaxed outfit she usually wore around the apartment, but something much closer to her chevalier livery, although without the usual adornments. The silver Vale signet ring glinted on her finger.

Marlow sat up. "Are you going somewhere?"

"An errand for Vale," Cassandra answered. It was not unusual for Vale to call upon Cassandra at all hours of the day.

"You're not staying for dinner?" Marlow asked, trying not to let on how disappointed she was.

"I need to get going, actually," Cassandra replied, with a glance at the clock hanging above the mantel.

"Want me to save you a plate?"

Cassandra shook her head, tugging on her boots. "I'll probably be late, so don't wait up."

Marlow waved her off; she was used to this by now.

"Marlow," Cassandra said, stopping at the threshold of the apartment.

It was both the use of Marlow's first name and the tension in Cassandra's voice that at the time had struck Marlow as odd, and later would be something that would keep her up at night. "Do you remember what I told you a few weeks ago?"

Marlow blinked at her. "Stop pranking the valet?"

"About what to do if I was ever . . . if something ever happens to me." Her eyes were locked on Marlow, the color like a summer sky before a storm.

"You said to leave Evergarden," Marlow said, brow creasing. "Mom, is something—?"

Cassandra's face relaxed into a smile. "No. Everything's fine. I just wanted to be sure you remembered. Be good, little Minnow."

She left through the door before Marlow could reply.

And that was the last time Marlow ever saw her.

In the weeks after, Marlow had taken this memory like a blade to her skin. She shouldn't have let her go. She should've gone after her. She'd known something was wrong.

But she'd done nothing.

It was time to fix that mistake.

The bridge wasn't exactly buzzing with activity, but there was a bored-looking crewmate sitting by the control panel who would probably not allow Marlow to just walk in and leaf through their logs.

Marlow fished out the stack of spellcards from her dress pocket and riffled through them until she found the one she was looking for buried at the bottom. Hoodwinking some unsuspecting sailor with an Urgent Distraction spell was well worth the chance to get another lead on her mother's disappearance.

Marlow pressed herself back against the wall and whispered the incantation, sending the card's amber glyphs hurtling into the sailor. A second passed, and then the sailor stood up abruptly, his expression flashing with panic. The spell had him convinced he had forgotten some urgent task on another part of the ship, and he quickly sped toward the door. Marlow ducked out of sight before he could spot her, and watched him dash down the corridor and disappear around the corner.

She darted into the bridge, knowing she had limited time before the spell wore off and the sailor realized there was no such task.

The bridge wasn't very big. The steering wheel and console panel took up most of the back wall, tucked below a wall of wide-paned windows that faced the front of the boat. Two chairs and some additional navigation equipment filled the space behind the console. Along the side walls were rows of wooden cabinets.

Marlow opened the first one and found stacks of neatly organized navigation charts. The second contained various tools and instruments. The third, to her relief, was filled with rows of clothbound volumes. Printed in neat lettering on the spine of each volume were the dates it covered. Marlow quickly scanned until she found the one labeled with last year's dates. She pulled it off the shelf, heart pounding as she paged through until she found the entry dated the day of her mother's disappearance. The fifth of the Ash Moon.

Her eyes skipped past all the various measurements and temperature readings until she found the column labeled for "course steered." The line read simply "berthed at Coral Marina." As did the following day's entry.

So the *Contessa* hadn't sailed anywhere that night. She stared down at the entries, bitter disappointment coursing through her. She'd gotten her hopes up too much that the *Contessa* would provide a solid lead. But if it hadn't left the harbor, what had Cassandra been doing on it?

Footsteps sounded outside the bridge and Marlow hurriedly closed the logbook and shoved it back into place before shutting the cabinet with a quiet *click*. She ducked out of the bridge and back into the corridor.

"You look lost, Miss Briggs."

Marlow jumped, heart rocketing into her throat as she whipped around to find a woman leaning against the wall, bright-green eyes fixed on Marlow expectantly.

Alleganza Caito was the personal chevalier to Aurelius Falcrest, and she was one of the last people Marlow would've wanted to run into at this precise moment.

Her midnight-blue hair was cut bluntly across her forehead and pulled into a sleek knot. She'd colored one stripe a venomous green, a color that reminded Marlow of nothing so much as the dart frogs that populated the rain forests in southern Corteo.

Her face was painted with dark-red spikes, two that framed her cheekbones and one that hooked down from her lower lip like a fang. They were the markings of the Zanne Rosse, an elite branch of the Vescovi army specializing in reconnaissance and interrogation. Aurelius Falcrest had recruited her from their ranks when she was still just a teenager, though the rumor was that by then she'd already proven herself one of their most effective agents.

Marlow could not recall ever having a direct conversation with the Falcrest chevalier before, but it was a chevalier's job to know everything about everyone, so it wasn't a surprise she knew exactly who Marlow was.

"I am lost, actually," Marlow said. "I was trying to find a better view and got turned around."

"Did you," Caito said. She had a low, husky voice, and if she wasn't so deeply unsettling, she probably could have given any member of the noblesse nouveau a run for their money in terms of beauty.

"I'll just go back down to the observation deck, I guess," Marlow said with a tense smile.

"I'm not sure that's the best idea," Caito said, "as I don't believe you were invited here today."

Marlow smiled. "It was last minute."

"I didn't realize you were still in contact with anyone in Evergarden, after what happened with your mother."

There had been no love lost between Cassandra and her Falcrest counterpart. Marlow always suspected Caito looked down on Cassandra. While Caito had been trained as an elite operative, Cassandra had earned her place as a chevalier in large part because of her connections to Caraza's underworld. Before being hired by Vale, Cassandra had been something of a con artist, grifting the moderately rich and making off with their money. Caito probably assumed that Cassandra had somehow conned her way into her job, too.

"Adrius invited me," Marlow said, pushing her hair off her shoulder and straightening her spine. "So I suggest you ask him whether or not we're in contact."

Caito arched a thin, dark eyebrow. "And does Adrius know that his guest is skulking around the crew's quarters, or should I ask him about that, too?"

Marlow held her gaze, tilting her head slightly and trying to project an aura of innocent confusion. "Like I said. I got lost."

Caito's gaze bored into her. "And if I go downstairs and check the ship's security log, what am I going to see?"

"Security log?" Marlow echoed, a light flashing in her mind.

"Of course," Caito replied. "Every guest on this boat was immediately logged the moment they stepped aboard, and their whereabouts on the boat recorded."

Of course. Marlow bit down on a smile.

"Shall I go take a look?" Caito asked with a slight air of menace.

"Marlow Briggs, is that really you?" A boisterous voice sounded from behind Marlow.

Marlow caught the irritation flickering across Caito's face before turning to find Cormorant Vale bustling toward her from the other end of the hall, his boyish face lighting up beneath his bushy blond beard.

"I heard a rumor you were here this afternoon!"

Cormorant Vale had always been a pleasant figure amongst the noblesse nouveau, and had treated Marlow, the daughter of his chevalier, with kindness. It had been with Vale's permission that Marlow was able to be educated alongside the children of the Five Families and their courtiers. The arrangement was unorthodox, but in many ways, so was Vale.

"Adrius kindly invited me," Marlow said, dipping into a little curtsy out of habit. "We ran into each other at the ballet the other night."

"Wonderful, wonderful!" Vale beamed. He glanced at Caito. "Ah, Alleganza. I believe Aurelius was looking for you."

Caito's expression was placid, but Marlow sensed the irritation simmering beneath. "Of course." Her gaze slid over Marlow like ice. "Do be careful, Miss Briggs."

With that she turned on her heel and strode away.

"It's wonderful to see you, Marlow," Vale said warmly. "I've been worried about you ever since Cassandra . . ."

"You don't need to worry about me," Marlow said quickly. "I'm fine."

In a softer tone, he said, "I wanted to extend whatever help I could after she . . . after it happened. Your mother was an excellent chevalier. She was important to the Vale family, I hope you know that. And that makes you important, too. She would want to know you're taken care of."

Marlow glanced up at his face, his brow creased with concern. Maybe even a hint of grief.

"I am," Marlow assured him. "I can take care of myself."

"If there's anything, anything at all that I or the Vale name can do for you, you'll let me know, won't you?"

Marlow worried her lip between her teeth. Here was a chance to maybe get more information about what her mother had been doing that night. But she didn't want to show all her cards. Whether Vale knew anything about Cassandra's disappearance or not, she could guess how he might react to finding out Marlow was looking into it—not so differently from how Hyrum had reacted.

"There is one thing," she said lightly. "The night my mom . . .

disappeared. She said she was going out to run an errand for you. It sounded important. You don't remember what that was, do you?"

Vale's face crinkled into a frown. "I didn't ask Cassandra to do any errand that evening. Are you sure that's what she said?"

Marlow studied his face, the tight crease of his frown and the cloudy confusion in his light-gray eyes, and found that she believed him. Whatever Cassandra had gone to do that night on the *Contessa*, it hadn't been at Vale's request.

"I'm probably misremembering," Marlow said. "You didn't see her at all that night?"

Vale shook his head. "I believe that was the night I attended the Annual City Philanthropists Gala. They were honoring the Vale family for our contribution of healing spells to the city's public hospitals."

"Oh," Marlow replied. "Right."

Vale looked apologetic. "I'm sorry. I—I wish I knew more about what happened to Cassandra. It pains me that you've been left with so many unanswered questions." He gave her a small, sorrowful smile. "If there's anything else, don't hesitate to ask."

"Of course."

A horn sounded from the deck above, signaling the start of the next race. "Well, shall we get back out there? This race is sure to be a real nail-biter."

Marlow hesitated. She had to get downstairs to see the security logs. "I'll, um—see you out there?"

Vale looked at her questioningly.

"It's just, you know. A little overwhelming to be around everyone again." Not exactly a lie.

Vale's expression turned understanding. "Of course. Say no more." He gave her another smile and then turned to go back to the party, whistling softly.

Marlow slipped down the hall and took the stairs to the control room below. The door was closed. She pulled out the long chain she wore tucked beneath her dress, withdrawing an enchanted magnifying glass. Holding it up to her face, she peered through the glass at the control room door. Ghostly threads of magic covered the door's handle like glimmering spiderwebs. Magical wards to keep people like Marlow out.

It was a fairly common ward that would sound an alarm when the door was opened. Likely there were only a few members of the ship's crew who had the key to open the door without triggering the wards, and Marlow didn't want to waste time tracking them down.

If she had an Incorporeal spell, it would be no trouble at all to get around the ward. Unfortunately, Marlow was not made of money.

She inspected the door more closely. It was airtight, which ruled out the possibility of enchanting something to slip underneath the door to open it from the inside. There was, however, a small port window through which she could see the inside of the control room. The glass was thick and double-paned—not as easy to break as she'd hoped.

Marlow flipped through her spellcards until she found a Heating spell—a more powerful version of the one she'd used to heat her tea at the Bowery—and cast it on the window. The sudden change in temperature cracked the glass. She used the hilt of the knife she kept tucked in her garter to break through it.

She glanced around the narrow corridor. There was what looked like a storage room a few doors down. She was able to break into it just with brute force, and found several lines of rope. She hacked off two lengths of rope with her knife and then returned to the control room.

She tied each length of rope into a loop large enough for her shoulders to fit through, and then placed them on the floor, one inside the other. Then she pulled out her Magic Tunnel spellcard and raised it above the ropes.

"Scavare!"

The glyphs rose from the spellcard and filled the circle inside the ropes with glowing purple light. Marlow picked up one of the ropes and folded it so that she could throw it through the opening in the port window. It landed on the floor of the control room and lay there in a lopsided circle.

With a deep breath, Marlow knelt beside the other rope circle. She plunged her hands through the glowing purple tunnel and then wriggled the rest of her body through it, pulling herself up into the control room and toppling ungracefully onto the floor.

Right above where she landed was a set of cabinets. She threw open the doors and found volumes and volumes of security logs. She scanned their spines until she found the one covering the first half of last year, and pulled it out.

She paged through it until she found the right date. The fifth of the Ash Moon.

Right underneath was the name *Cassandra Briggs*.

Marlow held her breath. Here it was, in plain black ink—proof that Cassandra had come here that night. It was even time-stamped for half past twenty bells.

There was only one other name in the log, time-stamped for twenty-one bells. *Armant Montagne.*

Marlow's stomach fluttered. She didn't recognize the name, but whoever this Montagne person was, he might've been the last person to see her mother.

All she had to do now was find him.

SIX

Adrius showed up at thirteen bells on the dot, wearing a goldenrod suit with a garnet waistcoat and a smile so sharp it could cut glass.

"Well, aren't you punctual," Marlow greeted him, stashing away notes about her mother's case. She had spent the morning scouring them for any mention of "Armant Montagne," but so far, she'd found exactly nothing.

"It's not like I had a choice," Adrius replied, voice clipped.

It took Marlow half a second to understand what he meant. She'd said *Don't be late* before leaving to search the *Contessa*. Thanks to the curse, Adrius had had no choice but to obey.

Guilt twinged through her—she'd have to take care how she spoke to him from now on. "Did you bring my money?"

Adrius swept over, pulling out several long strings of pearls and all but slamming them down on the desk. He braced his hands in front of him and leaned all the way into Marlow's space.

Propping her chin on her hand, Marlow met his thunderous gaze expectantly.

"If you were so desperate to date me, Minnow, you really should have just asked." It was exactly the type of comment she'd anticipated, but the unchecked acidity in his tone came as a surprise.

She pressed her lips together. "I'm sensing you may be displeased with my plan."

"Well, no wonder you're so good at breaking curses. Nothing gets past you, does it?" He smiled like a lion baring its teeth.

Marlow slid the pearls into an open drawer and then shut it firmly. "Look, whether you like it or not, this is the only way I'm going to be able to help you without anyone finding out about the curse. It's the perfect cover to let me investigate in Evergarden, and a good excuse for me to be nearby in case anyone gives you an order that needs counteracting."

It was all very logical and unassailable when she laid it out like that, Marlow knew. Despite that, Adrius's resentment still radiated off him, and Marlow tried to swallow down the sick mortification of being faced with Adrius's disgust at the thought of even *pretending* to be with her.

"Well, if it will help you with your *investigation*," Adrius said scathingly, pushing away from the desk, "how could I possibly say no?"

"It's not like I'm wild about the idea, either," Marlow said. It was just her wounded pride, that was all. "But if the thought of dating me is so offensive to you, just tell everyone I put a Love spell on you once we lift the curse. I really don't care."

"You should," Adrius said, lip curling. "If you knew what exactly you're risking."

Marlow propped her feet up on the desk. "What, your reputation? Thought you didn't care about that."

That was what the gossip magazines and the other noblesse nouveau said about him. Adrius Falcrest, the rebellious scion who did as he pleased, flouting propriety, damn the consequences.

But Marlow knew very well that that was as much a lie as anything else about Adrius. That he cared as much as anyone in Evergarden what people thought of him.

"I don't. But I *am* a Falcrest scion. Everything I do—*everything*—is watched, dissected, discussed by just about every living soul in Evergarden. You think this little ruse will make a good cover, but *I* think it will invite even more unwanted prying and speculation. Taking up with you would be a scandal—and please save me the self-righteous indignation, because you know it will be. And where there's a scandal, there's suddenly a lot of eyes and ears, precisely where we *don't* want them. Not everyone is going to be so easy to fool."

"Then I suggest you play your part well," Marlow said in a sugary voice.

"It's you I'm worried about."

"How sweet."

"The noblesse nouveau are not going to take kindly to a girl from the Marshes swooping in and snatching up one of the most eligible prospects in Evergarden. They'll consider it a slight, and they'll see *you* as an interloper. They'll be looking for any excuse to undermine our so-called romance."

Marlow hated that she felt stung by this. Not because she particularly cared what anyone in Evergarden thought of her, but because it drove home how much she didn't belong there, and never had. "Well, if my plan is so terrible, let's hear yours."

Adrius's eyes burned with contempt, but he said nothing.

Marlow swung her legs off the desk and stalked over to him, smug. "That's what I thought."

Adrius backed her into the desk, moving so fluidly she hardly had time to react. He didn't touch her, but she still felt pinned with his hands planted on the desk on either side of her, his eyes searing into hers.

She pulled her spine straight, raising her chin, refusing to let him see the heat that prickled over her skin at his sudden nearness.

"I just hope," he said in a low voice, "that you know what you've gotten yourself into."

Marlow had told Swift she didn't hate Adrius, but that had been a lie. Right now, she loathed everything about him, from the rich brown curls spilling over his forehead to the dark arch of his brow and the straight line of his jaw.

She put her palm against his chest and pushed him back.

He smirked, as if he'd just won something, and Marlow loathed that, too.

"Is that a yes?" she asked.

"It seems I don't have much of a choice," Adrius replied. "Besides, Gemma's probably leaked our little rendezvous at the regatta to half the gossip columns in the city by now. Denying it will only raise more questions."

"Glad we sorted that out." Glad that Adrius had taken the time to make it clear how repugnant he found the arrangement. She reclaimed her seat at the desk, pulling out a fresh notepad. "Now can we talk about the case?"

Adrius dropped onto the sofa. Toad wandered over from her usual sunbeam at the edge of Marlow's bed and butted her head against his hand. Adrius smiled—a real, unvarnished smile—and Toad hopped up to settle in his lap, her eyes squinting in pleasure.

Traitor.

He scratched her chin idly. "I've been meaning to ask, how *did* you become a cursebreaker? It doesn't strike me as a job someone simply decides to take up one day."

"It's a long story," Marlow replied. "And not what we're here to discuss."

Adrius raised an eyebrow.

Marlow blew out an irritated breath. She knew him well enough to know it would probably be quicker just to tell him. "A friend of mine was in a bad situation with one of the local street gangs. They cursed him to keep him loyal. I found out, helped him break the curse, and then I just figured, hey, maybe there were other people I could help in the same way."

"For a price," Adrius said.

"Yes, for a price," Marlow replied tartly. "This is Caraza. Everything costs something. You of all people should know that, considering your family is the one who decides what that cost is."

Adrius flicked a hand, like this was irrelevant. "There can't be that many people in need of a cursebreaker."

Marlow snorted. "Maybe not in Evergarden, but here? Where the Copperheads and the Reapers and the other street gangs have parceled up the Marshes between themselves? Curses are their main means of enforcing their control. Not to mention loan sharks, predatory landlords, jealous ex-lovers—trust me, the black market curse trade is thriving."

Adrius actually looked a little alarmed. From his gilded perch in Evergarden, he'd probably never spared a thought for what it was like for everyone else down in the muck of Caraza. "And you know a lot about the black market?"

"It's my job to know."

"It was also your mother's job," Adrius pointed out.

He was right. Cassandra's main duty as the Vale chevalier had been tracking down rogue spellwrights who sold spells and curses on the black market. The Five Families kept a viselike grip on the secrets of spellcraft—after all, it was the source of their power and wealth—and exacted harsh punishment on spellwrights who trafficked in illegal curses. Cassandra had had extensive knowledge of and plenty of contacts within the black market—knowledge and contacts that Marlow had been able to make use of in the past year as a cursebreaker.

"Let's talk about the case," Marlow said, before Adrius could press on the subject of her mother. "You said you think you were cursed about three weeks ago. What happened leading up to that?"

He craned his gaze up to the ceiling and worked his jaw. "I don't know. I suppose there was a party the night before."

That was hardly surprising. "What kind of party?"

He waved a hand. "Who knows. It doesn't matter. The only thing that made it significant was that Darian and Amara announced their engagement."

So they *were* engaged. "What else happened at this party?"

"The usual. Dancing, drinking, general debauchery," Adrius replied flippantly.

"I mean what did *you* do? Who did you talk to? Did anything seem strange?"

"To be honest, I don't remember very much after the toast," Adrius said. "I had a lot to drink."

"Is that normal for you?"

Adrius rubbed a knuckle over his brow, like Marlow was giving him a headache. "Is it normal for *you* to interrogate your clients like this?"

"I'm just being thorough."

"I don't see how my drinking habits are relevant."

Marlow resisted the urge to grind her teeth. She'd dealt with reticent clients before, but none who knew how to get under her skin the way Adrius did. "If you want my help, you're going to have to extend a little bit of trust to me."

He met her gaze mutinously and then looked away.

Marlow couldn't help but think about her mother, and how easily she gained people's trust. It was part of what had made her such a good chevalier—and before that, what had made her a good con woman.

A successful con, Cassandra told her once, *starts with establishing trust.*

Marlow dropped her pen onto the notepad and pushed it to the edge of the desk. "What do you know about curses?"

"My family produces over a third of all spells in the market," Adrius replied. "I'd say I know a bit."

"Cursebreaking isn't just about spellcraft."

"Oh no?"

"In order to break a curse, you need to know who cast it. Learn their weaknesses. What motivates them. Their secrets."

Marlow hadn't been lying when she said she'd never failed a case. Secrets just had a way of surfacing when she was around.

"What about people who break curses on their own?" Adrius asked. "Without burning the curse card?"

"That only happens in stories," Marlow said dismissively. "Break a curse with true love's kiss, or an act of true courage, or whatever they say in those fairy tales. None of that is real."

Adrius watched her through narrowed eyes.

"So if you want to break this curse, we need to find the curse card. And in order to do that, you need to tell me everything, even if you can't see how it's relevant." She let out a breath. If Adrius needed his hand held, then she would suck it up and hold his hand. "I asked about your drinking because if you *were* cursed at that party and can't remember it, it's possible that whoever cursed you compelled you to forget that it happened."

Adrius jerked upright, fast enough to startle Toad off his lap. "You mean they could just—order me to forget and I would?"

Marlow nodded. "The sorcerer who invented the spell—Ilario—did that to most of his victims. Historians don't even know the true extent of his crimes because so many of the people he targeted didn't have the slightest clue they were cursed until suddenly they were butchering their own families, or leaping to their own deaths."

"Something to look forward to, then," he said dryly. But she could see he was unnerved. His shoulders stiffened, like he was trying to brace against the horror of what he'd just heard. Like he was picturing the horrors *he* could be compelled to carry out with just a few whispered words.

"Who else was at the party that night?" Marlow prodded gently.

"Well, Darian and Amara, obviously. Silvan and his parents. My father. The usual crowd of noblesse nouveau and whatever hangers-on managed to swing an invite." Adrius paused. "Actually, I do remember seeing one person there who was a bit unexpected. Emery Grantaire—he stopped by to speak with my father. I don't know what about."

Marlow looked up in surprise. "What kind of business does the City Solicitor have with your father?"

"I have no idea. It was early in the evening—he gave his congratulations and then pulled Father away for a few moments. I'm pretty sure he left right after that."

It could be anything—the city government in Caraza was notoriously corrupt, with officials regularly taking kickbacks and other favors from the noblesse nouveau to relax regulations or push through pet projects or simply ignore unethical behavior. Marlow didn't know very much about the current City Solicitor, except that he was relatively young and new. In theory, the City Solicitor oversaw the investigation and prosecution of criminal endeavors within the city of Caraza. In practice, they got paid very nice sums of money to pretend such criminal endeavors didn't exist. Perhaps Aurelius had simply wanted to make sure the new City Solicitor knew his place in the city's hierarchy.

Still, she filed the information away for later examination.

"Well, I'm guessing at least one of the guests has a better recollection of that night than you," Marlow said. "We should talk to them. See if anyone saw you there. If you were alone with anyone that night."

Adrius sighed. "Fine. Darian and Amara's engagement party is in three days. Everyone who was there when they announced it will be in attendance. We should make an appearance anyway. It can be our first event as a *couple*."

"Perfect," Marlow said cheerfully.

Adrius paused. "The Vales are throwing it. At Vale Tower."

Vale Tower, home to the Vale family and their entire coterie. And once, a lifetime ago, home to Marlow and her mother.

"Great," Marlow said dispassionately. "I'll meet you there. In the meantime, let me know if you remember anything else important."

Adrius gave Toad one more scratch on the head and went to the door. He turned back to Marlow. "You've never been to a party in Evergarden, have you?"

He knew full well she hadn't, but the question somehow felt like a trap. Their friendship, such that it was, had mostly existed within the confines of their classes, Marlow's apartment, and the little terrace outside it. A private space, where the rest of Evergarden fell away and they could just be themselves—or so it had felt at the time.

Most of the time, that hadn't bothered her. Loath as she was to admit it now, she'd preferred having all of Adrius's attention to herself anyway.

"No," she replied. "I haven't."

"I thought not," Adrius said, and then went through the door, shutting it firmly behind him. The scent of amber and orange blossom lingered in the room even after he was gone.

Marlow couldn't help but wonder if he was recalling the same memory she was. The memory of the night he and Amara turned seventeen. The party the Falcrests threw that year had lit up the entire sky above Caraza. Marlow had seen the lights from her bedroom window in Vale Tower. She'd been staring out at them, trying not to imagine what might be happening at the party when she heard three slow, heavy knocks at the door.

It was late, too late for visitors, but Marlow had opened the door anyway and found Adrius standing on the other side, a smear of glitter under his eye.

"Hi," he said, leaning against the doorframe.

"Shouldn't you be celebrating?"

He shrugged and waltzed inside the apartment, like he always did. "I got bored."

"And came here," she said, hiding a question in it.

He draped himself along the couch. "I suppose I did. So you'd better entertain me, huh?"

And truthfully, Marlow had been about to go to sleep, but with Adrius grinning up at her from the couch, his suit lightly mussed and his curls a riot against the pillow, she knew there was no point in trying to deny him.

She thought about all the people who had been at that party tonight, dressed in their finery, alcohol and magic flowing freely in sparkling rooms. She thought about all the girls Adrius could have taken home with him.

Instead he was here.

A slow smile unfurled on her face. "Let me put on some shoes."

They'd snuck out of the tower, "borrowing" one of Vale's enchanted canal boats, which moved of its own accord when given a destination. It took them up past Crescent Canal, through the Outer Garden District. Adrius produced an enchanted music box that made it sound as if a string quartet were playing in the boat with them. He taught her the steps to the latest popular dances, laughing when she got them wrong. They hopped off the boat at Magnolia Street and strolled past empty shops beneath the canopy of white-pink blossoms. Adrius dared her to break into the Malachite Building, and with a few simple Lock-picking spells Marlow had swiped from her mother's stash, she'd managed it. They climbed up to the roof. From there, Evergarden seemed small and distant. They sat and stared at the sky, making up constellations and talking about anything and everything until the sun began to peek over the horizon.

"I didn't get you a gift," she'd mumbled sleepily into his shoulder, breathing in the scent of amber and orange blossom.

"Hm?"

"For your birthday." She was so tired she wasn't even sure what she was saying. "I'll get something for you. Anything you want."

For a moment she'd thought he hadn't heard her. Then she felt him exhale, his thumb just barely brushing against her bare shoulder underneath the weight of his suit jacket, which he'd tucked around her. "Anything I want?"

She had felt, in those small, twilight hours before dawn, that something between the two of them had shifted, just a little. Like the quiet, careful unfurling of a rosebud.

The next day, Marlow had shown up for their afternoon Civics class with a box neatly wrapped in ribbon, containing three different flavors of honey cakes that she'd painstakingly baked from scratch. She'd found Adrius loitering outside the classroom, along with a few of their other classmates.

"What do you have there, Briggs?" Silvan asked, the first of the gathered group to notice Marlow standing on the fringes.

She would have preferred to give it to Adrius in private, but it wasn't like honey cakes were a particularly intimate gift. So she held the box out to Adrius. "They're for you."

Adrius looked down at the box like it contained snapping turtles. "What? Why?"

"It's a birthday gift," she answered.

His brows pulled together in confusion. "Why would you get me a birthday gift?"

“I said I would,” she replied. “Remember? Last night?”

“Last night I was celebrating my birthday with my friends,” Adrius replied brusquely. “I don’t recall inviting you.”

For a moment, Marlow felt like laughing. Surely Adrius was joking. But as she stood there, staring at him in confusion, still holding the box of honey cakes, she could detect no trace of humor on his face.

“Could you imagine?” Silvan said snidely. “You know, Briggs, just because my father allows you to take classes with us doesn’t mean you’re one of us. None of us actually want you here.”

It wasn’t anything Marlow hadn’t heard from Silvan before, but still her cheeks burned with humiliation.

In the past, Adrius had *always* stepped in when Silvan was cruel to her.

This time, he said nothing, just stared at Marlow with bored indifference, as if he had never showed up at her door the night before, or danced with her on a canal boat under the stars, or watched the sunrise from high above the city.

The callous dismissal hurt far worse than any of Silvan’s barbed words.

“Right,” Marlow said hollowly, tears pricking at the corners of her eyes. “My mistake.”

She tucked the box of cakes under her arm and spun on her heel, hurrying away. Though not fast enough to avoid hearing another one of Adrius’s friends say, “She must have a crush on you, Adrius.”

Or Adrius’s reply: “Like I would ever be caught dead with *the help*.”

Marlow dumped the honey cakes into a trash can. Then she immediately changed her mind and fished them out, took them home, and ate all three cakes so fast she gave herself a stomachache, managing to make herself feel even more wretched than she already did.

She tried to tell herself that Adrius only acted that way because he was in front of the rest of his friends. He didn’t want them to know how close they really were, or that they’d spent the whole night together, even if it was all innocent. She told herself he'd show up at her apartment later, that they'd have it out, and he would apologize.

Except he never came. The next day, when she passed him in the hall, he'd looked right past her like she didn't exist.

Three weeks later, Marlow had left Evergarden for what she thought was for good. She'd vowed to herself then that she'd never trust anyone in Evergarden again—and certainly not Adrius Falcrest.

SEVEN

"Hey, Marlow," Swift said when Marlow walked into the Bowery the next afternoon. "If you were secretly romantically involved with the scion of the most powerful family in Caraza, you'd tell me, right?"

"Uh," said Marlow.

Swift grinned over the top of a copy of the *Weekly Gab*.

"Do you make it a habit of reading gossip rags or is this a special case?" she asked, shucking her jacket and joining him at the counter.

"I like to stay informed, you know that." He slapped down the magazine.

Marlow tilted her head to read the bold, dramatic headline splashed across the top of the page. *Falcrest scion spotted at the Summer Solstice Classic Regatta with mysterious new minx.*

Minx? Marlow pushed it off the counter. "Do people really read these things?"

"A lot of people, actually," Swift said, retrieving the magazine from where it had fluttered to the floor.

Well, maybe that was a good thing. The more rumors circulating about Adrius and Marlow, the more believable their supposed romance would be.

"Anyway, stop avoiding the question," Swift admonished. "It's not true, is it? Because that would be—"

"It's not true," Marlow said, cutting him off. "But . . . we're kind of hoping that people think it is."

"Ah," Swift replied, cottoning on immediately. "I thought you said you *weren't* taking his case. Actually, I think your exact words were 'I'd rather wade naked through Limewater Lagoon than work for Adrius Falcrest.'"

Marlow cleared her throat, shuffling through a stack of spellcards. "Well, if someone wanted to pay me a thousand pearls to wade naked through Limewater Lagoon, I might do it."

"*A thousand—*" Swift cut himself off with a swear, eyes widening. Then his face melted into a grin and he poked Marlow's shoulder. "So, I have my eye on this new record player . . ."

She batted his hand away. "I have to actually break the curse first, you know."

"You will," Swift said confidently. "And in the meantime, are you sure you're going to be able to convince everyone that you and Adrius are together?"

"I don't think I'll have to do much convincing, honestly," Marlow replied. "Everyone's just going to assume Adrius is being Adrius and, in a fit of rebellious pique, decided to scandalize Evergarden society by taking up with a girl from the Marshes. The scandal is what sells it."

"Well, you might want to work on selling it," Swift said, flipping through the magazine. "A lot of these hacks seem to think you're not really interested in Adrius at all, but heartlessly using him to get back into Evergarden society."

Marlow rolled her eyes. "Of course they do."

"There's one here that says you were 'a social pariah returning to stick it to the very people who scorned you a year ago.' I mean, yeah, they nailed it."

Marlow snatched the magazine away from him and rolled it up. "No more *Weekly Gab* for you."

"Hey!" Swift protested. "How else am I going to keep up with all the breaking news about which scion wore a new dress at what party?"

"Right, I'm sure there's a lot of important and noteworthy information to be gleaned from the pages of—" She stopped abruptly, blinking down at the rolled-up magazine. "Hang on. Do you still have some old copies of this? Or any of the gossip magazines?"

"Sure," Swift said. "They're, uh, good for killing mosquitoes."

"Can you bring whatever copies you have from around three weeks ago to my place after work?"

Swift's eyes narrowed. "Why?"

Marlow bopped him on the nose with the rolled-up magazine. "Because I asked you to."

"Swift," Hyrum called from the doorway where he stood with a box of spellcards. "I need you to go to Orsella's today and drop off some spell ingredients."

Marlow turned her head so quickly she nearly strained her neck. "I can go."

"You're on inventory."

"I finished inventory last night," Swift piped. "Marlow can go."

"You're going," Hyrum said bluntly, and then disappeared into the back room.

Swift shrugged and heaved himself out from behind the counter to follow.

Marlow waited at the door. Swift emerged moments later, a satchel of spell ingredients slung over his shoulder and a single raised eyebrow directed at Marlow.

"What?" Marlow asked. "He said you had to go. He didn't say I couldn't go with you."

"You're *awfully* eager to go to Orsella's," Swift said, shouldering past her. "Especially considering you're not exactly one of her favorite people."

"What are you talking about?" Marlow asked, pushing open the door and bracing against the wet slap of afternoon heat. "She likes me fine. She helped me on the Moon Thief case, remember? She's just cranky, like Hyrum. You don't understand because she's obsessed with you for some godsforsaken reason."

He grinned. "It's because I'm naturally charming and irresistible."

Marlow pinched his cheek. "That's exactly what I'm counting on."

Marlow dove out of the way as a bright-orange hex streaked past her. "Whoa!"

It hit the door, which shuddered dangerously and then started to smoke and blister. "Orsella, it's just me!"

"I know it's you, stupid," the tiny old woman behind the counter replied, a shotgun resting at her hip. "You think I shoot hexes at everyone who walks through my door?"

"Then why am I getting special treatment?"

"Because you're a pain in my ass, Briggs," Orsella replied, leaning the shotgun up against the counter. Her eyes went wide and her whole demeanor brightened as Swift entered the shop behind Marlow and heaved his satchel onto the counter. "Swift! I didn't see you."

"Afternoon, Orsella," Swift said. "Special delivery for Hex Row's most stunning black market broker."

"Oh, you charmer." Orsella fluttered at him, her dark eyes sparkling. "Let's see what we have here."

Marlow slid Swift a mocking leer as he and Orsella began sorting through the ingredients.

From the outside, Orsella's shop appeared to be a simple pawnshop. But the pier her shop fronted was known as Hex Row for a reason—almost all the businesses along it, from the Snapping Turtle Teahouse to Lucky's Bait & Tackle Shop, were black market fronts.

Orsella's real business was brokering—dealing curses and selling spell ingredients to spellwrights who needed a traceless way to get their hands on them. While the bulk of the Bowery's store of ingredients went to the Five Families' spell libraries, they siphoned off some here and there to sell to Orsella for a steeper markup.

If it had once bothered Marlow that the Bowery helped supply ingredients to the spellwrights who made the very curses she was hired to break, she had long since gotten over the moral implications. There was hardly a soul in the Marshes whose hands were totally clean of the curse trade, and in any case, Marlow couldn't do what she did without some contacts on the inside. And as far as contacts went, you couldn't do better than Orsella.

"Listen," Marlow said, sidling up to the counter. "When you're done with that, I need some information."

Orsella snorted. "I'm fresh out of favors, Briggs. I told you that last time, remember? We're square now. Actually we're *less* than square, because giving you Flint's name has landed *me* in a steaming pile of crocodile shit. Or I should say, Copperhead shit."

"They came here?" Swift asked, worry evident in his voice.

"Apparently *someone* caused a scene at the Blind Tiger."

Swift shot Marlow a disapproving look.

"They figured out it was me who tipped you off about Flint," Orsella went on. "They weren't terribly happy about that, I can tell you."

"Are you all right?" Swift demanded. "What did they do?"

She patted the shotgun leaning up against the sales counter. "I introduced them to Josephine, and she warned them off right quick."

Curse-dealing was not a job without its dangers, and Josephine, as

Orsella affectionately called the gun, was an important part of Orsella's business. Marlow still did not know exactly where Orsella had managed to acquire a shotgun that fired enchanted bullets, but she knew Orsella well enough not to bother asking.

She briefly entertained herself by imagining the lackeys Bane had sent to the store coming up against all five foot nothing of Orsella, enraged and blasting hexes at their heads. They'd probably turned tail pretty quick and decided that a tiny, terrifying old woman with a shotgun was not worth their time, and went back to their boss to say they'd put the fear of the Crocodile Goddess in her.

"But it's the principle of the matter," Orsella went on. "I don't have time for this muck, Briggs. I have a business to run."

"Hey, you're the one who sent me to the Blind Tiger in the first place," Marlow protested.

"And I'm certain I specified that you should *not* start any trouble."

"You might as well have told a mosquito not to bite anyone," Swift grumbled.

Marlow glared. "I didn't start it. Technically."

Orsella laughed. For such a small woman she was very loud. "You're a funny girl, you know that?"

This was not a compliment.

"So is that a no on helping me?" Marlow asked. "Come on, Orsella, you know more about this city than anyone."

Orsella fixed Marlow with a long, hard stare that could easily intimidate even the most hardened criminals in the Marshes.

"You want something from me, you can pay for it like anyone else," Orsella said, with a nod at the assortment of ingredient jars on the counter. "Tell me what you're after, we'll settle from there."

"Fine," Marlow said, pushing away from the counter. "I want you to tell me what you know about the Black Orchid."

It took a lot to catch Orsella off guard, but Marlow saw a rare flicker of surprise on her craggy face before it settled back into its usual frown. "Where'd you hear that name?"

Swift darted a worried glance at Marlow, clearly picking up on Orsella's unease.

"Not important," Marlow said. "You've obviously heard of them, though."

"Sure," Orsella replied offhandedly.

"What is it going to cost, then?" Marlow asked. "A bit of luck? I'm warning you, I don't think I have that much to spare."

"A memory," Orsella countered. "Nothing you'll miss."

"No," Marlow said firmly. As a rule, she didn't give up memories as spell ingredients, even seemingly insignificant ones. Logically, she knew Orsella was right—there were plenty of memories she wouldn't even notice were gone. People forgot things all the time on their own. But Marlow relied on her memory to do her job, and the mere idea of it being tampered with was too unnerving. She'd sooner give up a day of her life.

"A few tears, then?"

Swift barked out a laugh. "I'd pay to see you try to make her cry, Orsella."

Marlow jabbed her elbow into his ribs. "A few ounces of blood ought to be sufficient, right, Orsella?"

Blood was a common spell ingredient, and easy enough to relinquish without too much damage. That also meant it was not thought of as particularly valuable, although that depended on who was giving it. But it wasn't like Marlow was asking Orsella to go out of her way. She just wanted information.

But often what mattered in the Marshes was not how much an ingredient was worth, but how desperate the person trading it was. Orsella was well-known to be a fair broker, less likely than others in her position to take advantage just because she could. That didn't mean she was *lenient*, though.

"Make it worth my while, Briggs," Orsella retorted. "A pint of blood, no less."

"Deal," Marlow said at once, tugging off her jacket and offering her bare arm to Orsella, who busied herself with her bloodletting instruments.

"So," Marlow prompted, flinching as Orsella slid the lancet into the skin just below her inner elbow. "The Black Orchid. Who are they, exactly?"

Orsella didn't glance up as she set an empty jar down to collect the blood now running in a warm, thin stream from Marlow's arm. "Rogue spellwright ring. Their stuff is supposed to be top of the line. High-quality enchantments, hexes. Real innovative stuff."

"You deal for them?"

"No," Orsella replied. "No one does."

"What, they handle everything in-house?" Marlow asked dubiously.

Being a rogue spellwright was amongst the more dangerous vocations in Caraza. In order to become a spellwright, you had to train at one of the five spellwright academies run by the Five Families. It was a rigorous process, but a pretty fair deal—if you could manage to get accepted to one of the academies and actually make it to graduation without washing out, you were paid handsomely to make spellcards.

But in exchange for that investment, the Five Families demanded an extremely strict code of secrecy surrounding spellcraft. Partly this was due to competition between the families—each had their own vast library of spellbooks that they guarded jealously—but mostly it was how the Five Families collectively retained control of the spell trade.

Which meant a spellwright that stepped *out* of line was in danger of being hunted by one of the most powerful entities in Caraza—and that was where chevaliers like Marlow's mother came in.

So there were virtually no spellwrights who sold directly on the black market—they handled that business through people like Orsella, or gangs like the Copperheads, who could offer some semblance of secrecy and protection from the Five Families.

Orsella shrugged. "They don't really sell."

Marlow exchanged a confused glance with Swift.

"The rumor is they're fanatics," Orsella went on. "They want to disseminate spellcraft knowledge. Open the libraries to all. Destabilize the Five Families' oligopoly on magic."

"Good luck to them," Swift said blithely.

"Sounds like a great way to get killed," Marlow added. She had no doubt the Five Families would do whatever it took to stop a group like the Black Orchid.

"Their spells are supposed to be very impressive," Orsella said with a shrug.

Marlow did not say that a few flashy spells were hardly a match for all the might and power of the Five Families. Orsella knew that as well as she did.

But it did make her wonder what kind of spell her mother had been burning with the Black Orchid symbol on it. And how, exactly, she'd come across the spellcard to begin with.

"Is that all?" Orsella asked. She'd begun stanching the bleeding on Marlow's arm, sealing up the jar of her blood.

"One more question," Marlow said, adding pressure to the bandage Orsella had applied to her arm.

"Make it quick," Orsella replied testily. "I've got deliveries to make."

"Do you recognize the name Armant Montagne?" Marlow asked.

Orsella narrowed her eyes. "What's this about?"

"Case," Marlow replied smoothly. It was technically true.

Orsella glanced at Swift and cleared her throat. "He's a spellwright. Works at the Falcrest Library. That's all I know."

Something about the way Orsella wouldn't meet Marlow's gaze told her this wasn't the whole truth. Orsella was holding something back, but Marlow knew her well enough by now not to push. She'd given her enough to track Montagne down, at least, and Marlow would figure out the rest on her own.

"Now get out of here before you scare away all my customers." Orsella turned to Swift sweetly. "Swift, you should come by again sometime soon. My bike engine could use a tune-up. I'll make spiced persimmon juice."

"Sure thing," Swift replied.

Marlow rolled her eyes.

"Can't imagine what such a nice young man like you is doing hanging around her," Orsella sniffed.

"You and me both," Swift agreed, shooting Marlow a saccharine grin.

Marlow shook her head, already pushing out of Orsella's shop, her mind buzzing. If Orsella was right—and she always was—that meant a spellwright had met with Cassandra aboard the *Contessa* the night she disappeared. The same night Marlow had seen her burn a Black Orchid spellcard.

"Are you going to tell me what that was about?" Swift asked, jogging to catch up. "The Black Orchid? A Falcrest spellwright?"

"Like I said, it's for a case."

Could Montagne be a member of the Black Orchid? Had Cassandra been trying to track down the Black Orchid on behalf of the Vale Family? Maybe she'd managed to turn him and get him to give up the other members of the Black Orchid. Marlow's thoughts whirred almost too fast for her to keep up.

"Adrius's case?" Swift asked. "You haven't mentioned any others."

Marlow didn't answer, her attention pulled by the prickling feeling that someone was watching them. In the reflection of the water alongside the pier, she caught sight of a tall, dark-haired man in a storm-gray coat, walking about thirty paces behind them, gait slow and posture slouched.

She quickened her pace up Hex Row until she reached the juncture with the Serpent, the long, crooked causeway that connected the disparate enclaves of the Marshes like a backbone.

Marlow made a right turn on the Serpent, instead of going left.

"Uh, Marlow?" Swift said uncertainly. "That's not the way back to the Bowery."

"Let's just go this way," she insisted. She grabbed his wrist and dragged him over to a dinghy moored alongside the Serpent, selling newspapers.

"What's going on?" Swift asked in a low voice as they pretended to browse the headlines.

"The man on our left," Marlow said in a low voice. "The one wearing the gray coat. Did we see him on the way to Orsella's?"

Swift shifted subtly to glance over at the man. "I don't know. Maybe. You think he's following us?"

"Pretty sure," Marlow replied. She pulled Swift away from the dinghy and they filtered into the pedestrian traffic along the Serpent.

"Marlow," Swift said in a dark voice. "Is it a Copperhead?"

"I don't know." If it *was* a Copperhead, there was no telling what he might try to do to Swift and Marlow if he managed to corner them alone. This was exactly what Swift had warned her about.

"Well, let's not find out," he said grimly.

Marlow was more used to tailing people than *being* tailed, but she knew how to shake someone, and their best bet was the Swamp Market.

Enclosed by breakwaters and fronted by the crook of the Serpent, the Swamp Market was a dredged lake crisscrossed by hundreds of spindly docks. If the Serpent was the spine of the Marshes, then the Swamp Market was its heart. Every morning at sunrise, hundreds of flatboats, long-tailed gondolas, and narrow punts moored at the docks to sell everything from handcrafted clothes to buckets of squirming crayfish to enchanted objects of questionable provenance. By midday, the market was so filled with boats that it was almost impossible to see the waters of the lake beneath the tide of hulls.

With its thronging crowds, labyrinthine walkways, and few vantage points, it was the perfect place to lose a tail.

Marlow hurried Swift along one of the quays jutting out from the causeway, weaving between vendor boats and doubling back. Stopping at a boat selling fresh fruit from an upriver orchard, Marlow glanced subtly behind her. The man in the gray coat was about twenty paces away, ambling along the dock behind them.

"You still see him?" Swift asked.

Marlow nodded, heart pounding. If there had been any question before that they were being followed, now she was certain. And clearly, this was no amateur.

"Come on." She yanked Swift down the dock to a flatboat selling bowls of turtle soup out of a huge vat, with a row of stools and a bar to eat them at. They hopped onto the boat, veered around a man brandishing a ladle, climbed up on the stools and then dropped over the side of the boat onto the deck of the gondola beside it.

The flatboat rocked dangerously, boiling liquid sloshing up against the sides of the soup vat, threatening to spill over, before it settled back into the pot.

"Sorry!" Marlow called to the soup vendor, barely pausing before racing down the length of the gondola and scrambling on top of the low wooden cabin.

"What the hell do you think you're doing?" the gondolier blustered, charging over to them as Marlow helped Swift climb up next to her. "Get off my boat!"

"Sure thing," Marlow chirped. "We'll be right out of your hair."

The added height of the cabin allowed her to reach a rope ladder hanging down the side of a much larger barge.

"He still behind us?" she asked, holding out her hand to pull Swift up after her.

"I don't see him."

They emerged onto the deck of the barge and Marlow peered over the dock side. Somehow, seemingly impossibly, the man in the gray coat was making his way down a different dock toward them.

"Shit." She nodded at the stern of the barge. "This way."

They climbed, crawled, and leapt from vender boat to vendor boat, carving a jagged pathway through the Swamp Market, leaving irate vendors in their wake. But their erratic route seemed to do nothing to deter the man following them. He appeared around every corner.

Marlow was beginning to tire. "This isn't working."

"You're still warded against tracking spells, aren't you?" Swift asked, giving voice to Marlow's fear that somehow this man was using magic to keep them in his sights.

"Of course I am," she replied. It had been the first thing she'd done after breaking Swift's curse. Or else nothing would stop the Copperheads from hunting her down the minute she stepped out of Reaper territory.

She scanned the rolling tide of boats in front of them. "Okay, new plan." She stripped off her jacket, tossing it over Swift's shoulder, and then knelt to unlace her boots.

"What are you doing?" Swift asked.

"Going through the market doesn't seem to be working," she said, yanking off a boot and tossing it at Swift. "So I'm going under it."

Swift caught the boot and stared at her incredulously.

"You have a better idea?"

"Just don't drown," he replied.

Marlow pulled out a spellcard, flashing it at him. "That's what this is for."

It was an Endless Breath spell she'd picked up a few weeks ago after an unfortunate incident in Limewater Lagoon. She cast it quickly, the glyphs shimmering a bluish silver and floating down her throat, into her lungs.

"I'll meet you on the other side."

With that, she plunged into the briny lake, kicking her feet out behind her to dive below the mass of ships. The lake wasn't very deep, and she quickly found the slippery bottom, crawling through the muck to the other side of the market.

She emerged from the murky water at the western edge of the Swamp Market, between two gondolas selling fruit. She swam over to the jetty and scrambled up the muddy side of it, flopping onto the wooden path. She was sopping wet, covered in mud, and probably reeked of swamp sludge, but as she picked herself up, she was pretty sure that she had, at last, evaded the man in the gray coat.

With a breath of relief, she wrung out her hair and sloshed across the breakwater, ignoring the strange looks she got from the other pedestrians milling around the market.

The Bowery was only a few canals away—the most direct route took her over a narrow, muddy alley that wound behind two rows of shacks fronting the water. It reeked of fish guts and something sour that she didn't particularly want to know the source of.

The hair on the back of her neck stood up. She whipped around—the man in the gray coat loomed at the mouth of the alley, wreathed in the vaporous mist that steamed off the mudflats.

Marlow didn't care about pretenses anymore. Anyone who could find her this easily was someone she wanted the hell away from her. She took off at a run, her bare feet slapping over mud. She banked a sharp turn to squeeze between two shacks, and then stopped, breathing hard. Something pulled at her to stop running. Something that said she wanted answers, and the only way to get them was to confront her tail.

She pulled a spellcard out from her sopping pocket and crept back through the narrow gap between shacks. With a fortifying breath, she leapt into the alley.

A flash of movement to the right. Marlow spun, spellcard in hand, and caught sight of a fluttering gray coat.

"Melma!"

Copper glyphs swirled out from the spellcard and surrounded the man's feet, adhering them to the mud before he could escape into the shadows again.

Marlow stalked over to him. He didn't *look* like a Copperhead—no snake tattoo on his neck, and his sharp blue eyes lacked the malicious cruelty she usually saw in the Copperheads.

It was then that she realized this wasn't the first time she'd seen this man. He'd been a guest aboard the *Contessa*, one of dozens of people who'd gawked at her and Adrius. The realization sent a shiver of foreboding down her spine. It meant this man had access to her not only in the Marshes, but in Evergarden, too.

Even more reason to get answers.

"Why are you following me?" she demanded.

He looked at her impassively, then dropped his gaze to his feet. He waved a spellcard. Silvery-blue glyphs whispered out from the card and surrounded his feet. The mud fell away, Marlow's spell defeated.

He took one long-legged step toward her.

Marlow couldn't have moved even if she'd wanted to. To simply dispel a hex like that—Marlow hadn't seen that kind of magic before. A new kind of fear crept over her.

She looked back up to his face. "Are you Black Orchid?"

"A word of advice, Marlow," the man said. "Stop asking questions you might not want the answers to."

"What are you talking about?"

He advanced, cornering her against the back wall of a shack. "We know you've been asking about us." He loomed over her. "If you know what's best for you, you'll stop poking your nose where it doesn't belong."

Marlow drew in a shaking breath. This man *was* Black Orchid. First Hyrum's warning, and now this.

The man reached into his coat, pulling out a glimmering black spellcard. Marlow shut her eyes, bracing for whatever hex he had in store for her.

"Bruciare!"

A jet of bright-green glyphs shot toward the man from behind. He flicked his coat and the glyphs seemed to get completely absorbed, the spell rendered null.

Over his shoulder, Marlow caught sight of Swift at the end of the alley, spellcard in hand. His eyes were wide and shocked at the ease with which the man had countered the hex.

"Remember what I said, Marlow," the man said, and then he swept away, melting into the shadows.

Marlow just stood there, shaking against the wall, as Swift thumped down the alley to get to her.

"Are you all right?" he demanded, sounding half-hysterical. "Who the hell was that guy? Last I checked, the Copperheads don't have that kind of magic."

Marlow shook her head. "He's not a Copperhead. He's Black Orchid. They've been following me."

"What?"

"It's nothing," Marlow said. "Can I have my boots back?"

"That wasn't nothing," Swift insisted. "What the hell kind of case did you get yourself into?"

Marlow was silent for a long moment. Then quietly she said, "It's about my mom, okay?"

Swift sighed. "Marlow . . ."

"I know what you're going to say." And she did—it was why she'd avoided telling him. "But this is a new lead. A real lead. These Black Orchid people that Orsella was talking about . . . I'm pretty sure they have something to do with my mom's disappearance. I think they might know what happened to her."

"These people are clearly dangerous," Swift said. "*Really* dangerous."

Marlow was beginning to fear the same thing.

"Marlow, if you're being followed by these people, then it's probably because they don't want you looking into any of this."

"They can threaten me all they like," Marlow said. "But they can't stop me from finding out what happened to my mother."

If the Black Orchid thought they could scare her away, then they didn't know the first thing about her. If they'd done something to Cassandra, then Marlow was going to find out. And make them pay.

"The thing is, Marlow, I think you *will* figure it out," Swift said. "And that they're not going to like it when you do."

Marlow didn't say anything for a long moment, putting on her boots and shrugging on her jacket. Finally, she looked up at Swift's face. His dark eyes were concerned, but underneath that she could see the same fear she felt in her own heart.

"I can't give up, Swift," she said at last. "There's this thing my mother used to say. 'When the world takes a bite out of you, you bite back.'"

"Right." Swift looked away. "Just be careful not to choke."

EIGHT

"*Are you sure* you're not seeing this guy again?" Marlow asked through a bite of dense, delightfully tart apricot cake. She glanced at Swift, sitting beside her on the floor of her apartment, each of them poring over old copies of the *Weekly Gab* and the *Starling Spectator*. "I'd keep him around just for the sweets."

Swift chose another slightly stale tea cake that had been given to him by an overeager raconteur he'd met last week at the Charmed Grove Teahouse. "Definitely not. He was a good kisser, but for a raconteur he's a huge bore. Besides, you can just get your disgustingly rich new boyfriend to buy you all the tea cakes you want. They'll probably be frosted with gold." He batted away Toad, who had come over to sniff at the tea cakes with interest.

"Anything yet?" Marlow asked, glancing over.

"Would it help to know the twelve varieties of tea sandwiches that were served at the mayor's luncheon?" Swift asked.

"No."

"Then no."

Marlow let out a beleaguered sigh and flopped down, arms bent behind her head. "This is a waste of time."

"I'm honestly kind of impressed that Adrius stayed out of the gossip columns for three whole weeks." He flipped a page. "Hang on. This might be something."

Marlow lifted her head.

"Another column talking about Darian and Amara's engagement announcement." He pushed the magazine toward her. "Bottom paragraph."

Marlow read aloud: "'But it seems that it wasn't all smiles at the gathering. According to one source, Gemma Starling was seen storming out of a back room in tears. Who was she storming out on, you ask? None other than the bride-to-be's twin brother, Adrius Falcrest. Could this spat have something to do with the pair's brief but tumultuous affair that abruptly ended last fall?' And then there's an actual timeline of their relationship. Well, that's handy."

"So?" Swift prompted. "I mean, they had a fight the same night Adrius says he was cursed—that's suspicious, right? You think it could be her?"

Marlow ripped the page out of the magazine and folded it into a neat square. "It could be nothing. Maybe he insulted her dress or something. The timing makes it worth looking into, though."

Adrius had said he didn't remember the night of the party, but this could jog his memory. Maybe Gemma was still interested in Adrius—and maybe Adrius had told her those feelings weren't returned. And maybe Gemma had cursed him in retribution for his rejection. It sounded far-fetched, but Marlow had seen the absolute worst of human nature, and knew it was more than possible. The noblesse nouveau were already predisposed to histrionics when they didn't get their way.

Swift smirked. "Never thought I'd ever get you to spend an afternoon reading gossip magazines with me."

Marlow grinned. "Want to braid each other's hair later?"

He nudged her with his foot and Marlow threw a magazine at him, which led to a brief scuffle that sent Toad scampering under the desk for safety and ended with Marlow pinning Swift to the floor and shaking the empty box of tea-cake crumbs onto his face while he tried to dislodge her.

"Am I interrupting something?" a familiar voice drawled from the doorway.

Swift sat up so quickly he almost smacked his skull into Marlow's face. She tumbled off him, sprawling on the floor. Her gaze slowly climbed up to take in the sight of Adrius, leaning casually in the doorway wearing a persimmon jacket over a pale gold waistcoat.

Toad emerged from under the desk and trotted over to Adrius, chirping in joy and rubbing her head against his shins, pupils glowing again.

"To what do I owe the inexorable honor of your presence?" Marlow asked, picking herself off the floor and dusting the cake crumbs off herself. "I thought we weren't meeting until Amara's engagement party. As in, two days from now. I'm working on the case."

"Yes, you certainly seem very busy," Adrius said dryly. His gaze fell on Swift. "We haven't met. I'm Adrius."

Swift, still sitting on the floor, raised his hand in greeting. "Swift."

"Swift is assisting me with research on the case," Marlow said.

Adrius's jaw tensed. "You told him about the curse?"

"I know nothing," Swift said. "Well, I know you hired her, but that's it."

Marlow had considered telling Swift everything about Adrius's curse. If there was one person who could understand what it was like to be under a Compulsion curse, it was Swift. The Copperheads hadn't used an *actual* Compulsion curse on him, of course. Their curse had been cruder, and considerably more gruesome—for every order Swift refused, part of his hand would rot off. But their goal had been the same as whoever had cursed Adrius: to get Swift under their control and powerless to refuse their orders.

But Adrius had been clear about keeping the nature of his curse between the two of them, and Marlow couldn't afford to jeopardize his confidence in her this early on.

His gaze darkened. "Minnow, when I said no one can know—"

“If you trust me, you trust Swift,” Marlow said in a tone that brooked no argument. “That’s how things work around here. I didn’t tell him any sensitive details, and I won’t unless I have your permission. But curse-breaking requires some legwork, and Swift is the best there is.”

Adrius looked doubtful.

“Now seriously, what are you doing here?” Marlow asked.

“I’m here to take you on a date,” Adrius announced.

Marlow almost fell back against the desk. “What—now? Why?”

Adrius waved at the gossip magazines spread across the floor. “You’ve obviously read the columns. If we’re going to do this, we need to do it right. Think of it like a rehearsal before we have to perform in front of all of Evergarden.”

“This is research,” Marlow said, kicking the magazines under the desk. “And I don’t have time to—”

“She’d love to go,” Swift said loudly.

Marlow kicked him.

“Wonderful,” Adrius said. He spun and made a beeline for Marlow’s wardrobe, flinging open the crooked doors.

Marlow shot a glance at Swift, who just bounced his eyebrows the way he always did to communicate someone attractive had just entered his line of sight. Marlow narrowed her eyes. First Toad, now Swift. The effect Adrius had on the average person—or cat—was deeply infuriating.

“One condition,” Marlow called over to Adrius as he rummaged through her wardrobe.

“This looks relatively unobjectionable.” He emerged with a muted teal dress trailing from a hanger. “Although you really should go shopping. I see you weren’t lying about not owning just one dress—you have two. Actually, you know what, I’ll commission a few from Amara’s favorite maison, and have one sent over for the engagement party. Don’t pawn it this time.”

She snatched the dress from Adrius. "Did you hear me? If you really want to force me to spend my evening subjected to your *charm*, I'll need something in return."

"I know you probably don't understand the concept of a date, but they usually don't start with a negotiation of terms."

"I want you to take me to Falcrest Library," Marlow said. "Tomorrow."

Adrius's brow creased in confusion. "Why?"

"Research," she answered, sweeping around the partition that separated her bed from the rest of the flat. She threw off her shirt and stepped out of her shorts before tugging the dress over her head.

"They don't exactly do tours, you know."

"You're the son of the man who owns the place, I'm sure you'll figure something out." She resumed her struggle with the dress.

"Fine." She could practically hear his eyes roll.

"So," she heard Swift pipe up from the other side of the partition. "What's it like in Evergarden?"

Part of Marlow expected Adrius to ignore the question, and Swift, altogether. He would almost certainly consider someone like Swift beneath his notice in normal circumstances.

"Smells a whole lot better than it does here," he replied. "What *is* that?"

"Ah, the swamp stench," Swift replied knowingly. "You get used to it."

"I sincerely hope not."

Marlow slid on a pair of simple but nice pearly slippers and stepped out from behind the partition. "Let's get this over with."

Adrius leaned against her desk, flicking his gaze over her. The dress he'd picked out had a beaded, cream-colored bodice with a short but full teal skirt and a long train that cascaded to the ground in a river of satin. It was by far the most expensive piece of clothing Marlow owned—a remnant from her time in Evergarden that she hadn't quite been able to bring herself to part with.

Swift let out a low whistle. "You clean up nicely, Briggs."

Marlow gave him a sarcastic little curtsy.

"Here." Before Marlow knew what was happening, Adrius was stepping toward her. He swept the hair off Marlow's shoulder and pinned it back with some kind of hairpiece. She felt his fingers comb through the waves, and when she looked up, his face was inches from her own. She could see the long fans of his eyelashes and the small, fine curls just above his ear.

The air suddenly felt thick, like a summer squall was about to break open.

"There," he said, and stepped away. Despite the heavy humidity, Marlow shivered.

"Shall we?"

He held out an arm and Marlow hesitated before taking it. As he wheeled them back to the door, Marlow caught sight of Swift's face, and the entirely too gleeful expression on it.

"Have fun, you two," he said in an obnoxious, knowing voice as Adrius ushered Marlow out. "Not *too* much fun, though!"

"Don't forget to feed Toad!" she yelled over her shoulder as the door slammed shut behind them.

The sticky evening heat pressed in on Marlow as she trailed Adrius toward the dock, holding her train up from the muddy street. She couldn't help but glance over her shoulder every few steps, still rattled from being tailed by the Black Orchid. They could still be watching her now.

The Marshes were made up of hundreds and hundreds of enclaves of land, some natural and some man-made, connected by a weaving labyrinth of waterways. Flatboat water buses were the usual way of navigating the Marshes, but as they approached the dock, Marlow could see that Adrius had decided to travel in style.

"Adrius," Marlow said slowly. "What in the Ever-Drowning Mangrove is that?"

"That," Adrius said with a touch of pride, "is a state-of-the-art Falcrest personal zeppelin."

The vessel rested in the water like a boat, but attached to it was a huge white-and-gold balloon, easily four times the size of the buildings around it.

Marlow had never actually been on a zeppelin before. Thankfully.

"Minnow." Adrius's gaze was intent on her face. "You're not afraid of heights, are you?"

"No," Marlow lied.

"It's perfectly safe," he said breezily, leading her down the rickety dock.

The boat itself was larger than Marlow's flat. An elegant table was set up in the middle of the deck, with gleaming silverware and a white tablecloth strewn with bright flower petals. Bioluminescent lanterns lined the deck, making it glow an otherworldly violet. There was a small indoor cabin with glass walls, through which Marlow could see a cozy couch and shelves lined with glass bottles.

"Come on," Adrius said in a low voice, his hand at the small of her back. "I promise not to let you plummet to your death."

She jumped, and realized she'd been staring.

"Explain to me exactly how we're going to convince everyone we're dating if our date is taking place two thousand feet in the air?"

"They'll see us," Adrius promised, already climbing up the steps to the zeppelin. "Best to get inside for takeoff. It can get quite windy."

Marlow barely had her feet on the deck when she felt the zeppelin lurch beneath her. She stumbled forward, instinctively reaching out to steady herself, and her grip found Adrius's hand already out, waiting for her to take it.

"Thanks," she said curtly.

"You don't have to pretend to lose your balance just to hold my hand."

She yanked her hand back and marched through the door to the glass-walled cabin, Adrius laughing behind her. The zeppelin cut smoothly through the water—so smoothly, in fact, that Marlow didn't even notice the ship was lifting off into the air until they were already twenty feet up.

Below, several people had stopped in the middle of the street to stare. Their figures shrank as the zeppelin rose higher.

Disoriented, Marlow tore her gaze away and collapsed onto the couch, gripping a cushion fiercely.

"You and Gemma were alone together the night of the party," she said without preamble. "Do you have any idea what you were doing?"

At the bar on the other side of the cabin, Adrius turned back to her and raised an eyebrow. "Right back to your interrogation, I see. Don't you want to relax for a minute? Have a drink?"

Marlow was feeling far from relaxed, but when Adrius handed her a drink conjured magically from the bar, she took it begrudgingly.

"Gemma was seen leaving the room you were in together in tears," Marlow pressed. "You argued."

"How do you even know this?" Adrius asked. "Gemma certainly didn't tell you."

"It's my job to know." She took a sip of her drink, a coral-pink concoction that tasted like sparkling wine with a hint of tart fruit. "So? An argument? Any idea what it could've been about? Like maybe the fact that you abruptly broke things off with her six months ago?"

"We weren't together that long, and it was nothing serious."

"It wasn't serious to *you*," Marlow said, bitterness seeping into her voice. "What if it was to her? What if she was upset enough to do something drastic to get you back?"

"Something drastic, like curse me to obey her every command?" He laughed. "No."

"It's not *impossible*," Marlow countered. "I've seen some nasty curses from spurned lovers, believe me."

"Gemma would laugh herself to death if she heard you calling her my *spurned lover*," Adrius said. "Trust me. I don't remember what we talked about that night, but I can promise you it had absolutely nothing to do with Gemma being in love with me."

Marlow narrowed her eyes. "You're not telling me something."

"You told me that this wasn't going to work unless I trusted you," Adrius said. "Well, the reverse is true, too. You have to trust me when I say whatever happened between Gemma and me that night has nothing to do with the curse."

Marlow let out an irritated breath, but didn't press him.

The zeppelin rose higher, wheeling away from the crowded waterways of the Marshes, above the glittering skyscrapers of Evergarden, and toward the open expanse of Tourmaline Bay. Marlow's stomach lurched and she squeezed her eyes shut.

"You're sure you're not afraid of heights?" Adrius said with a smirk.

"Shut up," she muttered. When Adrius went instantly silent, she felt a pang of guilt. "Sorry. Don't shut up."

"Generous of you."

She eyed him. "How does that work, exactly?"

"What?"

"If I give you a command like that, how long does it last? Would it wear off? Or do I have to order you to do the opposite to counteract it? What are the limitations?"

He gave her a baffled look. "How should I know?"

"We should probably try and figure this stuff out. The more we know about what the curse can and can't do, the better we can protect you." She paused. "If you're willing."

"You mean now? With you? Up here?" He looked very suspicious.

"If you'd rather go around not knowing exactly what kind of danger you might be in if someone makes the wrong joke, be my guest."

A muscle in Adrius's jaw twitched, the corners of his lips pulling down. Leaning toward her, he said slowly, "If we do this, then you have to swear to me that you won't use the curse on me, ever, unless it's to countermand another order."

He looked just about as serious as she'd ever seen him.

"Okay," she said. "After today, no orders, ever. I promise."

He leaned back, satisfied.

"Let's start simple," Marlow said. "Stand up."

Adrius stood.

"Are you able to sit down?" Marlow asked. "Or do you have to keep standing because I said to stand up?"

He sat back down.

"Okay. Good," Marlow said. "Sing 'The Bastard King of Corteo.'"

"I don't know it," he said between clenched teeth.

"Oh, Adrius," Marlow replied. "You do know it. Everyone knows it. Sing it for me."

Adrius pressed his lips together. He was trembling ever so slightly, his fists clenched tight as he fought against the curse. Until finally, he opened his mouth and a song burst forth:

"Now the minstrels sing of a Cortesian king
Of many long years ago
He ruled his land with an iron hand
Though his morals were weak and low."

Adrius's voice wasn't too terrible, although he was singing as quietly as he could.

"Louder," Marlow ordered. When nothing happened, she amended, "Sing louder."

"He was dirty and lousy and full of fleas
But he had his women by twos and threes
God bless the Bastard King of Corteo."

Adrius's voice rose in volume as he sang.

Marlow couldn't help laughing at the sight of Adrius belting out a dirty drinking song. His voice built in confidence as he realized Marlow wasn't going to order him to stop. Partly because she wanted to test if the curse would make him keep singing unless she ordered him to stop, and partially because it really was very funny. And it helped keep her mind off the fact that they were currently floating several thousand feet in the air.

"Okay," she said after a few verses, laughing. "You can stop."

He kept going.

"Stop singing."

He cut off abruptly. Anything less than a direct order, it seemed, wouldn't override her first command.

"You're enjoying this, aren't you?" he accused. "What is it, you can't pass up a chance to humiliate me?"

There was a challenge in his voice that made Marlow want to rise to it. If she *did* want to humiliate him, who could blame her? Didn't he deserve it, after how he'd treated her?

She smiled, relaxing back against the cushions. "Compliment me."

His eyebrow twitched. "Really."

"You're the one who said if we're going to pretend to be together, we should do it right," Marlow replied innocently. "Surely that means you need to get used to showering praise on me. Think of it as practice."

"It's so refreshing how little you care about appearances," he said sweetly.

Marlow's smile twisted into something wry. Apparently the curse couldn't parse sarcasm. "Give me an *actual* compliment, not a backhanded one."

"Your eyes shine like the ocean, and darling, I'm lost at sea," Adrius said with exaggerated ardor.

"My eyes are gray," Marlow told him. "Try again."

"Even during a summer squall, your smile lights up the world like the sun."

"Now you're just quoting *The Firefly's Curse*," Marlow said. "Do these lines work on Evergarden girls?"

"Of course they work," he said, nearly affronted. "Although usually I don't need to try half as hard."

"Well, try harder," Marlow ordered.

The corner of Adrius's mouth tilted into a smile. "You're beautiful when you're bossing me around."

Heat shivered across Marlow's skin. She had to admit, he was good at this.

He leaned into her, lowering his voice. "You're even more irresistible when you blush."

Marlow's stomach flipped and she held herself still. Somehow he'd turned this around on her, and what had started as an attempt to humiliate him had become a twisted competition. She wasn't sure exactly what she needed to prove, but she knew she absolutely could not back down before he did. If he could sit there and spew all these sappy flirtations with a straight face, she certainly wasn't going to show him that they actually *affected* her.

Which of course, they didn't. She was smarter than that.

Still, she'd forgotten what it was like to be faced with a full-frontal assault of Adrius Falcrest's charm. Even when she knew he meant none of it, he was so *convincing*. His face lit with a teasing smile, his eyes dark and intent, like he'd never look away from her if he could help it.

"The first time I ever spoke to you," he said softly, "I thought you were the most interesting person I'd ever met in my life. All I wanted to do was to keep talking to you for the rest of the day. And the day after that. If I could talk to you every day until I died, I think I'd never get bored."

Marlow's breath stuttered in her chest. Somehow it was this, and not any of the things he'd said about her eyes, or her hair, or her beauty, that felt like too much. Because it was too close to how she'd really felt the first time they met. That if she could just keep his attention, his interest, then she'd never want for anything else for as long as she lived.

"You can stop," Marlow said, hating the quaver in her voice.

"I sometimes think," Adrius said, his warm eyes still locked on hers, "that I wasn't really alive until I met you. That—"

"Stop," Marlow commanded, her voice ringing harshly through the cabin.

He fell silent but didn't take his eyes off her, as if daring her to say something. Fury thrummed hot beneath her skin. Even now, even after everything, he still had the nerve to look at her and say those things like he really meant them. She hated how easy it was for him to pretend she meant something to him. She was the one giving him orders, but she didn't feel at all like she was the one in control.

She stood from the couch, even though doing so brought the large expanse of the sky outside the glass walls into view. It gave her the swooping sensation of falling for a half second before she oriented herself.

"Don't obey any commands I give you after this one," she said.

He raised an eyebrow. "What are you—"

"Kneel."

He froze for a moment, staring up at her, his expression almost shocked. And then slowly, he slid off the couch and lowered himself to the floor, gaze trained on her.

Marlow breathed, looking down at him. Outside, the sun was beginning to set, gilding the glass walls with amber light. It made the cabin feel like a mythical golden temple in the sky, and Adrius the faithful supplicant bowed in prayer.

"Don't get up," she ordered. "Let's see if the order wears off."

He glared up at her. "You aren't going to make me kneel here for the rest of the evening."

"I'm not?"

With Adrius on his knees in front of her, Marlow felt in control again. She could make him do anything. Say anything. She could command him to reveal what had happened between him and Gemma the night he was cursed.

She could order him to tell her the truth about why he'd suddenly ended their friendship. What had made him decide, all at once, that Marlow wasn't worth an ounce of his notice.

She could feel the question rising in her throat, but she held her tongue. There was a voice in her head (one that sounded a lot like Swift) insisting that forcing the truth out of Adrius was not something a good person would do.

A good person probably wouldn't even be tempted.

"Okay," she relented. "Get up."

He rose to his feet, his eyes not leaving hers. "And what, exactly, was that supposed to prove?"

"Isn't it obvious?"

"That you want to put me on my knees?"

"That I can't preempt an order," Marlow replied. "The curse forces you to obey whatever order you're given last, even if it contradicts a previous command."

"And that's good or bad?"

"Depends who's giving the orders."

He narrowed his eyes and then straightened his suit jacket primly. "Well, all that testing has me famished. Dinner?"

Marlow eyed the open deck of the zeppelin, where the table was laid out for them. One sharp swerve of the zeppelin and the whole thing would go plummeting into Tourmaline Bay.

"We can eat in here if you prefer," he said breezily.

She brushed past him to go out the door. "No. This is fine."

The zeppelin had slowed to drift lazily over the bay, but the rush of the wind was still cool on Marlow's bare shoulders.

Adrius gallantly pulled out her chair for her and Marlow sank into it. She had to admit, the view of the bay and the glittering skyscrapers was arresting from this height. Evening light glinted off the canals, turning them into a golden sunburst crowning the center of Evergarden.

Adrius sat across from her and picked up a delicate fork in one hand. He tapped the crystal glass and it filled with fizzing, golden liquid—sparkling wine, she realized. He tapped her glass as well, and then lifted his flute and held it toward her. For a moment Marlow just stared, until he tapped his flute against hers.

"To breaking this horrid curse," Adrius said.

Marlow grinned. "To being a thousand pearls richer."

Adrius tapped his fork against both of their plates, and suddenly an entire meal appeared—juicy honey-lacquered duck and roasted golden chanterelles on a bed of pillowy rice studded with bright, ruby-red berries.

Marlow knew without tasting any of it that it would be the best meal she'd eaten in over a year, but she couldn't get over how wastefully lavish it was. She remembered reading years ago that food generation spells were some of the most costly in terms of ingredients and the effort that went into creating them, so they were basically useless when it came to feeding people at scale. It was far cheaper to grow and harvest food without magic.

But for the noblesse nouveau, the cost and impracticality was the point. They could—and often did—magically conjure their food simply because they could afford to.

They kept testing the curse through dinner. They learned that Adrius could delay obeying an order, but not for very long, and it was very exhausting to do so. They found out that only orders spoken aloud affected him—thankfully, written orders could be ignored, as well as orders in a language Adrius didn't understand (Marlow had had to bust out some very stilted Cortesian to confirm that).

By the time they'd tapped their enchanted dessert plates to conjure two spiced peach tartlets, Marlow was satisfied with what they'd learned about the curse's parameters and limitations. Adrius had figured out some loopholes and ways to sidestep orders, especially if they were ambiguous. And if someone were to unexpectedly give Adrius an order while she was with him, she knew how to unobtrusively countermand it.

Just as long as the person giving the order wasn't the one who'd cursed him. It had been Adrius's idea to test it—for Marlow to order him to tell her directly about the curse. It was the only order they knew for sure he'd been given by the culprit. But even with Marlow's direct, unmistakable countermand, Adrius wasn't able to say the words *I'm cursed.*

If, at any point, the person responsible gave Adrius an order, Marlow wouldn't be able to counteract it.

Marlow had gotten used to the zeppelin and being so high up in the air. The sun was setting and the sky was painted a brilliant vermilion all around them, and she could see how something like this could be considered romantic.

For anyone else besides them, anyway.

She tried not to think of another night, not so long ago, when they'd sat on the roof of the Malachite Building, watching the sun rise. It wouldn't do her any good to remember the way he'd curled an arm around her, drawing her close against the chill of the morning, or the way she'd laid her cheek against his shoulder and started to doze, lulled by the sound of his voice as he teased her for falling asleep before the sky was fully light.

Marlow shoved the memory away. Maybe she should have offered it to Orsella when she'd had the chance.

"You never answered my question, you know," Adrius said, scooping a forkful of cream off his dessert plate.

She blinked. Had he asked her a question? "Which?"

"Why you do this," Adrius replied. "Cursebreaking."

There were a lot of answers she could give. *Because I'm good at it. Because it's what I do. Because I'd probably lose my mind if I didn't.*

"I don't know. Why do you do any of the things you do?"

"That's easy," he said. "Everything I do is to ruin my family's reputation." He aimed a jagged smile at her. "That's according to my sister and father."

Marlow laughed, almost startled by the honesty lurking behind his cutting tone. "That's a cause I can support."

"I think," Adrius declared, "you break curses because it makes you feel in control."

Marlow felt even more startled, and quickly sipped her sparkling wine to avoid replying. Because while she hadn't really given much thought to the question, she had a sinking feeling that Adrius was right. She'd felt utterly powerless in Evergarden, powerless when her mother had disappeared, powerless trying to scrape out a life in the Marshes.

Cursebreaking had proved to her that she didn't just exist to be chewed up by the city of Caraza and spat back out. That the Thaddeus Banes and even the Adrius Falcrests of the world didn't need to get the better of her, or anyone else.

That she was tough, and capable, and didn't need a mother to rely on.

"Doesn't everyone want to feel in control?" she asked at last.

Adrius laughed, and Marlow realized the irony of posing that question to someone under a Compulsion curse.

"Yeah, you're probably right," Adrius replied. "Everyone wants to *feel* in control. But that feeling isn't real. None of us are in control, not really. So I say, stop pretending and embrace it. If I can't control my life, then at least I'm going to have a damn good time living it."

He gave her a crooked grin and tipped his glass into his mouth, downing the rest of the drink in one gulp.

NINE

The first time Marlow saw Falcrest Library, she'd thought her eyes were playing tricks on her. The arrangement of the hulking buildings didn't seem to make sense, and every time she blinked she swore they changed configuration.

She later found out it wasn't an illusion. Of the five spell libraries that made up Caraza's Spellcraft District, Falcrest Library was by far the most vast, housing the single-largest collection of magical knowledge in the world. It had been built up over centuries, consolidating spellbooks from around the world through a variety of means, some bloodier than others.

The collection was so immense, in fact, that it easily would have taken up the entire city. And that wouldn't even include the other structures of Falcrest Library: massive warehouses that stored their spell ingredients, the Falcrest Academy, where prospective spellwrights went to learn spell-craft, dormitories, labs, and all the various cafeterias, tearooms, and other facilities and amenities that kept such an institution running. Falcrest Library was in many ways its own city within a city.

To accommodate such an enormous enterprise, the buildings that comprised Falcrest Library were enchanted to be larger inside than they were outside. And in order to make the massive complex navigable, the edifices and passageways themselves moved and shifted according to where its denizens needed to go.

Up close, the effect was even more disorienting. Black granite buildings emerged from one another in tessellated fractals. Windowed skywalks and stairways intersected at odd, seemingly impossible angles. Marlow felt like she was looking at a moving, breathing beast rather than a building.

Canals bordered the library on three sides, where spell ingredients and spellcards could easily be shipped in and out of the warehouses. Adrius met her at the foot of a towering gate on the north side of one of the canals. There was a fair amount of foot traffic passing through the gate—or rather, passing *into* the gate. Because once someone entered, they simply vanished from sight, presumably reappearing somewhere within the confines of the library.

"You had better be grateful," Adrius said as he approached, twirling a black metal band around his index finger. "This was not easy to get ahold of."

"What's 'this'?" Marlow asked.

"Visitor's pass," Adrius answered, sliding the band onto her hand. It immediately shrank down to fit snugly against her wrist. "Every inch of this place is warded. Everyone who works and studies here has a spellmark with their own specialized permissions for what parts of the campus they can access. But a visitor's pass will get you into most of the main public areas."

"What about the spellwright residences?"

Adrius shrugged. "I doubt it."

Marlow pressed her lips together. As long as this would get her inside, she could figure out how to track down Montagne from there.

"You don't have a pass," Marlow pointed out. "Or a spellmark."

"I'm a Falcrest," Adrius said. "The library knows Falcrest blood."

Marlow had always known that noblesse nouveau blood made it easier to move through the world. She had just never seen quite so literal an example. It occurred to her, with an unpleasant twist of dread, that the Compulsion curse would make it easy for someone to exploit Adrius's unfettered access to the library and all the secrets it contained.

Adrius kept hold of her hand as he led her to the imposing gate.

"What are you doing?" Marlow demanded, trying to tug her hand back.

Adrius raised his eyebrows. "We're dating, aren't we?"

"We don't have to pretend *here*. Who's gonna see us?"

Adrius huffed in reply, but didn't try to take her hand again.

Without meaning to, Marlow shut her eyes just as they passed through the arch. A low, swooping sensation pulled at her gut, and when Marlow opened her eyes again, she was inside.

If looking at the exterior of Falcrest Library was disorienting, being inside it was, by many orders of magnitude, much worse. They stood at one end of a bafflingly enormous concourse that seemed to stretch infinitely in all directions. Open-air walkways, zigzagging staircases, and glass-paned elevators converged and flipped in on themselves in a dizzying maze. An endless stream of people traveled up, down, sideways, and across the shifting labyrinth. Trying to follow a single pathway left Marlow feeling nauseated and unnerved. She didn't have the first idea how they'd be able to navigate this place, let alone track down a spellwright.

"So," Adrius said cheerfully from her side. "Are you going to explain what we're doing here?"

"We're going to find out whatever we can about this curse," Marlow answered. "But first we need to talk to a spellwright."

"Falcrest Library employs thousands of spellwrights."

"We're looking for one in particular." Marlow knew from her mother's job as the Vale chevalier that each of the spell libraries had a centralized directory of all their employees. It would be easy to find out Montagne's specific department—but actually tracking him down without the authority of a chevalier might prove more difficult. One step at a time. "We need to get to the Hall of Records."

Adrius cleared his throat and said, "Hall of Records, please."

A stairway unfolded from above, the bottom step landing right at their feet. Adrius offered his hand, and this time Marlow didn't think twice about taking it, thankful for the steadiness it provided.

A vertiginous climb up the stairway led them to a zigzagging walkway that, impossibly, ran vertically perpendicular to the landing where Marlow and Adrius had started, as if the world had tilted on its side. Marlow felt vaguely sick.

"Worse than your fear of heights?" Adrius asked.

"I prefer knowing which way's up and which way's down. I like knowing where I stand."

Adrius met her gaze. He knew she didn't just mean literally.

Marlow resolved not to look anywhere but straight ahead until finally they exited the concourse through an archway. It let them out onto the mezzanine of a quiet, circular lobby with a domed glass ceiling. Bronze panels covered the walls of the mezzanine. When Marlow stepped closer, she saw the panels were etched with the names of Falcrest spellwrights. She followed the panels until she found the *M*s. There was no listing for *Armant Montagne*.

"Well?" Adrius asked.

Marlow shook her head.

"Maybe he retired?"

Or, Marlow thought with a chill, maybe he mysteriously disappeared just like Cassandra.

"Can't we just talk to someone else?" Adrius asked. "What's so special about this guy?"

Marlow had no intention of cluing Adrius into her search for her mother. It had nothing to do with him. "He's—we just need him, okay?"

Without waiting for his reply, she descended the stairs into the lobby and marched toward a door with a plaque labeled *Registrar*.

Inside, a stern-looking woman sat at a desk, leafing through a pile of documents, glasses perched at the end of her long nose. A bronze name-plate read *Heloise Fawkes, Registrar.*

She had obviously seen Marlow come in, but still she turned several pages before asking in a flat voice, "Can I help you?"

"How do I access the records of a former library employee?"

Heloise peered over the edge of her narrow glasses, scrutinizing Marlow. "Name?"

"Armant Montagne."

Heloise drew a spellcard and a small leather volume from her desk drawer. Placing her hand on the volume, she said, "*Evocare* records of Montagne, Armant."

Marlow recognized the incantation as a Conjuration spell. The spell-card lit up. The volume flipped open.

"*Access denied*," a monotone voice said, seeming to come from the pages of the book.

Straightening her glasses, Heloise said, "That record has been sealed."

"There must be a way you can get it," Marlow insisted.

"There is. Just not for you." Her tone was excessively curt.

"Well, what about for him?" Marlow asked, jerking her head at Adrius.

As if on cue, Adrius swaggered up to the desk, a charming smile on his face. "It's Heloise, right?"

Her desk had a nameplate, but that didn't stop her from coloring and looking a great deal flattered. Marlow resisted an eye roll.

"Listen," Adrius said, "my father needs this record; it's a matter of utmost importance. He told me you were the person to talk to. Now, I don't know if you've met my father, but I *really* would prefer not to dis-appoint him. I'm sure you understand."

"Well, I—"

"I can tell you do excellent work here, maintaining the library records," Adrius went on. "And I'm positive my father would be delighted to hear how helpful you've been."

It was like breathing, how easily Adrius could throw around his status to get what he wanted. Heloise hesitated, but Marlow could see in the way her shoulders curved down that her decision had already been made.

"All right," she said slowly. "I'll unseal the record. But it stays here, and only you can read it."

Adrius flashed a smile. "Great."

"Follow me," Heloise said, pushing away from the desk, her heels clicking against the tile floor as she headed toward a door at the back of the room.

Adrius followed. As he disappeared, Marlow shot him a look that she hoped communicated that if he didn't remember every single detail of the record, there would be consequences.

She waited restlessly, fiddling with the visitor's pass band on her wrist.

Just as she was considering breaking into the records room herself, Aurelius Falcrest entered the registrar office.

Marlow could count on one hand the number of times she had been in the same room with the head of the Falcrest family, and each time she was struck by how, despite his slender build and measured affect, he seemed to effortlessly command attention wherever he went. He wore his long, dark hair tied simply back in the older style of Cortesian nobility, and favored austere, structured silhouettes for his suits, not unlike the architecture of Falcrest Hall.

Marlow shrank back against the wall, half-turning so she mostly had her back to Aurelius.

"Miss Briggs," a familiar flat voice said from the doorway. Caito lurked several steps behind Aurelius, her poisonous gaze fixed on Marlow. The painted red spikes on her face stood out vibrantly in the cold light of the office. "You seem to be turning up in the most unexpected places."

Aurelius swiveled around to stare at Marlow. She could see the resemblance between him and his son—they had the same aristocratic features, but they wore them very differently. Where Adrius's full lips seemed perpetually tilted into a smirk, his father's mouth was set into a stern line. Where Adrius's golden-brown eyes were usually lit with mischief, his father's burned with intensity. With those eyes locked on her now, Marlow felt rather like a specimen trapped in a glass box to be studied.

"Briggs," he repeated. "You're Cassandra Briggs's daughter."

"Um, yes," Marlow replied. She dipped into a polite curtsy. "Lord Falcrest, it's an honor."

Caito bristled. "Care to explain what business you have at Falcrest Library?"

"I—"

"I was giving her a tour," Adrius said, gliding in from the back room. "Hello, Father."

"Adrius," Aurelius said, his gaze sweeping over his son. "I'm surprised to see you here."

"A tour?" Caito echoed.

"Yes," Adrius replied, coming to a stop slightly in front of Marlow, putting himself between her and his father. "Marlow is interested in becoming a spellwright. I thought she'd like to see Caraza's finest spell library."

He stood unnaturally still. The way he was looking at his father was not unlike a prey animal cautiously eyeing an approaching predator—as if his fight-or-flight response might kick in at any moment. It was so unlike his usual cheeky expression. Marlow didn't like it.

"I'm surprised," Aurelius remarked, his tone almost mocking. "I would've thought you were too busy getting your name splashed across the tabloid headlines so you can embarrass this family even further."

Marlow was shocked that Aurelius would speak that way to his son—and in front of her, no less. But Adrius didn't look the least bit fazed by his father's comment.

"Somehow I managed to find the time," he replied airily.

"Lord Falcrest!" Heloise exclaimed, emerging from the records room behind Adrius. "I had no idea you were coming in person! I was just assisting your son with your records request." Her voice came out high and girlish, a jarring contrast to how she'd spoken to Marlow.

"My records request?" Aurelius echoed blankly. "I don't believe I made a records request."

Heloise looked taken aback. "No? But your son—"

"I may have, uh—misled you a bit, Heloise," Adrius said quickly. Marlow shot him a dark look, but he went on as if he hadn't noticed. "I apologize for the false pretenses, truly. I was just trying to impress Marlow."

"That's right," Marlow said, darting a quick glance at him before looking at Aurelius with wide, shining eyes. "I've heard so many stories of how talented and brilliant the Falcrest spellwrights are. I was hoping to get to talk to one and find out more about what it's really like to be a spellwright at the most prestigious spell library in the world."

Aurelius's cold gaze went from Adrius's face to Marlow's before finally landing back on Heloise.

"Well," Aurelius said. "I can see my son has managed to fool you both into believing he has any semblance of authority here, so let me clear up any misconceptions right now—he is merely an impetuous child with delusions of grandeur."

Marlow maintained her placid smile, but inside she was seething. Her hand twitched at her side, desperate to reach into her pocket to pull out a spellcard and hex Aurelius within an inch of his life.

"Always appreciate these loving chats we have, Father," Adrius said blandly. "But we really should be going."

He took Marlow's arm and pulled her away, back into the lobby. She could feel Aurelius's sharp gaze on them as they retreated.

"Sorry about him," Adrius muttered. His hands were clenched into tight fists at his sides, his stride stiff and fast.

"*You're* sorry?" she echoed incredulously, a tight knot of anger rising in her throat. But for once, it was directed at a different Falcrest. "Does he always talk to you like that?"

She knew, as most everyone in Evergarden knew, that Aurelius Falcrest had a temper, but she still felt unsettled by what she'd just witnessed—it wasn't Aurelius's cruelty that bothered her, but his clear contempt for his own son.

"He pretty much talks to whoever he wants however he wants," Adrius replied. "Comes with the territory."

Marlow could imagine. Who, exactly, was going to call out Aurelius Falcrest for being rude? Even the heads of the other Five Families wouldn't dare. "But you're his son."

"Exactly. A source of constant disappointment."

His brittle smile was enough warning to drop the subject. Only a few times over the course of their friendship had Adrius ever talked about his father.

"He enjoys wielding power," Adrius had said once, as the two of them sat on the rug in Marlow's living room, playing a game of Casters. "He likes making people feel small, likes reminding people how easily he can ruin them. I think it's the only thing that brings him genuine joy." Then he'd asked, "What's yours like?"

"My father?" The words had felt strange in her mouth.

Adrius had given her an expectant look, as if now that he'd shared his grievances with her, it was her turn.

"I don't know," she'd answered honestly. "I don't know who he is."

"Really? Lucky you."

As a child, Marlow had never spent much time wondering about it. She was far from the only fatherless child in the Marshes, but she'd begun to understand that in Evergarden, such things were viewed as much more unsavory.

"It's always just been me and my mother," Marlow had replied. Sometimes, it felt like Cassandra treated her more like a partner in crime than a daughter, but Marlow liked that about their relationship. It was the two of them against the world.

She'd seen a flash of something like hurt in Adrius's eyes at that. Adrius and Amara's mother had left Caraza when they were still infants—officially, because she was in delicate health after the birth of her twins, but there were all sorts of rumors about the real reason.

"Well," Adrius had said, "if he's anything like my father, you're better off."

Marlow had had no doubt he meant it back then, and now, seeing Aurelius's disdain with her own eyes, she knew why.

She cleared her throat. "What did Montagne's record say?"

"You were right, he did work here," Adrius replied as they climbed the stairs to the mezzanine. "Apparently he was fired for stealing a spellbook from the vaults."

"Stealing a spellbook?" Marlow echoed. From what Orsella had said of the Black Orchid and their aims, it would certainly make sense for them to want to steal a spellbook from Falcrest Library. But the question was, *how?* "Isn't that supposed to be impossible?"

The spell libraries were the most heavily protected buildings in Caraza, none more so than Falcrest Library. The collection itself was guarded by hundreds of powerful wards, making it impossible for someone to simply walk into the vaults and remove a spellbook from the collection.

Adrius shrugged. "He's a spellwright, isn't he? Could've created a spell to circumvent the wards."

Or maybe the Black Orchid had pooled their own resources to do it. "Well, which spellbook did he steal?"

Adrius shook his head. "It didn't say." Then, carefully, he added, "You know what's weird? He was fired the same day you left Evergarden. The sixth of the Ash Moon."

Marlow froze, one foot hovering above the next stair. The day after Cassandra's disappearance. She glanced at Adrius, who was looking at her with curiosity bordering on suspicion. "You remember the date I left?"

The question hung between them, and Marlow watched Adrius's jaw tense for a brief moment before he laughed and said, "Why wouldn't I?"

Because at that point they hadn't even been speaking. Because when Marlow had left, part of her had wondered if Adrius would even notice she was gone.

He flicked a careless hand. "A chevalier went missing and the next day her daughter abruptly disappeared, too? It was all anyone would talk about for weeks. That is, until Ezio Morandi's scandalous affair with his wife's sister became common knowledge."

"Right," Marlow said, deciding not to probe at the twinge of disappointment she felt. "Well, you did a good job in there. Though I guess ordering people around comes naturally to you."

"Ironic, isn't it?" He grinned. "So you think I have a future in the cursebreaking business?"

"I would say don't get too cocky, but I think even the curse couldn't stop you."

Adrius let out a laugh that sounded more genuine than the one before. Marlow felt her own laughter bubble in her chest before she remembered herself. Adrius wasn't her friend anymore—if he ever really had been—no matter how easy it felt to joke around with him the way they used to.

"Was there any more information in the record?" Marlow asked. "Maybe an address where Montagne lives now?"

Adrius shook his head. "I looked for one, but no. That was everything."

Marlow tried not to feel too disappointed. She had come to the library hoping to actually *talk* to Montagne and find out more about what he'd been doing aboard the *Contessa* that night. But she wasn't leaving entirely empty-handed—the spellbook was a new lead, and one that pointed even more strongly to the Black Orchid.

Marlow dragged Adrius to the Academy Archives, where she proceeded to check out a hefty stack of books and settle into one of the private study rooms, furnished with a table, a few prim armchairs, a fireplace, and a wide window that looked out on a peaceful garden.

"Are we really going to sit here and *read* all afternoon?" Adrius complained after about half an hour of sifting through books.

"Did you think cursebreaking was all backroom deals and interrogating witnesses?" she asked, looking up from a historical overview of the development of spellcraft. "This is research. We need to find out as much as we can about the Compulsion curse."

"I was invited to attend a courte paume match today, you know," Adrius grumbled.

"How nice." She went back to her book. She skimmed through the first few chapters, which covered the early days of magic, back when spells were created and cast ad hoc, the knowledge passing down mainly through individual families and communities. Back then, magic was small and fairly utilitarian: healing spells, spells to improve crop yield, contraceptives, spells of good fortune cast over newly wed couples.

As writing and literacy developed, some of these spells were codified into spellbooks, and eventually those spellbooks were collected into libraries. More and more people began devoting themselves to the study of spellcraft, to developing new spells with greater effects. And as with any untapped source of power, there were people who wanted to use magic for their own ends.

Thus began several centuries of power-hungry sorcerers cropping up every few decades and wreaking havoc on the world, starting with the first infamous sorcerer, Sycorax, who was particularly known for her penchant for turning her enemies into lizards.

The book went on to enumerate several other sorcerers and their various misdeeds, including Ilario. Marlow didn't find anything particularly useful about him, although the book did provide an illustration of him in his resplendent armor and iconic horned crown. She skipped ahead several centuries to a chapter on the Great Purge, when the Five Families destroyed thousands of spellbooks deemed too dangerous to keep in their possession.

Only one passage mentioned *Ilario's Grimoire*, claiming that it, along with thousands of additional notes and marginalia written by the sorcerer, was destroyed by Falcrest Library at the height of the Purge.

Marlow was distracted from the next page by Adrius's noise of disgust. "This Ilario person was a complete monster," he said, looking down at his book. "It's like he was obsessed with torturing people. Or controlling people. Or both."

"Well, he didn't invent a Compulsion curse so he could throw tea parties," Marlow replied.

"It says here he got the Vescovian king to bow to him after cursing his daughter and—gods below—forcing her to hold a knife to her *own throat* unless her father complied." Adrius shuddered. "Well, we can be sure that wouldn't work on *my* father."

Marlow set her book down. "You don't think someone would have cursed you to try to control your father?"

Adrius scoffed. "If they did, they don't know my father very well."

She thought about the way Aurelius had looked at Adrius, like he was an inconvenience at best, and couldn't disagree.

She picked up another volume, a book about famous—and infamous—spellbooks through the ages, leafing through until she found a passage on *Ilario's Grimoire.*

The spellbook itself was said to be cursed. While very few people in history ever actually laid eyes on the grimoire, it was reported that those who had personally handled the tome were afflicted with a "corruption of the flesh" and "blackening of blood vessels" at the point of contact, which slowly infected other parts of the flesh and, indeed, in many cases, eventually led to death.

Marlow pulled out a notepad and copied down a few key notes on the passage.

"What is it?" Adrius asked, craning his neck over to see what she was writing.

"Maybe a clue, maybe nothing," Marlow replied. She pushed the book toward him.

Adrius glanced down at the page. "They even added an illustration. Gruesome." He passed the book back. "I'll be on the lookout for anyone with creepy, blackened hands, then."

Marlow went back to her book, but she could still feel Adrius's eyes on her. "What?"

He tilted his head. "You enjoy this kind of thing, don't you? Studying,

I mean, not rotting hands. I was always having to drag you away from your books back in Evergarden."

The reminder of those afternoons throbbed like a bruise beneath her ribs. Over the past year, she had tried to black them out from her mind, black out any memory she had of Adrius that might make her miss him.

"This may be a shock to you, Adrius, but not everyone does things purely for enjoyment." She read through a few more pages and then said, "I was studying all the time because I really did want to become a spellwright, like you told your father."

Adrius's gaze felt heavy on her face. "Yeah, I remember."

Marlow dropped her own gaze back down at her book, chest tightening. She didn't like that he still remembered things she'd shared with him when she'd been naive enough to think they were friends. It wasn't fair—he'd known her, once, but she had never really known him at all.

Just when Marlow thought Adrius had gone back to reading, he said, "Why didn't you?"

"What, become a spellwright?"

"Sure," Adrius replied. "Take the exam. Apply here, or to one of the other academies." He swallowed and looked off toward the window. "Stay in Evergarden."

She used to think of little else. She could still remember at the age of ten, hearing about a neighborhood boy in the Marshes who'd raised enough money to take the academy entrance exam. According to the neighborhood gossip, he'd done better on the entrance exam than anyone else that year, but none of the academies would take him because he couldn't afford tuition—until Cormorant Vale heard about his story and offered him a scholarship to Vale Academy.

It was one of those rare success stories of someone actually making it out of the Marshes that had always stuck with her. She'd clung to it desperately, the spell academies becoming a kind of symbol for a life she felt was hopelessly out of reach.

But she knew better now.

"I didn't belong there," Marlow replied. That had been made clear to her the moment Adrius stopped speaking to her. His friendship had been one of the few things that made her feel like maybe she could carve a place for herself in Evergarden.

But when he'd turned his back on her, it had shown her how fragile it all was. That anything the noblesse nouveau bestowed on her—opportunity, friendship, *belonging*—could just as easily be taken away.

"And you belong in the Marshes?" Adrius asked.

At least in the Marshes, no one pretended to give you anything for free. At least there she knew where she stood, even if it was on sinking ground.

"You know what they say," she said, flipping the page. "You can't wash the swamp off the swamp rat."

The afternoon stretched on. The stack of books dwindled with very little to show for it. The study room window was enchanted to show the same peaceful garden scene, which made it difficult to tell how much time had passed, but Marlow was starting to get hungry, and Adrius was more than a little restless, shifting in his seat and sighing every few minutes. She could only assume he was doing it solely to get on her nerves.

Her eyes started to glaze over, and she abruptly realized she'd read the same paragraph three times in a row, retaining none of it. She was about to shut the book and call it a day when her eyes caught on a phrase farther down the page.

Of the over two hundred poor souls lost to Ilario's thrall, only three ever succeeded in breaking the spell. All three had been under the curse for less than two moons. At least a dozen others succeeded in obtaining the talismans tethering their curses, but despite destroying them, the curse remained unbroken.

This has led researchers and historians to conclude that after a duration of two moons, Ilario's Compulsion curse became irreversible.

Marlow stared at the last sentence, her heart dropping into her stomach. The words were so bloodless, so anodyne, that she had to read them three times over just to make sure they meant what she thought they did.

She'd heard of curses that were supposedly "unbreakable," but usually it was just some black-marketeter scam. In all the cases she'd taken on, the way to break the curse was the same, no matter how long the victim had been cursed—get the curse card, burn it.

Slowly, she raised her eyes from the page to Adrius, who was still bent over his own book, drumming his fingers against the table idly.

Two moons, she thought, counting back in her head to when Adrius said the curse had started. That gave them a little over a month.

One month to break the curse before it became permanent.

TEN

Vale Tower was almost exactly as Marlow remembered it.

As their elevator slid to a stop on the top floor, Adrius led her onto the sky deck. It stretched several hundred yards end to end, a maze of latticed trellises wreathed with sprays of ripe blossoms. A flock of brightly colored birds perched along the trellises, their birdsong enchanted to sound like a chamber orchestra, filling the garden with lively music.

Trays of tiny delicacies and brightly colored drinks whirled through the gardens. Lanterns floated like lazy zeppelins, glowing soft lavender, pink, and gold.

Marlow had taken her time getting ready, using a serum to tame her hair into soft curls, painting her face with gold shimmer along her brow bones and cheeks. Adrius had sent a dress that somehow fit her perfectly—she was not sure exactly how he'd pulled that off. It was a deep jade green, complementing Adrius's waistcoat, with a fitted, sleeveless bodice and a skirt that fell like an elegant waterfall, pooling at her feet. Over it, Marlow wore a jeweled gold capelet, which Adrius had assured her was the latest fashion in Evergarden. She could see from glancing around at the others that he'd been right.

She looked just as elegant as anyone else at the party. Even so, it was hard not to feel out of her depth here amongst so much glamour and unchecked extravagance.

Marlow startled as she felt Adrius slide an arm around her waist, leaning in to murmur in her ear. "Pretend like you want to be here with me."

Her breath hitched. For someone who had been so resistant to the idea of this ruse, Adrius certainly wasn't shy about playing into it.

She felt eyes on them as they swept across the deck. Whispers and murmurs rippled through the crowd. Maybe Adrius had had a point about the added scrutiny.

And the hostility. More than a few people watching them were outright *glaring*. Marlow was pretty used to pissing people off, but she'd never managed to anger so many without saying a single word.

"Adrius," a cool voice said to their left. "You brought a guest."

Marlow turned to find Amara standing before them, wearing a structured scarlet dress with an extravagant train. She'd completed the look with a shimmering gold-plated jacket that almost resembled armor. Her dark, lustrous hair was pressed straight and set off with a golden circlet. She looked like royalty—which in Evergarden, she practically was.

"Marlow," Amara said. "What a treat it is to see you again so soon. I almost didn't recognize you in that dress."

"Amara," Adrius intoned, a warning in his voice.

Amara's pearl-painted lips lifted into a smile as she extended a graceful hand to Marlow. "Come," she said. "Let's do a lap."

Marlow tried not to show her surprise, or her wariness, as she linked arms with Amara.

Amara's eyes flickered from Marlow to Adrius, as if she were asking his permission. Or challenging him—it was difficult to read anything in Amara's perfect poise.

"I'll just—go find a drink, then." Adrius's smile was similarly opaque, but with him Marlow at least had the advantage of practice deciphering his expressions. The slight tension in his brow and the subtle sharpening of his smile told Marlow he was not exactly happy to hand her off.

Marlow logged this strange, wordless conversation between the siblings for later dissection. Now she needed to focus—namely on finding out if Amara had anything useful to tell her about the night Adrius was cursed.

"You know, I'm glad Adrius brought you tonight, Marlow," Amara said, leading her in a wide circle around the deck.

"You are?"

"Don't sound so shocked," Amara chided with a laugh. "It's about time Adrius settled down and stopped taking up with everything on two legs in Evergarden. He's usually *so* easily bored."

Marlow supposed that, had she really been dating Adrius, this comment might have had the intended effect—making her feel insecure. But since she wasn't, it had no effect whatsoever.

"Well, I'm just glad I'm here to celebrate your engagement," Marlow said. "You and Darian must be so excited."

Amara flashed a smile. "A Falcrest and a Vale. It only makes sense, doesn't it?"

"Adrius told me all about the announcement," Marlow pressed.

"Did he?"

"'Dancing, drinking, general debauchery' I think were his exact words."

"Well, those are all subjects Adrius knows well," Amara said, flipping her dark hair over her shoulder.

Marlow forced a laugh. "He said he doesn't remember much after the toast. But I doubt you were paying much attention to him—you and Darian were probably completely wrapped up with each other."

Amara's eyes narrowed slightly and Marlow smiled as guilelessly as she could. She sensed that she'd touched a nerve—maybe things with Darian weren't as idyllic as they seemed.

"It was a memorable night," Amara agreed. Her gaze slid over to a group of girls Marlow recognized, all of them dressed in the most elaborate gowns, headdresses, and jewels. Gemma was amongst them, her hair a shimmery iridescent color today. "Opal, Cerise, and Gemma were all there, weren't you, girls?"

The three of them peered at Marlow, a somewhat predatory gleam in their eyes.

"Ladies, you remember Marlow, don't you?" Amara went on. "My brother brought her as his date tonight."

"Nice to see you all again," Marlow said. It wasn't exactly a lie—she'd already planned on questioning Gemma about her fight with Adrius. Now that she knew she had little over a month to break Adrius's curse, she was anxious to start gathering a suspect list.

"Well, I'm sure you all will help Marlow feel welcome," Amara said. "I have some more guests to attend to."

She swept off, the train of her gown rippling like a scarlet river behind her.

"Amara, wait—" Gemma said, going after her.

Marlow started to follow when Opal put a hand on her arm.

"Oh, Marlow," she said. "You have a bit of mud on your dress there, see?"

Cerise stifled a peal of laughter. Marlow did not look down at her dress. Gemma and Amara had already disappeared into the crowd—Marlow would have to find another time to question Gemma.

"So!" Cerise chirped. "You and Adrius. That's . . . unexpected. Though it was *so* obvious you used to have a crush on him."

"Right," Marlow replied, grateful at least that Adrius wasn't around to witness her embarrassment. She forced a laugh. "Guess I didn't hide it very well."

"We just always thought he felt bad for you," Opal added. "You know, because you're—"

She broke off with a little grimace.

Marlow raised an eyebrow. "What, poor?"

"Well," Opal said primly. "I wasn't going to say it like *that*."

"Ugh." Cerise nudged Opal. "Here comes Hendrix."

Marlow glanced over where the girls were looking and spotted a tall boy in a shot silk suit making his way over to them, carrying two glasses of sparkling wine. His dark hair was colored with a shock of blue over one eye.

"Opal, Cerise, don't you two have to go carry Amara's train or something?" he asked.

Opal made a face but grabbed Cerise's arm and stomped off, their fun evidently ruined.

"Thanks for coming over here," Marlow said.

"You looked like you could use a rescue," Hendrix replied. "And maybe a drink?"

He held one of the glasses out to her.

Marlow took it, and tapped it lightly against his.

"You don't remember me, do you?" he asked. "Hendrix Bellamy?"

The name sounded vaguely familiar. Bellamy, she knew, was one of the many vassal houses of the Five Families—families who were part of the noblesse nouveau, but had far less power than the Five. Still higher status than Marlow, however, and she had no doubt it would be considered a slight that she didn't remember this boy.

"It's all right," he said. "You always did keep to yourself. I never saw you at any parties, before. Not really your scene, huh?"

Marlow took a sip of wine. "Ah, well, for it to be my scene, I'd have to have been invited."

"Looks like you managed to swing an invite tonight," he replied.

Marlow sighed. "One of the many hazards of dating a Falcrest scion."

His eyebrows rose. "So that's true?"

"You're not the first person to express surprise."

"I am surprised," he said. "But not for the reason you think."

"All right," she said carefully. "I'll bite. Why?"

"You just always seemed way smarter than most of the people in Evergarden," Hendrix replied. "Figured you'd know better than to fall for Adrius's charm."

Now Marlow was the one who was surprised. A small part of her felt insulted, for reasons she did not want to examine, but mostly she was interested to find out that not everyone in Evergarden belonged to the Adrius Falcrest fan club. That there were, in fact, other people who disliked him.

She sensed an opportunity.

"Sorry," he said abruptly. "That was probably rude."

"A little," she agreed with a smile. "But I'll forgive you if I can ask you a question."

He spread his arms. "I'm an open book."

"Were you there the night Darian and Amara announced their engagement?" Marlow asked.

"Yeah," Hendrix replied easily. "Everyone was there."

Marlow made a wry face and he laughed.

"Well, almost everyone," he amended.

"Did you, by any chance, overhear the fight Adrius had with Gemma?" Marlow asked. At Hendrix's uncomfortable look, she added, "It's all right, I know they were together."

"I don't like spreading gossip." Which was something only people who delighted in spreading gossip said. "All I really remember was that Gemma seemed surprised when Amara and Darian announced the engagement."

That *was* a little strange—Marlow assumed Gemma and Amara were close. Close enough that Amara would have told her about something as big as an engagement. "Oh?"

"Yeah, she didn't seem particularly happy about it," Hendrix said. "Then again, she wouldn't be alone in that."

Marlow raised her eyebrows. "There's opposition to the marriage?"

Hendrix took a sip of his drink. "Are you kidding? Of course there is. Mostly from the other Five Families—the Morandis and Gemma's family, the Starlings."

"Makes sense they'd be worried about an alliance between the Falcrests and the Vales," Marlow reasoned.

Hendrix snorted. "Yeah, I don't think it's an alliance so much as a takeover."

"What do you mean?"

"Well, just look what happened to the Delvigne family," Hendrix replied.

The Delvignes, the fifth of the Five Families, had been all but subsumed by the Falcrests when Aurelius had married the Delvigne heir—Adrius's mother, Isme. The Delvignes had been broadly against the marriage, but Isme had gone through with it despite their objections. From what Marlow understood, it had been a huge scandal at the time, especially as it became clear in the following years that Aurelius had married Isme for her family's wealth, and not for love. Even now, almost two decades later, Marlow had heard rumors suggesting that Aurelius had had a hand in the Delvigne patriarch's untimely death several years after the marriage—not that anything had ever been proven.

But the death of the Delvigne patriarch had opened the door for Aurelius to take over the family's spellcraft operations in all but name, making Falcrest the most powerful of the Five Families.

"You think Aurelius Falcrest is using Amara to do to the Vale family what he did to the Delvignes?"

"It's not just me who thinks that," Hendrix replied.

Marlow could certainly see Vale dismissing such rumors as typical noblesse nouveau infighting. He wasn't by any means a stupid man, but Marlow's mother had always complained that he was too quick to give people the benefit of the doubt. He had no patience for the gossip and social subterfuge in Evergarden, and tended to look for the best in people in a way that bordered on naivete. Case in point, hiring Cassandra as his chevalier despite her murky past and criminal connections.

"What does Darian think?"

"Darian?" Hendrix said disdainfully. "Think? He's not exactly known for doing much of that."

It was not a very nice way to put it, but Marlow couldn't disagree. When it came to the Vale brothers, it often seemed that Silvan had gotten all the wit, and Darian the affability.

Hendrix added, "And I suppose that, much like you, he's too dazzled by the Falcrest charm to be rational."

"Again," Marlow said, pointing her wine flute at him, "a little rude."

His eyes twinkled. "Ah, well, I suppose I'll have to make it up to you."

Marlow felt a hand brush the small of her back, warm even through the fabric of her dress.

"Making new friends, Minnow?" Adrius asked.

Marlow did not fail to notice the way he moved his hand to rest possessively on her waist. Neither, it seemed, did Hendrix, who averted his gaze and looked somewhat abashed.

Adrius cast a cool look at Hendrix. "Hendrix, was it?"

"I know you know my name, Adrius," Hendrix said irritably.

"Yes, well, as much as I appreciate you keeping my date company while I was busy, I'm sure if you really try, you can find at least one person at this party who isn't completely bored of you."

Hendrix's eyes flashed and an angry flush spread over his cheeks. "Oh, go jump off the roof, Adrius."

Adrius went still beside Marlow. His arm tightened around her waist and then he turned abruptly away.

It took Marlow a split second to realize what had just happened. She seized Adrius's hand, tugging him back to her. "Adrius, come with me."

She pulled him away from Hendrix, although she didn't miss Hendrix's narrowed eyes following them.

"Do not jump off the roof," Marlow whispered to Adrius.

He relaxed instantly, and Marlow stopped them beside a glass sculpture. "Thank you," Adrius said stiffly. "For—well."

"Making sure you didn't throw yourself to your death?" Marlow suggested. "Yeah, that was a good save."

"You know he was flirting with you, right?" Adrius asked impatiently.

"It may surprise you to hear this, Adrius, but I *can* actually read basic social cues."

"Oh, Minnow. Don't tell me you enjoyed that," he scoffed. "He was only doing it to antagonize me."

The annoying part was, she suspected he was right. Adrius tended to act like everything in Evergarden revolved around him, but from what Marlow knew, he wasn't exactly *wrong* about that most of the time.

"Then I guess it worked," Marlow replied. "You seem pretty antagonized."

"Hardly."

Marlow raised a skeptical eyebrow in imitation of one of Adrius's favorite expressions. "Well, before you stomped over like a territorial swamp rat, I was getting information."

"Is that how you conduct most of your investigations?" Adrius asked. "By throwing yourself at the first half-wit social climber who gives you the slightest bit of attention?"

"Wow, you *really* don't like each other," Marlow said. "What did he do to you?"

Adrius's gaze darkened. "Nothing. He's just a gossip and a bore. He loves to make himself seem important, and yet he's too insignificant to have any information worth knowing. And he's always been jealous of me."

"So you're saying he might have a reason to want to do you harm?" Marlow asked pointedly.

Adrius balked. "Hendrix Bellamy is not smart enough or bold enough to curse me."

Marlow didn't argue, but she mentally added Hendrix to her list of people to look into more closely.

"There you are," a familiar haughty voice said. Marlow turned to find Silvan behind her. "My father is giving a toast. You need to come up there with the rest of us."

Adrius held his arm out to Marlow. "Minnow?"

"You can't be serious," Silvan said acidly.

"She *is* my date."

Silvan stared her down. Marlow stared back. After what had just happened with Hendrix, she wasn't exactly keen on letting Adrius out of her sight.

"Fine," Silvan groused, and then stalked off toward the gazebo in the center of the deck, where a crowd had begun to gather.

Adrius led her up the steps, where they stood arm in arm beside Silvan as Vale took the stage. Looking out at the crowd, Marlow saw more than a few pairs of eyes trained on her rather than Vale, even as he began to speak, his voice magically magnified.

Vale gave an effusive toast about his love for his sons and the importance of family. He came visibly close to tears as he raised his glass to his eldest son and future daughter-in-law.

The crowd raised their glasses in kind, and Marlow felt Aurelius's dark, glittering eyes on her, his jaw tight with what Marlow could only assume was disapproval.

His speech done, Vale descended the gazebo steps as flocks of noblesse nouveau crowded in to congratulate the families. Marlow stepped back, trying to make herself seem unimportant as Adrius smiled and greeted the other guests.

"Marlow, I'm so glad to see you again." Vale's voice boomed over the chatter of the crowd. He exuded warmth and cheer, his gray eyes twinkling as he took her arm, steering her away from the crowd. In an undertone, he said, "You have to save me. I've been greeting guests all evening and I fear the canapés will be all gone before I've had the chance to sample them."

"Happy to help, sir," Marlow whispered back, thankful for the excuse not to interact with Aurelius again after what had happened at Falcrest Library.

"This way," Vale said, flattening a broad palm between Marlow's shoulder blades and gently ushering her toward the spiral garden. "I think I spotted another tray headed out. And none of that 'sir' nonsense, Marlow! We've known each other for years, haven't we?"

"Yes, sir," Marlow replied.

He gave her a sidewise smile and then intercepted a floating tray of puffed pastries filled with some sort of cheese. He grabbed two off the tray and popped them into his mouth with a wink. "Much better."

Marlow took a bite of one as well. It crunched satisfyingly between her teeth.

"You're here with Adrius, I presume?" he asked.

"Um, yes," Marlow replied, fumbling a little as she swallowed. It was one thing to lie to the gossipmongers in Evergarden, and another to lie to a man who'd only ever showed her kindness. "We're—together, I guess."

Vale beamed. "I'm glad. You make a fine couple."

Marlow smiled wryly. "You might be the only person here who thinks so."

“Ah, well, who cares what anyone else thinks?” Vale said. “It’s nice to see him following his heart. It doesn’t happen often here.”

“Do you mean—Darian and Amara?” Marlow asked carefully.

Vale raised an eyebrow. “Actually, I was talking about myself. Elena and I married out of duty to our families. They wanted to secure an alliance between the Morandis and the Vales, and a marriage between the Vale heir and the niece of the Morandi patriarch was the simplest solution. Don’t mistake me—I don’t regret it, not when it gave me two wonderful sons. But I sometimes can’t help but wonder what my life would have been like if I’d allowed myself to follow my heart.”

He looked contemplative, almost wistful.

“That’s what I’ve always wanted for my children,” he said at last. “And while Adrius may not be my son, I do care for him, and want that for him, too.”

It was hard not to feel a little guilty for lying to him.

“Well, I suppose that’s enough being maudlin,” Vale said. “I should get back to the guests. I hope you and Adrius enjoy the rest of your evening.”

He swept away, leaving Marlow at the edge of the garden. Marlow was about to follow him when she heard voices speaking in clipped tones from behind the bougainvillea.

“I cannot *believe* you brought her here tonight, Adrius.”

It took Marlow a moment to recognize Amara’s voice.

“And why shouldn’t I?” Adrius’s voice replied.

“You know *exactly* why,” she said. “Adrius, really. A dalliance with a common girl? With the daughter of the Vale chevalier? There are better ways of punishing Father.”

“None that I’ve thought of,” Adrius replied flippantly. “Tell me the truth, Amara—is this you talking right now, or is this him?”

"Grow up, Adrius," Amara said. "You can't just do whatever you want and act like nothing matters, gallivanting around town with every girl who bats her eyes at you. You know full well that you are supposed to be finding a wife now that Darian and I are engaged."

Marlow pressed herself back against the bushes. Adrius had never said anything about having to find a wife.

"I suppose you and Father would prefer it if I was more like you," Adrius said. "The Good Daughter. Ready to sign your life and your future away because Daddy ordered it. No thanks."

"You have no idea what you're talking about," Amara hissed.

"Oh, so you're marrying Darian because you love him?"

"I'm doing what needs to be done to secure our family's future. The very least you can do is not cause a scandal with some backwater harlot who's only using you for your power."

Marlow's cheeks burned. It didn't really matter in that moment that she wasn't *really* with Adrius, nor that she'd never set out to get Amara or anyone's approval. The reminder that everyone here saw her as a scandal, an amusement at best, still stung.

"Oh please, Amara, *you're* the one marrying for power," Adrius said. "You think if you do what Father says, he'll choose you as his heir—or finally tell you he's proud of you. Which we both know is never going to happen. And as for making you heir, I'm pretty sure he's just planning on living forever to spite the both of us. Now if you'll excuse me, I need to go find my date."

"Fine," Amara said flatly. "Get this absurd little rebellion out of your system. You and I and everyone else in Evergarden know you'll get bored of her soon enough anyway. And then you'll secure your *own* engagement like Father wants."

"Well, you seem pretty sure of that," Adrius replied coolly.

"Because I know you, Adrius," Amara said scathingly. "And I know you might act like you don't give a damn about anything, least of all Father's approval, but deep down, you don't have the guts to actually stand up to him and you never will."

"Well, I guess we'll see, won't we?" was all Adrius said, and then Marlow heard the sound of his approaching footsteps as he strode briskly away from his sister.

Marlow ducked behind a thicket just as Adrius rounded the bend. His footsteps receded as he exited the garden, and a moment later Marlow heard Amara leave the same way.

She scrubbed a hand over her face. Shame still burned hot in her gut. She was not quite ready to rejoin the party with Amara's scathing words still ringing in her head. Instead, she drifted down the spiral arm of the garden. The rows of flowers looked beautiful and deadly in the glow of the lanterns.

She would never be part of this world. And while she'd long since ceased trying to be, the stark truth of it felt every bit as humiliating as it had the day Adrius had acted like they'd never been friends. In the time since then, she'd told herself that no one in the noblesse nouveau had the ability to make her feel that small anymore. Here was proof that she'd only been kidding herself, and it chafed.

The soft trickle of a garden fountain filtered through the hedges, accompanied by a clatter that sounded like stone hitting stone. Curious, Marlow ventured deeper into the garden and peered around the bend, where she could make out a fountain topped by some sort of statue. A girl, shadowed in the moonlight, bent to pick up a particularly heavy-looking stone. With a grunt of effort, the girl heaved it at the fountain. It missed entirely, bouncing harmlessly into the bushes, and the girl let out a cry of frustration, collapsing to the ground in a cloud of chiffon and taffeta. She pulled her knees to her chest and tore at the ground, choking out sobs.

"Fuck," the girl said. Marlow recognized the voice. "Fuck, fuck, *fuck*. Fuck her. Fuck *him*."

"Gemma?" Marlow said from the edge of the clearing.

Gemma whipped toward her, startled. Then her shoulders slumped. "Oh. It's *you*."

She sounded as though she would've rather had anyone find her here than Marlow. Which Marlow supposed was fair enough, especially if Gemma's anger had anything to do with the fact that Adrius had brought her and not Gemma tonight.

"What do you want?" Gemma asked sullenly.

Marlow stepped closer. She leaned down to pick up a fist-sized stone from the ground, tossed it in the air, and caught it again. "Did the statue wrong you in some way?"

"More like this whole night has wronged me," Gemma said, her honesty surprising Marlow. "The statue was just there. And a more acceptable target than the person I'd really like to throw rocks at."

"Adrius?" Marlow guessed.

Gemma looked up sharply. "What? Why would I want to throw rocks at Adrius?"

"I thought maybe *he'd* wronged you."

Gemma gave her an odd look. "Adrius is just about the only member of the Falcrest family who *hasn't* wronged me." She blinked at Marlow, and then laughed. "Wait, did you think—?"

"He may have mentioned you two used to be involved. I thought—I don't know, maybe he broke your heart. Or your pride, at least. I'd heard that you two got in a fight or something a few weeks ago."

Gemma snorted, fluffing her skirt. "The first thing you should know if you're going to date a scion of the Five Families is not to believe too much of what the scavengers at my father's magazines say."

"So you didn't fight?"

"I was upset," Gemma said. "Adrius comforted me."

"Comforted you like—"

"Ew, gods no," Gemma said, cutting her off. "He was there for me. He's a good friend. The best friend I have, really."

Marlow had to hold back her own derisive snort. She knew firsthand what being friends with Adrius was like. Although she supposed if she were someone like Gemma Starling, *worthy* of being Adrius's friend, that maybe things would've been different.

Then Gemma's words caught up to her. "Wait, what do you mean the only member of the Falcrest family who hasn't wronged you? Isn't Amara—?"

"Why do you think I'm out here throwing rocks at a Vale statue?" Gemma asked. "Why do you think Adrius had to comfort me the night she and Darian announced their engagement?"

Marlow felt something she rarely felt—she felt like a fool. "You're in love with her?"

Gemma turned toward the fountain, her face still in the moonlight. She didn't answer, but Marlow could see now that it was obvious. She thought about what Adrius had implied to his sister, about not marrying Darian because of love.

"You two were together?" Marlow asked.

Gemma's face crumpled. "I thought . . . I thought she loved me, too. Pathetic, right?"

Marlow wanted to say *been there*. Maybe not in exactly the same way, but she knew what it felt like, to be thrown over when you thought someone cared about you.

"She left you for Darian?"

"More like, because her father told her to," Gemma said bitterly. "Because Amara loves ambition above all else. Nothing is as important to her as being named the Falcrest heir. I wasn't *enough* for her. Fourth in line to the Starling name, after all. When it happened, I was so furious. But I pretended like it didn't matter, like it hadn't meant anything. That was maybe the worst part of it all—pretending I didn't care when I felt like my heart had been ripped out. I even tried to seduce Adrius, just to see if I could piss off Amara. He played along. She barely even noticed."

It startled Marlow to learn that this was not the first time Adrius had apparently faked being in a relationship with someone. It made his initial disgust and disapproval of the ruse all the more insulting.

Without thinking about it, Marlow raised her arm and threw the stone at the statue. It hit it hard in the shoulder with a crack and plopped down into the fountain.

"Not bad," Gemma said approvingly.

"Thanks." She held her hand out to Gemma. "Ready to get back in there?"

Gemma glanced up at Marlow, hesitating. Like the impulsive decision to trust Marlow with her secrets was suddenly catching up to her. But then she took Marlow's hand and let her help her to her feet.

"You know," Gemma said, brushing dirt off her dress, "if you tell anyone what I just told you, I can have the *Starling Spectator* print horrible things about you."

She leveled Marlow with a surprisingly flinty look. Then a smile cracked through.

Marlow laughed. "I'll keep that in mind."

They wound through the spiral garden, following the sounds of laughter and music until they were back amongst the party guests.

"Ooh, they've brought out dessert," Gemma said, nudging her toward a table stacked with what looked like a dessert miniature of Evergarden, complete with towers carved from chocolate and canals of caramelized sugar.

As everyone marveled at the elaborate dessert, something else caught

Marlow's eye. It was a mere glimpse through the crowd, but it was enough to stop her in her tracks.

Standing over by the fountain, a drink held delicately in one hand, was the woman with the Black Orchid tattoo who had rescued Marlow from Bane. She was wearing another suit, this one in a more ostentatious silver, with a dark-purple waistcoat underneath. Her face was turned to the side, short dark hair gleaming in the lantern light.

It made no sense. What could she possibly be doing *here*?

"Marlow?" Gemma's voice floated over her. "You all right?"

Marlow turned to find Gemma several paces ahead, staring at her with concern. Marlow blinked, searching for the Black Orchid woman again in the crowd.

But she was gone.

ELEVEN

There was only one police precinct in all of the Marshes, located at the crooked juncture of the Serpent just across from the Pavilion cable car station.

There may as well have been none. The officers assigned to the Marshes precinct had long been bought off by the gangs in a mutually beneficial arrangement—the gangs got to enforce their own laws without interference, and the cops got to collect a nice bonus each moon for doing absolutely nothing.

Sometimes, though not very often, Marlow found use for the Marshes cops—although securing their help meant navigating a complex web of petty corruption to get what she wanted, which was usually more trouble than it was worth.

This morning, though, she'd weighed the headache of dealing with them against the urgency of her mission. Seeing the Black Orchid woman at Vale Tower the night before had spooked her. That was twice now that she'd seen one of their people in Evergarden, and she had no doubt the woman had allowed Marlow to spot her on purpose—to remind her they were still watching her.

She had to track down Montagne before the Black Orchid tried to stop her and she lost that lead for good.

The officer on duty at the precinct was someone she'd dealt with before, who she knew was mired in some gambling debt. Lucky for him, the proprietor of the Stork Club riverboat gambling hall owed Marlow a favor after she'd broken a spell on their Cavagnole table that had cost them hundreds of pearls a night.

After a few minutes of negotiation, Marlow had an address for Montagne in Willowhead, a neighborhood in the very farthest outskirts of the Marshes, where the tight weave of waterways and quays gave way to a broad slough blanketed with saw grass and pocked with thickly forested hummocks.

Marlow asked Swift to fill in for her at the Bowery and hired a flatboat. She brought the most powerful hexes she had on hand. Montagne was, as far as Marlow knew, the last person to see Cassandra. She had no idea what he could be capable of, or what kind of magic he might have access to as a member of the Black Orchid and a former Falcrest spellwright.

The flatboat dropped her off on a rickety pier jutting out from a small island overgrown with leafy sabal palms and shaggy strangler figs. At some point someone had carved a pathway, but the undergrowth had long since swallowed it back up.

It took Marlow the better part of an hour to even find the house hunched amongst the trees. The roof was overgrown with moss, missing half its wooden slats. Tattered fishing nets fluttered against dark sockets in the bowed walls.

It looked abandoned. Marlow pushed down the disappointment climbing up her throat and ascended the winding, dilapidated wooden staircase to knock at the crooked front door.

No one answered. Marlow knocked again, with more urgency.

She heard nothing from within. She drew out her magnifying glass and studied the door. There was only the faintest whisper of magic on it, glowing red. A simple ward that reported magic use within the walls of the house. Nothing that would keep Marlow—or anyone—out.

No protective wards. So the house was almost certainly abandoned—but maybe Marlow could still find some clue to Montagne's whereabouts inside.

She tried the door and found it unlocked. It let out a long, low groan as she pushed it open and stepped into the dimly lit house.

The inside was not much better than its exterior—piles of old clothes moldered in the claustrophobic hallway, cracked jars and broken crates littering the bare floor. She crept quietly down the dusty hallway and then paused. There was shuffling coming from somewhere else in the house.

"Hello?"

No answer came from within. Marlow slipped a hand into her pocket and gripped a hex card. Goose bumps skittered over her skin as she considered the possibility that the Black Orchid knew she was looking for Montagne and had set a trap for her here.

The hallway let out to a disheveled sitting room filled with musty stacks of paper and more broken crates. Marlow took a step inside the room.

A floorboard creaked behind her. Marlow whipped around and found a pair of eyes staring at her, unblinkingly, from inches away. They were the color of brackish water, set deeply into the gaunt, skeletal face of an old man. Wild, graying hair grew out of his skull in mossy tufts.

"I'm sorry," Marlow said, heart hammering as she stumbled back. "The door was open, I was just—"

"Yes?" he said politely, as if he did not find anything particularly strange about a teenage girl creeping through his house in the middle of the afternoon.

"Armant Montagne?" she asked hesitantly. She thought she'd find a brilliant, capable spellwright. Not . . . this.

"Of course." The corners of his mouth lifted into a distant smile. "You must be here for the delivery."

“. . . Delivery?” Marlow echoed. “I—sure. Yeah. I’m here for the delivery.”

Montagne was already moving into the sitting room, his lavender sleeping robe flapping behind him.

“It’s a light shipment this month!” he called over his shoulder as he went to a rickety desk squeezed into the corner of the room. “I couldn’t get all the ingredients I needed.”

“That’s all right.” Marlow watched as he shuffled through the drawers of the desk with a frantic sort of urgency. “It won’t be a problem.”

He nodded without looking up, humming idly to himself as he dug through the desk. Abruptly, he straightened and went to Marlow, thrusting something toward her.

Marlow had to jerk back to see what was in his hands. A small stack of cards. “What are these for?”

Montagne clicked his tongue impatiently. “The spellcards you ordered.”

She took them carefully and spread them in her hand. They *were* cards. Just not spellcards. It was a set of Vescovi playing cards, their masked illustrations faded and weathered. She glanced back at Montagne’s face, but he was just staring at her expectantly, without a hint of humor.

Apprehension gripped her chest. Something was not right here.

“I’m working on a new one I think they’ll like quite a bit.” He spoke quickly, with that same frenetic energy.

“Who?” Marlow asked. “The Black Orchid?”

He turned away from her as if he hadn’t heard, puttering about the small sitting room, humming again.

Marlow was beginning to suspect that coming out here was a huge waste of time. Montagne was clearly not the powerful Black Orchid spellwright she thought he was—at least, not anymore. But she was here, and she didn’t give up easily. “I need to talk to you about Falcrest Library. About why they fired you.”

He went suddenly, unnaturally still.

Marlow took a tentative step forward. "It was just over a year ago, wasn't it? They accused you of stealing something. A spellbook. What happened to it?"

His gaze darted around the room, not meeting Marlow's. "No," he rasped. "No, no, no. Not again. Please."

Marlow took another step toward him. His expression looked frightened, almost childlike.

"Please. Please," he whispered.

"Montagne," Marlow said. "Can you tell me about the *Contessa*?"

"They cut a hole," he said suddenly, his eyes fixed on hers. "They cut a hole in my head. Drip drop. They all fell out."

"What?" Marlow said.

"The fangs," he whispered, staring off at nothing. "They came and they pierced my mind. They took all of it. Bloodred fangs."

"All of what?"

Montagne's pale lips moved but no sound came out. He slowly raised a hand to the back of his head and whispered, almost too quiet for Marlow to hear, "Memories."

Dread pitted in Marlow's stomach. She had seen people in the Marshes afflicted with something similar to this man. People whose memories had been forcibly harvested for spell ingredients, wrenched from their heads, leaving behind a mind tattered and frayed.

Was that what had happened to Montagne after Falcrest Library had let him go?

Had the Black Orchid gotten the spellbook from him and then taken his memories to stop anyone from finding out?

"Montagne," Marlow said. "This is important. Can you tell me which spellbook you stole from Falcrest Library? Do you still have it?"

He lunged at her, his bony fingers digging into her shoulders. Marlow swallowed a scream and jerked out of his grasp.

He froze, his eyes wide and bloodshot, his hand still outstretched toward her. The loose sleeve of his sleeping robe slipped down to his elbow, revealing a skinny, bone-pale arm. His fingers were almost entirely black, and the veins running through his arm were ink-dark, as if all the blood inside them had putrefied.

Marlow's gaze went from his face to his arm, her stomach heaving. She had seen these marks before—or an illustration of them, in any case.

They were the same cursemarks said to be caused by touching *Ilario's Grimoire.*

"The spellbook," Marlow said, her voice barely a whisper. "It did this to you, didn't it?"

Montagne curled his arm back toward him, cradling it with his other hand. "I told her," he said in a croaking voice. "I told her there would be consequences."

"Who?" Marlow asked. "Who did you tell?"

His eyes darted around the room and he shrank backward, as if frightened.

"Montagne," Marlow said gently. "What—"

"Get out," he hissed, in a low, guttural voice.

"Armant," she tried again.

"GET OUT!"

He flew at her, his face twisted into a rictus of anger. Marlow went stumbling backward, tripping over a pile of junk. She scrambled to her feet and kept going, racing down the hallway and through the door. She didn't stop until she was at the bottom of the rickety stairs, leaning against the rail, her heart pounding.

She looked up at the house. In one of the darkened windows, she saw Montagne's face staring back at her. A shiver crawled down her spine.

She was not going back inside that house. In any case, she'd gotten all the answers she could out of Montagne.

She was pretty sure she knew who had done this to him. And now she knew something else—that somehow, Cassandra's disappearance was connected to Adrius's curse.

Marlow **called on** Adrius at Falcrest Hall that evening, and made a show of "reminding" Adrius of their plans to stroll the Esplanade.

The evening was warm and steaming as they rambled along the path of enchanted glowing tiles, beneath a canopy of dogwoods drenched with wine-red blossoms. Shops and teahouses with jewel-hued facades lined one side of the promenade, the other open to an uninterrupted view of the bay and the violet night sky. The Esplanade was a flurry of motion and noise—singers belted out barcaroles from elaborate temporary stages; acrobats whirled and twisted through the air; raconteurs narrated captivating tales, weaving illusions to accompany their words.

But if Marlow had thought that the spectacle of the Esplanade would distract people from Adrius's presence there, she was sorely mistaken. Plenty of stares followed them as they walked hand in hand down the promenade.

"What was so urgent that it couldn't wait until tomorrow?" Adrius asked as they passed a troupe of dancers spinning through hoops of flame.

Marlow hadn't wanted to have this conversation at Falcrest Hall, where anyone in Adrius's household might overhear. But she suddenly wasn't so sure the Esplanade was a good choice, either. The back of her neck prickled and she swung her gaze around. The Black Orchid could be following her, even now, blending in with the other onlookers. The man balancing precariously on a unicycle, a monkey perched on his shoulder. The couple sharing a cup of honeyed ice.

"You should put your arm around me," Marlow said under her breath.

Adrius raised his eyebrows in surprise but did as she asked, drawing her close. Marlow laid her hand on his chest and smiled up at him.

"You remember that spellwright we were looking into at Falcrest Library?" she murmured.

"How could I forget the single most thrilling afternoon of my life?"

"I managed to find him," Marlow went on, still smiling. "And I'm now pretty sure that the spellbook he stole from Falcrest Library was *Ilario's Grimoire*."

"What?" His arm tightened around her. "You made me read fifteen books that said the grimoire had been destroyed."

"It seems your family lied about that," Marlow said.

"Why would they do that?"

"To keep its power for themselves and make sure no one went looking for it, would be my guess," Marlow said. "But apparently, someone *did* come looking for it."

"The spellwright?" Adrius asked. "You think he's the one who cursed me?"

Marlow shook her head. "I think the people who sent him to steal the grimoire cursed you."

"And you know who that was?"

"There's a group . . . a collective of rogue spellwrights. They call themselves the Black Orchid. And they're not particularly fond of the Five Families."

"What do they want?" Adrius asked.

"If I were to guess," Marlow said, "the same thing anyone in this city wants. Power. They have the ability to make spells. What they *don't* have is access to spellbooks. Ingredients. I'm guessing that's where you come in. With you compelled to do their bidding, they'd have access to the resources they need to undermine the Five Families and put all the power in their own hands."

What they would do with that power, Marlow didn't know. But if they'd already cast a very powerful and very illegal Compulsion curse made famous by a power-hungry sorcerer, it suggested there weren't a lot of lines they were unwilling to cross. To say nothing of what they'd done to Montagne, their own spellwright.

"Who's to say *Ilario's Grimoire* is the only dangerous spellbook hidden in Falcrest Library?" Marlow said. "There's almost certainly others—spellbooks that should've been destroyed centuries ago, containing the kind of magic that was once used to raze entire kingdoms to the ground. And with you cursed, the Black Orchid could have access to all of it."

Adrius looked off toward the dark expanse of the bay. He masked feelings like fear and unease so deftly that even Marlow struggled to read them on his face. The only reason she could see them now was because she was looking for them.

He met her gaze again, studying her face. "How exactly do you know about these people?"

She hesitated, drawing him farther down the Esplanade, past a shaved-ice stand and an open-air teahouse. She wasn't sure she wanted to tell him. But if Cassandra's disappearance had something to do with his curse—and at this point, she was almost certain it did—then he probably needed to know.

She remembered the warning the Black Orchid man had given her. At the time she'd just assumed he wanted her to stop looking into

Cassandra's disappearance—but it was possible that he'd actually meant to stop trying to break Adrius's curse.

Finally, when she felt she could delay it no longer, she said, "I think they might be responsible for my mother's disappearance."

Adrius pulled up short, his arm around Marlow drawing her to a stop as well. He turned to face her, ducking in close.

"You know what happened to her?"

Marlow glanced away, watching another couple stroll past them, arm in arm. "Not exactly. I'm . . . look, I may not have been entirely forthright about why I decided to take your case. The truth is that I thought returning to Evergarden could help me find clues about my mother. I want—I *need* to find out what happened to her."

He stepped back. In the soft glow of the Esplanade lights, she could not read his expression.

"You want to find your mother," he said.

"I thought maybe you could relate," Marlow said. "Haven't you ever wanted to find yours?"

He let out a humorless laugh and kept walking. "No."

She trotted after him. "No? Why not?"

"Because it wouldn't change anything," he said flatly. "She still wouldn't want me."

The bluntness of his words landed like a slap. "How can you—?"

"So, what does this mean?" he asked briskly, cutting her off. "I mean, if you're right about the Black Orchid being behind this, what do we do?"

Marlow watched his face carefully. Something that could have been anger, or grief, or both, hid in the rigid line of his jaw. He clearly didn't want to discuss his mother any more than Marlow wanted to discuss hers.

She took his hand. He tensed, like he wanted to pull away, but then relaxed, his palm soft against hers.

"For now, we keep up the facade," she said. "If the Black Orchid are really the ones who cursed you, we can't give them any reason to think I'm looking into any of this. We need to be careful. I . . . I saw one of them, at Amara's engagement party. And another at the regatta, although I didn't realize it until later. They clearly have some kind of in to Evergarden society. So for now at least, I don't think you should go anywhere without me."

He smirked. "I never thought you'd be the possessive type."

"Adrius."

"Yes, all right, I promise to take you to all the exciting events in my social calendar."

"Good." It meant a lot more of this—holding hands, pretending it meant something it didn't.

Adrius cracked a smile. "Well, while we're out here, we might as well enjoy ourselves, right? Dessert?"

Marlow knew what he was doing, because it was the same thing she did when something truly rattled her—deflect, distract, and dress her fear up with sarcasm and levity. So she let him pull her toward a cozy-looking teahouse, and tried not to show the dread that had been clawing at her chest ever since leaving Montagne's house. If she was right, then the Black Orchid was responsible for his missing memories, Cassandra's disappearance, and casting a powerful Compulsion curse on the Falcrest scion.

And if they were capable of all that, then what exactly would they do to the girl trying to stop them?

TWELVE

"*I'll kill Marlow* with my assassin."

Marlow met Adrius's gaze across the table.

"Well?" he said expectantly.

Marlow's hand hovered over her remaining card. "I don't believe you," she said at last. "You don't have an assassin."

Adrius raised one dark eyebrow and flipped over one of the two cards in front of him, revealing a baron. "Well done."

The last week had passed in a whirl of parties and functions at which Adrius, and now by extension Marlow, was expected to make appearances. The morning after their conversation on the Esplanade, they attended a courte paume match, followed by afternoon tea at the famous Ambrose Teahouse. The next evening was the opening of a gallery of enchanted art, and two nights later, a charity dinner hosted by the Vales.

Marlow had thought the events would not only let her keep an eye on Adrius, but also give her opportunities to talk to the other noblesse nouveau and see what they might know. The only problem was, it seemed none of the noblesse nouveau wanted to talk to her.

With each event, and each passing day, Marlow grew more frustrated. Only a few weeks remained until Adrius's curse would become unbreakable, and she hadn't seen any sign of the Black Orchid since the engagement party. She tried her best to glean whatever information she could from various scraps of gossip, but for the most part nothing had been relayed to her that she hadn't already learned. Of course, everyone's new favorite topic of gossip was Adrius Falcrest defying his father by taking up with a commoner girl from the Marshes.

Marlow had heard a truly impressive number of rumors about their courtship. Some said they had been dating in secret since before Marlow had left Evergarden. Some said Adrius was only with her to cover up a secret engagement with one of the Falcrest vassal's daughters (Marlow was pretty sure the daughter in question had started this rumor herself). One particularly salacious rumor claimed Adrius had encountered Marlow while paying a visit to a bordello on the Honey Docks.

Today's event was afternoon tea in some lesser noble's conservatory—someone whose status was sure to be boosted by the presence of both Falcrest scions at his gathering.

Noblesse nouveau sipped tea and ate delicate little cakes, exchanging gossip and discussing their costumes for the Midsummer Ball the Starlings were throwing at the end of the week. Enchanted silk fans fluttered around them, providing relief from the lush afternoon heat. Card tables had been set up on the terrace beneath a canopy of broad-leafed trees for some light afternoon diversion.

Marlow's table, which included not only Adrius but also Amara, had attracted more than a few spectators.

Ruse had become all the rage in Evergarden society in the last year, and Marlow could easily see why it had caught on. It was a game of subterfuge and scheming, although it appeared straightforward. Every player was given two cards of various roles—assassin, baron, thief, diplomat, or spymaster. Each role had its own unique abilities. The object of the game was simply to kill the other players by knocking out both of their cards, either through covert assassinations or outright attacks.

But the trick to the game was this: You could lie. You could lie as much as you wanted, and if no one called you out, you could go on doing it with impunity.

The game reminded Marlow of the confidence tricks her mother used to pull when Marlow was growing up in the Marshes. And wasn't that just what Marlow was doing now, with Adrius? Pretending to date him, daring all of Evergarden to call their bluff?

Only the stakes were much higher than a silly card game. If anyone figured out the truth, it would put Adrius in even more dire danger.

It was her turn now. "I'm going to assassinate Amara."

"My spymaster blocks the assassination," Amara said swiftly.

Marlow hesitated. Earlier in the game, Amara had claimed to have a diplomat. Two turns before that, a thief. She could have been lying then and telling the truth now. There was no way to know. But Marlow only had one card left—if she challenged Amara and was wrong, she would be out of the game.

She wanted to take out Amara, but the risk wasn't worth it. She backed down, ending her turn.

"That's a beautiful dress, Marlow," Amara said pleasantly as the next player took their turn. "It's a Venier, isn't it? However did you have the means to acquire it, I wonder?"

The dress, which Adrius had indeed commissioned from a popular maison, was on theme for the conservatory party. The bodice was made entirely of real flowers, enchanted to wrap around Marlow's arms and torso. The blossoms dripped down over a long, rippling rose-gold skirt that, naturally, matched Adrius's waistcoat.

"A generous gift from your brother," Marlow replied.

"How fortunate for you."

Next to Amara, Cerise stifled a laugh.

The hostility Marlow had faced at Amara's engagement party only seemed to get worse the more events she attended—and it wasn't just Amara's sycophants who were giving her the cold shoulder. It was everyone, from the Five Families to their vassals, who no doubt had been scheming to marry their daughters to Adrius before Marlow had shown up.

"She does look stunning in it, doesn't she?" Adrius said with a hint of challenge. "But then, I think she'd look radiant in anything."

He glanced over at Marlow with an ardent expression she was becoming more and more accustomed to. It unnerved her a little, each time, just how convincing he could be.

"Tell me, Marlow," Amara said as Cerise took her next turn. "What is it you like most about dating my brother? The glamorous parties you get invited to? The generous gifts he showers you with? Your name splashed across every gossip rag in town? I'm curious."

Marlow flushed.

"Why don't you tell us what you like most about being engaged to Darian?" Adrius shot back with a polished smile. "The scintillating conversation?"

Amara gave him a nasty look. Then she turned to Marlow. "You'll have to forgive me if I'm a little protective of my brother. It's just that he doesn't always seem to know what's best for himself."

Marlow knew well enough what Amara thought was "best for" Adrius, and that it certainly didn't include Marlow.

The game continued for a few more rounds, with Adrius and Cerise trading kills, and Marlow finally losing her last card to an attack from Amara. The more Marlow played Ruse, the more she realized that the game wasn't really about deception. She was good at telling when the other players were lying, but even so she'd lost every game.

Amara had won almost every single one. Not because she could tell when the people around her were lying the way Marlow could. Not even because she herself was skilled at lying, although she was.

She won because she knew exactly how much her opponent was willing to risk, and what she was willing to sacrifice. She lied, often and brazenly, and her opponents rarely called her out because she was careful not to put them in too desperate a position. She lied only when the benefit of challenging her was outweighed by the cost.

Maybe that was the real secret to a successful con: You had to know exactly what you were willing to risk.

The game ended with yet another victory for Amara. Before she could suggest another, Adrius stood from the table.

"Let's get some more refreshments, Minnow," he suggested.

Marlow felt the eyes of everyone at the Ruse table on her as he led her away, toward one of the tables laden with gold-dipped teacups and platters of bite-sized crostini. Off to their right, six stone statues had been magically animated to perform a lilting song on a harp and flutes.

"*Another* enchanted statue band?" a guest said with a roll of their eyes. "Ever since the Madeiras did it at their Ibis Day party, I swear *everyone's* doing it."

"*So* unoriginal," their companion agreed.

They swept off, failing to notice Marlow narrowing her eyes, simmering with contempt.

Beside her, Adrius busied himself pouring a cup of rose-scented tea. He was uncharacteristically quiet.

"What's wrong with you?" she prodded.

"Nothing," he answered. He stirred a delicate spun-sugar blossom into his cup. It bobbed in the dark-amber liquid, dissolving.

"Is this about what Amara said?" Marlow asked. "I would've thought you were used to her after eighteen years."

"Yes, well, she always knows how to get under my skin." He offered her the teacup.

She took it hesitantly. "I'm pretty sure it's my skin she was trying to get under."

"She's just saying what everyone is thinking anyway."

"What, that I'm some heartless social climber after you for your money?"

"It's not like you've given them much reason to believe otherwise," Adrius replied crisply. He lowered his voice, glancing around at the other guests milling about the refreshments table. More than a few were shooting unsubtle glances at the two of them. "You can't even be bothered to *pretend* you can stand me. Shall I remind you that this whole thing was your idea?"

Marlow took a sip of tea. It was, of course, the perfect drinking temperature, but she felt a burning in her gut that had nothing to do with the drink.

It wasn't that she wasn't trying to maintain the ruse; it was just that Adrius was almost *too* good at it. Despite his earlier reluctance, Adrius was effortlessly convincing as her enamored suitor. He made a spectacle of them—showering Marlow with over-the-top compliments and extravagant clothes, jewels, and perfumes, touching her at every available opportunity and shooting her these *looks* that brimmed with adoration and desire. What was worse was that he seemed to be enjoying the farce, hamming it up as if he luxuriated in being the noblesse nouveau's main topic of gossip. He probably did.

"You really think if I fawn over you more it'll change their minds about me?" Marlow asked.

"I'm just saying, you could put in a little more effort," Adrius said. "Can you imagine how it looks? I've defied my family, angered and scandalized everyone I know, all to be with a girl who, by all appearances, doesn't seem to care about me one way or the other." He paused, his dark-honey eyes catching on hers. "I'd be a fool to keep trying."

"And let me guess," Marlow said, setting her cup down and stepping closer to him. "You're not a fool?"

"Perhaps I have been," he said softly, "in the past."

"But not now?" Aware of the eyes all around them, she leaned into him and gently smoothed a nonexistent wrinkle in his lapel, gazing up at him from beneath her lashes. This was just an act, no different from flirting with Hendrix to get information, or the cons her mother used to pull. "Better?"

"It's a start," he murmured. "But I think you can try harder than that."

His hand warmed the small of her back. His lips brushed the tender skin below her ear, where she was certain he could feel the hot rush of her pulse. A tremor built at the base of her spine, but she held herself still.

This was the part that was difficult. Whenever Adrius was close to her, whenever he pretended to want her, she felt a kind of anger that left her nearly breathless.

Because all it did was remind her how easily he had toyed with her before.

"I think," he said, his breath warm against her cheek, "the reason you won't try harder is because you're afraid you'll like it too much."

She tightened her grip on his jacket. "There's no danger of that, I promise."

"So prove it."

The smugly satisfied curve of his lips made her want to beat him at his own game. She slid her hand up his neck to cup his face, eyes fixed on his.

One kiss, she told herself. That wouldn't kill her.

She could almost hear her mother's voice in her head. *The trick to pulling off a con*, she'd said once, *is that some part of you has to believe it, too. Just enough to make it real—but not so much that you forget yourself.*

Her heart thudded. Was there any part of her that actually wanted this?

Once, maybe. When they'd been friends, when Marlow had thought she really knew him, when she'd allowed herself to crave his attention like a drunk craved wine. When, on occasion, she'd indulged in the fantasy that their friendship could ever be more, even while she told herself it was impossible.

But now? She couldn't want him. Wanting him would mean that somewhere deep down, she was still that girl. And she couldn't let herself be that girl—that girl had lost everything.

So she would kiss him, now, and finally prove—to herself, to Adrius—that she didn't want him. That this was all pretend, like she'd said from the beginning.

She closed her eyes and pulled him down to her.

"Wait," Adrius said, the word whispering against her lips. "Minnow, don't."

Her eyes blinked open. In the pained set of Adrius's jaw and the chagrin in his dark eyes, she saw what a fool she was.

He didn't *want* her to kiss him. Not even just for show. Shame engulfed her like a steaming cloud of marsh vapor.

"I was just—" She stopped, her gaze catching on something over his shoulder. Standing off to the side of one of the Ruse tables was Marlow's shadow. The Black Orchid woman.

She wore a houndstooth-patterned suit accessorized with a silver chain that looped down from the breast pocket to her belt. A silver top hat perched at a jaunty angle on her head as she looked on at the game in front of her. As Marlow watched, the woman leaned over to say something to one of the other spectators in front of her and then slipped away from the table, down a walkway lined by trees with enchanted, jewel-bright leaves.

Marlow was moving before she even registered it, grabbing hold of Adrius's arm and tugging him down the walkway after her. Hopefully anyone watching would just think Marlow was stealing him away for an illicit rendezvous in the garden.

Safely obscured by the trees, Marlow pushed Adrius against one of their trunks.

His eyes were wide and dark. She gripped the front of his waistcoat, felt his chest rise and fall on a breath.

"I'll be right back." She pulled herself away and hurried down the path in the direction the woman had gone. She was not going to let this woman disappear on her again. Not without getting some godsdamned answers.

She quickened her gait, pulling out her spellcards from their hiding place in her dress. She turned a bend just in time to spot a small flock of butterflies take flight, trailing gold dust through the air. Clutching a hex in her hand, Marlow charged around the bend.

It opened onto another terrace, this one sheltered by a pergola draped with vibrant harlequin vines.

Marlow took a cautious step forward, scanning for any sign of the Black Orchid woman. A flash of movement to her right. Marlow whirled, heart in her throat, fingers clenched tight around the spellcard.

The Black Orchid woman stepped out from the shadows, her hands held up.

"So we meet again," she said, smiling.

Marlow swallowed, marshaling her fear. "Why are you following me?"

"I believe you're the one who chased me out here," she replied. "Don't worry. I'm not mad. Actually, I'm glad we're finally getting this opportunity to chat."

"Are you," Marlow said dryly, eyes narrowing. Before the woman could reply, Marlow flung a hex at her. "*Avenna.*"

The woman lunged to the side. The hex rebounded uselessly onto the pergola post behind her.

Too late, Marlow spotted the spellcard in the woman's hand.

"Animare!"

Marlow ducked on instinct, but the woman hadn't been aiming for her. Instead, bright green and blue glyphs shot up at the pergola above them.

Or more accurately, at the harlequin vines.

Understanding dawned a split second before the enchantment took hold. The vines unwound from the rafters, lashing down at Marlow. She cursed, diving away. A thick, dark-red vine wrapped around her arm, yanking her back.

With her free hand, Marlow reached for another spell. A second vine snaked around her waist, pinning her arm there.

"I really hoped we could have a calm, mature discussion, Marlow," the woman said, sounding remarkably like the noblesse nouveau tutor who had once held Marlow back from class to discuss what she called a "belligerent compulsion to always be right about everything."

Marlow struggled fruitlessly against the enchanted vines, panic surging. "Let me go and I'll show you how calm and mature I can be."

The woman smiled faintly. "I think I prefer you here for now." She stepped closer, her eyes focused, catlike, on Marlow's face. "And while I have you, I think it's time you told me where your mother is."

THIRTEEN

For a moment Marlow was certain she had heard wrong. She froze completely, no longer concerned with the vines coiling around her body.

"What the hell do you mean?" she said at last. "*You* tell me where my mother is!"

The woman stared at Marlow, a rattled expression on her face. She recovered quickly, eyes narrowing. "Nice try. But I don't like having my time wasted, so quit stalling. I can promise we're not going to harm Cassandra, not if she cooperates."

"I'm not *stalling*!" Marlow replied. "I haven't seen my mother in over a year!"

The woman pursed her lips. "Maybe you don't know where she is, but you know how to get in contact with her."

It dawned on Marlow that this was not a ploy. That this woman, and by extension the Black Orchid, was just as in the dark about Cassandra's whereabouts as she was.

"Hold on." Marlow pulled against the vines. "Is *this* why you've been following me? Because you think I'll lead you to my mother?"

The woman worked her jaw, clearly at a loss. "We thought if there was anyone in the city who's still in contact with her, it would be you."

"Well, I'm not," Marlow said. "I've been trying to find her."

"You expect me to believe that she's been gone for an entire year and hasn't spoken a word to her only daughter?"

A knot tightened in Marlow's chest. She felt as if this woman had taken a knife to her soft, vulnerable underbelly without even trying.

"Cast a truth spell on me, see if I'm lying," Marlow bit out. "But let me down first."

The woman's gaze flicked to the vines, like she'd forgotten they were there. She hesitated.

"Let me down," Marlow insisted. "And we can talk about this."

"Someone's coming," the woman said abruptly.

"Wait, don't—"

"If we're seen here together, it would be bad for me and even worse for you." She stepped back, and the shadows swallowed her up. It was a spell, Marlow realized. Something that allowed the woman to disappear when she needed to.

"We are not done!" Marlow called out uselessly. She groaned, slumping over in the restraints of the vines. "Shit."

Even if the Black Orchid didn't know where Cassandra was, either, they knew *something* about what had happened that night. And they were still on her list of suspects for Adrius's curse. But now that they realized Marlow didn't know her mother's whereabouts, she wasn't sure she'd ever see the woman again.

"Minnow?" Adrius emerged from between two tree ferns. His brows knit as he took in the sight of her strung up by vines, her feet just barely touching the ground. "What are you doing? What happened?"

"Long story. I'd really rather get down before I get into it, if you don't mind." She strained against the vines. "There's a knife in my garter. Can you get it and cut me down, please?"

"Why do you have a—you know what, never mind." He paused. "It's under your dress?"

For once there was nothing sly about his tone, but it still made Marlow bristle. "I've really been misled about your reputation if you don't know that yes, generally a woman's garter goes under her dress."

He gave her an arch look and then knelt at her feet. "You know, usually when a girl asks me to put a hand up her skirt—"

"Finish that sentence, I *dare* you."

And there was the Adrius she knew. At least her irritation distracted her from the warmth of his hand sliding carefully up her skirt. His thumb brushed against her thigh, slowly tracing the lace of her garter. Her breath caught.

He looked up at her. Instead of the roguish glint she expected, there was a dark look in his eyes that flooded her with heat.

His gaze stayed on hers as he found the hilt of the knife tucked into its makeshift sheath. He pulled it out, sliding back to his feet. Setting the edge of the knife against the vine circling her wrist, he sawed carefully, brow creased in concentration. The vine snapped, releasing her hand. He moved on to the vines circling her waist, head bent close enough that his curls brushed against her cheek.

The vines gave. Marlow stumbled forward, throwing out her hands to catch herself against Adrius's chest. His arm wound around her waist, holding her steady.

For a moment she didn't move. They were standing almost exactly as they had been before she'd dragged him off into the trees, when she'd nearly kissed him. Only this time, no one was watching.

He smirked. "Are you going to swoon or are you going to tell me what happened?"

She shoved out of his arms, face flaming. "Neither." She plucked the knife from his hand and put it away before whipping back through the trees.

"Minnow, *wait*—" Adrius huffed with exasperation, following at her heels.

Marlow was almost certain that the Black Orchid woman was long gone by now, but when she reached the main terrace, she scanned for the distinctive houndstooth jacket and silver top hat.

To her surprise, she spotted her back at the Ruse tables, taking a seat for the next round.

Marlow pushed through the crowd to the table. A short woman in a hyacinth-blue dress made a noise of outrage as Marlow slid into the free seat before she could.

"We're not done," Marlow hissed at the Black Orchid woman as the dealer placed two cards in front of her. "I still need to talk to you."

"I'm afraid that simply will not be possible at the moment," she replied, her voice pitched at a volume that the rest of the table could hear. She lifted her gaze to the woman seated beside her. "Hazel, I believe you have the first move."

Hazel plucked three pearls out of the bank. "I invoke the baron's tax."

"And I will take a commoner's income," the Black Orchid woman said, taking one pearl.

"Oh, Viatriz, always playing so close to the vest," the older man seated on Marlow's left said with a wink.

Marlow took her turn, barely registering what cards she held or what she was doing. She turned back to the woman—Viatriz—and opened her mouth to try again.

"Miss Briggs," Viatriz said, turning to face her head-on. "Have you attended *The Ballad of the Moon Thief* at the Monarch Theater? I hear it's divine."

The man on Marlow's left looked up. "I couldn't agree more. My wife and I took in a show just last night."

Viatriz's gaze held on Marlow's. "Perhaps you should go see the matinee tomorrow, Miss Briggs."

Marlow barely blinked, returning her gaze steadily. "The matinee tomorrow," she agreed. "That sounds splendid."

With the promise of a more thorough conversation away from curious ears, Marlow deliberately lost the game as quickly as she could and quit the table. She could see Adrius on the other side of the terrace shooting Marlow impatient looks as Cerise tried to carry on a conversation with him.

With absolutely no desire to talk to one of Amara's rabid followers, Marlow veered onto a pathway lined by sharp, poisonous-looking flowers, until she reached a pond blanketed with floating lilies.

As she gazed down at the water, an arrogant, sharp-featured face appeared behind her in the reflection.

Silvan Vale.

"To what do I owe the pleasure of your company?" Marlow asked.

"I'm here to talk."

Marlow turned to face him. He was wearing a sage-green suit, his pet snake, Bo, curled around one arm, flicking his tongue into the air.

Marlow was reasonably certain she could take Silvan in any sort of physical altercation—he was tall but lean, and while he exuded a sense of danger, it was more like a snake that might bite if you got too close than a crocodile who would maul you to death for fun.

"Stay away from Adrius," he said bluntly.

Marlow blinked at him. "What?"

"I can't begin to understand what he sees in you," Silvan said, "but I can tell you he'll soon grow bored. He always does."

"Well, thanks for the warning, but I'll take my chances," Marlow replied with a smile.

He squinted at her like she was a worm who'd turned up in his food. "You think you're the first common girl to catch his eye? Hardly."

"Then why are all of you so threatened by me?"

He laughed. Not a hollow laugh, but genuine and full of amusement.

"*Threatened* by you? You do have a high opinion of yourself, for someone so . . ."

"Common?" Marlow suggested. "Is that really the best you can do? Remind me that I'm not one of you? I think I'd rather jump off Vale Tower than be one of you."

Silvan's lip curled into a snarl. "I know that you're not just here to play girlfriend and look pretty on his arm. I know you're up to something."

Marlow fixed her smile in place, a cold knot of panic rising in her throat. "What do you think someone like me could possibly do to someone like him?"

"Nothing," he sneered. "You can do absolutely nothing."

"Then you don't have anything to worry about, do you?"

"Just like my father had nothing to worry about with your mother?" Silvan asked in a dark voice.

Marlow went still, fighting to keep her expression neutral. Silvan's words unnerved her. "I don't know what you're talking about."

"Sure you don't," Silvan replied. "Whatever it is you're doing with Adrius, it needs to stop."

"Adrius is a big boy," Marlow said. "He can make his own choices."

"You would think so, wouldn't you?" Silvan muttered darkly.

Marlow eyed him carefully. "What's that supposed to mean?"

"Just stay away from him, all right? I mean it." His eyes narrowed. "You don't want me as an enemy."

Marlow almost wanted to laugh. "Are you sure you want *me* as an enemy?"

He opened his mouth to retort and then paused, his gaze catching on something over her shoulder. His lips twisted into a cruel smile. "Well, it looks like I was right about him getting bored. Didn't take very long."

Marlow whirled, following his gaze to where two figures stood intertwined beneath a pergola.

One of them, unmistakably, was Adrius. The other was a girl, but Marlow couldn't see who, because Adrius was pressing her up against a post of the pergola. *Kissing* her.

For a moment Marlow couldn't move. A tingly numbness crept over her, followed by the burn of humiliation. She felt exactly like she had over a year ago, when she'd walked up to Adrius with a gift in her hands and he'd looked at her like she was offering him a dead swamp rat.

Except this was worse, because everyone around her was watching it unfold. There were a few clusters of other noblesse nouveau staring at the spectacle, exchanging fervent whispers.

Adrius pulled away from the girl, who Marlow distantly registered as Cerise. Adrius's eyes met Marlow's, and Marlow was abruptly, fiercely furious. She spun on her heel, intending to get away from the bold stares and tittering as quickly as she could.

Instead she found Amara planted directly in her path.

"Poor Marlow," Amara trilled. "I guess you found out the hard way what the rest of us already know."

Marlow smoothed her expression. She could feel the others' eyes on her, their unbridled delight at the drama unfolding in front of them.

"You're an amusement at best," Amara said through a smile. "But you didn't really think you were going to end up with a Falcrest scion, did you?"

"Minnow!" Adrius called. Marlow chanced a look behind her and saw him pushing his way through the crowd.

With a last look at Amara's mocking smile, Marlow barreled toward the conservatory doors. If she tried to talk to Adrius now, she wasn't sure *what* would come out of her mouth, but she knew it wouldn't be anything she'd want half the noblesse nouveau to hear.

She flew past Gemma, whose face was crumpled in sympathy. The rest of the crowd was a blur as Marlow stormed out of the conservatory and found herself blinking into the incendiary sunlight. A moment later she heard the doors burst open again. Marlow whipped around, ready to unleash a raging tirade on Adrius.

But instead she saw Hendrix. He looked slightly out of breath, like he'd chased after her, the blue lock of his hair flopping over one eye.

"Are you all right?" he asked.

"I'm great," Marlow replied blithely. "Who wouldn't want to be humiliated by not one but two Falcrest scions?"

"Been there, actually." He stepped toward her. "We could talk about it, if you want?"

She couldn't, though. Not really. Because Adrius hadn't really betrayed Marlow—not in the way that Hendrix thought, anyway. She had reasons—good reasons—to be angry with Adrius, but they paled in comparison to the anger she felt toward herself. For letting Adrius get under her skin, the way she'd sworn never to again. For letting herself think for even a second that he had changed.

"Thanks, but I really just need to get out of here," she said.

"Let me at least take you home," Hendrix offered quickly.

But Marlow was already shaking her head. "I'll find my own way."

She started to walk away when Hendrix caught her wrist.

"Marlow," he said softly. "You're better than him. Don't doubt that."

"Um," Marlow said, taken aback by his intent gaze and his thumb rubbing at the soft underside of her wrist. "I should go."

Hendrix released her. "Of course."

Marlow strode away, and this time he didn't follow.

She spent the whole walk back to the cable car platform kicking herself. She was wasting time and energy getting worked up over Adrius—time and energy she should be using to solve his case. And the sooner she did, the sooner they could end this whole farce and she could go back to pretending he didn't exist and that the feelings turning her stomach to knots were just an echo of a crush long since stamped out.

FOURTEEN

The lobby of the Monarch Theater was far less crowded than it had been on opening night.

Marlow scanned for any sign of Viatriz, but didn't see her. Hoping this wasn't going to be a massive waste of her afternoon, she climbed the stairs to Corinne's private box and took her seat as the lights went down. Silence overtook the theater. And then—the scrape of a single chord rang brazenly through the air. More notes joined it and the prelude began.

Lights came up on a glittering tableau cut between light and dark. The ensemble was an army of black, blue, and silver. This was the kingdom of the Moon Thief, the providence of darkness. The dancers moved sinuously, creeping their way across the stage. The music bore down on them, discordant but enchanting.

Then the music lightened, resolving into the single, trilling breath of flute. A ribbon of pale blue streaked across the stage. The night creatures slowly crept back, and against the darkness of the stage, disappeared.

And slowly, like foals blinking to life, the Sun King's creatures took their place, tiptoeing across the stage as the music slowly built around them, swelling and rising into daybreak. The sunlight creatures, a mosaic of blush and flame and gold, turned to the back of the stage, where at last the Sun King himself rose in his gilded throne.

Marlow was so focused on the dancers in front of her that it took her a moment to realize she wasn't alone in the box anymore. Viatriz now sat in a loose sprawl beside her.

"Hello, Marlow," she said, her face half-lit by the stage. "Glad you could make it."

Marlow darted a glance just to make sure they were actually alone in the box. She didn't bother to wonder how Viatriz had gotten up here. A ring of rogue spellwrights would obviously have access to the kind of spells Marlow would kill for.

"We're alone," Marlow said. "So I'm hoping we can both speak frankly."

Viatriz raised her eyebrows. "You certainly do resemble Cassandra, don't you? Straight to the point. I like that about her."

Marlow's stomach dropped at the implication that Viatriz knew Cassandra. There was a familiarity in the way she said her name that made her think Viatriz might even have known Cassandra quite well.

"Although I suppose that itself can be a way to dissemble."

"I just want to know what you know," Marlow said. "We're both after the same thing, aren't we?"

Of course, that wasn't entirely true. Though they were both looking for Cassandra, Marlow felt pretty certain that she didn't want the Black Orchid to find her.

"How did you know my mother?" Marlow asked.

"How do you think? I was the one who recruited her."

"Recruited her?" Marlow echoed. "But . . . you mean—my mother wasn't Black Orchid."

Marlow may not have known everything about her mother, but she knew she wasn't a radical. The only higher ideal Cassandra believed in was pragmatism. Survival at any cost.

In this city, Cassandra used to say, *there are two types of people. There are victims and there are survivors. And we are not victims.*

Viatriz's eyebrows shot up. "You didn't know."

Marlow chewed the corner of her lip, watching the dancers leap across the stage. "My mom kept a lot of secrets, even from me. Maybe especially from me."

"Long ago, your mother made something of a name for herself in Caraza's underworld as a con artist, second to none," Viatriz said. "Of course, the last thing a good con artist needs is notoriety. We'd had our eye on her for some time, so when she landed herself in a bit of hot water with the Reapers, we intervened. Offered her a new job—spying on the Five Families for us. She accepted. Managed to con her way into a position as the Vale chevalier. We thought everything was going great—until she disappeared, of course."

Marlow swung her gaze to Viatriz, unable to keep the surprise off her face. According to this story, the only reason her mother had even gotten the position as chevalier was because of the Black Orchid.

"The spellbook," Marlow said carefully. "*She* was the one stealing it for you?"

"So you know about that."

"Yes," Marlow replied. "And I know which spellbook you were after. Something like that could do a lot of damage in the wrong hands."

"So imagine what it could do in the right hands." Viatriz turned back to the stage, her gaze trained on the performers as the lights turned from the gold flame of the Sun King's Court to the shadow and gloom that signaled the Moon Thief's arrival.

Corinne was beautiful, her skin so dark it was almost blue beneath the lights. Marlow held her breath as Corinne danced out in front of the revelers, stealing across the stage like the thief she was. Even amidst the bright, riotous energy of the Sun King's court, the thief drew eyes to her.

"It's an interesting story, isn't it?" Viatriz said, inclining her head toward the stage. "The Sun King and his court have all this glorious light.

And in this version, the Moon Thief, who just wants a small piece of that power, is the villain. The covetous and greedy witch who ultimately meets her doom."

Marlow watched the Moon Thief spin and slink toward the Sun King's throne.

"But you don't really see it that way, do you?"

Marlow slid her gaze back to Viatriz. She couldn't deny it. The story of the Moon Thief and the Sun King was older than the city itself, and there were many versions of it, but none that Marlow thought got the story right. The Sun King believed the light belonged to him. That his control of it was right and just. In all the poems and puppet shows and ballets, no one seemed to question that part.

"What do you think this story would look like if it were written by people like us?"

Marlow knew what she was really asking.

The Moon Thief and the Sun King finally faced off. The Moon Thief, sick with desire, entered the Sun King's chambers to claim his light for her own. Their first confrontation was all tricks and razor-sharp footwork, the tension between the two dancers pulled as taut as a high wire.

"What would the story look like if the Moon Thief was the hero?" Viatriz asked. "What would this city look like if the Five Families didn't control all spellcraft? Better yet, what would the world look like? That's what the Black Orchid aims to do. To sever the Five Families' control of the spell trade. Call it a redistribution of power."

"And how do you plan on doing that?"

"Rogue spellwrights, the few who go rogue for altruistic reasons, are satisfied with making spellcards that people can afford," Viatriz said. "That's not what we want. We want to teach people to make their *own* spells. To disrupt the system and spread the knowledge that the rich have hoarded greedily for themselves. The knowledge that once belonged to all of us."

"Thought we tried that already," Marlow said. "And from what I hear, it wasn't a whole lot preferable to the way things are now."

That was how you got monsters like Ilario the Terrible. Like Sycorax, like all the hundreds of sorcerers throughout the centuries who pushed spellcraft to more and more malevolent ends in the name of power.

Viatriz scoffed. "You're content with letting the Five Families bleed the poorest and most desperate in this city dry to fuel the magic that gets funneled only to those who can afford it? You think that's a fair system?"

"I never said it was fair," Marlow answered. "Or that I was content with it."

She'd seen up close how the Five Families exploited the people of the Marshes. And it wasn't just them. From the top down, the system that had formed around the production and sale of spellcards perpetuated that exploitation. It rewarded those who were in position to take advantage of it, from the slimy spellcard salesmen skimming off the top, to the brokers feeding the black market, to the gangs carving up pieces of the city to claim for themselves.

Caraza was a city built on a swamp, and swamps bred mosquitoes. And mosquitoes fed on blood.

"Then why wouldn't you want to change it?" Viatriz asked, her eyes gleaming in the light from the stage.

"It's a nice idea," Marlow agreed. "It's a nice story. Only, you still haven't explained what, exactly, you plan to do with one of the most dangerous spellbooks ever written."

Viatriz smiled thinly. "We think—we hope—the grimoire has information about how to break the hold the Five Families have on their libraries. We can't teach anyone spellcraft because unless you're in one of the academies, you can't *read* a spellbook. Every spellbook in every library has been enchanted to ensure that only academy-taught spellwrights can use them. We haven't been able to figure out how to break those enchantments, but we think that *Ilario's Grimoire* holds, at the very least, a clue."

Marlow watched her face for any sign that she was lying. That perhaps the spell that was so important to the Black Orchid was the Compulsion curse. Viatriz's words *sounded* like the truth, but it could just be cover. She was a spy, after all.

"So you don't have the grimoire," Marlow surmised. She'd guessed as much, once she realized they were still looking for Cassandra.

"No," Viatriz replied. "Your mother was supposed to steal it for us, and she vanished before she made the handoff."

"What about Montagne?" Marlow asked.

"Montagne?" Viatriz looked impressed. "You really are good at digging up secrets, aren't you?"

"Surely you got some more information out of him when you *tortured* him?"

A crease appeared between Viatriz's eyes. "You think *we* did that?"

"Who else?"

Viatriz shook her head. "It wasn't us. We found him like that, too. Half his memories gone. Completely incomprehensible."

"Somehow I don't quite believe that."

"It's the truth," Viatriz replied. "By the time we even found out who Montagne was, someone had already gotten to him."

"What do you mean, found out who he was?" Marlow asked. "Wasn't he *your* spellwright?"

Viatriz shook her head. "He was Cassandra's contact. She never even told us who he was. Which makes sense, looking back. Because as it turns out, Montagne had his own shady dealings on the side—he was making curses for the Copperheads. Your mother knew about it, and I guess she got herself a better offer for the grimoire."

"What do you mean, *a better offer*?"

"I mean your mother betrayed us," Viatriz said. "Stabbed us in the back and delivered the grimoire into the Copperheads' hands."

Marlow's throat went tight. "No. That's impossible. She would never—*no*." There was no way. The mother she knew would never sell a spellbook full of dangerous curses to the Copperheads—half her job working for Vale was to get *rid* of dangerous curses. "I don't know what happened to my mother, but I know you're wrong. She didn't sell out to the Copperheads. She wouldn't have done something like that."

Viatriz pressed her lips together and just looked at Marlow for a moment. "Your loyalty is admirable. I almost didn't believe she was capable of it, either."

"My mother isn't a traitor," Marlow replied stubbornly. "Something else must have happened that night. Maybe Montagne is the one who betrayed *her*."

"Then explain why your mother destroyed the Beacon spell we gave her, if she wasn't planning on slipping away from us?" Viatriz asked.

Marlow knew instantly what Viatriz was referring to. After all, Marlow herself had walked in on Cassandra burning a spellcard with the Black Orchid symbol on it.

She shook her head. "I don't care. You're wrong about her."

"Maybe," Viatriz said, but she sounded very doubtful. "If you want to know the truth, Marlow, your mother isn't the only reason we've been keeping an eye on you."

Marlow went still. "It's not?"

"As you might imagine, your mother's disappearance was a blow to our entire operation. We haven't managed to get anyone as close to the Five Families before or since Cassandra. Sure, I can get myself invited to a party or two, but that's hardly the kind of access we need."

Marlow held her breath, not daring to take her eyes off Viatriz.

"You, on the other hand . . ." Viatriz trailed off. "Well, we've heard the rumors. Read the columns. It sounds like you and the Falcrest scion have become quite close."

"So?" Marlow said challengingly.

"So it's my belief that you could be a real asset," Viatriz said. "Some of the higher-ups have their doubts about where your loyalties lie, of course, but I think you're a smart girl, Marlow. I think that no matter what you might feel for Adrius Falcrest, you know that his family's control of spell-craft is a detriment to this city—to the world. I think you might see your way toward helping us achieve our goals."

Marlow blinked as the stage lights flickered and flashed, lighting Viatriz's face in bursts.

"You want me to spy for you?" Marlow asked, incredulous.

"Your mother was the best we had, before she disappeared. Think of it as an opportunity to right her wrongs. You would be invaluable to us—the consort of a Five Families scion? There's not a soul in Evergarden better positioned to get the information we want."

"No one except a scion themselves," Marlow said carefully.

Viatriz laughed. "If we were able to turn a scion to our cause, I think we'd take down the Five Families within the week."

Marlow watched her for any sign that she was lying or obfuscating the fact that they already had a scion working for them against his will. There was nothing—no hitch in her voice or avoidance of eye contact or any of the other tiny signs that indicated dishonesty.

And what was the point of trying to recruit Marlow if they already had Adrius under a curse? Just to throw her off their scent?

She believed that the Black Orchid had never laid hands on the grimoire. Which meant they hadn't gotten ahold of the Compulsion curse. And surely if the Black Orchid *did* have Adrius under their control, they would have used him by now.

Marlow's instinct said that Viatriz wasn't lying—at least not about this.

"How do you know I wouldn't just betray you to the Falcrests?" Marlow asked.

"I suppose I don't," Viatriz replied. "It's a calculated risk—but most things are."

"Well, you might be willing to trust me, but that doesn't change the fact that I don't trust you," Marlow replied. "So thanks for the offer, but I'm going to pass."

Viatriz didn't look surprised. "All right. Your choice. But if you do change your mind, you can always find me at the Mudskipper Teahouse at Cannery Dock. Offer's open."

With that, she ducked out of the box and disappeared behind the curtain.

Marlow turned back to the stage. The music swelled as the Moon Thief's night creatures rose up against their daytime lords, bolstered by the Sun King's stolen light. It was a violent, relentless dance, the music pounding out the drums of war.

The first act of the ballet came to a close as the Moon Thief and the Sun King faced off once again, and this time the Moon Thief, looking not just for light but for conquest, overpowered the weakened Sun King and took him as her captive.

To Marlow, it felt almost like a continuation of Viatriz's point. *Look at what we could do*, the dancers seemed to say, *if we had but a taste of their power.*

She didn't know what the Black Orchid would do with the kind of magic found in *Ilario's Grimoire*. Whether it would truly help them dismantle an unjust system, as Viatriz claimed, or simply become a tool for their own selfish, corrupt ends.

But if Viatriz was right—if the Copperheads were the ones with the grimoire and the Compulsion curse inside it—she didn't have to wonder what *they* would do with such power.

Marlow was halfway to her flat from the dock when she spotted them. Two Copperhead enforcers, bronze snake tattoos gleaming at their throats.

Stay calm, Marlow told herself as she eased to a stop a good fifty paces from them. *They're not here for you.*

"It's about damn time, Briggs," the bigger of the two said, spitting into the road. Marlow recognized him—an enforcer nicknamed the Ferryman, an allusion to the mythic figure who ferried the dead into the afterlife on a boat pulled by crocodiles. "We've been waiting here for hours."

The other Copperhead grinned, eyeing Marlow's dress as they advanced on her. "What's with the fancy getup? You just come from a *ball* or something?"

"You mean you didn't get an invite?" Marlow replied reflexively, her heart kicking in her chest. "And here I was hoping for a dance."

He sneered. "Cute."

She reached for the hexes tucked away in the pocket of her dress, and glanced subtly around. Fiero and Basil were in their usual spot, both of them frozen, watching the scene unfold. Likely wondering the same thing as Marlow—what were Copperhead enforcers doing stirring up trouble in Reaper territory?

They're not going to hurt you, Marlow told herself, even as the two Copperheads closed in on her. *They wouldn't dare.* If word got back to the Reapers that two Copperheads were causing trouble in their territory, there would be reprisals.

Marlow sucked in a breath as the Copperheads stalked right up to her.

"You better watch yourself, Briggs," the Ferryman warned, breathing into her face. "You think you're safe here? Well, I've got a message from Leonidas himself—you cross us again and you're dead. You show your face in Breaker's Neck again, and you're dead. You try and break a Copperhead curse and—"

"Don't tell me—I'm dead?"

He grabbed her so quickly, Marlow didn't have time to react or even to regret her words. He yanked her arm violently. Marlow stumbled, struggling to stay on her feet. She heard a faint crash and from the corner of her eye saw an overturned Pento board and Fiero gripping the back of Basil's shirt fiercely. They had to know it was futile to intervene—they'd only wind up pissing off the Copperheads worse and getting themselves hurt for their trouble. The best help they could offer her now was to bear witness to whatever the Copperheads did to her.

"Get off her!" a voice hollered from behind Marlow, followed by the pounding of footsteps along the dock.

The Copperheads actually froze for a moment, no doubt wondering who would be stupid enough to shout and sprint full tilt at two Copperhead enforcers.

Marlow could sympathize.

"I said get. Your hands. *Off* her," Adrius growled, lashing out to grab the Ferryman's wrist.

"Or what?" The Ferryman barked out a laugh. "You threatening me? Hey, Nero, I think this little punk's threatening us!"

Adrius tightened his grip, mouth curving around a feral smile. Marlow was suddenly certain of two things: One, that Adrius was about to punch a Copperhead enforcer in the face. And two, this would not end well for any of them.

She pressed Adrius back with a hand on his chest. "Let's just all take a breath."

The second Copperhead, Nero, went white, gaze fixed on Adrius's face. "You . . . you're . . ."

Marlow felt the rise and fall of Adrius's chest under her palm, the tight coil of fury as he stared the Copperheads down.

"The Falcrest scion," the Ferryman said with a cruel smirk. "Like mother like daughter, huh, Marlow? Just another rich man's wh—"

Adrius's fist cracked across the Ferryman's face.

The Ferryman reared back with a snarl. He froze there, as if realizing that he couldn't retaliate—not without facing very steep consequences.

He grabbed his partner instead, pinning Marlow with a hard glare as they shoved past her. "*You* are going to pay for that, Briggs. Don't forget what I said."

Marlow felt Adrius tense at the aggression, but thankfully he did not throw another punch.

"Give Leonidas my best!" Marlow couldn't help but call after them.

She turned to find Adrius staring at her, eyes dark with residual anger.

"Are you okay?" he asked.

"What the hell was that?" she demanded. "Since when do you know how to throw a punch?"

"Who were those guys?" he asked. "Why do they have it out for you?"

"Copperheads," Marlow replied. "And they don't really like anyone who gets in their way."

"Well, that's certainly something you excel at."

It was the little half smile that reminded Marlow she was blindingly furious at him.

"We can't all have your charms," she bit out. Her hand was still on his chest. Instead of pulling it away, she grabbed a handful of his neatly pressed shirt and shoved him to the side of the path. "What were you *thinking*?"

Adrius looked bewildered and a little indignant. "They were going to hurt you! The way he was talking about you, was I just supposed to—"

"Not *them*," Marlow gritted out. "The party. That kiss. Are you *so* incapable of keeping your pants on for *ten days* that you had to feel up the nearest willing girl? And for some reason you decided the best place to do that was in front of *every single person* we are trying to convince that we're a couple? You put my investigation *and yourself* in jeopardy because you just *had* to have your fun with—what's her name?"

"Cerise," Adrius replied automatically.

Marlow shoved him with both hands, a fresh crackle of outrage sparking under her skin. "What. Is. Wrong. With. You?"

She raised her hands to shove him again, but he caught them against his chest. For a moment they just stared at each other, Marlow's anger thrumming between them, as thick as the soupy evening air.

Adrius's lip quirked. "Are you done?"

Marlow seethed. "Are *you* done putting my investigation at—"

"It was an order, Minnow," he said. "Cerise ordered me to kiss her."

Marlow withdrew her hands and stepped back. "What?"

"You can begin your groveling apologies at your leisure," Adrius said with a wave. "'I'm so sorry, Adrius, I should have listened to you for one second instead of jumping to conclusions and running off—'"

"So Cerise knows about the curse?" Marlow asked, cutting him off.

"I don't—" Adrius ran a hand through his hair. "No? I mean, I don't think so."

"So she just . . . walked up to you and told you to kiss her for no apparent reason," Marlow said skeptically.

"She said someone dared her to do it."

"Who?"

"She wouldn't say."

"That's why you should leave the interrogations to me," Marlow replied. "Where is Cerise now?"

"Now? I'm not sure," Adrius answered. "But I know Amara was planning to go dancing at some exclusive speakeasy later tonight."

"Amara?" Marlow echoed. She remembered the way Amara had stopped Marlow just to gloat over Adrius's apparent infidelity at the garden party.

"Yes, and if you know Cerise, you'll know that wherever Amara is, that's where she's likely to be, too."

She closed her eyes briefly, centering herself. If there was one person with a vested interest in humiliating Marlow and breaking her and Adrius up, it was Amara.

If Amara had dared Cerise to pull that stunt, that meant *she* likely knew about Adrius's Compulsion curse. And that meant she could have been the person to cast it.

"Come on," Marlow said, hauling Adrius back to the dock. "We're going to that speakeasy."

FIFTEEN

After nearly two weeks of being publicly attached to Adrius Falcrest, Marlow had thought that she'd gotten used to being stared at. But nothing could have prepared her for how everything seemed to stop the moment she entered the Charm & Zephyr speakeasy. While the band continued to play and dancers kept whirling on the enchanted, floating dance floor, it seemed every other eye in the dimly lit hall was trained on Marlow.

She was still wearing the dress she'd worn to the Monarch, a deep sapphire and viridian gown with a beaded bodice and an open back. The silk fabric melted over her body, and in the dimness of the speakeasy, it glinted like bioluminescent light reflecting off water. She was fairly certain, however, that the whispers erupting from around the room had nothing to do with her dress.

Clearly, word had gotten around about Adrius's indiscretion the day before. Which was what she'd hoped. She'd decided that her best chance to get answers was to play into the perception that she and Adrius were fighting, on the verge of breaking up. Adrius had entered the speakeasy a half-hour before her to maintain the ruse.

It didn't take long to find Amara in the crowd, ringed by her usual cadre of adorers, including Cerise. Her tailored dress, in a dark, romantic shade of amaranthine, was far shorter than anything Marlow had seen her wear before, although it still had the sculptural, almost austere silhouette she seemed to favor. Her raven hair was swept off her neck and styled in a sleek, gleaming updo, displaying the silver engagement carcanet around her throat.

Marlow snagged a violet-colored drink off a passing tray. *This is just another case, Briggs*, she counseled herself. *Forget the charade. This is a case, and Amara is a suspect. You're here to get the truth.*

"Marlow!" Gemma greeted, her voice slightly too high. She wore a floaty, cranberry-red dress accented with black lace and had colored her hair burgundy, which coordinated well with the dark, lush furnishings of the speakeasy. "What a nice surprise to see you here."

"Yes, what an unexpected delight," Amara said in a flat tone. "I would've thought you'd want to avoid the crowds after the humiliation you suffered yesterday."

"I just came to tell you that you won, Amara," Marlow said. "You wanted to drive Adrius and me apart, and it worked."

Amara laughed, low and musical. "I don't see why you'd think *I* had anything to do with it. Cerise is the one who kissed him."

Marlow glanced over at Cerise, who looked like she wanted to sink into the floor. "Which she was dared to do. Weren't you, Cerise?"

Cerise's face matched her name. "I—"

"It's just," Marlow went on, still speaking to Cerise but watching Amara, "whoever dared you to do it was obviously using you to try and embarrass me *and* Adrius. I think I can guess who might've wanted to do that."

"Oh, Marlow," Amara said airily. "My brother already embarrassed himself the moment he showed up at my engagement party with you on his arm. Just because I think you're beneath him doesn't mean I'm going to waste my time with such childish antics. I mean, really. I'm about to get *married*. You honestly think I would devote that much time thinking about you, or any of my brother's flings?"

Marlow paused. Because while she very much thought Amara was just petty and vindictive enough to try to break up Marlow and Adrius, there were certainly easier ways to go about it if Amara did indeed know about Adrius's curse. She could, for instance, simply order Adrius to end things. And if the goal had been to humiliate Marlow, well—there were easier ways of doing that, too.

Amara scoffed. "There are more than a few people here who wanted to see you gone, Marlow. I'd suggest accusing one of *them*. Now, if you'll excuse me."

She swept away. Cerise made to go after her when Marlow reached out to grip her arm.

"Who was it?" Marlow demanded. "Who dared you?"

Cerise glanced at her coolly. "I don't see why it matters. Obviously, Adrius came to his senses about you. If I were you, I'd let it go and not embarrass myself any further."

She shook Marlow off and went to catch up to Amara.

Gemma lingered at Marlow's side. "Sorry about Amara."

"Yeah, what is it you see in her exactly?" Marlow couldn't help but ask. She winced. "Sorry. Sore subject, I guess."

Gemma shook her head with a rueful laugh. "Just something about those Falcrest siblings, I guess." She nudged Marlow. "For what it's worth, I'm not one of the people who wants to see you gone, Marlow. In fact, I'm kind of hoping you can find a way to forgive Adrius."

That took Marlow by surprise. "Why?"

"Well, for one thing, the last time you and Adrius fought he sulked about it *forever*. It was so annoying."

"Last time we fought?"

"Last year?" Gemma said. "After you left Evergarden he was *so* insufferable. He went around everywhere brooding and flirting with everyone, but he was so *miserable* about it, like he was doing it out of spite or something. Honestly, I was embarrassed for him."

Since when did Adrius need an excuse to be insufferable? "I doubt it had anything to do with me."

"I mean, he never said so, but he never said you two were friends, either. But we all knew because he used to hang around you so much. I used to catch him staring at you in class."

Marlow tried not to look as surprised as she felt. She'd never thought anyone in Evergarden had the slightest idea that she and Adrius were actually friends. "I didn't realize anyone noticed."

"There was also this one time that Hendrix made some kind of joke about you—"

"A joke?"

Gemma hesitated, biting her lip. "It was—something to the effect of girls from the Marshes having low standards. But . . . a little more crude than that. It really pissed off Adrius. He got all quiet and then verbally eviscerated Hendrix in front of *everyone*. Hendrix's social standing never recovered. And no one ever said anything about you in front of Adrius again."

"Wait—is *that* why Hendrix hates him so much?" Marlow choked. She did not know what to make of this. She had always assumed that back when she lived in Evergarden she'd been fairly invisible to the noblesse nouveau—immune to the gossipmongers because she was simply too unimportant to spread gossip about.

But if Gemma was to be believed, the real reason was that Adrius had all but publicly declared that anyone who said a bad word about Marlow would make an enemy of the Falcrest scion.

Gemma shrugged. "I don't know. I think he's always been jealous of him, but it certainly didn't *help*."

Marlow was struck suddenly with a wild thought—that perhaps Amara had been telling the truth. Maybe she *hadn't* dared Cerise to kiss Adrius. And maybe whoever had wasn't trying to humiliate Marlow, but Adrius.

Before the thought could fully coalesce, Adrius's voice rang through the din of the dance hall.

"Can I have everyone's attention?" Adrius asked. He stood on top of a table, visible even in the low light of the speakeasy. "I just want to get a few things off my chest."

"What is he *doing*?" Gemma half whispered.

Marlow wanted to know the same thing. This was certainly not part of their plan.

"I know you're all accustomed to reading about me in the gossip columns and whispering about me at parties," Adrius went on. "So I thought maybe it was time I give you the scoop directly."

Marlow fought through the rapturous crowd toward him. Something wasn't right. Adrius may have sounded like he was trying to titillate the crowd, but Marlow saw the tension in the way he held himself. He wasn't teasing—he was *stalling*.

Someone had ordered him up on top of that table.

"I'm sure you all know my sister, Amara, don't you?" Adrius said. "Perfect Amara Falcrest, who can do no wrong. Some of you have probably guessed that her engagement isn't quite as happy as it seems."

Well, there went Marlow's theory that Amara was behind this.

"See, Amara would do *anything* to please our father," Adrius said. "Including break the heart of the girl she *really* loves. Her best friend, Gemma Starling."

There was a shocked gasp as the crowd absorbed this information. All around Adrius, noblesse nouveau stared in astonishment, as if they could not quite believe this was happening. All of them, except one. Hendrix

Bellamy was staring at Adrius along with the rest of them, but he didn't look a bit shocked. He looked downright *gleeful*.

Someone called out, "Tell us more, Adrius!"

"Yeah!" another voice chimed. "Who's a better kisser—Cerise or Marlow?"

Heat rushed into Marlow's face.

Someone else cried, "Why'd you start dating Marlow, anyway?"

Marlow found Cerise and Opal standing together in the crowd. Opal shot Marlow a nasty look and called, "Tell us how you *really* feel about her!"

Marlow froze. She could see Adrius panicking, trying to bite back an answer. "Marlow Briggs," he said. "The girl who stole the heart of Evergarden's most notorious rake."

Panic flooded her. This situation had just turned from scandalous and embarrassing to utterly damning. Because if Adrius was compelled to tell everyone the truth about how he felt about Marlow, the jig was up. They'd all know their romance was a lie, and if Adrius kept talking, they would know exactly why.

"You've all been dying to know—why her?"

Everyone had fallen completely silent and still, hanging on Adrius's every word. His gaze found Marlow as she pushed through the silent crowd, and held there.

She had to stop this. She tried to make herself call out to him, to order him not to speak. The words stuck in her throat.

As dangerous as it was, she was just as hungry to know what Adrius might say as the rest of the vultures around her.

"What would make me fall for a girl from the Marshes, a girl without a title, without the power and prospects befitting a Falcrest scion?" Adrius asked. "The truth is, I'm—"

"Adrius, shut up and get down from the table."

Amara's voice rang out imperiously from across the room as she charged toward her brother.

Adrius's jaw slammed shut. A moment later he dropped down from the table.

"Exactly how much have you had to drink tonight?" Amara demanded, seizing hold of Adrius's sleeve. "I have to say, you've really outdone yourself. I didn't think you were capable of making more of a mockery of yourself, but now you've resorted to making up lies about me?"

Instead of replying, Adrius's gaze found Marlow as she strode briskly toward them. He looked wild-eyed and shaken. "Minnow, I—"

"Later," she said, and marched past the two siblings, heading straight for Hendrix.

He stood with his back to a wall, watching everything with a self-satisfied smirk.

Marlow sidled up to him with a sharp smile. "Hi there."

"Marlow," he greeted her, sounding surprised but not displeased.

"I wanted to take you up on your offer from yesterday," she said, touching his arm. "Can we talk?"

If Hendrix suspected what Marlow meant by *talk*, he did not show it. In fact, he looked as if he'd inferred another meaning entirely.

That would work fine for Marlow's purposes. The speakeasy had plenty of hidden alcoves and shadowy corners where patrons could steal away for a private moment or illicit tryst. Marlow sauntered off to one of the private balconies that ringed the main bar area. She didn't bother glancing behind her to see if Hendrix had followed, just leaned back against the rail and waited.

"I'm glad," Hendrix began, sweeping through the velvet curtain, "that you've finally come to your senses, Marlow."

"Oh, I definitely have," Marlow said as the curtain swung shut. "So, how did you do it?"

"Do what?" Hendrix asked.

"Exact your revenge," Marlow replied. "Adrius destroyed your social standing over a year ago, didn't he?"

Hendrix shrugged. "Something like that."

"That would've pissed *me* off," Marlow said, slinking closer. "One thing about me is I don't forgive easily. If Adrius had done that to *me*, I'd want to make him pay. Getting Adrius to humiliate himself in front of everyone? That would be a fitting revenge. Hard to pull off, though. But not for someone really clever."

Hendrix's eyes flickered to Marlow and she watched the praise hit its mark.

"Well," he said with a hint of smugness. "It just so happens that I know a secret about Adrius. Something no one else has figured out."

"Really?" Marlow asked with an impressed look. "What kind of secret?"

"Well," Hendrix said, puffing out his chest. "It seems that Adrius Falcrest is completely susceptible to orders. So I . . . gave him a few suggestions."

"A few suggestions?"

Hendrix shrugged. "I just told him to tell everyone the truth."

"So you're telling me," Marlow said, "that Adrius insulted you over a year ago and your completely normal and not at *all* disturbing response to that was to force him to publicly humiliate his sister and one of his closest friends?"

The smug smile dropped from Hendrix's face. "All I did was tell him to be *honest*. He's such a snake, I thought people should hear the truth about how he feels about all of us from his own lips. That was all him."

"And daring Cerise to order him to kiss her?" Marlow asked. "Was that all him?"

Hendrix tilted his chin up haughtily. "If you think that isn't something he would have done on his own, you're fooling yourself."

"It doesn't matter what he would have done," Marlow replied, "because you didn't give him a choice."

"I wanted to show you that you're better than him, Marlow." Hendrix covered her hand with his own, looking into her eyes. "You deserve better."

Marlow laughed, pulling her hand away. "No. You just wanted to take something from him. To show everyone you could. And what was your plan if I didn't fall into your waiting arms? Were you just going to take what you wanted anyway?"

Hendrix went pale, his expression scandalized. "Of course not! I would never—"

"You would *never*?" Marlow echoed incredulously. She was surprised by how angry she was. The righteous, protective rage building in her chest was not unfamiliar—she just never thought she would feel it on behalf of Adrius Falcrest. "Spare me. That's *exactly* what you did to Adrius, only worse because he *couldn't* refuse. You think you're so much better than him, than the rest of the noblesse nouveau, but you're not. Adrius may be a lot of things, but he would *never* curse someone for some sick revenge plot."

"You think *I* cursed Adrius?" Hendrix choked out.

Marlow arched an eyebrow.

"*Yes,* I manipulated the kiss between him and Cerise, and yes, I ordered him to tell the truth, but I didn't curse him, I *swear*," Hendrix insisted. "How would I even do that? Where would I even *get* a curse like that?"

That was a question she'd been mulling over since her meeting with Viatriz at the Monarch Theater. If the Copperheads really *did* have their hands on the spellbook as Viatriz suspected, then they could be selling Compulsion curse cards on the black market. But was someone like Hendrix Bellamy likely to have black market connections?

It certainly wasn't *impossible*, but it did strain credulity just a little. She already knew he most likely wasn't the person who had cursed Adrius—but if she sweated him a little, she could get him to at least reveal how he knew about it, and that might lead her to the real culprit.

"You *have* to believe me, Marlow," Hendrix pleaded. "I didn't do anything to Adrius! I just noticed something was off with him. The first time was at Amara and Darian's engagement party. I told him to jump off the roof and he just—reacted strangely. Almost like he was going to do it."

"I remember," Marlow said evenly.

"I started paying closer attention after that," Hendrix said. "And then, just a few days ago, I overheard Amara and Silvan."

"Overheard them doing what?"

"Arguing. About Adrius. Amara said she thought something was up with him. Silvan kept telling her not to worry about it, and finally Amara said she was worried Adrius was under some kind of spell. That he'd been avoiding her, and at first she'd thought he was hiding his relationship with *you*, but then she started to suspect it was something else. She suspected Silvan knew something about it."

"What did Silvan say?"

"He kept telling her to drop it," Hendrix replied. "It got heated. He didn't exactly *threaten* her, but it was close."

Hendrix, of course, could have been making up this entire conversation, but Marlow didn't think so. It sounded similar to the conversation Marlow had had with Silvan at the garden party. But while that conversation, strange as it had been, made some kind of sense, Marlow couldn't see any reason why Silvan would get so heated with *Amara* of all people. They may not have always gotten along perfectly—both of them, frankly, were too high-strung—but she was about to marry his brother. They were practically family already.

So why would Silvan try to threaten her, unless he was hiding something?

"After that, I started to wonder if Adrius really *was* under a spell," Hendrix said. "It was such an absurd idea, but I thought—what do I have to lose? So I put it to the test, at the garden party. I dared Cerise to order him to kiss her, and it *worked*. And then . . . tonight."

Marlow narrowed her eyes. "You know what, Hendrix? I do believe you. I think you're a pathetic, spineless little barnacle, but I believe you."

Hendrix's eyes flashed. "Come on, Marlow, he *deserved* it—"

"Let me stop you right there," Marlow ground out. "If you breathe a single word about this curse to anyone, if you so much as utter a *hello* to Adrius, I am going to hex your balls to rot off. If that doesn't sound fun, let me tell you—it is far, far more gruesome than whatever you're imagining."

Hendrix looked faintly nauseated. "You're—joking, right? I mean I can see you're angry, but—"

"You haven't seen me angry," Marlow said with an edge of violence. "Do as I say, and you won't ever have to. Got it?"

He nodded mutely.

She smiled and simpered, "So glad you've finally come to your senses, Hendrix," before turning on her heel and blowing past the curtains.

She walked almost directly into Adrius. They both stumbled back. Adrius's expression was slightly amazed.

He broke the silence first. "You don't really have a hex that will rot someone's balls off, right?"

She flipped him a coquettish smile and skirted past him, into a dimly lit alcove with a low ceiling and an intimate little couch. "A girl can't give away *all* her secrets."

Adrius followed her in, ducking close before asking, "So what happened? Did he—?"

Marlow shook her head. "He's not the one who cursed you. He only figured it out. Is Silvan here?"

"Silvan?" Adrius echoed. "No. This isn't really his scene. How can you be sure Hendrix didn't cast it?"

But Marlow had already moved on. "Did you tell Silvan about the curse?"

"No," Adrius answered. "I can't tell anyone, remember?"

"Well, Silvan knows."

"He—he *can't*," Adrius said, bewildered. "Did Hendrix tell you that? He's a liar."

"Maybe, but I don't think he was lying about this," Marlow answered. "I talked to Silvan the other day, at the garden party. He made some vague threats, and at the time I brushed it off because—well, it's Silvan. But now . . ."

"What are you saying?" Adrius asked, but Marlow knew he already understood.

"You need to be careful around him," Marlow warned, her hand on his elbow.

Adrius jerked out of her grasp and stared at her, stunned. "You think he did this, don't you? You think my *best friend* cast a Compulsion curse on me. Gods, Marlow."

"Yes, I do," Marlow replied stoutly. "And you need to keep your voice down."

"It wasn't him," Adrius bit out, low and fierce. "I would trust Silvan with my life. You know what you said about your friend Swift? That to trust you is to trust him? That's how it is with me and Silvan. For all his flaws, he's the most honest person I know. He didn't do this."

"That's different," Marlow replied. "You aren't me and he isn't Swift. This world . . . the noblesse nouveau . . . no one here can be trusted. You all have too much to lose."

"That's what you think of us, isn't it?" Adrius said in a quiet, cold voice. "Of *me*. You think this world is just like a game of Ruse, that we're all ready to stab each other in the back at the first sign of weakness. It's not true."

"Isn't it?" Marlow demanded. "You may not see it because you're the Falcrest scion and people would jump from Vale Tower if it meant getting your favor, but Evergarden is a more brutal world than the Marshes. You're naive if you believe otherwise."

Adrius shook his head. "It's not Evergarden, it's *you*. You didn't used to be like this. You used to be able to trust people."

"I used to be able to trust *you*," Marlow said before she could stop herself. "And look how that turned out."

The words hung between them—the first real acknowledgment that Adrius had hurt her. That she had held on to that hurt all this time. She flushed, and felt at once foolish and bitter as Adrius looked away from her. There was shame on his face, and something akin to hurt. "Minnow—"

"Never mind," Marlow said, suddenly desperate not to hear what he might say. "Just—let's not."

His eyes searched her face, and it felt not unlike the way he looked at her when they'd played Ruse, trying to determine if she was bluffing.

Whether he got his answer or not, Marlow couldn't tell. He set his jaw, flashing an edge of a smile. "Whatever you say. Let's just get on with it, then."

"Get on with what?"

He pinned her with an icy look. "We still have to get back together, remember?"

Right. To the rest of the noblesse nouveau, they were broken up after Adrius's indiscretion. Now Adrius had to pretend to win her back so she could stay close to him. Which, now that she suspected that Silvan knew about the curse, seemed more vital than ever.

"Fine," she agreed. "Let's get on with it."

With a deep breath, she turned and stalked back into the main room.

"I don't want to hear it, Adrius," she said, pitching her voice just loud enough that the surrounding partygoers would hear. As expected, they ceased their conversations to take note of whatever drama was unfolding.

"Wait, just let me explain," Adrius insisted, following close at her heels.

Marlow spun to face him, her skirt flying out in a dramatic sapphire swirl. "Explain *what*? You kissed someone else."

"It was a mistake." Adrius's eyes were intent on hers, imploring. "It didn't mean anything. If I could take it back, I would."

Marlow's stomach fluttered. Adrius was good at this. He looked and sounded so sincere. From the corner of her eye she could see that their theatrics had attracted even more attention from the crowd. They'd already gotten one show tonight, and they were ready for act two.

Adrius stepped toward her. "I never meant to hurt you."

"Well, you did." There was a quaver in her voice she hadn't put there intentionally. Because Adrius *had* hurt her—and she'd never gotten to tell him that. Not until now, surrounded by prying eyes, under the guise of a fake betrayal.

She started to turn away.

"Wait," Adrius said. "Please. I can't lose you again."

Again. The word struck her like a hex. *Again* meant he'd lost her before. *Again* meant more than this fake estrangement they'd put on for show. *Again* meant some part of him was thinking about the last time he'd lost her.

Suddenly, Marlow didn't know if she could listen to Adrius beg for her forgiveness when the lie they were spinning to their audience was so close to the real hurt she still held on to. She had driven herself mad over the past year trying to understand what had happened between them, whether their friendship had ever been real, whether she had been a naive fool to trust him.

A breath shook loose from her chest. "How can I trust you again?"

Pain flickered across his face, there and then gone like the flash of lightning in a summer storm. His fist tightened at his side and then he was striding toward her, conviction blazing in his eyes.

"I know I messed up. I was just—stupid, and scared because I realized what I feel for you is real. I told myself it wasn't, because for so long it was easier just to pretend that nothing really mattered to me. But you do, Marlow. And I'm—I'm sorry." His voice cracked. He was close enough to touch now, his eyes dark and sincere. Marlow could find no trace of artifice there, no sign that this was all part of an act.

"I'm sorry I ever made you think otherwise," he said softly. "I'm sorry that I ever hurt you."

The rest of the crowd had gone completely silent, breathlessly awaiting her reaction. This was the part where she was supposed to fling herself into his arms and kiss him, telling him that all was forgiven.

She couldn't do it. The lines had blurred too much, the fake hurt bleeding into the real one. How could she help but hear Adrius's words as the apology she'd longed for so many times over the past year? But she didn't—couldn't—know if it was the truth or a mockery of it.

The longer she stood there, with her heart in her throat, the more she felt Adrius could see everything written on her face—the damning evidence that she still felt something for him.

It was too much. Marlow turned and fled the room. Adrius called after her.

She kept going, past the couples floating through the air on an enchanted dance floor, the dim lights of the speakeasy spinning around her. She just needed space. She needed to get away from the eyes on her.

She needed to breathe.

She threw herself through the curtains, out onto a terrace blanketed in fragrant blossoms and strung with twinkling lights. She gulped in a lungful of sweet, damp night air.

It was then that she noticed the lone figure standing in the corner of the terrace, plucking the petals off an iris.

"Guess I'm not the only one who needed some air," Gemma said. Her hair and dress were as perfect as always, but her eyes were rimmed with red as if she'd been crying.

"Are you all right?" Marlow asked, stepping toward her.

Gemma let out a watery laugh. "I've been better. I'm pissed at Adrius. Amara won't even look at me." She tossed the iris to the ground. "What about you? I heard a little of that, in there. It sounded . . . intense."

Something—maybe the quaver in Gemma's voice, or the smudged line of paint beneath her eye—made Marlow want to be honest. "I just wish I knew if he meant any of it."

Gemma folded her arms over her chest. "I get it. I wish I knew if Amara had really meant any of the things she said to me before . . ." She wiped at her eyes. "You know, she was the one who kissed me first. *She* started it. And then she walked away, like none of it mattered."

"You want to talk about it?" Marlow offered.

"Not really." She locked eyes with Marlow. "You want to get drunk with me?"

Marlow considered the wisdom of the idea. "Yeah."

With a smile, Gemma hooked her arm through Marlow's and led her back inside. She plucked two glowing blue glasses from a passing tray and handed one to Marlow.

"To the Falcrests," Gemma said sarcastically, clinking her glass against Marlow's before taking a hearty swig. Marlow smiled and took a sip of her own. It shivered down her throat, cool and bright and sweet.

Gemma came up for air giggling. "Have you ever had Zephyr Elixir before, Marlow?"

Marlow froze, wondering for one wild moment if she'd been too quick to trust Gemma. Maybe this was an elaborate prank and the drink would turn her into a frog or something.

At the look on Marlow's face, Gemma dissolved into laughter. "Relax. You'll like it."

A light, floaty feeling came over Marlow. Gemma laughed, and Marlow realized she actually *was* floating. She let out a small gasp and reached for Gemma's arm, afraid she would simply float up to the ceiling. But she remained hovering gently just a foot or two off the ground.

Gemma grabbed her hand and spun her through the air. "Let's dance!"

Marlow was happy to let Gemma tug her along, and soon she found herself twirling through a crowd of dancers, some of them floating, too. The band played a joyful, riotous number as Marlow locked hands with one partner and swung to the next. After a song or two, the effects of the drink were beginning to wear off, but there was Gemma shoving another drink into her hand, this one a deep emerald that made her breathe harmless green flames. Then there was a clear drink filled with what looked like iridescent confetti that made sparks shoot out of her fingertips as she swayed and moved to the music.

Marlow felt light and free in a way she hadn't in years. In a way she'd maybe never really felt before. She felt like golden light was pooling around her, like for once she had her own magnetic pull instead of being caught in someone else's orbit.

At one point, Marlow spotted Amara through the crowd, glaring daggers at Gemma and Marlow. It seemed like the funniest thing Marlow had ever seen, and she laughed herself silly until neither she nor Gemma remembered what they were laughing about.

"I never knew you were this fun!" Gemma yelled over the music.

"Me either!" Marlow yelled back, and they burst into fresh peals of laughter.

Someone grabbed her hand and spun her as the music soared into a crescendo. She spun again, and as the world swung to a stop, the line of dancers parted and Adrius emerged, striding toward Marlow with purpose, his gold-and-ruby jacket glowing like a warm flame beneath the dim lights.

"There you are," he said, coming to a stop in front of Marlow. There was something dark and heady in his molten gold eyes, something that made blood pound furiously in Marlow's veins.

The dancers converged, shoving Marlow forward. Adrius caught her hand, his other arm going around her waist as he whirled her gracefully in time with the music. All at once, they were dancing, pressed close in the crush of bodies. Marlow's dress moved like liquid when Adrius spun her. Her skin felt impossibly warm in all the places he touched. The scent of amber and orange blossom filled her head as he ducked his face close to hers. She could see the gleam of perspiration along the ridge of his brow.

"Come with me," he murmured.

For a wild moment Marlow felt like she was the one who had been cursed, because she had no choice but to obey. Adrius guided her to the edge of the dance floor, his hand feverishly hot against her bare back. The crowd parted for them readily.

She imagined what they all must be thinking as Adrius steered her back onto the terrace. That he was dragging her off for an illicit tryst in the middle of the party, and in the privacy of the terrace he would push her against the ivy-covered wall and kiss her, his mouth warm and lush and sweet with wine, his hands tangling in her hair and rustling in her skirt.

Marlow's breath caught in her throat as Adrius maneuvered her beneath a trellis, backing her into the wall, out of sight. She felt overheated, confused, her head swimming from the lights and the drinks and the scent of the flowers thick and sweet in the air around them.

"This should be private enough," Adrius murmured, his warm breath ghosting against her lips.

"Okay," she said. She felt she would agree to anything he said at that moment. In the quiet of the terrace, she was overly aware of the rise and fall of her chest beneath her beaded bodice. All she could see was the image she'd conjured, of the two of them entwined in the dark amongst the ivy.

She wanted it. She was dizzy with how much she wanted it. She reached for him.

He stepped back. "That was a good performance. I wasn't expecting you to walk out, but I think it worked in our favor."

And she remembered—this wasn't for her. It was never for her. "Right."

Adrius's eyes narrowed, assessing. "Are you drunk?"

"What? No." She swayed back against the trellis. "Maybe."

"Didn't know you had it in you." He looked at her a little questioningly. "I should get you home."

"You don't have to—"

"Minnow," he said firmly. "Let me take you home."

She did not have the will to protest, just followed behind him as he led her back inside, her hands clenched in the fabric of her skirt to keep them from shaking.

They left the speakeasy and boarded a private boat that navigated the canals of the Outer Garden. Marlow flopped back against the silk cushions, staring dizzily up at the stars. The quiet splash of water and the low song of the canal frogs filled her ears. The night air felt cloying and sultry against her skin. Adrius sat across from her, just out of reach. He wasn't looking at her, but out at the water, and something about that filled her with simmering irritation.

"Everyone at the party thinks you're taking me home to ravish me in my bed," she informed him.

It worked—he glanced at her, his expression annoyingly neutral. "I'm sure most of them could tell you're in no state for ravishing."

"I'm fine." She stood—a mistake. The combination of the swaying boat and the fizz of enchanted alcohol made her stumble. Adrius was there to catch her, but the pitch of the boat sent them both tumbling into the cushions.

Her dress pooled around them. They were as close as they had been on the terrace. Marlow could feel the heat of him underneath her. She could see his eyelashes in the pale moonlight, hear his slightly elevated breathing. His arm tightened around her.

He set her down beside him.

She slumped back against the cushions. "There wouldn't be any ravishing anyway, since we're only pretending."

"I don't need a reminder, Minnow, I'm well aware." His face looked pinched in the moonlight.

"You're very good at it," she said. "Pretending. You've got everyone fooled. Your best friend. Your own sister. But not me."

She had not meant to say that, had not meant to give away how very close she'd come to buying into her own godsdamned ruse for those few hazy moments on the terrace. But she'd stopped being able to make sense of what she was doing, what she was trying to hide and from whom.

"I'm not trying to fool you," Adrius said after a long pause.

"Good," she said, closing her eyes.

They spent the rest of the boat ride in silence.

Back in her flat, after Adrius shuffled her up the stairs, there were no heated looks, no lingering touches. Even when Adrius helped her out of her dress, it was with indulgent patience, like he was helping an unruly toddler change into sleep clothes.

In just her slip, she tumbled into bed, the room spinning around her. Adrius knelt to remove her slippers, fingers curling gently around her ankle. Her breath fluttered in her chest. She closed her eyes, and when she opened them again, he was pulling a soft knitted blanket over her, tucking it around her shoulders.

No one had tucked her into bed in years. The last time that she could remember was when she'd been sick one night, and her mother had taken the evening off to make her tea and pet her hair and put her to bed, singing a soft, familiar lullaby. The scent of vetiver and bergamot had clung to her sheets even after Cassandra had retreated to her own room down the hall. It was a rare moment of tenderness from her mother, but one Marlow had cherished.

A knot of emotion squeezed her chest and she closed her eyes again, breathing sharply to keep the tears at bay.

Adrius gently swept her hair off her face. "Good night, Minnow."

She grabbed his wrist before he could move away. Their eyes met in the dark. A strange compulsion to tug him under the covers with her, to make him stay, welled up in her.

Instead, she released him, closing her eyes as he backed away. A moment later she heard the soft *click* of the door of her flat closing, and the sound of his footsteps creaking down the stairs.

Toad jumped onto the bed and curled up beside her as dread settled heavily in Marlow's chest.

"Toad," she moaned pitifully, "how could you let this happen?"

When she'd taken Adrius's case, she'd been confident she could fool the rest of Evergarden into believing their little hoax. She'd been right.

But it was only now, with the echo of Adrius's touch still lingering on her skin, that Marlow realized that the person she had fooled the best was herself.

SIXTEEN

There were few things that could distract Marlow from pursuing a lead, and the newfound realization that she *might* still have feelings for Adrius certainly wasn't one of them.

Even with everything that had happened the night before, she hadn't forgotten what Viatriz had told her at the Monarch Theater. She knew what she needed to do next, and as nauseated as she already felt, she was ready to do it.

"You're a hard man to find," Marlow said as she strolled up the steps to Orsella's veranda, where Swift sat elbow-deep in motor oil and bike parts. A glass of coral-bright persimmon juice sweated on the handrail.

Swift grunted, working something loose on the bike. "Depends who's looking. Socket wrench?"

Marlow handed him the tool. "I talked to the Black Orchid."

That got Swift to look up from his work. "You didn't think to bring me along as backup?"

"I don't think you get a plus-one to clandestine meetings with secret rogue spellwright rings," Marlow said with a shrug.

"Well, you're still all in one piece and it doesn't *sound* like they shredded your memories, so I'm guessing it went well?"

She filled him in on everything Viatriz had told her as Swift sat, patiently listening and wiping the sweat from his forehead with a motor-oil-stained rag.

"There's no way your mother sold a Falcrest spellbook to the Copperheads," Swift said. "Right?"

"Right," Marlow echoed. A stab of doubt throbbed painfully under her ribs. "But what if she did?"

"Why would she?" Swift asked.

"I don't know," Marlow replied. "That's the whole problem. When it comes to her, I *never* know. I certainly didn't know she was working for the Black Orchid."

Even before she'd disappeared, Cassandra had sometimes felt unknowable. As if the more pieces Marlow tried to gather of her mother, the less she was able to fit them together.

"I need to know, Swift," she said. "I—I have to."

Swift looked at her carefully. "What do you mean?"

Marlow chewed the corner of her lip. "I have a plan," she said, although what she really had was the vague outline of one, "and I'm going to need a favor."

Swift stared at her. Then he swore. "You can't be serious."

"If the Black Orchid is right, then the Copperheads have *Ilario's Grimoire*. And they know what happened to my mother."

"Marlow," Swift said in a deadly serious voice. "*No.*"

She met his gaze. "You know I wouldn't ask unless I had no other choice."

"That is such a load of shit. You don't have a choice? *I* didn't have a choice!" Swift roared. "I didn't have a choice when Leonidas cast that curse on me. I didn't have a choice when he ordered me to do things I can barely *live with*! Do you know the last thing I did with my hand before I lost it?"

Marlow swallowed. She had seen Swift angry before, but never like this. Never with this dark shadow of hatred and desperation flickering behind his eyes.

"I held a gun in it," he said slowly. "I held a gun to the head of an innocent man."

Marlow's chest heaved. Swift had never told her exactly what had happened in the days before she'd tracked him down and learned he'd been conscripted by the Copperheads. He'd told her about the curse they put on him, and she'd seen the rotting flesh of his hand for herself, so it hadn't been hard to guess: The Copperheads had ordered Swift to do something so repugnant, he had chosen to lose his hand rather than obey.

She'd never asked what it was. And he'd never told her, until now.

"The things I had to do," Swift said haltingly, "the person I had to become, just to survive. I . . . became someone that I don't recognize anymore."

"Swift," Marlow said miserably.

"You can't ask me to do this," Swift said, staring her straight in the eyes. "You can't ask me to go back there. Back to *him*."

She dropped her gaze, shame and disgust flaring hot in her cheeks. Because she knew exactly what she was asking of him, and it still didn't stop her.

"Adrius doesn't have a choice, either," she said quietly.

"What do you mean?" Swift rasped.

"The grimoire," Marlow replied. "It has the one and only known recipe for a Compulsion curse."

Swift's eyes widened. "Are you saying that Adrius—?"

"Yes," Marlow replied. "And if the Copperheads have the grimoire, then they have the Compulsion curse. We can't let something like that stay in Leonidas's hands. Think of what he'd do with something that powerful."

Swift's chest rose and fell on a heavy breath. His grip tightened on the wrench. "There has to be another way. I can't do it, Marlow. I—I *won't*."

Marlow pressed her lips together and nodded once, a pit forming in her stomach. "Okay. I get it."

Swift slumped with relief. "Good. We'll just have to—"

"I'll go alone." Marlow swung to her feet. "My plan would be easier with you there, but it'll still work."

"Marlow," Swift said, starting after her. "*Marlow!*"

But Marlow was already marching down the stairs, leaving Swift calling after her.

The crowd at the Blind Tiger was bigger than it had been on Marlow's last visit. And much, much rowdier.

Dark-violet and sickly green lights strobed over the teeming mass of people drinking, brawling, and writhing on the makeshift dance floor. Dancers hung in metal cages suspended from the ceiling, juggling flames and casting phantasmal illusions. Music thumped through the bar, rattling Marlow's teeth.

It took Marlow about thirty seconds of scanning the crowd to spot some Copperheads, their tattoos gleaming in the strobing lights. A *lot* of Copperheads. On the one hand, that was exactly why Marlow had come back here. On the other, she hadn't anticipated being quite this outnumbered.

Her pulse picked up and Marlow slipped into a chair at the first open table she saw. She kept her hood up, her hands clenched in her lap.

She spotted Bane a second later. He was hard to miss, swaggering through the crowd in an eye-searing orange three-piece suit, flanked, as always, by two Copperhead lackeys. One of them she recognized as the Ferryman, the enforcer Adrius had struck.

Over at the bar, a flash of ice-blond hair caught her attention. Marlow turned, watching the person who had just stepped up to order a drink.

A person who had absolutely no business being in a Copperhead joint.

Marlow's mind stuttered to a halt. For a moment she almost could not make sense of what she was seeing. Because there was no way that *Silvan Vale* was currently standing in the middle of the Blind Tiger, surrounded by Caraza's most notorious gangsters.

Except he was. His skin looked almost bruised in the bioluminescent light. Marlow spotted Bo's body peeking out under his sleeve like an electric-blue bracelet.

Marlow was so stunned by the sight of him that it took her far too long to realize that Bane and his cronies had stopped directly in front of him.

Silvan slowly lifted his gaze, a familiar sneer curling his lip. Bane leaned in and said something that Marlow couldn't hear.

Disbelief thundered through her. Her mind scrambled to come up with *any* reason that Silvan Vale would have business with the second-in-command of the Copperheads. She could only come up with one.

Silvan had cursed Adrius.

It was far too great a coincidence to mean anything else. Silvan had bought the Compulsion curse from the Copperheads. He had cast it on Adrius at the engagement announcement.

The only question was, *why?*

As Marlow grappled with this realization, the music abruptly cut out. The crowd quieted to low murmurs before petering into tense silence. The click of metal boot heels echoed through the bar. Dread brewed in Marlow's gut.

Leonidas Howell, leader of the Copperheads, stepped out from the crowd. Marlow could almost feel the weight of every held breath in the room. Anyone who frequented the Blind Tiger knew enough to understand that if you were paid a personal visit from Leonidas, you were about to have a very bad night.

Next to Bane in his bright-orange getup, Leonidas looked almost refined in a dark, charcoal suit. A simple gold earring dangled from his ear. In one hand, he held a gold chain that leashed his favorite pet: a twelve-foot-long crocodile named Sycorax who stalked behind him, yellowed teeth protruding from his massive jaws.

Bane was bombast and bluster, relying on his loud voice, huge frame, and ostentatious clothes to do most of the work of intimidation for him. But as scary as Bane could be, at the end of the day he was just a bully, using fear as a tool to keep everyone around him in line.

Leonidas was a different breed. He was rangy and lean, and he held himself like a clenched fist. Unlike Bane, fear wasn't a tactic for him—fear was the whole point. He was driven by a pure passion for violence.

But he and Bane did have one thing in common—they both loved an audience.

Leonidas prowled up to Silvan. He lifted Silvan's glass off the bar and took a slow sip. Smacking his lips with an exaggerated sigh, he said in a silk-smooth voice, "To what do I owe the pleasure of your visit, Mr. Vale?"

Silvan narrowed his eyes at Leonidas, darting a glance at Sycorax. "Who are you?"

Marlow rose quickly and ducked through the crowd to get closer.

Leonidas smashed the glass down at Silvan's feet and roared, "You think you can come into *my bar* and ask me who I am?"

Beside him, Sycorax whipped his tail, a growl rumbling from deep in his throat.

Silvan stood stiffly, his whole body cowering. The other Copperheads surrounding him were similarly frozen. Even Bane looked nervous, and it wasn't hard to imagine why.

Nothing could control Leonidas's rage once it was set off. Not even the threat of bringing down the wrath of the Five Families. If Leonidas snapped and hurt a scion of one of the most powerful families in Caraza, he would basically be signing the death warrant of *all* the Copperheads.

The only person Marlow would want to piss off less than the leader of the Copperheads was the head of one of the Five Families.

Bane was clearly making the same calculation, his beady eyes darting between Leonidas and Silvan with increasing panic. The moment was a knife balanced on its point. They were all just waiting for it to fall.

Then Leonidas burst into loud, gut-splitting guffaws.

There was a discordant moment of startled confusion, and then the other Copperheads started to laugh along with him, some of them clearly bewildered but following their leader's cue anyway.

Silvan did not look the least bit mollified by this abrupt switch in mood. Nor did he seem to appreciate the lean, sinewy arm Leonidas slung around his shoulders.

"You!" Leonidas crowed, jostling Silvan playfully. "I like you. You've got *gumption*."

Silvan's expression made it clear he could not have been more offended than if Leonidas had spat in his face. As if he could think of no greater insult than a lowlife like Leonidas presuming to *touch* a Vale scion.

Leonidas clasped the back of Silvan's neck, drawing him close to his side, and whispered something that made Silvan go pale.

The next thing Marlow knew, Leonidas was shoving Silvan down onto a nearby table with a loud bang. Drink glasses went smashing to the ground and the two people who had been occupying the table leapt up and scampered back toward the crowd.

Leonidas's grip on the back of Silvan's neck kept him pinned facedown on the table as he struggled futilely.

"Get off me!" Silvan yelled, his temple pressed against the table. "You can't do this! Don't you know who my father is?"

Without being told, two more Copperheads swooped toward him, pinning his arms.

"Oh, I know all about your daddy," Leonidas said, leaning over Silvan. "A big man in his big castle." He dug a pinky into his top row of teeth, picking something out and flicking it onto Silvan. "Thing is, his castle's *way* over there on the other side of the city. And you? You're in *my* house."

He released his hold on Silvan, letting his two lackeys keep him pinned while Leonidas pulled out a stack of spellcards. "Your daddy and his fancy friends aren't the only ones who can make spells. I'm building my own little kingdom right here in the Marshes, selling the kind of curses that would keep your daddy up at night. Want a sample?"

One of the Copperheads pulled Silvan's sleeve back and wrenched Bo from his wrist. They held the snake toward Sycorax, who snapped his jaws. Bo hissed, a few sparks emitting from his mouth.

"No!" Silvan cried, thrashing. "No, *don't*!"

"So which curse do you want to test out first, daddy's boy?" Leonidas leered. "The one that makes your eyes shrivel up like little raisins? Or how about one that makes you bleed out of every orifice?"

Silvan had ceased trying to reason with Leonidas, but was struggling harder than ever, snarling like a caged beast.

Marlow's heart kicked. Whatever Silvan was doing here, whether he had cursed Adrius or not, she wasn't about to watch him become an experiment for all of Leonidas's most gruesome fantasies. She had to do something—and fast.

"Leonidas," Bane said hesitantly, stepping toward them. "Maybe we should—"

"*Oooh*, this is one of my favorites," Leonidas went on, holding up a spellcard and ignoring Bane entirely. "It will make you cut off your own fingers, one at a time. That sounds fun, doesn't it? Sycorax hasn't eaten at all tonight—maybe I'll feed him your little snake, and then each of your fingers for dessert."

Gripping a hex card in one hand, Marlow wove through the crowd until she was standing mere feet away from the table where Silvan was pinned.

She hesitated at the edge of the crowd. Was she about to do this? Risk her life for Silvan Vale, a boy who had only ever treated her with derision?

She glanced at his face, still pushed down against the table and screwed up with sheer, consuming panic. It was almost hard to see him that way—Silvan, who was always so impossibly polished and regal, reduced to a struggling beast in the jaws of an even more dangerous predator.

Leonidas held up the curse card.

"*Bruciare!*" Marlow cried, aiming her hex at one of the Copperheads pinning Silvan to the table.

He stumbled back with a startled yelp, clutching at his face. "It burns! It *burns*!"

With one arm free, Silvan thrashed toward his other captor and sank his teeth into his arm. Marlow spared a brief moment for surprise—she hadn't thought Silvan had that kind of savagery in him. Then she was charging forward, seizing Silvan and hauling him away from the Copperheads.

"Wait, *Bo*!" Silvan cried, pulling against Marlow's grip.

Marlow looked behind her, spotting the blue coil of Bo's body thrashing in the grip of one of the Copperheads. He hissed, emitting bright blue sparks.

"*Vertigini!*" she yelled, aiming another hex card at the Copperhead. It was a fairly minor hex, intended to make the target lose their sense of balance, but it did the trick. The Copperhead flailed back. Bo launched into the air and dropped to the ground, slithering lightning fast across the floor.

"Come on!" Marlow yelled. Silvan knelt midstride to let Bo slither back into his sleeve as Marlow yanked him toward the exit.

Two huge, muscled bouncers blocked their path.

"Shit," Marlow swore, skidding to a stop and patting her pockets. "I'm out. What do you have?"

Silvan looked at her like he had never seen her before. "What?"

"Hexes, Silvan!" Marlow replied. "What kind of hexes do you have?"

"Why would I have hexes?"

Marlow almost wanted to laugh. Here was the scion of one of the most successful spellcrafting families in Caraza, who had access to magic most people would never see in their lives, and he didn't have a simple hex to get them out of here. Because why would a boy raised in the lap of luxury, surrounded by opulence, *need* hexes? He was protected everywhere he went by nothing more than his name.

But Marlow didn't have time to dwell on the irony, because Leonidas was stalking toward them, a panther with his prey in his sights.

"Well, well, well." His teeth gleamed like pearls in the green light. "Look who it is, boys! Our favorite little cursebreaker."

The Copperheads flanking Leonidas hooted with delight. There wasn't a single one of them that wouldn't love to see Marlow get ripped to shreds for freeing Swift from their clutches and making them all look like fools in the process.

"It must be my lucky day. I owe you a present, Marlow, and I've been waiting an awfully long time to give it to you." Leonidas held up a curse card. "Let's see you break this curse."

SEVENTEEN

Marlow's first thought as she stared into Leonidas's grinning face was, *Swift was right.*

Her next, embarrassingly, was that she would never see Adrius again.

Tears gathered in the corners of her eyes as Leonidas slunk toward her. Behind him, Sycorax growled. The gold-and-silver ink on the curse card flashed in the sickly light.

Leonidas had already threatened Silvan with a slew of gruesome curses, but Marlow knew whatever he'd picked out for her would be something far worse. He'd waited too long to corner her like this—helpless, terrified, completely at his mercy.

And she knew too well that Leonidas had no mercy. Whatever he had planned for her, he was going to draw it out.

He was going to make it hurt.

"Leonidas!" a voice called from the doorway. A wonderful, beautiful, *familiar* voice. "Let them go."

Swift strode toward them from the entrance of the speakeasy. He had come for her. After everything he'd said, he'd still come. The soaring surge of affection she felt for Swift was eclipsed only by her dread of what Leonidas would do to him.

Leonidas's eyes widened with delight. "It *is* my lucky day. I should've known when Little Miss Cursebreaker showed up that you wouldn't be far behind. Well, that just makes this moment even sweeter—Marlow Briggs will finally get what's coming to her, and you get to watch."

"Let her go," Swift said steadily. "Let them both go, unharmed, and I'll—I'll come back. I'll take the cursemark again. I'll be a Copperhead."

Marlow started toward him. "Swift, what the f—"

Swift turned, leveling her with a cold glare. "Stay out of this, Marlow."

Marlow's heart plummeted into her stomach. He couldn't do this. Not for her.

Leonidas smiled. "Awfully arrogant to assume we'd even *want* you back, Swiftie. That ship has sailed."

"I don't think it has," Swift replied coolly, stepping toward him.

Leonidas's eyes tracked Swift's movement, and Marlow could practically see his mind working. When Swift had freed himself from the Copperheads' curse, he'd violated the most important rule Leonidas held—that he was not to be disobeyed. Yet here was Swift, still walking around, nearly unharmed.

The chance to punish Swift for the crime of defying him was too tempting for someone like Leonidas to pass up.

He stalked toward Swift. "I want to hear them," he said. "Say the words, Swift. Say you're mine, and your friends go free."

Swift's jaw clenched. He shut his eyes, his hand twitching at his side.

"No," Marlow gasped. She couldn't watch this. She couldn't bear it. "Swift, you *can't*."

"Swamp Market."

It took Marlow a split second to register the words. And a half second more to react, dropping to the ground and pulling Silvan with her.

By that time, Swift had pulled Josephine out from where it had been hidden at his hip and fired the gun point-blank at Leonidas. Silver and black glyphs engulfed him. When they cleared, Leonidas stood still, his hand half-raised, his mouth open, his face a rictus of surprise. Completely frozen.

Swift blasted his second shot over Marlow's and Silvan's heads into Bane's chest. A swarm of bees exploded from the enchanted bullet, buzzing and stinging Bane and anyone in his general vicinity.

Bane screamed.

The entire bar erupted into pandemonium, with most people either fleeing from the bees or hiding beneath tables and behind the bar. The Copperheads, catching on to what was happening, charged toward Swift from all corners of the room.

Marlow scrambled to her feet, dragging Silvan up with her and shoving him toward the exit with the fleeing crowd.

Swift fired another hex at the closest Copperhead. The man flailed for a moment and then instantly plummeted up toward the ceiling, as if gravity had been suddenly reversed.

Another Copperhead leapt at Swift from behind, tackling him to the ground. They grappled, Swift attempting to shove the man off and keep his grip on the shotgun at the same time.

Marlow skidded to a halt. "Swift!"

Swift glanced up, meeting her gaze, and flung Josephine as hard as he could toward her.

Marlow caught the gun, cocked it, and fired a spell straight into Swift's assailant's face. Dark-green glyphs enveloped him, and when they cleared, the Copperhead looked up at Marlow, let out a bloodcurdling shriek, and ran as fast as he could in the opposite direction.

A Fearmonger hex. Orsella had a flair for the dramatic.

Marlow pulled Swift to his feet. "Gods below, Swift, you scared the absolute shit out of me." She reached into his bandolier and grabbed two more enchanted bullets, reloading Josephine.

"*I* scared *you*?"

Marlow paused to fire another hex at a charging Copperhead. He stopped, wobbled, and then started to tap-dance on the spot.

"I can't believe you stole Josephine," Marlow said.

"Borrowed," Swift corrected. "And you're just mad you didn't think of it first."

"Of *course* I'm mad I didn't think of it first!" She blasted another hex at a charging Copperhead, slowing his movements to one-tenth their normal speed.

"By the way, where the hell did he come from?" Swift asked, jerking his thumb behind them.

Marlow followed his gaze to where the fleeing crowd had begun to thin and spotted Silvan, grappling with a Copperhead. Silvan was putting up a fight, while Bo hissed and snapped at the Copperhead's fingers, a jet of sparks shooting out of his mouth.

Marlow sighed, grabbing more bullets to reload Josephine.

Swift shook his head and strode toward Silvan. He aimed one good punch at the Copperhead's jaw and he fell to the ground, howling in pain. Silvan whirled, fists up like he was ready to fight Swift, too.

Swift held up a placating hand. "Calm down, tough guy, I'm not gonna hurt you."

"Who the hell *are* you?" Silvan spluttered.

"I'm the guy who just saved your rich ass," Swift replied, grabbing Silvan's arm and hustling him toward the exit. "*Twice.* Now, move."

Marlow followed close behind, pausing only to shoot another spell at the Copperheads for cover before crashing through the hatch with Swift and Silvan.

The three of them spilled out into the hulking carapace of the dreadnought. Marlow fired off the last bullet through the hatch, knocking back a Copperhead who was charging toward them.

"Marlow, come on," Swift said impatiently, climbing up the steel ladder to the plankway, Silvan just ahead of him. "This way!"

Marlow spotted a familiar motorbike parked on the plankway.

"You stole Orsella's motorbike, too?"

"*Borrowed.*" He grabbed the handlebars and glanced behind him. "Come on. Those hexes'll wear off in about two minutes and there are gonna be a lot of pissed-off Copperheads crawling all over these docks. I don't know about you, but I'd prefer to be long gone by then."

They piled onto the motorbike and sped into the night.

Swift had barely stopped the motorbike outside his flat by the time Marlow hopped off, seized a handful of Silvan's shirt, and shoved him up against the edge of the water.

"Hey—!"

She hoisted Josephine and leveled it at his chest. "Tell me what you were doing at the Blind Tiger."

"Or what?" Silvan sneered. "You'll shoot me?"

Marlow raised her eyebrows and cocked the gun.

"Marlow." Swift kicked the bike off. "Calm down."

Marlow whipped her head to look at him. "He's the one who cursed Adrius!"

"*What?*" Silvan cried. "Why would I curse my best friend?"

"Oh, I don't know," Marlow said breezily. "Maybe because his family is planning on gutting your family for everything its worth?"

"*Marlow,*" Swift said again, with more urgency. "We need to get inside. Now."

Marlow glanced over at him. "You sure?"

The warding on Swift's flat made it impossible for anyone to find—unless of course that person had already been there. It was how they'd kept the Copperheads from hunting him and forcing him back into their ranks. It also meant that once they took Silvan inside, he would become one of only four people who could access Swift's flat.

"We're exposed out here," Swift said impatiently. "Let's just go."

Lowering Josephine, Marlow grabbed Silvan's arm and marched him through the door to Swift's flat. "Upstairs. Now."

Swift trailed behind them, making irritated noises. When they got to his flat, he bolted the door behind them and then disappeared into the kitchen. Marlow steered Silvan through the mess of the main room, which was littered with various engineering projects—typewriters and pocket watches, brass-trumpeted phonographs, boxy cameras. The radio he'd gotten from the pawnshop next to the Bowery hissed on the side table.

Marlow shoved Silvan down on the couch. "Talk."

"At least let me change out of this shirt before you interrogate me," Silvan said, plucking at it with disgust. "Who knows what kind of fluids were in that place."

"Oh my—*here*." Marlow stomped over to Swift's dresser and lobbed the first shirt she could find directly at Silvan's head. "Now explain what you were doing skulking around a well-known black market crime den."

"What were *you* doing there?" Silvan shot back. "Or is that just one of the many charming establishments you frequent here in the Marshes?"

"*I* was trying to find out who cursed Adrius," Marlow replied without missing a beat.

"How do you know he's cursed?"

"How do *you*?"

Silvan looked affronted. "He's my best friend. And he's really not the best at hiding things. I know when something's wrong with him. Dating *you* was my first clue."

Marlow was pretty sure she was the one who should be affronted.

"If you want to know the truth, I thought you were the one who cursed him."

Marlow thought back to their confrontation at the conservatory. She had to admit, the explanation that he had been warning her off in order to protect Adrius *from* her made sense.

It still didn't explain what Hendrix had overheard. "What about Amara?"

"What *about* her?"

"She asked you about the curse," Marlow said. "If you weren't the one who cursed him, why did you try to keep it from her?"

"How do you even—" Silvan cut himself off with a frustrated noise. "Never mind. Yes, I wanted to keep Amara from knowing, but that doesn't mean I *did* it. That just means I know Amara too well."

"Meaning?"

"She doesn't exactly always have Adrius's best interest in mind," Silvan replied. "Or rather, she and Adrius don't really agree on what his best interest is."

"You think she'd take advantage of the information," Marlow surmised. It was the same conclusion she'd come to; she was just surprised that Silvan was so clear-eyed about the possibility. "You don't trust her."

"Not with him," Silvan agreed.

Marlow thought this over. "All right," she said in a measured tone. "Say I believe that you're not behind Adrius's curse. That still doesn't explain what you were doing in Copperhead territory."

Silvan blew out a noisy breath. "I was following *you*."

"Excuse me?"

"Like I said, I thought you had something to do with Adrius's curse," Silvan sneered. "So I followed you."

"Gods below," Swift grumbled from the kitchen.

"What's wrong with him?" Silvan asked, peering through the doorway at him.

"He thinks you're an idiot," Marlow replied. "Which you are. Only a scion would imagine he could walk into a Copperhead joint without consequences."

Swift snorted as he came in from the kitchen, handing Silvan a cup of tea. "Only a scion or, I don't know, *Marlow Briggs*."

Marlow shot him a glare.

Silvan eyed the tea as if it might bite him. Bo slithered out from his sleeve, tasting the steam pouring from the cup with little flicks of his black tongue. He exhaled a stream of soft blue bubbles, which Marlow assumed meant he was content.

"What do the Copperheads have to do with Adrius?" Silvan asked carefully.

"One of their black market spellwrights possibly made the curse," Marlow answered. "But I don't know for sure."

She didn't mention the grimoire. She no longer thought Silvan had cursed Adrius, but she didn't exactly trust him, either.

That didn't mean he couldn't be useful, however.

Marlow pushed to her feet. "Okay. Here's what's going to happen—you're going to stay here with Swift until I say you can leave."

"*What?*" Silvan exclaimed. "What am I, your prisoner?"

"No," Marlow said, "but considering the leader of the Copperheads just tried to curse you, I'd say they have a vested interest in making sure you're no longer around to tell your father what they did. So you might want to consider lying low."

Silvan eyed the broken clock on the wall, the softly spluttering radio, and the pile of unidentifiable machine parts in the corner. "Exactly how is this shithole supposed to be safer than Evergarden?"

"*Shithole?*" Swift echoed.

"Evergarden's plenty safe—it's going back out in the Marshes that isn't," Marlow said. "And you happen to be standing in the one place in this entire half of the city that the Copperheads can't set foot in."

That was all true—Marlow was just leaving out the part where she needed to keep Silvan away from Evergarden in order for her plan to work.

"So I'm stuck here with your goon until—what? The Copperheads forget I exist?"

"Until I handle it," Marlow said curtly.

Silvan sneered at her and then stomped off to the kitchen, where he began noisily rifling through the cabinets.

Marlow glanced at Swift apologetically. "I promise you won't have to put up with him for long. One night, at most."

She expected Swift to argue, or crack a joke, or demand that Marlow explain her plan. But he just narrowed his eyes and said, "Fine."

"And I'm going to need to take Josephine with me."

"Okay."

His tone was flat, his face carefully blank, but Marlow knew him too well to be fooled.

"Just get it over with," she said wearily. "Yell at me some more or—whatever you're going to do."

Swift met her gaze evenly. "What would be the point? You're just going to ignore me and do whatever you want anyway."

"What I *have* to do."

"Oh, like you had to go to the Blind Tiger?" Swift asked. "Like you had to almost get yourself *killed*?"

"But I didn't," Marlow said. "I'm fine. We're fine. Because of you. Because you came for me."

"Of course I came for you," Swift said. "I was always going to come for you, but the point is that I shouldn't have had to. You put me in an impossible position, and you don't even realize how selfish it was."

"Fine," Marlow said, jaw set. "Next time, I'll leave you out of it."

Swift thrust his hand toward the kitchen. "Forcing me to babysit a spoiled rich boy is leaving me out of it?"

Marlow leaned over to glance at Silvan, who seemed determined to inspect every item inside Swift's kitchen.

"I can hear every word you're saying," he informed them. "This apartment is tiny." He held up a package of dried sardines between two fingers, wrinkling his nose. "Can't you afford anything the least bit palatable? Even Bo won't eat this."

"Sorry, Your Highness, I ran out of gourmet snake food yesterday," Swift sniped. He shot Marlow an emphatic glare.

"This is the last time I ask for your help," she promised.

"That isn't what I meant," he said, frustrated.

"You want me to stop putting myself in danger," Marlow surmised. "I get it, but you can't just—"

"I want you to stop acting like you have all the answers all the gods-damned time!" Swift exploded. "You think you have everything figured out, that you can stay one step ahead of everyone forever."

Marlow clenched her jaw, biting down on the angry words that threatened to spew out of her. Swift was just worried about her, and pissed. He would get over it.

"That's what makes me a good cursebreaker."

"Yeah? Well, it also makes you a shitty friend," Swift replied. "So do whatever it is you think you have to do, go throw yourself into danger like always. You obviously don't care how I feel about it, so I'm done trying to talk you out of it."

"Good," Marlow spat, slinging Josephine over one shoulder. "Because I'm sick of hearing it."

"You two seem close," Silvan commented snidely.

"Shut up," she heard Swift snap, right before she slammed the door behind her.

It took Marlow much longer than she would've liked to track down Bane. By the time she did, it was midmorning, and he was bent over beside a burlesque club on the Honey Docks, spewing his guts out into the murky water below.

"Rough night?" Marlow asked.

Bane grunted. "If you're going to kill me, do it quickly."

He braced himself on the wall and tottered around blearily. But when he realized who he was talking to he froze, eyes flashing with malice. "*You.*"

His face was swollen and distended with bee stings. His usually impeccable suit was rumpled and torn in places, and there were flecks of what looked like vomit in his beard.

He looked like a man defeated. Marlow was exhausted, angry, and fed up, but the pitiful look in his eyes brought her a small spark of satisfaction.

"You have a lot of guts showing up here, I'll give you that," he growled. "You're a dead girl walking."

"I'm shaking," Marlow replied dryly, Josephine balanced at her hip and pointed straight at him. "But you've got it backward, Thad. You're the dead man walking. And I'm pretty sure you've figured that out because you just blew five hundred pearls at a burlesque club and woke up wallowing in your own vomit, waiting for someone to come put you out of your misery."

Bane pressed a knuckle to one side of his nose and blew out noisily.

"You really mucked this one up," Marlow went on. "You think a man like Cormorant Vale is going to let some lowlife gangster threaten his son and *get away with it*? You're lucky Swift and I showed up when we did. Imagine if the Vale scion had actually gotten *cursed*."

"That was all Leonidas!"

"Oh, well I'm sure if you explain it *real nicely*, the person Vale hires to kill you will understand," Marlow said. "Your boss sure likes to throw his weight around, but he's not too big on thinking through the consequences, is he? That's what he has *you* for. So tell me, Thad, how *are* you planning to get out of this with all your organs intact?"

"Shut up," Bane barked. He was sweating.

Marlow blew out a breath. "If you want my advice, you should consider being more polite to the girl who, *one*, has a gun pointed at you, and *two*, has the power to save your ass from getting merced by one of the most powerful men in the city."

"The hell are you talking about?" Bane demanded.

"As of right now, Cormorant Vale has absolutely no idea what you and your buddies tried to do to his son last night," Marlow said. "I can make sure it stays that way. For the right incentive, of course."

"You know where the little brat is?" Bane eyed her. "No, you don't. You're bluffing."

"He's somewhere safe," Marlow said. "In my protection. And he'll stay quiet, as long as I tell him to. Your problems can magically disappear. All I want in return is ten minutes of your time."

"No."

Marlow cocked the shotgun.

Bane threw a hand over his face. "Don't shoot that fucking thing at me again. Fine. Ten minutes."

Marlow smiled and balanced Josephine against her shoulder to pull a spellcard out of her jacket pocket. "Great choice, Thad."

Bane lurched back. "Whoa, you're not casting shit on me, Briggs." He squinted in suspicion. "What is it?"

"Would you believe me if I said it's a hangover cure?"

By his expression, the answer was an emphatic *no*.

"Bargainer's Burden," Marlow said. "I'm sure you're familiar."

The spell was designed to uphold verbal agreements between two parties. Break the agreement, and your tongue would wither up and your teeth would start to fall out. It was brutal and effective, common in the circles Bane ran in and favored by loan sharks in particular, because it saved them the trouble of tracking down and threatening clients who missed their payments.

You just had to be very, very careful in how you worded the agreement.

Bane eyed the card and then eyed Marlow. "Fine. But I know every trick in the book, so don't even think about trying anything."

"Wouldn't dream of it," Marlow muttered. She returned Josephine to the bandolier's holster and raised the spellcard. "*Affare!*"

Yellowish-green glyphs burst from the card and swirled around them.

"I am going to ask you ten questions," Marlow said. "You are going to answer them, and answer them truthfully. In exchange, I'll ensure that Silvan Vale doesn't say, write, or insinuate a word to his father about the events of last night."

"Doesn't say a word to *anyone*," Bane growled.

"I can't promise that," Marlow said. "How's this: I will ensure that Silvan Vale doesn't say, write, or insinuate a word about what happened last night to anyone who wasn't at the Blind Tiger. Deal?"

Bane eyed her outstretched hand warily. "Fine. Deal."

They shook on it. The glyphs encircled their clasped hands, binding the agreement.

"I want to know what happened on the fifth of the Ash Moon last year."

Bane tensed almost imperceptibly, his eyes darting to the other end of the alley. "What about it?"

"Did you, or any of the Copperheads, see my mother that night?" Marlow asked.

Bane bared his teeth. "Yes."

A chill crept up Marlow's spine. "Where?"

"The marina."

"How did you know she would be there?"

"Montagne tipped us off," Bane answered.

So he *had* sold Cassandra out. A small part of Marlow couldn't help but feel relieved. The Black Orchid was wrong—Cassandra had never been working for the Copperheads. It was a setup.

Marlow raised Josephine and pointed it at Bane's forehead. "What did you do to my mother?"

"Whoa, whoa, put that down!" Bane exclaimed. "I didn't do shit to her."

"Then what happened?" Marlow demanded, biting the words out.

Bane glared. "We showed up at the marina, found Cassandra just like Montagne said. Got a few good licks in, but—your mother, she's a crafty one."

Marlow's heart thudded. "She got away?"

"Yes."

"And the spellbook?"

Bane whistled. "In the wind along with her. Leonidas was not very pleased about that."

Relief washed over her. The Copperheads hadn't gotten their hands on either Cassandra *or* the grimoire. "What did you do to Montagne?"

"What do you mean?" Bane asked. "Nothing. Montagne was a good spellwright. Great at making curses. In fact"—Bane smiled, pressing his tongue against the back of his teeth—"he's the one who made the curse we used on your friend Swift."

Marlow held very still, willing herself to stay calm.

"We were trying to help him out by getting rid of Cassandra, so she couldn't add him to her little racket."

Marlow narrowed her eyes. "What racket?"

"Cassandra was blackmailing him," Bane replied. "She knew he'd been making curses for us and threatened to expose him."

Marlow finished the thought. "Unless he stole *Ilario's Grimoire* for her."

"Sure, that was her first condition, but it wasn't going to be her last."

"What are you talking about?"

"Come on, Marlow," Bane taunted. "Don't tell me you didn't know. Your mother was *very* good at her job—knew exactly how to root out the rogue spellwrights making curses under Vale's nose. And she was generous, too—instead of turning them in she'd cut them a deal. They could keep making curses so long as they gave her a third of the profit. Pretty easy choice if you're a spellwright."

Marlow clenched her jaw. Bane had to be telling the truth, otherwise Bargainer's Burden would punish him. But she still wanted to call him a liar. How could her mother do such a thing? How could Marlow not have known?

"She had the perfect grift going, right under Vale's nose." He laughed. "In fact, we should really be thanking her. If it weren't for her looking the other way for so long, I doubt we could have cornered the curse trade so quickly." He grinned. "Face it, Marlow, your mommy was a curse-slinging crook, just as bad as the rest of us—"

Marlow fired Josephine before she could stop herself. The hex hit

Bane square in the swollen face, enveloping him in pale-green glyphs. When they cleared, Bane slumped back against the alley wall, coughing. A few slugs and worms fell out of his mouth.

"You bitch," Bane wheezed. A fat worm slithered from his mouth. "We had an agreement!"

Fury crackled through her veins.

"I never said I wouldn't hex you. Should've been more specific, Thad."

She walked away, making it all the way around the club and onto the muddy thoroughfare before she had to stop, doubling over against the side of a cigar shop and dry-heaving into the street.

When Marlow took on new cases, she always gave her clients the same warning—that in order to break a curse, Marlow would have to dig up the truth. And that meant having to live with whatever she uncovered.

She thought of Corinne, and how heartbroken she'd been when Marlow had revealed her friend as the culprit bent on sabotaging her. She thought of Adrius, staunch in his faith that his best friend would never do anything to harm him.

Marlow had believed she could make herself impervious to the kind of betrayal she'd felt when her mother disappeared, when Adrius had abandoned her. She thought she could armor herself with the truth. With one particular truth—that the people you love will always let you down.

Apparently, she hadn't learned that lesson well enough.

EIGHTEEN

All Marlow wanted to do after leaving the Honey Docks was go home, collapse into her bed, and preferably not move for the next sixteen hours.

First, though, she had to go relieve Swift of his scion-minding duties.

"I see you're still alive," Swift said when he opened the door.

"I just came to tell Silvan he can go home now." She lifted Josephine. "And to return this."

Swift took the gun. "All right," he replied in a detached voice. "I'll tell him."

Marlow peered into the flat. "He *is* still here, right? You didn't murder him or anything? Not that I'd blame you."

She meant the joke as a kind of peace offering, but Swift didn't so much as smile. He just pushed the door open wider so Marlow could see Silvan heaped sullenly on Swift's beat-up old armchair, letting Bo wind his way up his arm and curl around his neck like a bright-blue necklace.

"Oh, you're here," Silvan said. He was still wearing one of Swift's shirts, although Marlow noted it wasn't the same one she'd tossed at him the night before. "Have you negotiated my release, then?"

"Something like that," Marlow replied. "You're safe to go back to Evergarden—on the condition that you never speak a word of what happened last night to *anyone*."

Silvan stood, stretching languorously. "Fine."

"I mean it, Silvan," Marlow said menacingly. "One wrong word and I will ruin your life in ways you can't even imagine."

He yawned, brushing past Swift and stepping out into the entryway where Marlow stood. "You know, you're really not as scary as you think you are."

"Silvan."

"You have my word," Silvan promised, his frost-blue eyes locked on hers. "It's up to you whether or not that's something you can trust."

Marlow searched his sharp, haughty face. Adrius had said Silvan was the most honest person he knew. And as much as Marlow might dislike Silvan, she could find no evidence to the contrary. She'd never known him to lie or dissemble. He was certainly honest about how he felt about people, and never bothered with fake niceties or games like so many other noblesse nouveau. What you saw with Silvan was exactly what you got.

"Okay," she said with a nod.

Silvan turned away with an imperious huff.

"Bye, Your Highness," Swift said, waving from the doorway.

Silvan whipped around to stare at him and, for some reason, went red.

Marlow turned back to Swift, too. He shut the door in her face.

"I take it he's still mad," she said.

"I don't really have time to discuss your feelings, Briggs," Silvan replied, making his way down the rope bridge that connected Swift's porch to the dock. "I need to get out of this godsforsaken place before I start to smell."

"Do you even know where you're going?"

He did not. And as tempted as Marlow was to leave him stranded in the Marshes, she also knew the longer he was gone from Evergarden, the more questions people would start to ask.

"Let me take you to the Pavilion," Marlow offered.

"The what?"

"Cable car station."

Silvan spent the entire walk taking equal offense to every puddle of mud, dock vendor, and strange smell they encountered.

When they finally arrived at the bustling rotunda of the Pavilion, he shuddered. "I am never coming back here again."

"Probably for the best," Marlow agreed.

He looked down his nose at her. "I suppose I'll be seeing you tonight at the ball?"

"Ball?"

"The Starlings' Midsummer Costume Ball. You're going with Adrius, aren't you?"

Marlow winced. "That's tonight?"

She and Adrius had already discussed attending together, but that had been nearly a week ago. The very last thing she wanted to do at this moment was get dressed up and go to yet another ridiculously extravagant party. There was also the fact that she would have to face Adrius for the first time since the night at the speakeasy.

None of it sounded appealing. She wanted to go home. She wanted to sleep, regroup. She needed to process the last twenty-four hours, reckon with yet another dead end in her mother's case, and figure out where to go from here.

But Adrius was running out of time and Marlow was out of leads. In two weeks' time, the curse would become unbreakable. She *had* to figure out who had cast it before that happened.

"Swift told me what you do," Silvan said suddenly. "You're trying to break Adrius's curse, aren't you? That's the reason he started bringing you around?"

"I—yeah, something like that." It had become far more complicated in the past few days, but Silvan understood the heart of the matter.

"He said you're good at what you do," Silvan said.

"I'm one of the best." It wasn't a brag.

"Then since I made you a promise, you're going to make me one, too," he said. "When you find out who did this to Adrius, you tell me. So that I can make them pay."

His voice was a fierce growl she'd never heard from Silvan before. His eyes burned into hers like blue flames. What had Adrius done, she wondered, to win the unwavering loyalty of someone like this?

"Okay," she said. "Deal."

The Starlings' Midsummer Costume Ball was, as the *Weekly Gab* put it, the event of the season. Adrius always went as the Sun King, and so it was fitting for Marlow to go as the Moon Thief to match. It was a bit of a cheeky choice. If the noblesse nouveau were determined to see Marlow as an interloper, then she may as well dress the part.

She called in her favor at the Monarch Theater to borrow Corinne's new understudy's costume, which was enchanted so that the dress and its wearer could all but disappear into the shadows.

The costume was incredibly elaborate, made of impossibly dark, impossibly delicate material that glittered like stars when the light struck it. She wore her hair pulled back into an elegant updo, with loose curls framing her face and a silver tiara of twin crescent moons and a dark onyx gem.

She wouldn't be the only person there wearing an enchanted dress. Everyone was sure to show up in their most outrageous, over-the-top outfits, each trying to outdo one another.

All the scions were to be formally introduced upon entering the ballroom, so Marlow met Adrius in a staging room so they could enter together.

When he walked into the staging room, Marlow couldn't help but stare. He was luminous in the Sun King costume—outfitted in a suit that resembled golden armor, a circlet glinting in his chestnut curls and golden paint shimmering on his warm brown skin. He looked like a hero out of a fairy tale—which, Marlow supposed, the Sun King was.

Marlow rose as he neared. "Hi," she said, her voice sounding faint to her own ears.

His gaze flicked over her, but she could read nothing in his expression.

Marlow was struck by the uncomfortable realization that she had wanted a reaction. That when she'd put on this costume and spent all that time doing her hair and painting her face, she had done so anticipating Adrius's expression when he saw her.

In the face of his non-reaction, she felt a swoop of disappointment.

"What do you think?" She made her voice steady, forcing a sly smile to her face. "Aren't you going to compliment me?"

She expected him to say something over-the-top and flirtatious like he had so many times before.

Instead, he looked away. "What would be the point? We're alone in here."

Her chest tightened. Obviously, something had changed since the speakeasy. She knew what had changed for her—the realization that all Adrius had done to convince the noblesse nouveau that they were in love had, humiliatingly, made Marlow *actually* fall for him. Or at least come close. She felt she was on the precipice, that one good strong wind might blow her over, but she still had a chance to pull herself back from the edge.

"Adrius—"

"They're about to announce us." He turned abruptly and strode to the curtains that led out to the balcony of the ballroom.

From the other side of the curtain, the marshal's voice called out, "Adrius Falcrest and his guest, Marlow Briggs!"

The curtains swept aside, and only now did Adrius offer his arm to Marlow. She took it, and together they glided onto the balcony. A dazzling smile overtook Adrius's face and he threw up his free hand to wave to the applauding crowd below.

It seemed that their display at the speakeasy the other night had won over a few noblesse nouveau. Everyone liked a dramatic love confession.

They paused at the railing, Adrius circling her waist with one arm. Marlow flashed a smile to the crowd and started to move away. But before she could get too far, Adrius lifted a hand to her jaw and gently tilted her face back toward his. A frisson of heat sparked through her. Adrius leaned in, brushing his lips to the corner of her mouth. Light enough that it barely whispered against her skin, but enough that everyone watching them would see it. Heat erupted in her chest and her cheeks as Adrius released her and drew back. His eyes pinned her with a look that held the promise of something that belonged in darkened rooms.

It wasn't a look meant for her, Marlow knew. None of this was meant for her.

They descended the stairs to clear the balcony for the next couple, and not for the first time, Marlow was struck by how easily Adrius slipped into and out of this role, and how woefully unprepared she was each time he did.

She distracted herself from the weight of his hand at her waist by taking in the opulent ballroom and the equally extravagant costumes of the guests. On one side of the room, a long, floating glass bar gave way to a waterfall of pale-gold sparkling wine. On the other, an orchestra of enchanted instruments played a rousing song. The ceiling was enchanted to look like the sky during a magnificent sunset. Guests wore lavish costumes that lit up, transformed, defied gravity. Several people sported actual, functioning wings of gossamer silks and iridescent feathers. One woman had enchanted a small flock of parakeets to trail after her, chirping out a tune. Another had a towering headdress with waterfalls cascading off it.

Marlow turned back to Adrius. "About Silvan—" she started to say, but Adrius turned away from her to grab two glasses of the iced wine that had been specially prepared for the evening, handing one to her.

He tipped his back and then surfaced with a brilliant smile. "Let's just enjoy the evening, all right? Just this once."

Marlow sipped at her wine. "It's not him. That's all I was going to say."

"Well, gosh, Marlow, I'm glad you were able to suss that one out," he said blithely.

"You're still angry at me."

"Nope," he answered. "Not angry."

"You've barely looked at me unless someone was watching."

He looked at her then. There was a dark heat in his eyes, something that sweltered against her skin like the sultry night air. "Satisfied?"

"Why are you acting like this?"

"Why don't you figure it out?" Adrius bit out. "You're Marlow Briggs. You know *everything*, don't you?"

The words hit her like a slap to the face. A harsh echo of the accusation Swift had hurled at her.

"I'm getting another drink," Adrius said, striding away, though there were plenty of glittering trays floating about with various concoctions.

Marlow stood frozen in his wake, stomach knotting. Not since the beginning of this ruse had Adrius been so obviously angry with her. Even then, he hadn't been *cold*. It reminded her too much of those last few weeks in Evergarden, of trying to catch his gaze. Watching his attention glide effortlessly over her, as if their friendship had been nothing. As if *she* was nothing.

"I *love* your costume!"

Gemma emerged from the crowd, her green eyes bright on Marlow. She was dressed as the Butterfly Queen from a popular Cortesian opera, complete with a crown of actual butterflies fluttering their spectacular black-and-orange wings atop her hair, which today was a brilliant shade of amber.

"Yours is great, too," Marlow said as Gemma air-kissed her cheek.

At Gemma's elbow, Silvan, wearing a suit patterned with iridescent scales, acknowledged Marlow only with a glare.

"Welcoming as always, Silvan," Marlow said wryly.

"Silvan here had quite the night, didn't you?" Gemma said with a sly smile.

Panic flooded Marlow. She had made it *very* clear what she would do to Silvan's life, reputation, and particularly sensitive appendages if he breathed a word about the Blind Tiger to anyone. But when she met his gaze, she saw her own frantic horror reflected on his pale face. She blinked, and his expression snapped back into sneering indifference.

"I have no idea what you're talking about."

"Oh, come on, don't be coy. Darian said you went out last night and came home this morning wearing someone else's shirt." She leaned toward Marlow conspiratorially. "Want to take bets on who the mystery man is?"

Marlow bit down on a laugh, thinking gleefully about how Swift was going to react when she told him he'd unwittingly become the subject of the latest Evergarden gossip.

With a twist of her stomach, she remembered that Swift wasn't speaking to her.

"Darian should keep his mouth shut," Silvan hissed. "Since when do you two trade gossip anyway?"

Gemma's eyes widened with delight. "Must be someone you really like if you're *this* testy about it."

Silvan threw a surreptitious glance at Marlow and then straightened his spine, looking off into the crowd. "I'm going to find my brother and tell him to mind his own godsdamned business."

Gemma's gaze followed his retreat, and then drifted over to the orchestra pit. "Speaking of romance, I think they're about to start 'The Lover's Cotillion.'"

"The what?"

Gemma stared at her. "You've never been to the Midsummer Ball, have you?"

"No, but—"

"The ball always opens with 'The Lover's Cotillion.' All the couples dance it. It's tradition."

"That doesn't actually matter, does it?" Marlow asked.

Gemma looked at Marlow like she had said something truly appalling, but there was a fond quality to her gaze, as if Marlow was a beloved pet who had just tracked mud over the rug. "It matters if you don't want every gossip magazine in town to start speculating that you and Adrius are on the outs. *Are* you?"

Marlow met Gemma's wide green eyes. Gemma liked to gossip, and perhaps that made her a poor choice to confide in. But the delicate crease in her brow and the way her perfectly painted lips tugged down made Marlow realize she wasn't asking with the intent to find gossip, but because she actually cared. And Marlow found herself saying, "Honestly, I don't really know."

"Well, I hope you can figure it out, whatever it is," Gemma said. "Adrius, he's . . . different, when he's with you."

Marlow swallowed down her unease. *He's different,* as in, Gemma could sense he wasn't quite himself. As in, she sensed the ruse.

"Are you all right after the other night?" Marlow asked, redirecting her.

Gemma let out a huff. "I'm still mad at Adrius, obviously, even though I know he didn't *mean* to hurt me. But he can't just go spilling everyone's secrets the second he has too much to drink. It's like he has no control over himself."

Marlow tried not to react to the inadvertent truth of Gemma's words.

Gemma's eyes widened as she caught sight of something over Marlow's shoulder. "Speaking of . . ."

Despite the warning, Marlow was by no means prepared for Adrius's hand at the small of her back and his voice low in her ear.

"May I have this dance?"

The sweet scent of sparkling wine wafted over her as Marlow turned to face him. She wondered if the wine waterfall was enchanted to be particularly potent, because while Adrius didn't quite look unsteady, there was a certain glassy, relaxed look on his face that suggested he'd had a few glasses.

She nodded uncertainly and he took her hand, leading her to the dance floor where the other couples had begun to line up. The cotillion was an older style of dance, where rather than couples twining in each other's arms the entire dance, they danced with other couples in a series of different formations, coming together and drawing apart in turns.

The orchestra took up a low, sensuous tune as the couples bowed to one another and the dance began. Marlow was not particularly well-versed in the cotillion figures, but the dance was slow and simple enough to follow along with the other couples. She let her gaze wander over the dancers, and easily picked out Amara and Darian. Just beyond them, Gemma looked on with a heartbroken expression.

When Marlow glanced back to Adrius, she was surprised to find him gazing intently at her as they moved through the next sequence of the dance.

"It suits you," he remarked as they came together again, shoulder to opposite shoulder.

"What does?"

They slowly circled each other.

"Your costume," he replied as they separated again. "You asked me what I thought of it, before."

They wove through the other couples and came to a stop on either side of the line.

Marlow wasn't sure how to reply. "Yours suits you, too."

"The Moon Thief in the Sun King's court," he mused as another pair of couples circled around them. "The only question is, what have you stolen?"

Marlow's gaze followed him as they separated again, her heart quickening and her skin buzzing with sudden nerves.

"I think I know," he murmured, his hands a warm brand against her hips as they whirled back together. "'You have stolen my breath.'"

He was quoting the original Sun King poem that the ballet had been based upon, his voice low and velvety, so like the one he'd jokingly used aboard the zeppelin—but if this was a joke, it was at her expense.

They had both stopped dancing, the other couples moving seamlessly around them.

"'And I fear if I'm not careful,'" Adrius went on, an accusatory glint in his eyes, "'you'll steal my heart, too.'"

Warmth blossomed over Marlow's skin. Her heart dropped into her stomach, beating where Adrius's hands spread against her waist.

His face dipped closer to hers. The bottom curve of his lip glistened in the lamplight, wet with wine.

The crowd broke into applause, shattering the taut air between them. The dance had ended. Adrius seemed to snap out of his fog of wine at the same moment, releasing her and stepping back to applaud along with the others.

From the corner of her eye, Marlow spotted Amara weaving through the other dancers toward them, Darian and several other hangers-on at her heels.

"I didn't believe it, but it seems the rumors are true," Amara said. She was dressed as the Maiden of the Sea, with a carapace bodice encrusted with white pearls, and an elaborate headdress to match. "You really are back together."

"I guess we just can't stay away from each other," Adrius replied, wrapping an arm around Marlow's waist.

Amara scoffed. "You've been seeing each other for what, a week?"

"Almost three weeks," Adrius shot back. "But I've known how I felt for much longer than that." His gaze was focused intently on Marlow now. She felt caught in it, like a small creature mired in silt. "In fact, I've known for over a year. Ever since the night we turned seventeen."

Marlow's heart thumped hard in her chest. Her breath stuttered. It felt forbidden, somehow, for Adrius to bring up that night, especially in front of Amara.

"Marlow wasn't even invited to that party," Amara said.

"You're right," Adrius replied. "Which is why I slipped out early to go see her. We watched the sun rise on top of the Malachite Building, and I remember thinking I'd pass up every Evergarden party if it meant I could be with her."

Marlow stiffened. Anger roared hot in her chest. She desperately wanted to pull out of his arms and flee the dance floor. Adrius was making a mockery of what their friendship had been, what that night had meant to her, and she couldn't do a thing about it in front of these people except stand next to him and smile as if he hadn't just twisted the knife in the wound of their ruined friendship.

"I should have told her that night," Adrius went on. His expression was wistful, tender, and even Amara's sycophants were starting to look a little dreamy. "But by the time I found the courage, she'd left Evergarden. I thought I'd missed my chance."

"So this really has been a long time coming," Darian said thoughtfully. "I had no idea."

That's because it's not true, Marlow thought bitterly. It was just a pretty lie, embellished with a sliver of truth. She couldn't even look at Adrius. Couldn't face those warm, soft eyes, the way they brimmed with devotion, like he meant every lie on his lips.

"Looking back now, I suppose I was a bit heartbroken," Adrius said, his voice tinged with pain.

Anger seized her. *She* was the one who'd gotten her heart broken.

Suddenly, she needed to be anywhere that wasn't here.

"Excuse me a moment," she said, pushing out of Adrius's arms and hurrying off the dance floor.

She made it as far as the stairs before Adrius caught up to her.

"Minnow, wait."

She whirled around, and immediately realized they were in plain view of plenty of other costumed guests. Taking hold of Adrius's arm, she steered him behind the stairs.

When they were safely out of sight, she turned and dropped his arm. "What the hell do you think you're doing?"

"Exactly what you told me to, Minnow. *Pretending.*" His eyes were sharp and challenging, nothing like the tender look he'd given her in front of Amara.

Heat flooded her. "Well, I'm glad it's so godsdamned easy for you. But I guess you have the practice, right? After you pretended to be my friend for so long."

"What are you talking about?"

Fury pounded through Marlow's veins, as hot and unrelenting as a summer squall, blotting out all rational thought. She couldn't even feel embarrassed; she was too angry. All she could think was that she had to know—she *had to* understand what had made Adrius turn on her a year ago. She didn't know who her mother was or who had cursed Adrius, but she could at least have this one answer.

"Last year," she said, choking the words out. "You just turned your back on me out of nowhere. What happened?"

Adrius's eyes dropped to the ground, his jaw tensing. His chest rose and fell on a ragged breath. The longer the question hung between them, unanswered, the more Marlow wanted to take it back.

Instead, she hardened her voice and pushed toward him. "What was it? The poor, hapless little minnow was interesting for half a second, but then you got bored?"

He met her challenging gaze, his body bowing toward hers like some invisible tether dragged them together. "Yes. That's it. I lost interest."

Marlow stared up at him, disbelief welling up inside her. Not at Adrius's answer, but at herself. For caring in the first place. For being stupid enough to let Adrius Falcrest pull her in again.

A jagged laugh splintered from her throat, its edges sharp with the knowledge that if she didn't laugh, she would surely cry.

And there was no way she was letting him see her cry.

She started to walk away to go back to the dancing and the sparkling waterfall and the beautiful people with all their terrible secrets.

"Marlow."

She stopped despite herself, despite everything telling her to flee. Maybe it was the fact that he'd called her by her name instead of that mocking nickname. Maybe it was because his voice was weighted with something that almost sounded like regret.

But that was all he said. No explanation. No apology. Just her name.

She kept walking.

The lights of the ballroom swirled dimly as Marlow crossed it, wanting to put as much distance between herself and Adrius as she could. Past the whirling dancers and fizzing glasses, Marlow caught sight of someone lurking at the edge of the room. A flash of venomous green, a swift, slinking stride.

Caito.

Marlow stopped where she stood in the middle of the ballroom, her body making a connection before her mind had caught up. Armant Montagne's face flashed behind her eyes. She could almost hear the soft rasp of his voice.

They cut a hole, he said, his dark-green eyes fixed on hers. *The fangs. They came and they pierced my mind. They took all of it. Bloodred fangs.*

Marlow stared at Caito across the room. At the dark-red markings of the Zanne Rosse that hooked down her face like bloodred fangs.

NINETEEN

"I need a spell."

Orsella looked up at Marlow in the entrance of her shop, a cigarette dangling from her lips.

"And *I* need a foot massage and a bottle of gin, but you don't hear me complaining about it, do you?" she carped. "By the way, don't think I didn't hear about the little stunt you pulled the other night at the Blind Tiger. With *my* gun, no less."

"Swift is the one who brought it—take it up with him," Marlow replied, striding toward the counter. "In the meantime, I'm here on business."

Orsella narrowed her eyes. "Fine, I'll bite. What sort of spell do you need?"

"The most powerful ward-breaking spell you have," Marlow replied. "Something that can get me through any ward, but won't leave a trace that I was there."

Orsella sighed, long and low. "Do I even want to know?"

"Do you have it or not?"

Orsella took a drag from her cigarette. Smoke curled through the wan air. "Might take a few days."

"I don't have a few days," Marlow said. "I need it by tomorrow night."

Tomorrow night was Amara and Darian's wedding eve banquet, to be held at Falcrest Hall. It was Marlow's best opportunity to search Aurelius

Falcrest's office—which was sure to be protected by the most powerful of wards. Without a powerful spell of her own, there was no way Marlow was getting inside.

She knew now that Caito was the one who had tortured Montagne. Which meant she, and therefore Aurelius, had found out that Cassandra had stolen *Ilario's Grimoire*. There was no doubt that Caito would have tried to track her down to get it back—and she'd most likely succeeded. Marlow doubted that Aurelius would have let her keep her job otherwise.

There was also the fact that neither Caito nor Aurelius had ever tried to question Marlow about her mother's disappearance. Which meant they were no longer looking for her.

Since the night of the Midsummer Ball, Marlow's mind had been crowded with nightmares. Horrible imaginings of all the ways Caito could have hurt Cassandra. Maybe she'd done the same thing to her that she'd done to Montagne. Maybe Cassandra was out there somewhere, haunting the streets of Caraza like a ghost, unable to even remember her own daughter.

Marlow had to know.

"Tomorrow night," Orsella echoed. "Fine. But it'll cost you."

Marlow reached for her bag of pearls.

"Not pearls," Orsella said.

Marlow raised her eyebrows. "How much blood?"

Orsella shook her head. "What you're asking for won't be easy to get my hands on. You want a spell that powerful? I'm going to need something premium in return. A spell ingredient I can't get from just anyone."

There were certain types of spell ingredients that only the most desperate people gave up, because they had no other choice. There was no telling what Orsella might ask for—Marlow's voice, her left eye, a year of her life. Her ability to dream, or feel anger or love or joy. Her most cherished memory.

"What do you want?" Marlow asked, almost afraid to voice the question.

Orsella's green eyes glittered. "How badly do you need this spell?"

Despite having been Adrius's girlfriend for almost three weeks now, Marlow had not set foot in Falcrest Hall for over a year.

Adrius greeted her in the grand entryway outside the banquet hall, looking, for the first time that Marlow could remember, less than perfectly put together. It was subtle enough that anyone else might not have even noticed—his deep burgundy jacket was impeccably pressed and fitted, his curls gleaming like burnished bronze. It was only the slight shadows under his eyes and the tense set of his jaw that gave him away.

Marlow dearly hoped that he could get past whatever had gotten under his skin—tonight more than ever, she needed him to put on his best Adrius Falcrest smile and charm everyone into believing they were just a young couple in love, there to celebrate the union of the Falcrest and Vale families.

"I wasn't sure you were coming."

Marlow gave him her sweetest smile, eyeing the other guests lingering in the entryway. "Of course I came."

"I—here." He held out his hand. Draped across his palm was a thin silver chain with a small moon and sun charm on it.

"What is this?" she asked.

"An apology," he replied. "The other night—"

"You don't have to—"

"I do," he said. "I was . . . upset. That's not an excuse. I—"

"It's fine." She grabbed his arm, squeezing slightly in warning. There were more than a few pairs of eyes on them. "We're fine."

"Somehow I don't really believe you."

Marlow shook her head. No matter what was going on between them, she was here for one reason and one reason alone—to solve a mystery. Everything else could wait. "What does it matter, Adrius? We can pretend everything's fine, at least. Isn't that what we do? Pretend?"

Adrius gave her a stormy look. "Right."

"Just—here." She held out her wrist. His fingers grazed the delicate skin there as he fastened the bracelet. She wondered if he could feel how fast her pulse was racing.

"We should find our seats," Adrius said, leading her into the banquet hall. Marlow breathed a sigh of relief as they stopped at two chairs halfway down the table from where Amara and Darian were seated as the guests of honor. Perhaps the embarrassment of Adrius bringing Marlow as his date would mean they'd be seated far away from anyone who mattered.

"Well, isn't this a treat."

Marlow snapped her head up, blood going cold. Seated directly across from her was Aurelius Falcrest. His tall, slender frame was sheathed in a suit of luxurious black silk with a high, rigid collar that made his long face look even more severe. His eyes pierced Marlow like twin blades of obsidian.

Marlow smoothed her expression into something demure and polite. As far as Aurelius knew, she was just some insignificant girl, probably desperate to get his approval. That was the lie she needed to sell, and she was going to have to put aside all her complicated feelings about Adrius and sell it.

"Lord Falcrest," Marlow said. "It's an honor."

"Yes, well, I suppose it's time we get to know each other, Miss Briggs," he said.

Adrius eyed his father with mistrust as they took their seats. Plates appeared in front of them with the first course—tender baby clams drizzled with a bright, decadent sauce that looked almost like blood.

"Tell me more about yourself, Marlow," Aurelius commanded, swishing his glass of wine. "I want to understand what it is that draws my son to you."

Impress me. If Marlow really was just here as Adrius's girlfriend, then she would want nothing more.

"There's not much to tell," Marlow replied lightly.

"You were educated here alongside my children and the other scions, weren't you?" Aurelius pressed. "That's unusual, for a chevalier's daughter."

Marlow didn't allow herself to react to the mention of her mother. "You're right, it was unusual for me to receive such an opportunity. I was very fortunate. Especially since that's how Adrius and I met."

"Your mother," Aurelius said abruptly, sending Marlow's heart rate rocketing. "She's an interesting woman. It must have been difficult for you when she . . . vanished."

You bastard, Marlow thought fiercely, spearing a baby clam with her fork. "It was, yes."

"And you still have no idea where she went, do you?"

Marlow's fingers tightened around her fork, pulse speeding. He didn't suspect she knew—how could he?

"Father," Adrius said in a warning tone.

"What?" Aurelius asked. "I thought you'd be glad for me to take an interest in the girl you claim to love."

Adrius looked ready to leap across the table. He shot Marlow a look of thunder. Marlow could not tell where his anger was truly aimed—at her or his father.

"Adrius, it's all right. I have nothing to hide from your family." She looked Aurelius in the eye. "No, I don't know where she is. I wish I did."

Aurelius took another sip of wine. "And how did you enjoy your tour of Falcrest Library?"

Marlow's heart stuttered. The sudden change in topic was no coincidence. He *knew.* He'd figured out the real reason Marlow and Adrius had gone to Falcrest Library.

"It was fascinating," Marlow replied with a smile. She touched Adrius's elbow. "Adrius was an excellent guide."

To Marlow's great relief, their second course appeared on the table—butterflied lobster tail on a bed of creamy rice cooked with saffron. The dish was served with individual pitchers of rich, buttery sauce to pour over it. Only two more courses until everyone retired to the adjoining terrace for the traditional Wedding Eve candle-lighting ceremony, and Marlow would have her opportunity to slip out—and search Falcrest's study.

"So tell me, Marlow," Aurelius said. "What is it you see in Adrius?"

There was a cruel tilt to Aurelius's smile, as if he couldn't possibly imagine what might be worth valuing in his own son. It made her want to wipe the smile off his face. Instead, she reached over and took Adrius's hand on top of the tablecloth.

"Well, for one thing, he's never begrudged me my background, or where I came from," Marlow said. "When I first came to Evergarden, no one wanted anything to do with me. But Adrius never cared. He got to know me, because it didn't matter to him that I'd grown up in the Marshes."

"Indeed not," Aurelius agreed. His tone made it clear he viewed this as a failing rather than a virtue.

Marlow stared into his cold, black eyes. "Adrius sees the truth in people—and in himself."

"You find that an admirable quality, I suppose?" Aurelius asked.

"Yes," Marlow answered at once. "It's rare that a person sees themself clearly. Most people lie to themselves about who they are and what they stand for because they don't want to face the truth that they're flawed just like everyone else. They want to believe that they're better, somehow."

"Well, I'm sure you're right about that," Aurelius replied. "My son, at least, is aware of his many shortcomings."

Marlow felt Adrius's hand tense in hers. She traced his profile—jaw tight, eyes averted, an angry flush of color in his cheeks. She gripped his hand more firmly.

"Maybe you see him as weak," she said to Aurelius, "because he refuses to use his power in the way you do. Maybe you think him insouciant because he acts like he doesn't care about anything. But I know he does care, deeply, about the things that are important to him. Even—perhaps *especially*—when those things aren't important to people like you."

"Well," Aurelius said, ripping into his lobster tail with a delicate fork, "you certainly are opinionated, aren't you, Miss Briggs? It seems as if you feel you have something to prove."

"I don't have anything to prove to you, sir, except that I care about your son a great deal." Adrius's gaze moved to her face, and Marlow forced herself not to look away.

Some part of you has to believe the con, she thought. *Just enough to make it real—but not so much that you forget yourself.*

It was too late for that. She just didn't know if Adrius realized it yet. She couldn't tell from his dark-eyed gaze whether he'd figured out that everything she'd just said to his father was true.

The rest of the dinner passed agonizingly slowly, but finally Amara and Darian made the announcement for everyone to go out to the terrace for the ceremonial candle-lighting. Marlow waited until she saw Aurelius get sucked into conversation with the Morandi family before slipping off toward the doors.

Adrius blocked her path. "I need to talk to you."

"Not now," Marlow gritted out, maneuvering around him.

"Minnow—" He grabbed her wrist, whirling her right up against his chest. If she leaned up on her toes, they would be kissing.

His lips parted on a breath. Her pulse pounded against his thumb. She watched the delicate fan of his eyelashes as his gaze dropped to her lips. He swayed toward her. Heat ignited in her gut.

Her hands shook as she pulled them out of his grip. "I have to go."

She spun away from him and didn't let herself look back as she wove through the milling crowd out of the banquet hall.

She crept to the next floor of Falcrest Hall, winding through the hallways. It wasn't hard to find Falcrest's office—other than perhaps the ballroom and the main dining chambers, it was the grandest room in the estate. And given the number of meetings a man like Aurelius Falcrest took, it would be easily accessible from the main concourse.

Marlow peered down the third-floor hallway and spotted two glass-paned doors at the end. Instinct told her she'd found the right place. A quick detection spell revealed that the coast was clear.

The glass-paneled doors unlocked without much resistance to a fairly standard lock-picking charm. They opened into the least inviting parlor Marlow had ever set foot in. It was all gleaming, polished surfaces and austere, sculptural furnishings that would not have looked out of place in a museum gallery. To one side, a wall of geometric windows looked out on the moonlit arc of Crescent Canal. Straight ahead was the heavy, dark wood and brass door that led to the inner chamber of Aurelius's office.

Marlow pulled the magnifying glass out from under her dress and held it up to her eye. Dozens and dozens of shimmering, ghostly wards crisscrossed the door, spreading out along the wall. She wasn't sure she'd ever encountered a room as heavily warded as this one.

She fumbled with the spellcard Orsella had dropped off earlier that evening. She had promised Marlow it would get her through any ward undetected. Marlow just had to trust that she was right.

"*Grimalde*," she whispered. The card's glyphs glowed silver and blue. They swirled through the air, coalescing into a single, glowing shape. A key. Marlow grasped it with shaking fingers and slid it into the door's keyhole. Holding her breath, she twisted until she heard a quiet *click*.

Holding the magnifying glass back up to her eye, Marlow watched as glowing silver glyphs spiderwebbed out from the keyhole and spread along the door, turning the wards silver and then dissolving them into thin air.

Marlow let go of a breath in a rush of relief. Quietly, she eased open the door and slipped inside the office.

It looked like every other room in Falcrest Hall—a soaring ceiling, floor-length windows, dark, imposing furniture with gleaming brass and gold designs. And like the rest of Falcrest Hall, there were secrets hidden here. Marlow just had to figure out where.

She went first to the desk, rifling through the drawers. She found mostly papers—various correspondences, crisp sheafs of Falcrest letterhead—and a few stacks of spellcards. Marlow didn't have time to sift through everything—her priority was *Ilario's Grimoire*. She moved onto the bookshelves lining the far wall. She found thick volumes of history and business theory, as well as various enchanted objects of unknown use. But nothing related to her mother or the grimoire.

Her stomach sank. This whole risky endeavor was going to be for nothing.

Footsteps echoed on the marble floors of the hallway, soon joined by indistinct voices. Marlow's pulse jumped in her throat as they grew louder, nearing the office. She scrambled to the door, slipping through and pulling it shut before diving behind one of the sofas in the parlor.

A moment later the glass doors pushed open and the voices filtered through clearly.

She recognized Amara's, tight with anger, as it rang through the room.

"I am doing everything you've asked of me—I've *done* everything you've asked, and still, *still* somehow you're making *him* heir?"

Marlow had to stifle a gasp of surprise. Aurelius had made Adrius heir? It didn't make sense.

"Your brother is very capable," Aurelius replied, not even bothering to make it sound like he believed it.

"Adrius has made a mockery of himself and this family for *years*," Amara said, fury chewing through every word. "I'm the one who secured a marriage with Darian while Adrius refuses to even entertain the prospect of finding a suitable match. I'm the one who wants to see this family succeed, not tear it down in a fit of pique! He will ruin us."

"You are acting just as childish as your brother," Aurelius said. "Are you going to throw a fit because you didn't get what you wanted? You expect that to change my mind?"

There was silence for a moment. Then, in a low voice, Amara said, "Maybe I won't marry him, then."

"Then don't." Aurelius sounded bored. "If you think that will get you what you want."

As much as Marlow disliked Amara, she couldn't help but feel a little angry on her behalf. She had broken her best friend's heart and entered an engagement with a boy she didn't love just to please her father, and still it wasn't enough. Aurelius had denied her the one thing she most desperately wanted.

Adrius was right about his father. Some part of him *enjoyed* it—denying Amara what she wanted most and knowing that even then, she wouldn't defy him because it would only prove him right about her.

"I know about the investigation," Amara said suddenly. Marlow almost choked, certain that somehow Amara meant *her* investigation, but then she continued, "I know the City Solicitor is looking into us. You spoke with him the night we announced the engagement. I heard you. He has something on you, doesn't he?"

"It's low-level. It won't touch me," Aurelius replied dismissively.

"Don't lie to me," Amara said at once. "He has something on you, something bad enough to take you down. Then what—Adrius will be in charge? You're going to bring us all down with you because you're too stubborn to see that *I* am this family's future."

"Our family's future is secure, I've made sure of that," Aurelius replied icily. "You are too shortsighted—you always have been. You don't see the bigger picture. *That* is why I didn't make you my heir. Now go back to your fiancé and play your part."

Marlow thought for a moment that Amara might stay and continue the argument. But with a huff of outrage, she stormed out of the parlor.

Marlow expected Aurelius to follow shortly after, but instead she heard his footsteps click past her, and then the sound of his office door opening and then closing him within.

She waited for a heartbeat, and then two, to see if he might emerge again. When he didn't, she slowly raised herself to her feet. She needed to get out of here as soon as possible, and return to the reception before anyone took note of her absence. She rose, creeping as quietly as she could to the door, praying that Aurelius stayed in his office.

She had hardly taken three steps when the parlor doors suddenly flew all the way open, the sound splitting the silence like thunder as Adrius stormed inside.

His gaze found her by the drawing table. "*There* you are. What the hell are you doing in here?"

Every inch of Marlow lit up with terror. After all the care she'd taken to conceal herself, she'd been made. Aurelius knew she was here. She had a chance—the faintest, grasping chance—to convince him she was just what she appeared to be: a lovestruck girl.

She leaned back against the table, trying not to betray her panic. "Hoping you would come find me, of course. I saw the door open and I thought this was the perfect place to get you alone."

Adrius's shadowed face creased with confusion. "What are you—it doesn't matter. I need to talk to you, and it can't wait. Here is as good as anywhere."

It really wasn't, especially with Aurelius inside the office, able to overhear every word. Marlow made her voice low and sweet—warm honey poured over rich cake. "I was thinking we might do something else."

"What?" He seemed genuinely baffled, and Marlow could not blame him. She would explain it all to him after. "There's no one else up here, Marlow, it's just us."

"Right," Marlow said, wishing she could wordlessly communicate that there *very much* was someone else there. "Exactly."

"I—" He stared at her, uncharacteristically caught off guard. Then, with sudden determination, he pushed toward her. "Maybe this is foolish, but I don't care. I can't take it anymore. What you said back there, Marlow, I need to know—did you mean it?"

There was a desperate note in his voice.

"Of course I did." Through the fog of her panic, she wasn't even sure what Adrius meant. She would say whatever it took to keep up the ruse.

He looked stunned. "Gods. I know I've been an ass, but this—it's been *torture*. Pretending to be with you when—when all I—"

Shit. Aurelius already suspected too much, and Adrius had basically revealed their whole charade. That their entire relationship was fake.

But Adrius was still talking, and in her panic, Marlow couldn't think how to stop him. "—I thought that's all it was for you. I thought you still hated me, that you could never—I didn't think—"

"Adrius." Marlow blurted the first idea that flickered through her mind. "Kiss me."

Adrius's lips parted in surprise. The only movement of his body was the rise and fall of his chest as he pulled in a ragged breath.

Marlow had barely caught up to what she'd just said when suddenly Adrius's eyes went hard and blazing. The next thing she knew, he was backing her against the table, one hand at her waist and the other tangling in her hair as he crushed their lips together.

Heat rolled through Marlow like thunder. It was as if every touch and lingering gaze had built and built between them like storm clouds until at last, now, the sky broke open, pouring down on them like a sudden, devastating tempest.

It swept her up, driving every scrambled thought from her mind except the one that told her she had wanted this for almost as long as she'd known him, that she had spent every moment until this one fighting as hard as she could not to give in to it. But now it seized hold of her and Marlow forgot why she'd ever wanted to resist.

Her feet left the floor as Adrius lifted her onto the table, fitting himself between her legs. Marlow hauled him closer, clinging to him with a kind of desperation that should have felt shocking. She wanted him closer still, wanted the heat of him pressed flush against her, wanted to keep him there.

One of his hands was bunched in her skirt. The other trembled as he cupped her face.

It was that tiny quiver that struck Marlow like a hex. Her mind caught up to her. Clenching her fist in the fabric of his suit, she gave him one hard shove, breaking the kiss.

Adrius stumbled back.

They stared at each other in the dark, both of them catching their breath. Adrius's suit was in utter disarray, his hair mussed and his eyes dark. Everything about the sight of him begged Marlow to pull him in for another kiss, even as horror flooded her. She felt sick with the knowledge of what she had just done.

She had *ordered* Adrius to kiss her.

"I—" Adrius started.

Before he could say anything else, the door of the office flew open and Aurelius strode into the parlor.

He stopped, arching an eyebrow as he took in the sight of them. With that expression, Marlow suddenly saw the resemblance between him and his son. "I see that I'm interrupting."

TWENTY

If Marlow weren't so terrified, she would have been mortified. She scrambled off the table, yanking her skirt down.

"We were just—" Adrius began.

"Having a tryst in my parlor?" Aurelius suggested. "I can see that."

"Father—" Adrius tried again.

"Leave us," Aurelius said. His gaze bored into Marlow.

She hesitated. The last thing she wanted to do was leave Adrius alone with someone likely to issue orders. If he commanded Adrius to tell him the truth, their entire ruse would be over. She couldn't risk it.

"Adrius," Aurelius said, still looking at Marlow. "Leave us."

A tremor shook Marlow's spine as she held herself perfectly still.

Adrius tensed beside her. "What are you—"

"I said," Aurelius spat. "Get. *Out.*"

Even if Adrius had wanted to defy his father, the curse would not allow it. It forced him from Marlow's side and through the door. Marlow didn't dare take her gaze off Aurelius to look at the expression on Adrius's face.

The glass doors swung shut behind him.

Aurelius moved toward the windows. Marlow watched him, hardly daring to breathe, and heard the soft clink of glass as he poured two drinks from a crystal decanter sitting on an elegant bar cart. He offered one to Marlow.

"To soothe your nerves," he said.

Nothing short of a powerful sleep enchantment would soothe Marlow's nerves at this precise moment, but she took the glass. It was heavy, solid, and thick-rimmed.

Aurelius swirled his own glass so the liquid caught the light. "You can be under no misconception that I approve of your relationship with my son, but I must admit I do somewhat admire you, Miss Briggs."

Marlow did not know what to say to that. "Why?"

"To go through the world alone as you have . . . that takes courage. Especially when you know what a dangerous place it can be," Aurelius answered.

Marlow didn't miss the threat in his words. "Well, I guess I don't scare that easily."

"No, I suppose you don't," Aurelius replied with a hint of humor. "Although perhaps you'll agree that there comes a point where courage begins to look a lot like foolishness."

Marlow's gaze dropped to the glass in her hand. It occurred to her that Aurelius had not yet taken a sip of his drink. She tilted her own so that it caught the light and noticed a faint, glittering tinge.

It was cursed.

"Shouldn't we get back downstairs?" Marlow suggested, her voice coming out just a little desperate. "Everyone will wonder where you've gone."

"Oh, I wouldn't worry about that," Aurelius replied. "I doubt anyone will miss us. Let's toast, shall we?" He raised his glass. "To courage. And prudence."

Marlow clinked her glass against his, hard enough that some of the liquid sloshed onto his expensive rug.

"Oh!" Marlow exclaimed, falling to her knees to dab at the wet spot. She tucked her other hand into the hidden pocket of her dress. "I'm so sorry."

"Leave it," Aurelius said curtly. "I said—"

"*Melma!*" Marlow exclaimed. Magic swirled from the card clutched in her hand and turned the floor beneath Aurelius's feet into a thick, gluey mud.

Marlow did not wait to see his reaction. She ran.

Aurelius Falcrest just tried to curse me.

No matter how many times Marlow repeated the phrase in her head, she couldn't quite wrap her mind around it.

But even in her state of utter disbelief, Marlow knew one thing—she had to get out of Falcrest Hall.

"Marlow."

Of course Adrius was waiting for her, just outside the banquet hall. He looked agitated, his curls in disarray like he'd been running his hand through them. Or maybe that was from her hands.

"I can't—I have to—I have to go," she stuttered out, pivoting toward the entrance hall.

He grabbed her arm. "That kiss—"

"It was a mistake," she said desperately. "I'm sorry, I—I'm so—"

"A mistake?" he echoed. His eyes were wide, unguarded. "Marlow, that was—"

"I know," she said. "I panicked, I didn't mean to do it, I just wanted you to stop talking so your father wouldn't find out."

"My—" His expression hardened to stone. "You knew my father was there. It wasn't real, was it? You were just . . ."

"I have to go," Marlow said again. "I'm sorry, I—I'll explain later."

"No," Adrius said abruptly, releasing her. "There's nothing to explain. I get it."

He brushed past her to the terrace, where the rest of the party waited. Marlow's stomach churned with guilt. In his haste to get away from her, Adrius nearly bowled into Vale, who was headed toward the doors. Marlow watched as they exchanged a brief word before Adrius shook him off and threaded through the crowd. Vale watched him go, his brows pinched in concern.

Marlow turned back to the entrance hall. She couldn't just walk through the front door the way she'd come in. There was no doubt in her mind that every single member of the Falcrest staff had been instructed to detain her on sight. She could try climbing out a window, but she'd still need to get beyond the gates, and there was no way she was scaling them in her dress.

"Marlow," a warm voice greeted her. Marlow whirled to find Vale in front of her. "I just saw Adrius in an uncharacteristically foul mood. You two didn't quarrel, did you?"

"Something like that," Marlow replied.

"Well, Falcrests can be awfully . . . intractable," Vale said delicately.

Marlow shook her head. "It was my fault."

Vale smiled gently. "I'm sure you two will work it out. No need to let it spoil your night."

A sudden thought occurred to her—maybe she *could* walk out the front door. Falcrest's guards wouldn't try to detain her in front of a witness. It would cause too many unseemly questions.

"Actually, I need to be getting home," she said.

"Well, then, please let me walk you out," Vale offered. "I was planning on slipping out myself—my duty here is done and I find my tolerance for socializing rapidly declines after twenty-one bells."

"Thank you, that would be—most appreciated."

Vale offered his arm and Marlow took it, unable to hide her relief and hoping he would just chalk it up to a desire to avoid any awkwardness with Adrius.

As they made their way down to the atrium, Marlow wondered what Vale would do if she told him the truth—not about Adrius and the curse and the kiss, but about Aurelius and the cursed cup of wine. About the fact that she was more and more certain that he had something to do with Cassandra's disappearance. Why attempt to curse Marlow otherwise? Why try so hard to intimidate her at dinner?

It was unlikely Vale would believe her, of course, but if she somehow managed to convince him, what would he do? Would he want revenge for his former chevalier? Or would he, like everyone else in this city, be forced to let it go, to look away because Aurelius Falcrest was too rich and too powerful to face consequences?

Marlow wanted to think that Vale would do what was right. But it was hard to believe it.

"How are you getting home?" Vale asked once they were outside the gates of Falcrest Hall, winding down the long path to the boathouses. "Shall I summon a canal boat?"

Marlow wasn't sure she *should* go home. Would she be safe there? There was the looming threat of the Copperheads, and the possibility that, having been thwarted in his attempt to curse her at Falcrest Hall, Aurelius could send someone to wait for her at home.

Evergarden wasn't safe. Neither was the Marshes.

"I'll take a cable car," Marlow said, and bid him good night.

She needed somewhere off the map entirely. Somewhere no one would know where to look for her. Somewhere with a fortress of magical wards, enough magic to make her all but untraceable.

There was only one person Marlow knew outside of Evergarden with that kind of magic.

Marlow hurried to the edge of the pier, wishing she had her jacket so she could pull her hood over her head. Her aubergine-and-turquoise dress was far too flashy and fine to go unnoticed in this part of the city, but there was nothing she could do about that. At least she could be fairly certain that Falcrest hadn't had her followed—even if he'd put a tail on her, between the cable car and the two flatboat taxis weaving a circuitous route through the industrial district, she'd long since lost them.

She waved down a flatboat as it approached along the canal.

"Cannery Dock, please," Marlow said as it pulled up to the pier.

The flatboat cut through the water and Marlow sat, clenching her hands in her skirt and praying to the Ever-Drowning Mangrove that this wasn't the worst idea she'd ever had.

But if there was anyone with the kind of magic that could hide Marlow from the most powerful man in the city, it was the Black Orchid. And while Marlow didn't exactly trust them, they were working against the Falcrests and hadn't tortured anyone or tried to curse Marlow, so that was three points in their favor.

Viatriz had told Marlow at the Monarch Theater that she could find her at the Mudskipper. Marlow just had to hope she could convince Viatriz to help her.

The boat pulled to a stop before Marlow was ready. She paid the fare and stepped unsteadily onto Cannery Dock, anticipation buzzing under her skin as the taxi rowed away.

The night air had cooled, but the shallow, marshy water was still warm enough to let off trails of steam that settled in thick clouds. They made the green dock lights look wan and ghostly. Beneath the cackling song of the bullfrogs, Marlow could hear the quiet splash of large shapes moving beneath the dark waters of the canal. Crocodiles, most likely.

At the mouth of the pier, a form appeared in the mist. A human form.

Marlow froze. The figure stepped toward her, and in the thin light of the moon, Marlow saw the dark-red markings on her face.

TWENTY-ONE

Marlow trembled as Caito unholstered a black hilt from her hip. With a flick of her wrist, a metal rod erupted from the hilt, glowing with magic.

Marlow took a shaking step back. She knew what this was—a far more dangerous version of the same tool that sat locked behind the counter at the Bowery. A memory harvester.

"You've been poking your nose where it doesn't belong," Caito said. "You really shouldn't have done that. I'm afraid we can't permit you to keep walking around, knowing what you know."

Dread writhed in Marlow's gut. "What is it you think I know?"

Caito smiled. "Very cute that you think you can get information out of an expert interrogator."

"Worth a try, right?" Actually, Marlow was just stalling, trying to scrape together an escape plan.

"This really doesn't need to be difficult," Caito said. "Just let me take some of those pesky memories off your hands, and we can both be on our way."

Marlow stepped back. "Like how you took Montagne's memories?"

"Montagne made things difficult," Caito replied. "You won't do that, will you, Marlow?"

"And my mother?" Marlow couldn't keep the fury from her voice. "Did she make things difficult, too?"

Caito's eyes flashed. "Your mother stole from us."

"What do you call what the Falcrests did to *get* those spellbooks in the first place?" Marlow asked. "How does one family get control of such a vast collection of magical knowledge? By asking nicely?"

"All right," Caito said, advancing, "I guess you're going to make things difficult."

The only escape that didn't involve submerging herself in canal muck was past Caito and up the stairs to the street level. In her dress pocket, Marlow had three spellcards—a Rebounding spell, a Blinding hex, and a Ring of Fire spell.

Caito leapt toward her.

"*Accendere!*" Marlow cried, flinging the ring of fire toward Caito.

Caito dove out of the way of the flames, just barely avoiding getting singed—but enough to clear Marlow's path. Pulse pounding in her head, Marlow launched herself up the stairs.

From behind her, Caito choked out, "*Spianare!*"

The stairs beneath Marlow's feet flattened into a smooth ramp. Marlow pitched forward, her feet flying out from under her. She hit the ramp hard and slid back down where Caito waited. Twisting around, Marlow kicked out, landing a hard blow to Caito's shin. Caito buckled against the wall. Marlow scrambled to her feet, but Caito seized a handful of her skirt and threw her back to the ground.

Marlow landed hard, biting her own tongue. Her head swam.

"It didn't have to come to this," Caito said, standing over her. "You shouldn't have gone digging for secrets."

Marlow was too dizzy to speak, staring up at the thick, dark clouds swallowing the knife-thin moon. Caito knelt over her, one hand gripping Marlow's jaw like a vise. She held her head still as she lowered the harvester to Marlow's temple. Marlow thrashed against her hold, scrabbling fruitlessly at Caito's arms.

"No!"

Caito wrenched Marlow's head to the side. Her cheek scraped against the rough ground. Her breath punched out of her in labored, panicked bursts. The shining back of a spellcard glinted on the ground a few feet from Marlow's face. One that had slipped out of her pocket when Caito threw her.

Seized with desperation, Marlow flailed her arm out to try to grab it.

Caito touched the harvester to Marlow's temple. It flared hot and bright with magic.

Marlow stretched her arm until she felt it would break and closed the spellcard between two fingers. She nudged it over. The rebounding spell.

"*Invertire!*" she gasped, just as the harvester plunged its magic into her head.

Images flashed through her mind, alien and disorienting. They moved too quickly for her to make sense of them, faces and snatches of conversation rippling and dissipating like smoke.

These were memories, Marlow realized. When she'd used the Rebounding spell, the memory harvester had shown her Caito's memories.

Marlow was drowning in a sea of them—flashes of Caito training as a Zanne Rosse, Aurelius's stern face, the gilded rooms of Falcrest Hall, the dizzying concourse of Falcrest Library.

And then Armant Montagne's face, struck with fear. Marlow reached for the memory like a life raft, and instead of fading away like the others, Montagne's face flickered into sharper relief.

"I didn't tell her anything!" Montagne cried, panicked. Even in his terror, Marlow could see this was a different Montagne—one still in full possession of his faculties. His eyes were clearer, his face fuller than the skeletal old man she'd found in the swamp.

The memory was through Caito's eyes, so Marlow didn't see her, but she heard her reply. "She knew about the grimoire."

"I didn't tell her," Montagne insisted. "She already knew about it when she came to me."

"Where is she?"

"I don't know! I gave her the grimoire and got out of there."

"Stop wasting my time."

Before Montagne could reply, Caito thrust the memory harvester against his temple. Montagne let out a terrible scream, his face twisting grotesquely.

The memory shifted. A woman wearing the black uniform of a chevalier stood on a bridge looking down at the water, her back to Caito. Marlow recognized the golden curls gathered into a braid over one shoulder, the slope of her broad but slender shoulders, even the way she stood with one hip cocked up.

"You're too late," Cassandra said without turning around.

"Where is it, Briggs?" Caito demanded. "Does the Black Orchid have it?"

Cassandra's shoulders tightened.

"Oh yes, I know who you're working for," Caito said. "I know enough to get you locked up for life. Tell me where the grimoire is and maybe we can make a deal."

"I destroyed it."

"This isn't one of your little cons, and I'm not a mark," Caito spat. "You didn't destroy the grimoire—you couldn't have. The protective enchantments—"

"It wasn't easy," Cassandra said, turning to face Caito at last. "But it had to be done."

In the moonlight, Marlow could see the markings—black veins creeping up her mother's wrists, just like she'd seen on Armant Montagne.

"Don't lie to me," Caito snapped. "The Black Orchid wanted *Ilario's Grimoire* for a reason, and it wasn't to destroy it."

"Has it occurred to you that the Black Orchid and I don't agree on everything? As far as I'm concerned, no one should have that kind of power. Not them, and certainly not Aurelius Falcrest." She stepped toward Caito, the moonlight slashing a pale line across her face. "I know what he's already done. I know what he has hidden in Wisteria Grove."

There was a pause before Caito spoke. "I'm sure I have no idea what you're talking about."

Her voice was perfectly flat, but her hesitation said everything—Cassandra had rattled her.

"I wasn't about to risk my life stealing a spellbook from the most powerful man in the city without a little insurance," Cassandra said. "If Falcrest wants to make sure his secret stays secret, you'll let me go. Forget about the grimoire—we'll all pretend it was destroyed two centuries ago like the story goes."

"Or," Caito replied, igniting the memory harvester, "I can pry that secret from your mind, and then track down whoever it is who told you and pry it from their mind."

Cassandra squared her shoulders. "You can try." She reached for her spellcards.

Caito was quicker. She flicked a wrist, and a dart shot out of her leather gauntlet. It struck Cassandra's chest. A dark-green miasma exploded out of it, enveloping Cassandra. For a moment Marlow couldn't see her.

The cloud dissipated, revealing Cassandra stumbling back.

"What did you do to me?" Cassandra demanded, coughing. She could hardly keep herself upright.

"Disorientation hex," Caito replied coolly. "It'll wear off. So just stay still, and don't—"

But Cassandra was already backing up, crashing against the flimsy bridge railing. It groaned under her weight, and when Cassandra tried to lever herself up against it, it gave way with an earsplitting metal shriek.

She plummeted down, down, down into the dark water below.

Caito leaned over the broken railing to stare at the ripples in the water. It was silent as she waited one minute, two, three. Cassandra didn't surface.

Caito looked down at the Falcrest signet ring on her hand and twisted it once. In a blink, she was no longer standing on the bridge, but back inside Falcrest Hall.

The memory dissolved. In its place, Marlow stared up at Caito's grimacing face.

Thunder roared through the sky. Dark clouds burst open in a sudden deluge.

"You . . . you killed her," Marlow gasped over the pounding rain.

"You should learn from your mother's mistakes, Marlow," Caito said. "Don't end up food for the crocodiles like her."

Fury ignited in Marlow's gut, consuming her fear. Her mother was dead, and Marlow wanted someone to *pay*.

She reached for her last spellcard, squeezing her eyes shut. "*Oscurare!*"

Light blazed behind Marlow's eyelids. When she blinked them open, Caito was clutching at her own eyes. The memory harvester clattered to the ground.

Marlow reached up, scrabbling for Caito's hand. She grasped it tightly, yanking it away from Caito's face at an awkward angle, and used the momentary advantage to grab hold of the Falcrest signet ring and twist it.

Caito vanished.

Marlow heaved out a labored breath. The enchanted stone inside the signet ring had transported Caito back to Falcrest Hall. Where soon, the Blinding hex would wear off, and Caito would come back for Marlow and finish the job she'd started.

Numbly, Marlow rolled over, pushing herself onto her hands and knees. Something glinted in the mud a few feet away. Marlow picked it up—the moon and sun bracelet Adrius had given her. She pocketed it and then limped to the end of the dock to switch on the light to signal for a taxi. Wrapping an arm around her throbbing ribs, she waited in her rain-soaked dress.

A question pulled at her mind like the tug on a fisherman's line. She sensed it below the churning waters of her thoughts, waiting for her to reel it in and gut it open.

She pushed aside the shocking, devastating grief of her mother's death. Set it down, shut it behind a door and backed away, past the horror of Caito's memories, the violence of their fight. She walked herself all the way back to the moment she had stepped onto the dock and found Caito waiting for her there.

The question surfaced, squirming and gasping for an answer.

How had Caito found her?

No one had known where Marlow was going. *She* hadn't even known her destination until after she'd left Falcrest Hall, and she hadn't told a single soul. Caito couldn't have used a tracking spell on her, either— Marlow was warded against them.

If she didn't figure out how Caito had found her, and quickly, then it would only happen again. And Marlow was pretty sure she wasn't going to survive a third encounter with the most powerful family in Caraza.

A water-taxi pulled up to Marlow's dock as she grasped for an answer that made sense. She boarded in a daze, and only realized the boat hadn't started moving when the driver huffed out an impatient "Destination?"

"Sorry," Marlow stuttered. "Uh—"

She sucked in a sharp breath. She *had* told someone where she was going tonight. She'd told the water-taxi driver.

Somehow, Caito must have been listening in. *Spying* on her. She had to have planted something on Marlow, something enchanted with an Eavesdrop spell. Maybe someone had slipped it into her dress at dinner, or maybe Aurelius when he'd handed her the cursed wine, or . . .

Marlow's stomach dropped into her knees as she reached into her pocket and pulled out the delicate crescent moon bracelet.

Or someone had fastened it around her wrist and it had stayed there all night. Hiding in plain sight like a crocodile in the shallows. Like the truth that Marlow had been too stupid to see.

Adrius had betrayed her.

TWENTY-TWO

Marlow staggered back to her flat, fury and panic roiling through her body. Toad leapt down from the kitchen counter to greet her, butting her head against Marlow's knees and letting out a warbling meow. With shaking hands, Marlow held out the delicate silver bracelet. Toad sniffed at it and then her eyes lit up pearlescent blue.

Marlow flinched back and threw the bracelet across the room as if it had grown claws. Her knees went out from under her. Toad had only confirmed what Marlow had figured out on her own—the bracelet was enchanted with an Eavesdrop spell. She shut her eyes and gasped in a breath, palm pressed to her mouth.

Maybe Adrius hadn't known what the bracelet was. Maybe he'd been coerced to plant it on her. Or ordered.

But she couldn't shake the feeling that this made a sick sort of sense. It would explain why Adrius had been acting so erratic the last few days. His anger toward her, the cutting remarks. He must have realized Marlow was looking into his family. And while Adrius might play the rebellious son when it suited him, deep down he was still a Falcrest.

There was a knock at her door, loud and urgent enough to startle her. Marlow scrambled for a spell, any spell she could use to defend herself.

"Who is it?" she called, her voice hoarse and shaking.

"Minnow, it's me." Adrius's words came muffled from the other side of the door. "Let me in."

Marlow froze, her mind churning. Why would Adrius come here? He probably had no idea that Marlow had figured out what he'd done. Maybe his father had sent him, hoping to coax Marlow into another trap and finally finish what he'd started tonight.

She heard Adrius sigh. Something thumped softly against the door, like he was leaning on it. "I need to talk to you." Then quieter, "Please."

Maybe Adrius hadn't come alone. Maybe he was waiting for Marlow to open the door, Caito lurking in the shadows behind him.

Marlow crept to the door and curled her hand around the knob. She should tell him to leave. *She* should leave—grab Toad, climb through the window, and find a place to hide out until she could come up with a plan. That was the smart thing to do. The thing least likely to get her killed.

"Fine," Adrius snapped, with a bang like his palm hitting the door. "Shut me out again. It's not like I haven't gotten used to it by now."

Before Marlow could reconsider, she yanked open the door. Adrius stood on the threshold, wide-eyed, his chestnut curls disheveled like he'd been running his hands through them. A quick glance at the stairwell behind him revealed no sign of Caito, or anyone else. Fury poured through Marlow's veins. She seized Adrius by the front of his shirt and backed him up against the stairs.

"How could you do it?" she demanded, her voice coming out more desperate and broken than angry. "How could you do that to me?"

"What are you—" His wide, surprised expression sharpened as he took in her appearance. "You're hurt."

Marlow knew she was a mess, still soaking wet from the storm, dress torn, face smeared with mud and blood, eyes wild and frantic.

He cupped her face, the tenderness of his touch a counterpoint to the cold fury in his voice. "What happened? Who did this to you?"

Marlow jerked away from his touch, disbelief surging into rage. "Who do you *think* did this to me? What exactly did you imagine would happen when you helped your father *spy* on me? Did you think he was going to give me a stern lecture? Even you're not that naive."

"What?" Adrius said, his voice barely a whisper. He dropped his hand. "Are you saying he did this to you?"

"Don't, just—don't," Marlow said. "I know the bracelet was enchanted. I know Caito and your father have been listening in on me. I know that's how Caito found me tonight. And earlier, with your father, the cursed wine—did you know what he was going to do?"

Disbelief and hurt rippled across his face. Marlow felt sick. He'd thrown her trust back in her face once before. She should have known better than to make that mistake a second time.

When he spoke, his voice was a harsh rasp. "You really think I would hurt you? That I could *ever* hurt you? How—how could you think that?"

"Because I don't know who you really are!" The words burst out of her, and Marlow realized with alarm that she was on the brink of tears.

Adrius's jaw clenched, his eyes burning. "You're the *only* one who knows who I really am."

"Stop it." She balled her fists in her sopping skirt, trembling. As if she could squeeze out all the parts of her that had ever let him close. "Just—tell me the truth, Adrius."

The words hung between them.

Adrius swallowed. "Is that an order?"

It had slipped out by accident. A desperate, broken plea—not a command. She could take it back.

But she had to know. She had to know before the not-knowing killed her. Before the jaws of the beast closed on her, before the storm swept her up and drowned her, before this city and its secrets swallowed her and spat out some weak and mewling creature.

"Yes." She looked him in the eyes as the words left her lips, and she knew there was no going back. "I order you to tell me the truth."

Adrius looked at her like she'd slapped him. "You want the truth," he said in a quiet, glacial voice. "Fine. *Fine.* The truth is, if that bracelet was enchanted, I had no idea about it. I gave it to you because I wanted to give you something beautiful, something that might make you think of me even just for a fleeting moment, because the truth is you're all I think about, you're all I've *thought* about for the past year. The truth is, when I saw you standing in the lobby of the Monarch that night I barely even knew what to say to you—I just knew I couldn't let you disappear on me again. The truth is, I have been in *agony* these past few weeks pretending to have something I've wanted almost since the moment I met you. The truth is, Marlow, this whole time I never lied about the way I feel about you. Not once."

Marlow took a wavering step back, something like horror crashing over her. These were words she'd ached to hear for longer than she could admit, but they were wrong, all wrong, pouring out of Adrius like bitter, caustic poison.

"Well?" he snarled. "Aren't you going to say something? This is the truth, Marlow. This is what you wanted to hear."

"I—" Marlow choked out.

But the curse would not let Adrius stop, not yet. "Or did you want to hear that on my seventeenth birthday, I spent the entire night wishing you were there? That I left my own party to come see you because the only time I ever felt like myself was when I was with you. And the next day, I was cruel to you, because all I wanted to do was tell you, and I couldn't tell you because I knew what would happen. I knew what my father would say, what Amara would do, and the truth is, I was a coward."

Marlow couldn't breathe. Adrius wasn't lying—*couldn't* lie—but she didn't understand how this could be the truth, how she could have been so wrong about Adrius, about *everything*.

"Then you walked out of my life," he said quietly. "And I was the one left behind, feeling like the biggest fool in the world."

"Stop," Marlow said, finding her voice at last. "You don't have to say anything more, Adrius, I'm—"

"No." His gaze rose to meet hers, heated and dark. "You ordered me to tell you the truth, so here it is: When I got cursed, you were the *only* person I trusted."

The words suffocated her. They reached inside her. She knew that their truth led to another, the same way she knew it when a clue led to an answer.

This was her answer: He hadn't betrayed her. He had trusted her.

Maybe that's all love was. Handing someone a knife and trusting that they wouldn't cut your throat.

And if that was the case, maybe Marlow just wasn't capable of it.

"But you didn't trust me back," he said. "You still don't. Maybe I earned that, maybe I deserve it, but I can't—I can't do this. I can't pretend anymore. And I can't trust you. Not when you've just done the one thing you swore to me you wouldn't do."

"Adrius—"

"We're done," he said, his voice as hard and sharp as obsidian. "Whatever this was—a business arrangement, a fake relationship, a *case*—it's over."

"What about the curse?" she said, desperate. "If you don't break it before the next moon, it will be irreversible. What are you going to do?"

"I don't know," he answered. "But I know I don't want to see you again."

And because Marlow had ordered him to tell her the truth, she knew that this was it. She'd messed up. She *knew* she'd messed up. She'd done something so unforgivable, Adrius would rather risk his own life than put it in her hands again.

"Goodbye, Marlow." He cast her one last look, filled with hurt and longing, and pushed past her to descend the stairs.

"Adrius—" Marlow called after him. But there was nothing she could possibly say to make him change his mind, to forgive her. She could only watch him walk out of her life.

TWENTY-THREE

Marlow knocked on Swift's door at just past midnight, Toad wriggling under one arm, her heart hammering in her chest.

It was late; Swift might be asleep already. Or he was awake and still too angry to even look at Marlow.

The door creaked open and Marlow exhaled. Dim green-blue light splashed across Swift's familiar features. His eyes were bloodshot, his jaw tight, but at least he didn't slam the door in Marlow's face.

Toad launched herself out of Marlow's arms and slipped through the door before Marlow could speak. Concern shadowed Swift's gaze as he took in her injuries and her torn, muddy dress.

Wordlessly, he opened the door wider and stepped back.

Something inside her crumbled at that one simple gesture, and before Marlow knew what was happening, her eyes flooded with tears and she crashed, gratefully, into him.

"Hey," he said, folding his arm around her. "You're safe. It's okay."

She hadn't cried in so long. Not since those first few days following her mother's disappearance, when she'd felt more abandoned and alone than ever before. But she felt the tears rising in her like floodwaters, and she had no strength left to dam them up. They spilled out, shaking her like windows rattling in a storm.

Swift just drew her closer and nudged the door closed behind her.

Wiping the salt from her eyes, Marlow said, "Are you still mad at me?"

His hand was warm and solid on her back. "Yeah. And I'll still be mad at you in the morning, so we can fight about it then."

Marlow choked out a laugh that was half a sob as Swift led her to his bedroom and handed her clean clothes to sleep in. She pulled them on, wincing at the twinge in her ribs when she lifted her dress over her head. When she was done, she crawled into Swift's bed and curled up on her side, soothed by the sound of his voice from the kitchen as he chattered to Toad.

Every part of her ached, from her bloody knees to her grief-filled heart, and she wasn't sure if she deserved Swift's love and care, but she clung to it anyway—the one thing that this ravenous city hadn't taken from her yet.

Marlow startled awake in the blackness of Swift's room. The only sound was Swift's soft, slow breath from the other side of the bed, and occasionally Toad's little snores from where she was squished improbably between them.

Marlow had been dreaming of her mother, but the dream slipped through her mind like silt through hands. Only one image lingered. It was herself, gazing into a mirror and seeing her mother's face staring back at her. A bird with feathers like flames perched on the palm of her hand.

She knew what memory her dream had plucked that image from. It was from a day not long after their move into Vale Tower.

She had been standing in her bedroom when she heard her mother's voice call from the living room.

"Come here, Minnow," Cassandra said. "I want to show you something."

Marlow poked her head out the door, peering into the living room.

Her mother was standing behind her writing desk, hands resting on the back of the chair. "What is it?"

Cassandra held out her hand. "Come here."

Marlow obeyed. A mirror with a thin bronze frame hung above the desk. Cassandra put her hands on Marlow's shoulders, positioning her so that she was looking into the mirror dead-on.

"What do you see?"

"What do you mean?" Marlow asked, impatient. "It's a mirror. I see myself."

Cassandra let out a displeased huff. Sometimes she got into these strange moods, where she would look at Marlow, studying her face as if she was searching for something. Marlow never knew what. Traces of Marlow's father, maybe. A man Marlow had never known, a man who Cassandra had never spoken of.

"Watch this," Cassandra said, picking up a spellcard from the writing desk. "*Fantasma.*"

The illusion unfurled from the spellcard, shaping itself into a tiny kingfisher whose feathers were the color of a vivid sunset. Marlow held out her hand and the illusion came to perch on her fingers. It trilled out a little warble. It looked real, as real as anything else in their apartment. As real as Marlow.

But when she looked back into her reflection, all she saw was her empty outstretched hand.

Cassandra met her gaze in the reflection. "This is a Mirror of Truth. It reflects things as they are, not as they appear. It sees through illusion and disguise. So, what do you see?"

Marlow stared at her reflection and let out a slow breath. She saw herself as she was. A girl who wanted to make something of herself before the world could convince her she was insignificant. A girl who had never wanted to belong in the Marshes, who wasn't sure she belonged in this gilded tower, either. A girl who hoped for a better future, but never expected it.

She glanced up at her mother and saw that she was studying her own reflection in the mirror. What did Cassandra see?

It felt forbidden to even wonder. As close as they were, there was always a part of her mother that felt unreachable. She treated Marlow like a partner, a confidant, a sidekick—but only when it suited her. Even to Marlow, Cassandra was a cipher.

Marlow remembered gazing into the Mirror of Truth, knowing that for all the mirror's magic, it could never show her the truth of who her mother was. But it was then, standing beside her, each of them looking at the other's reflection, that Marlow wondered for the first time—did Cassandra even know?

She'd thought when her mother searched her face, she was looking for the parts of Marlow that belonged to her father. But maybe it wasn't that at all.

Maybe, all along, Cassandra had been looking at her daughter, trying to find herself.

The next morning, after Toad was fed and Marlow was dressed, sipping on a warm mug of tea—Swift had even given her his last chocolate-filled biscuit, which nearly made her start crying again—the whole story spilled out.

"I think," Marlow said when she was done recounting the last forty-eight hours, "I really messed up."

Swift snorted. "Really? Which part? When you tried to break into the office of the most powerful man in Caraza? When you accused a boy who is obviously, painfully in love with you of betraying you? When you used his curse against him after swearing that you wouldn't? When you did *all of this* without once coming to me for help?"

"You made it pretty damn clear you weren't interested in helping me anymore."

"I never said that and I never *will* say that," Swift said firmly. "I'll always have your back, Marlow. No matter how pissed off I get. You know that."

She did know that. It was why she'd come here last night, when she'd had nowhere else to go. And that was part of the problem, wasn't it? Because the deeper Marlow sank into the morass of this city and the people who controlled it, the deeper she pulled Swift in, too.

She couldn't help but think of her mother. While she might never know why Cassandra had done everything she'd done, she thought maybe she understood why she'd kept so many secrets. She hadn't wanted to pull Marlow into the mess she'd made. But maybe if Cassandra had understood her daughter better, she would've known it was impossible to keep Marlow from diving in headfirst.

"For what's it worth, I *am* sorry," Marlow said. "I'm sorry I dragged you into my mess. I'm sorry you're still in it. You're too good a person to leave me out in the cold, but maybe you should have. Then at least you'd be safe."

"You and I both know, there's no such thing as safe in this city," Swift said. "No matter what kind of danger you're in, I'll be right there next to you, okay? I never wanted you to leave me out of it. I just wanted you to *listen* to me."

"I can do that," Marlow said. At Swift's arched eyebrow, she amended, "I can *try* to do that." She blew out a breath and sank deeper into the chair. "What I did—Adrius is never going to forgive me. There's something wrong with me, isn't there?"

"Do you want an itemized list, or is this more of a yes or no question?"

Marlow glared.

"Look," Swift said, "I know you really well and I know you're not exactly the easiest person to get close to. You let people in only on your terms and you guard your secrets closely. But then you act like you have a right to everyone else's secrets. And the more you feel vulnerable to someone, the less you trust them. So you start looking for reasons not to."

Marlow looked away, her grip on the teacup tightening. She'd *asked* Swift for his opinion, after all. She could hardly complain that he'd given it.

"I'm not saying I blame you. I know better than most what this city can do to a person," Swift went on, his voice gentler now. "You put yourself in a lot of dangerous situations in pursuit of the truth, but when it comes to your heart? You do everything in your power not to risk it. And falling for a scion of the most powerful family in Caraza, whose father may or may not want you dead? Pretty much the riskiest move there is."

"And I fucked it all up," Marlow said.

"Yeah," Swift agreed. "Did you really think Adrius had betrayed you?"

Marlow blinked. "What do you—"

"Or did you just *want* to believe that?"

Marlow opened her mouth to spit out some reflexive reply and then closed it again to really think through what he was asking. Of course she didn't *want* to believe that Adrius had betrayed her. But it had been easy to jump to that conclusion because some part of her had been waiting for Adrius to hurt her again. Some part of her had expected it. Some part of her had felt *relieved*.

"You fucked it all up," Swift repeated. "I think, to you, that was the only option. Because what if it was real? Then you'd have to take the risk."

Marlow let out a dry laugh. Wasn't it the same reason Adrius had walked away from their friendship a year ago? He'd been too scared to confront the fact that she actually mattered to him, and all the risk that came with that.

"You ruined things with Adrius because that was the only way to stay in control of the situation."

Gods, Adrius had been right about her.

"This is why you never date anyone for longer than two weeks, isn't it?" Marlow said, nudging Swift's arm.

"We're not talking about my love life." His expression darkened. "What we *should* be talking about is what the hell you're going to do about the fact that the most powerful family in Caraza is out to get you."

Marlow had been trying not to think about that all morning.

"You can hide out here for now," Swift said. "But you're going to have to come up with a plan eventually. You're capable of a lot of things, Marlow, but I don't think even you can stop the Falcrests."

She met his gaze and knew they were both thinking the same thing—that *no* one could stop them.

A sharp rap on the front door echoed through the room.

They looked at each other, alarmed. There was only one—well, now two—people it could be, thanks to the wards that protected Swift's flat.

Swift moved toward the door quietly.

Whoever it was knocked again, more urgently. "Open up, Swift!"

"Orsella?" Swift said, exchanging a baffled look with Marlow.

"Who else?" came the gruff reply. "Open your godsdamned door before someone sees me."

Swift raised his eyebrows at Marlow. She gave a slight nod—Orsella could be trusted. Swift unlocked the door hurriedly and Orsella burst through it like she owned the place.

Her gaze instantly fell on Marlow. "Oh, good, thought I might find you here."

"You did?" Marlow said, more confused than ever. "Why?"

"To hide from the Copperheads," Orsella said, like this was obvious.

Swift and Marlow exchanged another look.

"You *are* aware that they're after you, right?"

Marlow blew out a breath. "I mean, what else is new?"

"No, you don't get it," Orsella said sharply. "This is not like before. Leonidas declared open season on you. *As in*, the Copperheads no longer give a swamp rat's ass about whose territory you're in or whose protection you're under. They want you dead, and if the Reapers want to kick up a fuss about it, then the Copperheads are ready to go to war over it."

"*What?*" Swift demanded. "They can't—"

"That goes for you, too," Orsella said, tipping her head at him. "Figured you already knew about it by now."

"I've been a little busy," Marlow grumbled. But she couldn't completely hide the fear that Orsella's words had struck into her heart. Before, the danger of the Copperheads had been confined to their own territory, but if what Orsella said was true, then nowhere in the Marshes was safe. The Copperheads would hunt them down and the Reapers would have two options—strike back and possibly incite an all-out gang war, or relinquish their protection and let the Copperheads do whatever they wanted to her. Neither option ended well, at least not for Marlow.

"You need to get out of the Marshes immediately," Orsella said. "Maybe the city altogether."

"Leave Caraza?" Marlow echoed. "You can't be serious."

"Marlow," Swift cut in quietly. "Maybe she's right. I mean—is there anyone left in this city who doesn't want you dead?"

Orsella glanced between them. "Look. I know someone. A smuggler, works fast and clean. It'll cost you a pretty pearl but he can get you out."

"And go *where*?" Marlow demanded.

"Vescovi?" Orsella suggested. "The Cortesian colonies? Anywhere that's not here."

Marlow closed her eyes, tried to picture it. Growing up in the Marshes, she used to imagine setting out on adventures, leaving the stinking, soggy city behind her. Seeing the snowcapped mountains of northern Vescovi, the lush rain forests of the southern Cortesian Empire. The endless grass sea of the Aristan frontier.

What was really holding her here anymore? Adrius was done with her. Swift would go with her—she knew that without having to ask. They could strike out together, find some corner of the world to be the home that Caraza could never be. Somewhere they could build a life on ground that didn't try to suck them down into the mud with every step.

"Face it, Briggs," Orsella said. There was an unfamiliar note of sympathy in her hoarse voice. "This city's done with you. Best to get out while you still can."

Marlow went to the window and looked out at the hot, thick clouds crouched low over the sluggish waterways. She knew what had happened to her mother now; she'd dredged the truth out of the mire. But the case was still unfinished. There were still more questions, more secrets to uncover.

She turned to Swift. "What do you think I should do?"

"I think you should get the hell out of this city as fast as you can," Swift answered without hesitation.

It was what her mother would have done. Take what you can get and get out while you can. That was the rule Cassandra had lived by.

"But I know you," Swift went on. "I know you'll never forgive yourself if you do. As annoying as it is, it's the thing I love about you, Marlow. You don't give up."

Marlow wasn't her mother. She lived by a different set of rules. A set of rules that said if there was a chance to bend one small part of this irredeemable world to her will, then she had to try. Even if it killed her.

Because if she didn't, if she surrendered to the cold-blooded apathy of this city, if she accepted selfishness as the only way to survive, then she might as well be dead.

She looked at Orsella. "Maybe this city is done with me, but I'm not done with it. My mother died knowing a secret about Aurelius Falcrest. Maybe it has the power to take him down and maybe it doesn't. But either way, I'm going to find out what it is."

Orsella was already shaking her head. "You still haven't learned your lesson about sticking your nose where it doesn't belong?"

"Guess not."

Swift cleared his throat. "Uh—what are you planning on doing, exactly?"

"Haven't figured that part out yet," Marlow admitted. "Right before she died, my mother said she knew what Falcrest was hiding in Wisteria Grove. That's at least a place to start."

"So what are you going to do, canvass the neighborhood?" Swift asked. "'Hi there, are your neighbors harboring any dark, potentially ruinous secrets for Aurelius Falcrest?' Even if that got you anywhere, you know the minute word gets back to Falcrest that you're poking around, Caito will come after you again."

"Swift's right," Orsella said. "No matter what you do or how careful you are, a man like Aurelius Falcrest is always going to be one step ahead of you."

Marlow had learned that, quite literally, the night before. She opened her mouth to say so, and then stopped, her mind tracing out the beginnings of an idea. A plan.

"You're right," she said, "and that's exactly where I want him to be."

TWENTY-FOUR

Marlow tapped her fingers impatiently on the side of the canal boat, waiting for Swift to reemerge through the gates of Falcrest Hall.

Under normal circumstances, he would not have been able to simply stroll inside, but with the entire staff bustling around to prepare for three nights of festivities to celebrate Amara's wedding, it had been easy enough to slip in amidst the scores of florists, caterers, entertainers, and backup staff.

Relief coursed through Marlow when she finally spotted Swift meandering down the stone pathway with his arms full of flowers. He passed the boathouse, making for the dock where Marlow's boat was moored.

He handed her the flowers and stepped onto the boat. Marlow raised her eyebrows at him. He gave her a grin and a thumbs-up, signaling he'd been able to confirm Caito was currently inside Falcrest Hall.

Now it was Marlow's turn.

"I can't stop thinking about the secret my mother knew about Falcrest," she said, toying with the bracelet on her wrist.

"You're going to drive yourself crazy," Swift replied.

"I know, but—Wisteria Grove. That's where mom said it was hidden—whatever *it* is."

"So?"

"I went through all my notes about my mother's disappearance,"

Marlow said. "And last night, I found something. She'd written down an address in Wisteria Grove. There wasn't any other information, but . . ."

"You think it's where Falcrest was hiding this secret?"

"Yes," Marlow replied. "I could be wrong. But if I'm right . . . I need to know. I'm going to go there, now."

"All right," Swift said. "But be careful."

She grinned, and slid the silver crescent moon bracelet off her wrist. It caught the late afternoon sun, gleaming.

As far as Caito and Aurelius knew, Marlow had never discovered the Eavesdrop spell Caito had cast on the bracelet. Which meant as long as Marlow had the bracelet on her, Caito would be listening. The Copperheads had been staking out her flat, so Marlow had asked Orsella to go and retrieve the bracelet, pretending she was going to the Bowery on business.

She really owed Orsella for that one. And for taking care of Toad while Marlow figured out what to do about the Copperheads.

And for the spellcard currently tucked in Marlow's pocket.

"You better make it out of this," Orsella had warned her, "because I've got a lot of favors to collect on."

Marlow dropped the bracelet into the canal.

"You think Caito bought it?" Swift asked as they both watched it sink. "You just *happened* to find the address to this place in your mother's things?"

There was no address, of course. Marlow had scoured through everything she had of Cassandra's countless times. There wasn't anything mentioning Wisteria Grove, and there never had been.

But Caito didn't know that.

Before Cassandra had learned how to con men out of their money, she used to steal it more directly—by picking pockets.

Once, when Marlow was young, she had asked Cassandra how she knew which pocket to steal from.

"It's easy," Cassandra had replied with a laugh. "You make them show you."

She'd taken Marlow to the Pavilion cable car station, a notorious hunting ground for cutpurses. She'd pointed out a man in the crowd and told Marlow to bump into him—the more conspicuous the better.

"When he walks away from you, watch him."

Marlow had done as asked, and sure enough, after the man was done yelling at her to watch where she was going, he patted his jacket pocket to check for his pearl purse, revealing exactly where he kept it. So when Cassandra walked up to him two minutes later pretending to ask for directions, she easily slipped her hand into the pocket while distracting him with a coquettish smile.

So, how do you find out the most closely kept secret of the most powerful man in the city?

Easy: You make him show you.

Marlow looked across the canal to the gates of Falcrest Hall. "Guess we'll see."

It wasn't long at all before Marlow saw Caito's distinctive bright-green-striped hair as the woman slunk through the shadow of the gates.

"Here we go," Marlow said, pulling the spellcard out—the spellcard that had cost more than half her upfront fee from Adrius. "I'll meet you at Cannery Dock. If I'm not there in two hours—"

"Then I'll come find you," Swift said firmly.

She shook her head. "Swift—"

"Marlow."

Marlow swallowed down her objections. "All right. Fine." She held the spellcard out. "*Diventare ombra!*"

The glyphs around the edge of the spellcard lit up with magic. Marlow could feel it crackling over her skin. With a sudden jolt, Marlow was thrown out of her body, slamming against the side of the boat.

That's what it felt like, anyway. What had really happened was that the Shadowstep spell had turned Marlow into her own shadow. Her body still lay exactly where she had left it, inert. Swift would watch over her until Marlow returned.

As a shadow, Marlow couldn't speak or touch anything. It wasn't an invisibility spell—that was far beyond what Marlow could afford—but as long as she was careful, she could follow Caito undetected. She moved along the dock to the exterior wall of the boathouse, where Caito had just entered. With the afternoon sun low in the sky, there were plenty of shadows for Marlow to hide in.

Caito unmoored one of the Falcrest canal boats. Marlow darted into the boathouse and slipped into the floor of the boat. Just as she had hoped when she'd spun her little story, Caito headed up Crystal Canal, the northwestern spoke of the five canals that radiated out from Evergarden. Wisteria Grove was one of the handful of residential neighborhoods in the Outer Garden District, where the upper classes who had not quite achieved the status of the noblesse nouveau lived.

Marlow's first thought about what Falcrest could be hiding there was that it was perhaps a mistress, but she'd quickly thrown out that theory. Lots of powerful men had mistresses—that was hardly the kind of secret that could destroy him. Even an illegitimate child seemed unlikely.

It had to be something worse—worse than bastard children, worse than possessing banned spellbooks, worse than the myriad other things men like Aurelius Falcrest got away with every day in Caraza.

Caito finally moored the boat next to a nondescript house, nearly identical to the others along the canal. It was large, though nowhere near as grand as any of the homes in Evergarden, with a wide porch and an upper gallery, both trimmed with thin white columns and gleaming railings.

Caito stepped onto the dock and swung open the wrought-iron front gate, striding past the row of neat hedges that bracketed the front steps.

Marlow slipped through the rails of the gate and stayed back in the hedges as Caito stomped up to the front door and unlocked it with a wave of a spellcard. She waited until Caito had stormed inside and slammed the door shut behind her before sliding through the tiny gap beneath the door.

The sight that greeted her was not what she expected. Caito stood on the threshold of an elegant sitting room just off the front entrance. She was not alone. An older woman sat on a plush couch, pouring a cup of tea. She wore a flowing silk robe, her gray-streaked black hair pinned back with a gem-studded comb.

With a jolt, Marlow realized she recognized her. Her portrait hung in the atrium of Falcrest Hall.

Isme Falcrest. Adrius's mother.

"To what do I owe the pleasure of this visit, Caito?" Isme asked, lifting the delicate teacup to her lips.

"I don't have time for games," Caito snapped. "Who's been here, Isme? Who have you talked to?"

"Talked to?" Isme echoed. She let out a harsh laugh. "You must be joking."

"Do I look like I'm joking? Tell me who's been here."

"Only you, dear Alleganza," Isme simpered. "My sole visitor. Stay for some tea, won't you?"

"What about a girl?" Caito asked. "Nosy, blond, *highly* irritating?"

"No one," Isme said sharply. "Just like there's been no one for years."

Years? Adrius said his mother had been out of Caraza for the past decade. Could she really have been here all along? *Why?*

"Amara's wedding is this evening," Isme said, abruptly changing topic. "I saw it in the news."

"Isme—"

"I won't speak to anyone. I won't do anything. But please, *please*—I want to see her. It isn't right for a mother to miss her daughter's wedding day." There were tears shining in Isme's eyes. The teacup shook in her hands. "Ask him, Caito."

"Aurelius made his decision," Caito replied flatly. "You're too much of a risk, especially now with the City Solicitor breathing down his neck."

Isme let out a half-crazed laugh. "A *risk*? A woman compelled to follow every order she's given is a *risk*? Aurelius must be losing his touch."

Marlow was suddenly very glad she couldn't speak, because she didn't think she'd be able to stop herself from gasping.

Isme rose to her feet, a ferocity in her dark eyes that reminded Marlow of Adrius. "The man that you so happily serve took *everything* from me. He stole me from my family, forced me into a marriage I never wanted, used me to pillage my family's fortune, and then, when I bore him two children, he took them from me, too. I ask—no, beg—for this one thing. I just want to see my daughter get married."

Marlow was frozen, unable to tear her gaze away from Isme.

She was cursed. Aurelius had used the Compulsion curse on her—*years* ago, it seemed, to acquire her family's fortune.

This was the secret he thought would ruin him.

Marlow took in the heartbroken look on Isme's face, the expression crumpling her features. It was the same expression that had been on Adrius's face when he'd first told her about the mother who had abandoned him. Marlow hadn't thought she could loathe Aurelius more than she already did, but this—it was unspeakably cruel.

Caito was unmoved. "If anyone comes knocking on this door, you will not open it, you will not speak to them, you will contact me immediately, and I'll deal with them."

She turned before Isme could choke out a reply and then stopped short, her eyes pinned to Marlow's shadow on the wall. Marlow moved back toward the door, but she was too late.

Caito swore. "*Briggs.*"

Marlow did the only thing she could—she fled.

TWENTY-FIVE

"*Aurelius Falcrest cursed* his own wife" were the first words out of Marlow's mouth once Swift had broken the Shadowstep spell.

"What?"

"That's what he's been hiding," Marlow said, pacing down the dock. "That's what my mother knew. That's what—" She stopped. Caito had mentioned the City Solicitor. So had Amara, last night at the wedding eve banquet.

If *this* was what the City Solicitor was investigating, then maybe Amara had been right. Maybe Aurelius was afraid the investigation could bring him down.

She remembered Aurelius's dismissive reply. *Our family's future is secure, I've made sure of that.*

Marlow clapped a hand over her mouth, her stomach lurching.

"Swift," she said, her voice shaking. "I think I know who cursed Adrius."

"You think Falcrest—" Swift cut himself off. "Why would he do that?"

"Because," Marlow said, "he needed a contingency plan. The City Solicitor has him under investigation—if he found evidence of what Aurelius did to Isme, he would lose control of the Falcrest family. No matter what else he's done, the other Families wouldn't let him get away with cursing one of their own."

Realization dawned on Swift. "So he cursed Adrius so that even if he was forced to step down from the family, he'd still remain in control."

"That also must be why he's rushing Amara's wedding," Marlow said. "He has to make sure it happens before the other Five Families find out what he did. He's going to use Adrius to keep hold of the Falcrest fortune, and use Amara to take control of the Vales, just like he did to the Delvigne family. Then he'll really be untouchable."

The wedding. That was her chance—maybe her *only* chance—to warn Adrius. Caito had seen Marlow's shadow. She knew Marlow knew about Isme. Once Aurelius was informed, Marlow's chances of getting Adrius alone long enough to tell him the truth would drop from slim to nonexistent.

Marlow's only shot was to get to the wedding and talk to Adrius before his father took drastic measures to keep him away from her.

Less than two weeks remained before Adrius's two moons were over and the curse became permanent.

"I have to go," she said to Swift. "I have to warn Adrius."

"You mean go to Amara Falcrest's wedding?" Swift asked. "Where Aurelius himself will be?"

"I'm not going to get another opportunity," Marlow said. "Aurelius will order Adrius not to speak to me. Or maybe even keep him locked up the way he did to Isme."

Swift shook his head. "This is such a godsdamn terrible idea, but fine. We'll go back to Falcrest Hall."

"We?" Marlow echoed. "I'm not getting you involved in this." Immediately, Swift tried to interrupt, but she spoke over him. "Swift, right now you can't even go home, and that's *my* fault. The Copperheads are going to try to hunt us both down, and I need to know that you're going to be safe."

"Where exactly am I going to go that's safe?"

Marlow already had a plan. "The Mudskipper Teahouse. It's where Viatriz told me to go if I ever wanted to contact the Black Orchid. It's one of their fronts, I guess. Go there, tell them the truth about what happened to my mother, and ask them to give you their protection from the Copperheads."

"Can we even trust them?"

"Honestly, I'm not sure," Marlow admitted. "But I know the Copperheads are scared of them, I know they have the magic to protect you, and I don't see another option."

Was Marlow just sending Swift into danger once again? Viatriz had convinced her the Black Orchid didn't mean her harm, but what would they think when someone they'd never met before showed up at their secret hideout asking for their help?

"Tell them I sent you," Marlow said. "Tell them in exchange for safe haven, I'll give them information that could take down the Falcrest family. Once I warn Adrius about his father, I'll come meet you and tell them about Isme."

Swift still looked wary. He blew out a slow breath. "Okay. But I'm *only* doing this because if you get yourself into trouble with Aurelius Falcrest, the Black Orchid might be the only people who can help you. And since I'm being so agreeable, it would be nice if, as a personal favor to me, you tried not to get yourself killed."

"Deal," Marlow said, holding out her hand.

Swift ignored it, wrapping his arm around her in a fierce hug. "I'm serious, Marlow. You're my best friend. If anything ever happened to you, I don't know what I'd do with myself."

"You're my best friend, too," Marlow said, squeezing him back. "Good luck."

"*I can't thank* you enough for coming with me," Gemma said as she and Marlow approached the entrance of Falcrest Hall. "I don't know if I could have faced today alone."

"What are friends for?" Marlow replied, scanning the crowd ahead of them.

It seemed half the city of Caraza had garnered an invite to Amara's wedding. Photographers lined the entrance of Falcrest Hall, ready to snap pictures of the arriving noblesse nouveau in all their finery.

Gemma reached out and smoothed the sleeve of Marlow's borrowed dress. It was bright turquoise with shimmering gold accents, and just as ostentatious as the rest of Gemma's wardrobe. Gemma herself had opted for a gown that faded from deep plum to pale rose, her hair gathered off her neck in lustrous, shining cinnamon coils.

"Adrius isn't going to be able to take his eyes off you," Gemma said.

Marlow laughed darkly. She hadn't exactly gone into detail about how Adrius had left things between them. "If he can even bring himself to look at me."

Gemma looked wistful. "I just thought . . . well, it seemed like what you two had was . . ."

"What?" Marlow asked.

Gemma met her gaze. "Real."

Marlow could only laugh again. With a stab of guilt she remembered Adrius's words.

I never lied about the way I feel about you.

She shook off the thought. That wasn't why she was here.

Gemma dazzled the photographers and onlookers as they made their way up the steps. Marlow concentrated on not betraying her apprehension at being in the same room as Aurelius Falcrest. Before she knew it, they were sweeping through the grand double doors to the atrium.

The wedding guests mingled in the grand, open space of the atrium, sipping glasses of wine and trading gossip about the other attendees. Marlow could feel their eyes rake over her, whispers rippling across the room at the sight of her on the arm of yet another scion. No doubt this would fuel accusations of Marlow being a ruthless social climber.

"Come on, I see Silvan," Gemma said, leading Marlow by the arm toward the back of the room.

Silvan stood aloof in a silver suit near the entrance of the ballroom, where the ceremony would take place. As far as Marlow could tell, he was alone.

"What is she doing here?" Silvan asked, lip curling with displeasure as Gemma and Marlow reached him.

"She's my date," Gemma replied.

Silvan gave her a withering look. "I didn't realize your taste in girls was as terrible as Adrius's."

"Where is he?" Marlow asked, heart pounding.

Silvan shrugged. "Not coming."

"What?" Marlow felt winded. "Why? This is his sister's wedding!"

"You didn't hear?" Silvan asked, a little haughtily. "He left Falcrest Hall last night. Spent the night in one of the guest quarters in Vale Tower. He basically renounced the Falcrest name and refuses to speak to his father."

Gemma looked as shocked as Marlow felt. "Why would he do that?"

Silvan shrugged again, looking at Marlow. "He didn't want to say. I figured it had to do with *you*."

"I thought you said you weren't together anymore?" Gemma asked.

"We're not." Whatever the reason for Adrius's departure from Falcrest Hall, it was a good thing. It meant he was out of his father's reach—for now. "Is he at Vale Tower now?"

"Probably," Silvan replied. "My father was trying to convince him to come to the wedding, going on and on about how important family is, but I'm not sure how—" He broke off, gaze going to the doors. "Well. Looks like whatever Father said worked."

Marlow followed his gaze, her chest tightening at the sight of Adrius on the threshold, framed against the vermilion sky. He wore an onyx-black suit with a waistcoat patterned in gold. Every inch of him was immaculate, from his chestnut curls to his crisp collar to the implacable mask of his expression. He looked entirely, untouchably perfect—save the dark circles beneath his eyes.

Marlow was moving toward him before she'd even thought about what she was doing.

"Marlow!" a jovial voice boomed. Cormorant Vale emerged through the crowd, beaming.

Several heads turned toward her—including Adrius's. She couldn't interpret the expression that flashed across his face, only that it was closer to panic than joy.

Marlow turned her attention to Vale, dropping into a stiff curtsy and mustering a smile. "Congratulations on the wedding."

Vale beamed harder, and Marlow felt a pang of pity. Vale just wanted his son's happiness. He had no idea what Falcrest was plotting, what this marriage would end up doing to the Vale family. Unless Marlow found a way to stop him.

"I'm so glad you could be here to celebrate with us," Vale said.

"Me too," Marlow agreed hastily, moving toward Adrius again. "I just—I really need to talk to . . ."

Vale glanced over to Adrius and then gave Marlow a twinkling look and a pat on the shoulder. "Ah, say no more."

Adrius was still watching Marlow as she approached.

"What the hell are you doing here?" he demanded.

Marlow sensed more than a few pairs of eyes on them. "I need to talk to you. Now. Alone."

“You shouldn’t be here,” Adrius said coldly.

“Adrius—”

“Excuse me,” a voice to Marlow’s left said in a chilly tone. “Are you Marlow Briggs?”

Marlow turned, her stomach sinking. Someone requesting her by name was not a good sign. Her gaze fell on a tall woman wearing Falcrest servant’s livery, blinking at Marlow expectantly.

“What do you want with her?” Adrius asked brusquely.

“The bride is requesting to speak with you,” the servant said. “I’ll escort you to the bridal suite.”

Marlow couldn’t think of a good reason why Amara would want to talk to her. Unless she knew everything her father had been up to, and was willing to finish the job herself.

Marlow slipped her hand into her pocket and touched the hilt of the knife strapped to her side. If this was an ambush, she would be ready.

“Let’s not keep her waiting,” the servant said impatiently. “Or cause a scene.”

Marlow turned to Adrius. “Please, Adrius. You know I wouldn’t have come if it wasn’t important.”

“Marlow—”

Before Adrius could say anything more, the servant took Marlow’s elbow and led her through the crowd and into the ballroom. They exited through a side door into a long corridor lined by mirrors, and then through a set of ornate double doors. They entered a lavish sitting room furnished in cream and rose gold. At the back of the room, in front of a huge, gilded mirror, stood Amara. She wore a gorgeous tiered ruby wedding dress beaded in gold. An ornate headdress balanced atop her head, her raven hair elaborately pinned up in shining curls. A small army of servants crowded around her, fixing her dress and accessories.

Her eyes, painted with gold, met Marlow’s in the mirror.

"Leave us," she said to the servants. They backed off at once and exited the room, along with the servant who had brought Marlow. Leaving the two of them alone.

"Congratulations on your wedding," Marlow offered.

Amara whirled, her skirt moving like a wave behind her, her eyes dark with anger. "Surely you know why I summoned you."

Dread dripped down Marlow's spine.

"I want to know exactly what you think you're doing at *my* wedding after what you've done to my family," Amara said in a sharp, cold voice.

"After what *I* did?" Marlow repeated. "I haven't done *anything* except try to—"

"Please," Amara scoffed. "Spare me. Thanks to *you*, my brother has renounced the Falcrest name. He has left Falcrest Hall. He's not even speaking to Father."

"I fail to see how that's my fault."

Amara went on like she hadn't heard her. "Luckily, we've managed to keep all this out of the gossip rags for now, but it's only a matter of time until everyone in Evergarden finds out. I will *not* have my brother's ridiculous tantrum overshadow this marriage."

"You mean this marriage that you don't even want?" Marlow asked. "Maybe you should take a page from your brother's book."

"What is that supposed to mean?" Amara demanded.

"It means you're not in love with Darian and you're only going through with this because your father wants to use you to take over the Vale Family."

Amara flinched. "You don't know what you're talking about."

"Really?" Marlow asked. "You're about to break your best friend's heart because you're too much of a coward to stand up to a father who treats you like a pawn instead of a daughter. You've been playing his game your whole life, yet you have no idea what he's really capable of."

Amara's face went very still. When she spoke again, her voice was like ice. "I just wanted to tell you to your face that you are not welcome at my wedding. And if you ever come near my brother again, I will *ruin* you." She called out, "Leland, Terra, please escort Miss Briggs *out* of the building and ensure she doesn't return."

Two servants appeared from the doors flanking the suite, gripping Marlow roughly by the arms.

Trapped between her captors, Marlow felt her slim hopes slipping away. Aurelius Falcrest would get away with his heinous plans. He would ruin the Vales and condemn Adrius to a fate as horrifying as his mother's.

She grasped desperately for something to say, anything that would stop Amara from tossing her out before she could warn Adrius. "Do you want to know the real reason your mother isn't here to see you get married?" she asked as they dragged her toward the door. "It's because *he* didn't want her here. He has kept her away from you your whole lives—"

"Get her out of my sight!" Amara snarled.

The servants dragged her out of the room and down the corridor. They banged through the door into the ballroom. At this point, many of the guests had already taken their seats for the ceremony. Marlow could feel dozens of eyes on her as the servants marched her along the edge of the ballroom. Whispers broke out as she passed, and she knew they must all be speculating about what Marlow could have done to get herself thrown out of this wedding.

Amongst the seated guests, Marlow spotted Adrius. Their eyes locked. He looked stricken, and angry, but underneath that she could see his confusion. She turned her head as the servants led her through the doors and back into the now-empty atrium.

Or rather, the nearly empty atrium.

"Leland, Terra," a deep, familiar voice said just as they reached the antechamber. "You can leave Miss Briggs here. You're dismissed."

Marlow turned to face Aurelius as the two servants quickly bowed and took their leave without hesitation.

Behind the closed doors of the ballroom, the orchestra began to play.

"Do you recall that little chat we had the other night?" Aurelius said at last. "About the line between courage and foolishness?"

"Was this when you tried to get me to drink cursed wine?" Marlow asked, taking a step back.

"If you were wondering," Aurelius went on as if he hadn't heard her, "you crossed that line the minute you left that night. Had you not run off so suddenly that evening, you would've known that you were always going to be perfectly safe. So long as you cooperated."

"Cooperated with your plan to forcibly remove my memories, you mean." As Marlow spoke, she reached slowly into the slit in her skirt, grasping the hilt of the knife strapped to her garter. She pulled it out slowly, keeping it hidden behind her skirt. "No thanks."

"Listen to me very carefully," Aurelius said, advancing. "You are in over your head. There is only one way for this to end: I *will* win. Because I always win. The only question is whether you will still be alive to see it. And the only person who can answer that question is you."

Marlow's heart thudded. She had no doubt that Aurelius was right. She'd managed to outsmart him once—she didn't think he'd make the same mistake again.

"Get away from her!"

The shout cracked across the empty atrium. Marlow and Aurelius both looked up to find Adrius barreling toward them, a frantic sort of fury in his eyes. He planted himself in front of Marlow, facing his father, one hand braced behind him as if to keep Marlow back.

"I told you," he said in a low growl, "if you *ever* went near her again—"

"Settle down, Adrius," Aurelius said calmly. "We're just clearing a few things up. Isn't that right, Marlow?"

"Adrius, you should—you should go," Marlow said haltingly.

"I'm not leaving you alone with him."

Even after what she'd done, Adrius was still trying to protect her.

"You and your sister and your *dramatics*," Aurelius said scornfully. "No one is in any danger here."

As if he hadn't just threatened Marlow's life thirty seconds ago.

"Then what's going on?" Adrius demanded.

This was it, Marlow realized. Her last chance to warn him. She looked at Aurelius. "Do you want to tell him, or should I?"

"Tell me what?"

She didn't take her eyes off Aurelius. "Your father used Ilario's Compulsion curse on your mother. He kept her away from Evergarden, away from *you*, so no one would find out. But someone *did* find out, didn't they?"

Aurelius looked as cold and composed as ever.

"My mother," Marlow said, grip tightening on the hilt of her knife. "And she paid for that knowledge with her life. But now . . . now your secret's in danger of getting out. You can bury a lot of your misdeeds, but you can't bury this. You know you're going to go down for this, but you've made sure that when that happens, you won't lose control of Falcrest Library. That you'll secretly still be in charge, even if not in name. So you made Adrius your heir and you cursed him so he would *have* to obey you."

Adrius stared at his father with unrestrained horror.

"That is utterly ridiculous," Aurelius said.

"Then why did you make Adrius your heir?" Marlow demanded. "You would never entrust the Falcrest empire to him unless you *knew* that you could control him."

"I made Adrius my heir because unlike his sister, I knew his ambition wouldn't get the better of him," Aurelius spat. "Because he has none. He would only ever be a figurehead, and the Falcrest legacy would be safe. But I did not curse my son."

"No, you cursed your wife," Marlow said, "*and* your son. And you're not getting away with it."

Aurelius's eyes narrowed. "You are a troublesome girl with quite a fanciful imagination."

"Adrius," Marlow pleaded. "You have to believe me."

Adrius met her gaze, his eyes wide. "I—"

From within the ballroom, bells began to chime, signaling the end of the ceremony.

Slowly, Adrius reached over to pluck Marlow's knife from her grip. His face was strangely blank, no trace of the alarm and anger from before. He looked calm. Almost docile.

Without warning, Adrius stepped forward and thrust the knife into his father's chest.

TWENTY-SIX

Marlow watched the blade plunge into Aurelius's chest. He crumpled to his knees, blood soaking his clean gray suit.

Shock froze her in place. She couldn't make sense of what she was seeing. One moment she had been trying to convince Adrius his father had cursed him, and the next—the next he was stabbing him.

But this wasn't revenge or uncontrolled rage. Marlow had seen the look on Adrius's face. He hadn't chosen to take the knife and thrust it into his father's chest.

It was the curse.

At her feet, Aurelius coughed, choking on his own blood as it gushed out of him.

He killed my mother, Marlow thought.

Adrius raised the knife again.

He killed my mother. He might not have cursed Adrius, but he was far from innocent. He deserved to pay for Cassandra, for Isme, for what he'd tried to do to Marlow.

All she had to do was nothing. She could stand here, and Aurelius would never be able to hurt her again.

And Adrius would live the rest of his life knowing he'd murdered his own father.

No. No matter what Aurelius had done to her, she wasn't going to watch him die. She wasn't going to let Adrius kill his own father.

Adrius swung the knife down. Marlow lunged, shoving him back. The blade tore through her dress and clipped her side. Pain bloomed over Marlow's ribs.

"Minnow," Adrius gasped. The trancelike look on his face was gone. His expression was broken open with horror and fear. The knife was still clenched in his fist. Marlow seized his wrists, pressing them back as he tried to slash at her again.

"Stop," Marlow commanded. "I order you to stop."

Adrius struggled against her hold. "I *can't*," he said, frantic. "I—"

Fear scrabbled at Marlow's insides. The person who had cursed Adrius had ordered him to do this. The person whose orders couldn't be overridden.

"Minnow," he pleaded. "You have to leave. Please, before I—"

Marlow sucked in a shaking breath, eyes locked on the knife he was trying to drive into her. The orders must have been to kill his father, and to kill anyone who tried to stop him.

"I'm not going anywhere," she said in as soothing a voice as she could. She had never seen Adrius so terrified.

"You have to get out of here," he kept chanting. "Please. Please, don't make me do this."

"You can fight this, Adrius," Marlow said. Her grip on him was slipping. He *couldn't* fight this—she knew that. They both knew that. But she couldn't leave him. "Remember—remember what you told me? You could never hurt me, Adrius. Say it again."

"I—" He cut himself off with a ragged breath. "I could never hurt you."

He was too strong. The blade was at her throat. She strained against him. He fought against himself.

She found his wild, terror-filled gaze and said, "I'm sorry."

Her apology splintered like the roots of a mangrove, each root one of the many wrongs Marlow had done. Betraying his trust that night.

Failing to break the curse before it destroyed him. Being too stubborn to admit what he meant to her.

The blade's edge bit into her throat. There was no more time for apologies, for promises, for words.

Marlow surged up to her toes and kissed him. He gasped against her lips.

Maybe it was the surprise. Or maybe it was Adrius's will breaking through for just a moment. But as Adrius kissed her back, his grip on the knife loosened.

Marlow didn't hesitate. She wrenched the blade from his hand and shoved him back as hard as she could. He crashed to the floor.

They stared at each other, stunned. The only sound in Marlow's ears was the pounding of her own heart.

Then the doors of the ballroom burst open and the cacophony of the wedding party poured into the atrium.

Marlow tore her gaze from Adrius to see guests spilling through the doors, Amara and Darian arm in arm at the head of the crowd.

Marlow had two, maybe three seconds before the crowd spotted them. She turned to Adrius, still on the floor, frozen in shock.

"Adrius," she said in a low voice. "Tell *no one* what happened here."

Amara saw them first. She stopped dead in the middle of the atrium, her gaze flicking over the scene in front of her. Her father, bleeding on the marble floor. Her brother, sprawled at Marlow's feet.

And Marlow, splattered with blood, holding the knife.

Amara's heels skittered across the floor as she dashed to her father's side, her skirt and train a scarlet cloud behind her.

"Help him!" she shrieked, her voice ringing through the silent atrium. "What are you all doing standing around? Someone *help him*!"

Several people sprang into action, crowding around Aurelius. Healing spells bathed him in blue light.

Tentatively, Darian knelt to help his new wife to her feet. But Amara snatched her hands away from him, whirling on Marlow.

"You did this," she snarled, angry tears shining in her dark eyes. "You have been out to get my family from the beginning. Guards!"

Several members of the wedding's security team snapped to attention at once. They wore a mix of Falcrest and Vale livery.

"Disarm her and detain her," Amara commanded.

Marlow didn't try to resist as the guards surrounded her. She let them take the knife from her hand and restrain her arms behind her, clamping her wrists with warded cuffs.

"What are you—hey!" Adrius protested, scrambling to his feet. "Don't touch her, don't—she didn't *do* anything! Amara, don't—"

Marlow looked at him and found herself focusing on the strangest details. The damp sweat gathering above his furrowed brow. The disheveled curl sticking out behind his ear. The shape of his mouth as he pleaded for Marlow's life.

If the truth of what had just happened got out, everyone would know that Adrius had been cursed. There was only one thing Marlow could do to protect him now.

She raised her chin and looked Amara in the eye. "You're right. It was me."

She swept her gaze over the silent crowd. Gemma was standing near the doors, looking dazed and sick. Silvan had planted himself at Adrius's side, his eyes narrowed in suspicion. Behind him stood his father, his typically jovial demeanor sobered. His gray eyes tracked Marlow, softening with something like pity or sympathy.

"Amara is right," Marlow declared. "I killed Aurelius Falcrest."

TWENTY-SEVEN

There was still blood on Marlow's dress when the Falcrest guards shoved her into the holding pen of the precinct.

Somehow, that was the worst part of this—that Marlow had to sit on a cold metal bench with a man's blood all over her.

She could not let herself think beyond the blood, because if she did then she would have to think about what was going to happen to her. She would have to think about the eyes of the cops in the precinct pinned on her. About how those cops were all but owned by the man whose blood was crusted in the fabric of her skirt.

She would have to think about how, when they transferred her from the precinct to the city jail, she would be locked inside there with hundreds of other criminals. How some of those criminals wore a bronze snake tattooed around their throats. How easy it would be for any one of them to gut her in a corridor, smother her in her sleep, slip something into her food.

She would have to think about the look of quiet devastation on Adrius's face when the Falcrest guards had led her away. And how there was a very real chance that she would never see him or Swift again.

Instead, she thought about the moment Adrius had taken the knife from her hands. She studied it in her mind, searching for clues. No one had been around. Whoever had given Adrius the order must have done so beforehand, but phrased it so that it wouldn't be triggered until—until what? Was it something Aurelius had said? She thought back to their conversation, to her own accusations.

She had been so *sure* it was Aurelius who had cursed his son. Now she wasn't sure of anything, except that Adrius was still cursed and Marlow no longer had any idea who was responsible.

A voice broke through the turbulent swirl of her thoughts. "Where is she?"

Marlow jerked her head up, gripping the edge of the bench and clamping down on her fear.

A man wearing a sharp suit and a pleasant smile strode toward her with the relaxed confidence that came with authority. He was familiar, but it took Marlow's panicked mind a moment to place him.

"Sir," the cop stationed next to Marlow said in surprise. "We weren't expecting—"

"Marlow Briggs, right?" the smiling man asked her, ignoring the cop entirely. "Pleased to meet you. I'm Emery Grantaire, Caraza's City Solicitor."

Marlow's throat went dry. "I know who you are."

What she didn't know was what he was doing here.

He turned to the cop next to her. "Let's get those cuffs off her, shall we?"

The guard hesitated.

"Come on now, we don't have all day."

The cop hesitated. "Sir, this girl is a confessed murderer—"

"Let's assume," Grantaire cut him off, "that as the City Solicitor I am perfectly aware of who this is and what she has allegedly done. Let's *also* assume that I have the authority to have her released into my custody without incident. Sound good? Or shall we go to my office and have a little chat?"

The cop swallowed, looking from him to Marlow. She did not envy the position he was in.

"All right," he grunted at last. "She's your responsibility."

"Much obliged," Grantaire replied.

"Not that I'm not grateful," Marlow said as the cop uncuffed her, "but what the hell is happening right now?"

Grantaire smiled. "It seems you have friends in high places, Miss Briggs."

"News to me." *Enemies* in high places, sure. But her heart leapt when she thought of Adrius. Had he somehow arranged this? Marlow had ordered him not to reveal the truth about what had happened to his father, but could he have gotten around that somehow? Or simply used his power and position to set her free?

It was the only possibility that made sense.

Grantaire looked amused. "Do you need anything? A drink of water?"

"You don't happen to have a change of clothes, do you?" Marlow asked, looking down at the bloodstains on her dress.

"Fetch Miss Briggs a clean set of clothes," Grantaire said to the cop.

Ten minutes later, Grantaire led her out of the precinct and into a private canal boat.

"I can't go back to the Marshes," Marlow said as Grantaire slid into the seat across from her.

He smiled. "We're not going to the Marshes."

Their boat docked at the Vale Tower private boathouse.

Marlow trailed Grantaire, bewildered, as they strode through the grand lobby to the elevator bank. She was silent as he summoned one and loaded Marlow into it.

“Top floor,” Grantaire said, and off they went, shooting up so fast Marlow’s ears popped.

At the top floor, the doors opened with a soft chime, revealing a warmly lit sitting room. Grantaire led her briskly to the double doors at the other end. He knocked once, and the doors swung open to a stately office furnished with plush chairs and a heavy desk of dark wood.

Behind the desk stood Cormorant Vale.

He smiled when he saw them. “Emery. Thank you for getting her here safely. You have my deepest appreciation for your assistance in this matter.”

“Anything for a loyal friend,” Grantaire replied, but there was an edge to his voice. “I was hoping for a word, actually.”

He gave Vale a meaningful look that Marlow could not parse. Vale just smiled mildly. “Of course. Why don’t you have a seat in the parlor while I talk to Miss Briggs. Help yourself to some tea, and I’ll be with you in just a moment.”

Grantaire looked like he wanted to push, but evidently thought better of it, smiling sunnily. “Of course.”

He whisked back through the double doors, leaving Marlow and Vale in the office alone. Vale’s suit was the same one he had worn to the wedding—a deep, midnight-blue jacket over a cream waistcoat. His expression, usually alight with twinkling mirth, was drawn and serious.

He circled the desk, striding toward Marlow with purpose.

Marlow tensed. Vale’s burly arms went around her, drawing her into a gentle embrace.

Whatever Marlow had expected him to do, it wasn’t that. She could only stand there, stunned, until eventually he pulled back, his hands still braced on her arms.

“Marlow,” he said warmly. “I’m so sorry for all this. But you’re all right now. You’re safe.”

"You . . . ," Marlow said slowly. "You got me released?"

"Of course," he said. "I had to make sure you were out of Amara's reach. My daughter-in-law wants blood for what happened to her father."

"Then why are you protecting me?"

"Did your mother ever tell you how we first met?" he asked. "It was eighteen years ago, but I still remember it like it was yesterday."

Eighteen years ago? Cassandra had never said she'd known Vale before she was hired as his chevalier.

"I was not yet head of the Vale Family—just a young man who thought he could change the world. I thought I could bring fairness and justice to this city. I was sheltered, naive. Your mother was not—she'd lived a life so vastly different from mine, yet that only made her more intriguing. She opened my eyes to so many things. I wanted to protect her from the ruthlessness of this world, this city."

Marlow's throat felt tight. "So you're trying to protect me because . . . what, you couldn't protect her?"

"Not quite," Vale said gently. "The truth is, Marlow, as much as I wanted to be a good, faithful man, I was never strong enough to resist the pull I felt toward your mother. But now, when I look at you, I can't find it in myself to regret falling in love with her."

Marlow stared at him, the conversation they'd had at Amara's engagement party echoing in her head. About a loveless political marriage. About how Vale wished he'd been brave enough to follow his heart.

He'd been talking about her mother.

"If there is one thing you should know about me, it's that there is nothing more important to me than family. That I will do anything to protect mine." He cupped a warm hand over her shoulder. "To protect you. My daughter."

Marlow couldn't speak. This couldn't be real. His daughter. A *Vale*.

She shook her head. "No, that's . . ."

Vale's voice was gentle. "Why would I lie about this?"

Marlow couldn't come up with an answer. Yet—it couldn't be true. Her mother had always said it was just the two of them. They were a team. It was them against the world.

"Then she lied to you," Marlow said, her voice shaking.

"She didn't even want me to know," Vale said softly. "The moment she came to work for me as my chevalier, I suspected. Your age, of course, was a clue. But she didn't admit it to me until just before she disappeared. I think some part of me knew all along, though. Or perhaps just hoped. It was one of the reasons I insisted you be given the same education as my sons."

Marlow didn't need to be told why Cassandra had wanted to keep it a secret. Being Vale's daughter—particularly an illegitimate daughter—was dangerous. It meant being a part of the noblesse nouveau in a way she'd never be able to escape. She knew her mother didn't want that for her. Things were dangerous enough without that target on her back.

Vale went to his desk and unlocked one of the drawers. He pulled out a letter, folded and creased, like it had been read many times. "She gave me a letter, explaining all of it, and told me she didn't want you to know. I . . . I wanted to respect her wishes. I regret that now. I wish I had told you immediately. I wish I had taken a firmer hand in ensuring your protection after she disappeared. But today . . . that, at least, was something I knew I had to do."

Marlow swallowed, her eyes trained on the letter. She was still so desperate, so hungry for anything of her mother's. "Can I read it?"

Vale smiled sadly and tucked the letter back into the drawer. "I'd prefer you didn't. Not now, at least. There are . . . certain aspects of our relationship that I'm not the most proud of. And there are things in here that I'm not sure your mother would want you to know."

Marlow felt the hot sting of tears in her eyes. She blinked them away furiously.

"I know this is a lot to take in," Vale said gently. "If you need some time to process, I can take you to your room."

"My room?"

"Of course," Vale replied. "You will always have a place here, Marlow—if you want it."

Marlow thought about the desperate fear that had been humming in her veins since the moment Aurelius had handed her a cursed glass of wine. Since Caito had ambushed her in the middle of the night. Since the Copperheads had declared open season on her.

Danger lurked around every corner, and yet here, for what felt like the first time in her life, someone was offering her safety. A place where no one could touch her, a wall put up between her and those who would hurt her.

She didn't know if she had it in her to trust something like that.

"Don't you want to know?" she asked. "Before you offer me a—a place in your home, don't you want to know why I killed Aurelius?"

Vale's gray eyes studied her face. She'd never really noticed how similar the color was to her own. At last, he said, "They didn't tell you?"

"Didn't tell me what?"

"Aurelius isn't dead," Vale said. "He's gravely injured. I don't know what will happen, in the end, but—he isn't dead."

"I still stabbed him," Marlow said. "Don't you want to know why?"

"I suppose I want to know why you lied about it."

Marlow stiffened, startled. "I didn't."

Vale's expression was gentle. "I know that you and your mother had a . . . particular relationship. Cassandra liked her secrets. I'm not surprised that you learned that from her. But I would like if you and I endeavor to be honest with each other. We've had enough secrets, I think."

"What makes you think I'm lying?"

Carefully, Vale said, "I know that Adrius and his father argued the night before the wedding. That Adrius threatened his father, and Aurelius disowned him."

According to Amara, it was Adrius who had disowned the Falcrests, but Marlow didn't make this correction.

"I suppose you're taking the fall for him out of love?" He shook his head. "I can't fault you for that. Love is the most noble cause in this world. But, Marlow . . . I beg you to reconsider. Don't throw your life away for a boy who would cast you to the side the moment it benefits him."

"You don't know what you're talking about," Marlow said, her tone too sharp against the man who had just offered her shelter.

But Vale only looked at her with sympathy. "I know you must believe that he loves you. And perhaps even he believes it. But when reality sets in, he will leave you to hang and do what he must to protect himself and his reputation. That is what the Falcrests know. That is who they are."

"You're wrong about him," Marlow said, but her voice shook.

Vale smiled. "Maybe. But this is your life, Marlow. I will do everything in my power to protect you, but there is only so much I can do if you continue to stand in the way of the truth."

The truth. If only Marlow knew what that was.

"I'm sure you must be very tired," Vale said. "Give me just a moment to thank Grantaire for his assistance, and then I can take you to your room."

He brushed past her to go to the office doors. Marlow moved aside. As the doors swung shut behind him, instinct seized hold of her and she lunged for one of them, stopping it just before it clicked all the way shut.

Vale's voice filtered in from the parlor. "My apologies for the wait."

"I hope you know this is no small favor I just did you," Grantaire replied. His tone was light, which paradoxically made him sound more threatening.

"I know what I asked you to do," Vale replied steadily. "Though I'm not sure it constitutes a favor, given that you already owed me."

"Owed you for what, exactly?" Grantaire asked. "Tipping me off about Falcrest's wife? I'm fairly certain that served your interests, too."

Marlow's stomach dropped. So Grantaire *did* know about Isme. She had guessed as much, but she'd *never* thought that Vale knew anything about it. Had Cassandra told him?

"If you mean my interest in cleaning up this city, then I suppose you're right," Vale replied.

"Cleaning up the city," Grantaire echoed scornfully. "Sure. Or maybe you just wanted Falcrest out of power."

"I am far from the only person who wants that."

"Well, I suppose it doesn't matter now," Grantaire said blandly. "You realize how this looks, don't you? Your son, married to his daughter moments before Aurelius gets a knife to the heart. You, calling in favors to protect the girl who did it."

"As I'm sure you know, the truth is often quite different from how things appear," Vale said. "Marlow Briggs is innocent."

"A hundred wedding guests heard her confession."

"Has it occurred to you that perhaps the young lady had reason to lie? To protect the real culprit?"

"You think Falcrest's son did it," Grantaire said. He was obviously sharp.

"That's not for me to say," Vale answered. "But I will say that Adrius Falcrest had far more to gain from his father's death than Miss Briggs."

"And why is that?"

"Because Falcrest made him his heir."

Grantaire was silent for a moment. Then he said, "Well, I'm sure the truth will come out one way or another."

In Marlow's experience, the truth came out only when you dug it out with your bare hands.

"If that's all," Vale said, "please allow me to escort you out."

"I think I can find my way down an elevator."

"I insist."

Marlow heard the chime of the elevator, and then the sound of the doors closing. She moved away from the doors and walked over to Vale's desk, perusing the neat row of trinkets along the edge. A porcelain tray held a small cache of pens. A small, carved wolf howled up at the ceiling. A gold watch with a calendar set into the face. An hourglass filled with black sand on a circular stand. Marlow touched the stand, rotating it so the hourglass turned over, and watched the sand stream back down.

She knew, of course, why she had gone to the desk, and it wasn't to look at the trinkets. It was because her mother's letter was tucked inside the drawer, calling to Marlow like a beating heart.

Vale didn't want her to read it. Marlow very badly wanted to.

She heard Swift's voice in her head, saying, *You act like you have a right to everyone else's secrets.*

Maybe she did. But this wasn't just anyone's secret—this was her mother's.

She slid open the drawer.

There wasn't much inside. A small jewelry box, which contained a pair of sapphire cuff links. A spellcard for an Illusion spell. And the letter, folded up and tucked away in the back.

The paper had that stiff, warped feeling that indicated something had spilled on it. When Marlow unfolded it, she saw that in fact some of the ink had been smudged. It was still legible enough, though it was much shorter than Marlow expected. But then again, that was just like her mother—she never gave away more than she had to.

Marlow started to read.

Cormorant,

You may think I owe you the truth, but you're wrong. I don't owe you anything. But here it is anyway.

Eighteen years ago, you fell in love with a woman who didn't exist. She—I—was not who I said I was. You wanted to save me. I wanted you to think that you could. That was the con. But then you offered me a life I never could have dreamed of, a life where you would have loved me.

To me, the choice was clear: Your love or my freedom. We both know which one I chose.

I wish I could tell you I regretted it ever since, but that would be a lie. And as I said, this letter is about the truth.

The truth is this, Cor. Marlow is yours. I know you've always suspected it. I planned never to tell you, but I'm out of options.

When I came to you two years ago and asked you to hire me as your chevalier, I knew you wouldn't deny me. Just as I know you will not deny me now. This letter is my last resort to make sure that even if I can't protect myself, I can still protect our daughter.

Whatever happened between us, I know you will make sure she's safe. You might be the only one who still can.

She had signed the letter with a simple *Cass.*

Marlow stared at the letter, and read it twice over. She felt like she was looking at her mother's last words. When she held the letter close to her face and breathed in, she could even smell her perfume. Bergamot and vetiver. When Marlow closed her eyes, she could almost feel her mother in the room with her. Teasing her. Snapping at her. Rolling her eyes and smiling that familiar, mischievous smile.

Gods knew she wasn't a perfect mother, but she was *Marlow's*.

The sound of the elevator chime jolted Marlow back into the present. She folded the letter and placed it back where she'd found it, pushing the drawer shut and darting over to the doors just as Vale pulled them open.

She turned, smiling like she'd just been idly waiting for him to return.

"I'm sorry about that," Vale said. "Let's get you settled in, shall we?"

It wasn't until they were walking down a familiar hallway that Marlow realized when Vale had said her rooms, he'd meant the ones she'd lived in with Cassandra.

Her steps faltered when they reached the door.

"Is this all right?" Vale asked. "I thought it might be nice to be somewhere familiar. But if you'd prefer another room—"

"This is fine," Marlow said.

Vale patted her shoulder. "Well, I'll let you get settled. I'll conjure some dinner and fresh clothes for you. We'll talk in the morning."

Marlow thanked him and waited until he had retreated down the hall to open the door.

It was like stepping into the past. Everything in their apartment was exactly as she had left it the morning she'd departed Evergarden. Her mother's favorite paintings, landscapes depicting mangrove forests and swamps thick with vegetation. The lavish kitchen with all its enchanted cookware and conveniences. The ornate dining room chairs that had always made Marlow feel like a princess from a story when she sat in them.

Marlow had scoured these rooms the morning her mother vanished, searching for any kind of clue as to where she had gone. She still remembered the frantic terror clawing at her chest when she realized Cassandra wasn't coming back.

It was disorienting, being here now, knowing what she knew. To be amongst her and her mother's belongings, realizing that the only thing in the apartment that had changed at all was Marlow.

In the corner of the sitting room, her mother's desk sat in its typical disarray—pens scattered amongst a few candles and books. The Mirror of Truth hung above it, a thin film of dust coating the glass. Marlow picked up a cloth from the kitchen and sat down at the desk. She lifted the cloth to wipe away the dust and then paused, her gaze catching on a glass bottle sitting innocuously at the corner of the desk. Her mother's perfume bottle.

Tears gathered in Marlow's eyes as she pulled out the glass cork and lifted it to her nose. The scent of bergamot and vetiver lingered, but the bottle itself was empty.

Empty, because the night Cassandra disappeared, Marlow had startled her and she'd knocked it over, spilling perfume across a pile of papers.

Marlow remembered her mother's letter, hidden away in Vale's desk. The paper had been stiff and warped, the writing slightly smudged. It had smelled lightly of bergamot and vetiver.

Her stomach dropped, just as that familiar prickle of instinct crawled up her spine.

That letter was what her mother had been writing when she spilled the perfume. Cassandra had given it to Vale that night—the night she'd disappeared.

Or at the very least, Cassandra had left the letter for him that night before going to meet Montagne. But—no. Marlow knew her mother. She'd be more careful than that. She would've handed Vale the letter directly, because she wouldn't have risked the possibility of someone else stumbling upon it and learning the truth of Marlow's parentage. And Vale had said that Cassandra *told him* she didn't want Marlow to know about the letter, admitting he'd spoken to her.

Which meant that Vale had seen Cassandra the night she died.

It didn't necessarily mean anything. But then, why hadn't Vale told her? Why had he insisted he hadn't seen Cassandra at all that night?

He'd told Marlow that he was at the Annual City Philanthropists Gala, being honored with some award. Marlow had easily confirmed his attendance from coverage of the event in the papers. According to the *Contessa*'s security log, Cassandra had already been aboard to meet Montagne at half past twenty bells—the gala would have still been underway. And Cassandra had left the apartment at just past twenty bells—not enough time for her to have intercepted Vale at the gala before arriving at the marina.

So the only time Cassandra could have gone to see Vale was *after* Montagne had handed off the grimoire.

But hours later, when Caito finally tracked her down, Cassandra no longer had the grimoire with her. She'd told Caito she'd destroyed it, but what if she'd lied?

What if, along with the letter, she'd handed it over to Vale?

Marlow unspooled the thought inch by inch.

Vale had known about Isme's curse. He'd said as much to Grantaire. He'd admitted he wanted Falcrest out of power, even though he was marrying his son to Falcrest's daughter.

He'd known that Aurelius had named Adrius his heir.

Adrius Falcrest had far more to gain from his father's death than Miss Briggs, he'd said to Grantaire. But if Adrius was under Vale's control, it gave Vale something to gain, too.

Whoever had ordered Adrius to kill Aurelius intended for him to do it at Amara and Darian's wedding. There would've been other opportunities, but they'd waited until then to strike. Why? Because whoever wanted Falcrest dead needed to make sure the marriage would be secured before it happened?

Everyone in Evergarden thought Vale was a fool to let his son marry Amara, that he was opening himself up to a takeover, but Marlow knew Vale was smarter than he let on. If Aurelius was out of the picture entirely, Vale could use the marriage alliance to his own advantage. Tying one Falcrest scion to his family, and gaining control of the other. That put him in a very powerful position.

Adrius almost hadn't even showed up to the wedding. Silvan had told Marlow that it was *Vale* who'd persuaded him to come.

But maybe he hadn't persuaded him at all. Maybe he'd simply ordered him to.

She dropped the cloth and sat back in the chair. This was foolish. A wild theory, with little proof. Yes, there were pieces that fit, but—Marlow had been wrong before.

And Vale had just saved her life. He'd offered her a place in his home without conditions or expectations.

The more you feel vulnerable to someone, the less you trust them, Swift had said. *So you start looking for reasons not to.*

Was that what this was? Was Marlow looking for a reason not to trust Vale so she wouldn't have to open herself to the risk of letting him care about her?

She didn't know. But either way, it would be better for her to put this away. To leave it alone.

She remembered what she had told Hyrum when she'd asked about her mother and the Black Orchid. *Secrets can't protect me. Only the truth can.*

After everything, she wasn't sure she believed that anymore. Sometimes it was better not to know. Sometimes it was safer.

But no matter how badly the truth hurt her, no matter what danger it put her in, Marlow would always rather know.

TWENTY-EIGHT

Marlow slept fitfully and woke to the sound of rain outside her window. Staring at her familiar bedroom ceiling, she almost believed she had woken up in the past. That it was a year ago, and her mother was still alive.

The rain outside made the tower feel muted. Like she was sitting in the eye of the storm.

She padded into the living room and sat down at her mother's desk. Her suspicions about Vale had not subsided. But that was all they were—suspicions.

She picked up the empty perfume bottle. All it proved, really, was that Vale had lied about seeing Cassandra the night she'd died. It didn't mean he had the grimoire. It didn't mean he'd cursed Adrius.

She sat back in the chair, peering at her own reflection in the mirror. There was nothing different about it, of course. The Mirror of Truth showed her exactly as she was. She might keep some things close to the chest, but she'd never disguised the truth of who she was. There were no illusions.

A knock at the door startled her from her thoughts.

There was only one person who knew Marlow was here, so she wasn't surprised when she opened the door to find Vale standing on the other side.

"I have news," he said. "Can I come in?"

Marlow stepped back and gestured inside.

He paced past the dining table and then turned back to face her. "I've just come from Falcrest Hall."

A spike of fear pierced her. Falcrest Hall, where Adrius was. Adrius, who was still cursed, possibly by Vale.

But before her worries could spiral, he continued, "I went to ask my daughter-in-law to consider a full pardon for you."

"What?"

There was no way. Amara *hated* Marlow, since long before she thought Marlow had tried to kill her father.

"Obviously, as Aurelius's daughter, her word will carry a lot of weight with the rest of the Five Families," Vale went on. "If we can secure her support, they will see fit to issue the pardon."

"You might as well have asked her to hand over Falcrest Library," Marlow replied. "Amara isn't going to go for it. She's not exactly my biggest supporter."

"Well, I suspect that Amara herself may have her reasons for wanting the matter of her father's attack to be put to rest quickly and cleanly, before any more doubts or questions as to what truly happened can arise." Vale gave her a pointed look. "There are, naturally, more than a few rumors flying around."

He meant rumors about Adrius, no doubt.

Marlow crossed her arms over her chest. "What did you offer her?"

"Nothing that is worth as much to me as your safety," Vale replied. At her unconvinced look, he said, "Really, don't worry yourself over it."

"I thought you said you wanted honesty between us," Marlow reminded him.

Vale gave her a wry look. "So I did. All right, then. Honestly, I told her the truth. That you are my daughter, and that I didn't want the union of our two families to be fractured by this unfortunate situation."

Marlow was momentarily speechless. "You really told her that I'm—?"

"Of course," Vale said, cutting her off. "Unlike your mother, I never intended to hide it. That's something else I wanted to discuss with you. I would like if, in the course of the next few days, I could introduce you to the rest of my family as my daughter."

Marlow didn't try to hide her surprise. Vale really meant it when he said she was family now. He was going to tell his wife about her. His sons.

Her *brothers*, Marlow realized with a disorienting lurch. She hadn't really thought about it last night, but being Vale's daughter meant Silvan and Darian were her brothers—half brothers, at least. The thought of being related to Silvan was mildly horrifying. She resolved not to think about it for now.

"We can talk about that later," Vale assured her. "Once we get your pardon sorted out."

"I'm grateful for your help," Marlow said, "but you're wasting your time."

"Well," Vale said with a smile. "Even so, I'm not going to give up. This—you—are too important."

Marlow turned away from him and moved into the living room, pacing in a slow circle. She gripped the back of the chair tucked into the writing desk. She could almost hear Cassandra's voice in her head. *In this city, you've got to look out for yourself first.*

"I told you," Vale said, striding toward her. "I'll do whatever it takes to protect you."

Marlow looked up. When her gaze met his kind gray-blue eyes—almost the same shade as her own—she found that she believed him.

"I don't know how to thank you," she said, shaking her head. "I don't—"

He crossed the rest of the distance between them, bracing his hands on her shoulders. "You don't need to thank me, Marlow. We're family."

She nodded, tears gathering in her eyes as she stepped into him. He wrapped his arms gently around her, and she turned her head to the side, resting it against his shoulder, facing the Mirror of Truth above the writing desk. In it, she saw a father and daughter reunited, tucked into an affectionate embrace.

It was an image she had thought for so long was impossible. Her whole life, she'd only had her mother. Cassandra, who in her imperfect way had taught Marlow to get what she could from a world that, time and again, seemed only to take from her.

But now, the world had given her something. A father. Someone who wanted to protect her the way no one ever had before. Marlow was surprised by how much she wanted what she saw in the mirror. A place where she could belong. Someone who would take care of her, no matter the cost.

She was surprised by how much she wished she could have it.

Her eyes traced the strong line of Vale's arm around her, shielding her. A bulwark against whoever might try to harm her.

Her gaze went to the reflection of his hand wrapped around her shoulder. She had to brace herself against the shudder that went through her.

In the Mirror of Truth, his fingers were inky black. The veins running through his hands and up his arms were dark, infected with the same cursemarks that had marred Montagne, and Cassandra, and every single person who touched *Ilario's Grimoire*.

Vale had done it. He had gotten the grimoire from Cassandra. He'd used it to put Adrius under a Compulsion curse. Ordered him to kill his own father.

He'd gotten away with all of it, and now there was no one left to stop him.

No one except Marlow.

ACKNOWLEDGMENTS

It's not an easy thing to bring a book forth from your mind and into the real world, but I am lucky enough to have help from some incredible people in that process.

The first thank-you goes to you, dear reader, for braving the dark, steaming corners of Caraza (unless you skipped to the acknowledgments, in which case, thank you for picking up this book! I hope you keep reading!).

Thank you to Hillary Jacobson and Alexandra Machinist for believing in Marlow and this book from the very start, and, as always, for pushing me to do my world-building homework. Thank you also to the rest of the team at CAA.

Thank you to my editor, Brian Geffen. Somehow, we did it again! Every time I convince myself I'll never turn a ramshackle first draft into a real book, your insights and unwavering faith make it possible. A huge thank-you to Samira Iravani and Michael Rogers for bringing Marlow to life and giving this book the gorgeous cover it deserves. Thank you also to the rest of the team at Holt Books for Young Readers and MCPG: Carina Licon, Starr Baer, Alexei Esikoff, Ann Marie Wong, Jean Feiwel, and the many others involved in bringing this book to the world.

My earliest readers have my deepest gratitude for all of their incredible feedback, encouragement, advice, and enthusiasm. Scott Hovdy and Ashley Burdin, where would I be without your mystery expertise? Meg RK, as always, thank you for pushing me on the romance. Alexis Castellanos, Axie Oh, and Erin Bay, you were the very first people to read chapters of this book and tell me it wasn't complete nonsense. Akshaya Raman, my constant deadline buddy and brainstorming partner, I am so sorry for making you brainstorm the infamous Office Scene a dozen times and then abruptly trashing everything. As always, thank you to the rest of the writing crew, without whom I would be lost: Tara Sim, Amanda Foody, Janella Angeles, Kat Cho, Amanda Haas, Mara Fitzgerald, Charlie Herman, Melody Simpson, and Madeline Colis.

Thank you to Erica for beachside and hot-tub brainstorm sessions, and helping me work out the finer details of Caraza. To Sean, for enthusiastically reading the first chapters of this book before I knew what the hell I was doing. Thank you to the rest of my family: Mom, Dad, Riley, Julia, Wilder, Charlotte, and of course Curry, who might not be able to detect curses but can always tell when I need a good distraction.